THE
THIRSTY
EARTH

ALSO BY DAVID VALENTINE BERNARD

The Last Dream Before Dawn
The Raw Essentials of Human Sexuality
Intimate Relations with Strangers
How to Kill Your Boyfriend (In 10 Easy Steps)
God in the Image of Woman

THE
THIRSTY
EARTH

DAVID VALENTINE BERNARD

SBI

STREBOR BOOKS

NEW YORK   LONDON   TORONTO   SYDNEY

Strebor Books
P.O. Box 6505
Largo, MD 20792
http://www.streborbooks.com

ISBN 978-1-59309-461-4
ISBN 978-1-4516-9579-3 (ebook)
LCCN 2013933641

First Strebor Books trade paperback edition August 2013

Cover design: www.mariondesigns.com
Cover photograph: © Keith Saunders/Marion Designs

10 9 8 7 6 5 4 3 2 1

Manufactured in the United States of America

For information regarding special discounts for bulk purchases,
please contact Simon & Schuster Special Sales at 1-866-506-1949
or business@simonandschuster.com

The Simon & Schuster Speakers Bureau can bring authors to your live event. For more information or to book an event, contact the Simon & Schuster Speakers Bureau at 1-866-248-3049 or visit our website at www.simonspeakers.com.

For the brothers—Michael, Callistus, Angello, Petroc, and Andrew. Slowly but surely we seem to be getting to where we need to be.

When fools are aware that they are fools—and are willing to admit to their foolishness—there is no problem. Unfortunately, fools are rarely self-aware; and even when they are, they rarely have the courage to shun their foolishness. They allow themselves to be seduced by it; they incubate it within themselves, give it a fertile breeding ground, and go out amongst others, spreading their disease. This is how foolishness spreads throughout a society.

BOOK ONE
ALONE

Sometime during the night, a mango fell from the gigantic tree behind the house and banged into the galvanized steel roof like a missile. Startled, Shango cried out and rose from his bed; in the room across the hall, he heard his grandmother shriek as the mango ricocheted off the roof and landed in the yard. Yet, it was one of those things that one got used to during mango season. Within seconds, Shango lay down on his side, yawned, and allowed the dream world to reclaim him.

He slept soundly and peacefully; in fact, *hours* later, when the morning sun was rising over the mountains, Shango was in the same position on the bed. He was not yet awake, but his thoughts—about a pretty teacher at his high school—were too orderly to be dreams.

On the wall, to the left of his bed, there were magazine clippings of places he wished to visit: glossy images of the Eiffel Tower, the Statue of Liberty, and other tourist destinations. His mother had moved to New York City five years ago—when Shango was seven—and her absence had set off a wild yearning for the outside world. In fact, with the exception of his grandmother, all his other relatives were in America now. America was the paradise of his personal religion—which meant his mother, his uncle, and all the island's other emigrants, were the chosen people of God.

Others, like himself, who were still stuck on the island, were like sinners who had been left behind to suffer for their sins. However, since his God was a forgiving God, every day was a chance for redemption. His mother had been working on his immigration papers for years now—and he had again come in first in his class at school—so it was only a matter of time before he joined his mother, in that better world....

To the right of Shango's bed there was a window with a sweeping view of the forest and the mountains. Birds were singing in the trees that surrounded the house; others were busy rooting about in the rich volcanic earth that had bewitched the European colonizers four hundred years ago. As one of the birds cried out insistently, Shango inhaled deeply and scratched the side of his neck—but the bed was warm and comfortable, and the day seemed too young for him to be bothered. In fact, he hugged his pillow tenderly now, and was about to sigh contentedly, when something stung his arm!

He opened his eyes in time to see the mosquito rising into the air. It was plump from feeding—gorged with so much blood that it was struggling to fly. Something about its fitful flight mesmerized him for a moment; but when the mosquito landed on the wall, between his pictures of the Great Wall of China and the Sphinx, Shango sucked his teeth angrily.

The thing had been feeding on him all night! Even now, it only seemed to be waiting for its next chance to feed. Shango saw his slipper on the floor, and reached down to grab it. He was moving deliberately now, like a lion stalking its prey. He was dressed in a pair of shorts and a t-shirt, both of which were dingy. As soon as he was free of the sheets, he sprang at the wall, his slipper poised for the death blow. He swung, and the slipper collided with the wall with a loud *crack*—but Shango looked on in disbelief, then growing rage, as the mosquito glided past his ear and headed toward the window.

The bed was between him and the window: Shango jumped onto the bed and swung at the creature again. The mosquito was slow and fat, but as those little bastards never flew in a straight line, Shango kept missing. The rage escalated into full-blown madness as the creature zigzagged in the air and eluded him. Then, when he saw it was about to escape out of the window, the rage exploded in him, and he threw the slipper with all his might!

Unfortunately, the moment the slipper left his hand, Shango remembered there were glass louvers in the window; and so, the horror was etched into his face as the slipper smashed through the glass. The sound was deafening; he instinctively ducked, as if he expected the entire house to come crashing down on his head.

When he looked back at the window, a queasy feeling came over him—so that he sank to his knees. Even though a few shards of glass still stuck tenaciously to their moorings, he saw, right away, that the louvers were damaged beyond repair—and that his grandmother was going to *kill* him! He waited for the sound of her approaching footsteps; he braced himself for her angry screams and her *blows*…but there was nothing. He frowned.

Staring out of the window, at the verdant mountains in the distance, he saw it was a bright, sunny day. From the height of the sun, he suddenly realized it was at least seven in the morning—and that he was hopelessly late for school! There was a moment of panic as he thought about the headmaster's cane; but after a few seconds, a new, unnamable terror left him staring blankly into space. His grandmother had never let him sleep this late before—not on a school day anyway. Suddenly numb, he turned from the window and found himself moving toward the doorway. There was not actually a door there—only a sheet over the doorway. He pushed the sheet aside and stood staring across the hall, at the sheet that covered his grandmother's doorway. Her sheet's floral pattern had become faded with age, and it was getting frayed around the edges, but Shango stared at it expectantly, as if his grandmother would emerge from behind it at any moment. When that did not happen, he opened his mouth to call to her— but in the room behind him, another piece of glass escaped from its mooring and fell to the floor with a loud crash. Once again, Shango held his breath and waited for his grandmother's wrath, but there was nothing....

He had no idea how much time had passed. Eventually, he willed himself to move. When he stretched out his arm to push his grandmother's sheet to the side, he saw his hand was shaking. To distract himself, he moved ahead quickly, almost pulling down the sheet in his haste. Yet, once he was in the room, urgency turned into uncertainly, and he stood there frozen. He opened his mouth to call to her, but the words stayed locked up inside of him—as if his unnamable fears had taken them hostage.

Since his grandmother's curtains were drawn, it took a few moments for his eyes to adjust to the darkness. When he saw his grandmother was still in bed, the sense of urgency came over him again, and he moved toward her. However, when he finally saw her face, he gasped. Her eyes were open; her teeth were bared— like a wild animal's—and in that moment of confusion, he figured she was angry because he had come into her room without knocking.

Suddenly agitated, he was about to explain himself—and the broken louvers. Yet, as the seconds passed, he saw his grand-mother's eyes were unfocused and blank. For the first time, he noticed the bedspread was entangled around her limbs; her willowy arms still clutched the sheet, as if it had come to life during the night and tried to strangle her. The only thing he could do was stare. Maybe another twenty seconds passed before he allowed himself to acknowledge she was dead—and that she had died horribly. When he did, he found himself backing away from the bed.

He wanted to run, but his limbs refused. In fact, it was as though his grandmother's corpse had some kind of gravitational pull on him. He struggled to be free of it; the effort was so taxing that he did not even have the strength to turn his back on it. All he could manage was to back away. Then, after what seemed like hours of this strange gravitational struggle, Shango once again found himself beyond the doorway, staring at the kitschy floral pattern on the sheet. His mind was hopelessly lost now. Time seemed to unravel as he stood there; but when a bout of light-headedness came over him, he stumbled back to his bedroom and collapsed onto the bed.

His heart was racing. There was something he should be doing—some *adult* thing—but his mind still refused to move. He was staring at the wall blankly, sinking deeper into shock, when the mosquito suddenly flew into his field of vision. He sat up on his elbows, staring in disbelief as it once again landed on the wall. It was the *same* mosquito! He didn't even bother to use a slipper this time: he sprang from the bed and slammed his palm into the wall. His hand stung from the impact, but the mosquito evaded him again! Once more, it flew toward the window. Shango leapt onto the bed and tried to *smash* the mosquito between his hands—but the thing darted away at the last moment. He sprang at it again—however, as he was off balance, he found himself toppling from the bed. He instinctively put out his right hand to brace his fall; but at the last moment, he remembered the broken glass was still lying on the floor. He cried out as the shards sliced through his palm; but by twisting his body, he was able to roll away from the glass as he fell to the ground.

Blood was gushing from his hand now. The pain was not that bad, but he suddenly found himself sobbing uncontrollably. *His grandmother was dead!* He lay there for about a minute or two, surrendering himself to the grief. He sobbed until his body ached from it and his throat was sore.

In fact, the grief possessed him *totally*. It fed on him the way a fire fed on a forest—it was horrible and devastating; but eventually, when there was nothing left to burn, the fire petered out, and there was nothing left but smoldering ash. Shango felt empty now; at the same time, after his outpouring of grief, he felt like his mind was working again. He sat up, wiping away his tears with his left hand. His right hand was still bleeding: he stared down at his bloody palm. The blood was not gushing out any-more, but there were still about half a dozen shards embedded in his palm. The biggest one had sliced into the fleshy part of his hand, between his thumb and index finger. It had practically gone all the way through. For a moment, Shango felt a budding sense of panic—but there was only one thing to do, so he grabbed the shard and pulled it out. He winced at the pain, and grimaced as the blood spurted out; but at the same time, having something to do made him feel real again. It occurred to him he had to wash his hand, and bandage it. That was the *adult* thing to do. He had to contact the authorities about his grandmother, and call his mother in America, to let her know… An anxious feeling came over him when he realized he was alone on the island now. For a moment, the panic threatened to return—but the voice of adulthood told him it was pointless, so he rose from the floor and headed out of the room to wash his hand.

Once Shango left his room, he again stood staring at the sheet in his grandmother's doorway. After a few seconds, it occurred to him his bleeding hand was making a mess on the floor. When he looked down and saw it, he had a sudden fear that his grandmother would charge from behind the sheet and *brutalize* him. People of his grandmother's generation didn't just beat you: their sadistic genius rose to the level of an art form, so that your *fear* of the punishment was always worse than the actual punishment. His grandmother's preferred method was sending him into the forest to find a stick for her to beat him with—and God help him if he picked one that was not to her satisfaction!

Anyway, when he looked down and saw the mess the blood had made, years of psychological conditioning were triggered instantly. Soon, he was running through the small, neat living room, heading to the kitchen. The kitchen was essentially a storage room. There was no sink, no stove…none of the usual kitchen appliances. There was a window—but at night, his grandmother locked a piece of board over it—so the room was dark now. Suddenly wary of the darkness, Shango stopped on the threshold of the kitchen and stood looking around the small chamber. The only features in the kitchen were some handmade wooden cabinets and a worn wooden countertop that at the moment held two kerosene lanterns. Everything was handmade, or crudely fashioned—but the house was neat and tidy. Everything was in its place, and something about that reassured him, as if it were all a testament to his grandmother.

He moved to the kitchen door now—which was in fact the only door in the house. There was a handmade rush mat to the side of the door. Two sets of "outside shoes" were lying on the mat—one for Shango, and the other for his grandmother. He slipped into his shoes, then reached for the doorknob with his left hand.

The door did not have a lock, but his grandmother closed it at night to keep out rats and the mountain spirits she *swore* she had seen countless times. Then, once Shango opened the door, he found himself looking at the outside world.

Even on the hottest days, the back of the house was always cool—since the gigantic mango tree shaded it from the blazing sun. The tree rose into the heavens, blocking out the sky and the apex of the mountain. According to his grandmother, the mangoes were part of their personal covenant with God. Over seventy years ago, when Shango's grandfather was on his way to digging ditches in World War II Europe, the man had spotted the huge mangoes on one of the larger Caribbean islands. Fearful of the cold, hostile world at the end of his journey, he had taken one of the mango seeds with him on the ship, as a kind of memento; then, as he was sailing across the Atlantic, God had appeared to him in a vision and told him the seed would keep him safe and be an aegis against all the evils of men.

Understandably, by the time his grandfather landed in Europe, and war began raging around him, he had found himself holding the seed in his hands when he prayed—like a sacred relic. He had caressed it and surrendered himself to every form of idolatry.

By the time he returned safely to the island, he had been like a Crusader returning from a holy war. However, when he had tried telling the islanders about God's will, their souls had been too corrupt to accept God's blessings. Bewildered, he had trekked away from the town in the valley, in search of a sacred place to renew his soul. Hours later, when he emerged from the forest and found himself on this mountain land, it had seemed like paradise to him. He had planted the seed that day, before deeds had been signed and man's laws had been verified. The land had been God's gift; so, once the seed began to sprout, Shango's grandfather had seen it all as a sign that God had extended His blessings to the land and all who would live on it.

The man had built the house by hand, harvesting timber from the surrounding trees. After that, he had found Shango's grandmother—an impressionable girl from the country, who had seemed willing to accept God's plan for them. As the years passed, cement and plaster, and store-bought furniture, had been added to the house. A procession of children had followed—six in all. Shango's mother had been the last, but three of the six had died in childhood. One had died from a fever, one had drowned during an Easter excursion to the beach, and another had been hit by a car while walking down the mountain to the valley. Of the three children to make it to adulthood, one became enamored with the "gifts" some of the visiting cruise ship tourists provided, and soon died from a mystery illness that ravaged his immune system. The island had been harsh to their family; nevertheless, when Shango's grandfather succumbed to a stroke fifteen years ago, he had died believing he was in paradise, protected by his covenant with God.

S hango was still looking up at the tree dreamily. In a week or two, the mangoes would be ripe, and he would climb up into the tree to gorge himself. He unconsciously smiled at the thought—but then, unexpectedly, he began to sob as he remembered his grandmother. In years past, he would always pick the first mangoes of the season for her. That strange little ritual was gone forever; and all at once, the simple joys of mango season seemed lost forever...

Immediately outside the kitchen door, a deep cement ditch ran the length of the house. The ditch diverted the deluges that swept down the mountain during the rainy season. A cement plank between the kitchen door and the ground allowed people to bypass the ditch; but every once in a while, when Shango was rushing, he would fall into the ditch and scrape his shins. At those moments, his grandmother would yell at him for not looking where he was going, then she would douse his wounds with the stinging over-proof rum she used to treat all his cuts and bruises.

Shango sighed, wiped away his tears, then stepped across the plank. The outhouse was to the right, behind some bushes. His grandmother had made him paint it a few months ago, in a futile effort to keep termites from devouring it. Like the main house, the outhouse was dilapidated and ugly—even when it was freshly painted. Shango looked away from the structure, vaguely ashamed of his poverty, then he turned left, toward the sink.

Given the remote mountain location, the government had never gotten around to providing water and other utilities. There was no electricity, and no indoor plumbing. Like most of the structures on their land, the freestanding sink looked like it had been constructed from scavenged and leftover parts. Its base was concrete; the pipes and basin were old and rusty, as if they had come from a junkyard. As for the water, it came from a mountain stream about one hundred meters away, and was conveyed to the house through a system of pipes. A little further up the mountain, behind some guava trees, there was a shower, and a tank that stored the water from the stream.

Twenty years ago, Shango's uncle had celebrated his success in America by sending down money for the storage tank, pipes and sink. After experiencing the joys of America firsthand, he had sworn he would drag his boyhood home into the modern age. He had shipped a gas-powered generator from America, and hired a contractor to wire the house. Yet, even though the rooms in the house still had light bulbs screwed into their sockets, the generator had quickly rusted in the tropical climate. Worse, rats, or some other pests, had eaten away at the wires, as if they were candy. Elaborate plans to expand the house and install indoor plumbing had also fizzled. Nature had been too strong for the grandiose plans of men; so, with the passage of time, the overseas relatives had grown weary of their struggle against the mountain. They had concentrated on their new lives in America, and left his grandmother to the old ways.

Now that his grandmother was gone, Shango had no doubt that he would be joining his mother soon—within days, if not *hours*. Once he was gone from this place, nature would brush aside all his uncle's attempts to bring the modern world to the mountain. The pipes would rust and seep into the earth, the wood would rot, the cement would return to dust, the path through the forest would become overrun with vines and trees; and when all trace of Shango's family was gone from the land, his grandfather's decades-old covenant with God would finally come to an end.

In truth, Shango was still in shock. He looked back at the open doorway absentmindedly, asking himself if his grandmother was really dead. He was tempted to go back and look, but his bleeding hand was proof that it had all happened. In fact, while he had stood there daydreaming, the blood had dripped down his arm, onto his shirt and pants. Suddenly coming to his senses, he rushed to the sink, turned the tap and allowed the cold water to wash out his wounds. The sensation was soothing; he took a deep breath...

Once he had finished cleaning his hand, he washed his face and arms to clear away the blood. At last, he closed the tap and stood looking at his hand. For the most part, the bleeding had stopped, and all the wounds seemed clean. He nodded approvingly, then thought of the work ahead: bandage the wounds, head into town to inform the authorities—

He suddenly remembered the cellular phone! It had not rung in months, but it occurred to him he could use it to call his mother and the police. Shango's uncle had brought the phone when he visited five years ago—along with a solar battery charger (since there was no power to charge the phone otherwise). The charger and phone had been his uncle's last attempts to bring technology to the mountain. In the beginning, his mother would call every Sunday, like clockwork, and they would have long, meandering conversations about how everything would be perfect when they were together in America. However, over the years, her calls became less frequent—so that now, somehow, it had been six months since he had even heard his mother's voice. More troublingly, the last few times they talked, his mother had seemed rushed; when Shango lingered too long, she had pointedly told him she was late for an appointment or headed out of the door. ...And the last time he had seen her was when she visited at Christmastime four years ago. He had met her at the airport, and looked on in amazement as she sashayed out of the plane with sparkling new clothes. She had brought a sack of presents— just like Santa Claus—and had smiled more than he had ever seen her smile in his life. Everything about her had seemed transformed—enhanced by her brief sojourn in paradise. When she left, they had cried and hugged, but she had reminded him that God would reward their sacrifices.

By then, Shango had been a true believer. To prove himself worthy of God's grace, he had endured all the necessary hardships. Even while the loneliness got the better of him, he had told himself that it would only be a matter of time before he received heaven's reward. …Unfortunately, his childish expectations had been crushed the following Christmas, when his mother said there was not enough money for her to visit. A plane ticket would only eat into her savings and prolong the amount of time they were forced to be apart. Paradise required sacrifices, and God only blessed those who were resolute in their tasks, so they would all have to tighten their belts and make do with what they had.

In lieu of a visit, she had sent him some money to buy a present; and as soon as his grandmother handed over the money, he had rushed down to the town to get a remote-controlled car that had looked spectacular in the store's display case. In fact, he had spent half a year ogling it on his way to and from school. Unfortunately, as was so often the case, when he brought the toy home, it had only lasted two days before one of the wheels fell off. His grandmother had scolded him for his weakness, pointing out that he should have used the money to buy school books or something more practical. To her, his choice of toy had been especially stupid—since he could not afford new batteries anyway! Shango had sulked in his room for a few days; but after a while, his old religion had returned, and he had reminded himself that this was only another one of God's tests. In this way, each new disappointment had been proof that God was watching over him—and that his moment of deliverance was drawing near.

With the passage of time, his mother's one-year absence became two; two years became three; and now, somehow, it had been *four* years since he had seen her. Nevertheless, Shango's faith was absolute, and he would not waver.

Shango moved from the sink and headed for the kitchen door. After leaving his outside shoes on the mat, he entered the house. He needed a bandage for his hand, but there was nothing like that in the house. He could cut up one of his old shirts to make a bandage. However, when he looked down at his palm and saw the blood had stopped, he could not bring himself to go through the trouble. Similarly, since he lacked the courage to douse his palm with his grandmother's overproof rum, he put that idea out of his mind as well.

Instead, he focused on his plan: get the phone from grandmother's bedroom; call his mother and the police. He nodded his head and set off down the corridor, but his pace slowed after a few steps. Other than his bedroom and his grandmother's, there was a third one at the end of the corridor. It used to be his mother's room, but a demon had attacked him in there, while he was napping.

His stomach clenched as those old thoughts filled his mind; his pace slowed further, and a pained expression disfigured his face for a few seconds; but knowing he had no choice but to get the phone from his grandmother's room, he forced himself to move to her doorway.

After taking a deep breath to steel his courage, he pushed aside the sheet and looked inside. The curtains were drawn, so the room was still relatively dark. The darkness unnerved him. His grandmother's form was just a shadow on the bed—and he did not like the idea that he could not see her face. Indeed, at that moment, Shango remembered some of his grandmother's obeah stories—about reanimated corpses. Suddenly terrified, he stared at her shadowy form, looking for the slightest sign of movement. The voice of adulthood chastised him for such stupid thoughts, but he still stood in the doorway tentatively, holding the sheet.

Light: the room needed light! He grasped the sheet tightly, then he twisted the bottom of it, so that he could tie it in a loose knot.

That was better. Now, he needed to open the curtains. There was a window at the foot of his grandmother's bed. He went to it quickly. When he realized his heart was racing, he only pushed himself faster. He pulled the curtains apart in a brusque motion. The light was good. He opened the glass louvers to let in some fresh air, then he stood there breathing deeply. That was better.

When he felt sufficiently calm, he turned and looked at his grandmother. Her facial expression was still horrible. He found himself staring at her again—in case her eyes moved—but since her expression had not changed from what he remembered, his fears about mountain demons and reanimated corpses faded away for the moment. Besides, he did not have the strength of will (or the courage) to *keep* staring, so he looked away and went to his grandmother's dresser. The dresser was one of the household's rare pieces of store-bought furniture; but like everything else, it had become faded and chipped with age. It was perpendicular to the bed, against the wall; and on top of it, there were about a dozen black and white pictures of relatives—most of whom Shango had never met.

When he opened the top drawer, the phone was lying right there, next to his grandmother's neatly folded underwear. Yet, the obeah stories were still in the back of his mind; and once he had grabbed the phone, he found himself fleeing the room. After two steps, he remembered the solar charger. His grandmother kept it in its original box, under the dresser. Shango glanced at his grandmother, half-expecting her to be in a different position, or climbing out of bed to grab him. His fears told him to leave the solar charger and *run*, but his grandmother had not moved—and he definitely did not want to have to come in here again—so he darted back to the dresser, bent down, grabbed the box, and fled the room.

Once he was in the corridor, he pushed past the sheet in his doorway and entered his bedroom. He was breathing heavily again. The voice of adulthood was annoyed with him, but Shango did not care anymore.

He placed the box on the bed before looking at the phone. His grandmother usually kept it turned off—since his mother and uncle only called on Sundays. He pressed the button on the side, to turn it on. The start-up screen appeared, and the phone played a joyous tune. While the phone was displaying a message about searching for the network, a creepy feeling came over Shango, so that he turned back toward his doorway. The sheet still covered it, but he had a sudden fear that something might leap at him from behind it. He approached it anxiously, then he pulled it to the side the way people did in horror movies—as if expecting someone or something to be standing there. Mercifully, the corridor was still empty; and from where he was standing, he could see his grandmother's feet on her bed. As far as he could tell, she was still lying in the same position, but he knew he was coming undone.

First, he placed the phone on the bed; next, as a precaution, he grasped the sheet in his doorway, twisted it, and tied it in another loose knot. When that was done, he instinctively looked across the corridor again, into his grandmother's room, to check that her feet were still in the same position on the bed. When he caught himself, he looked away uneasily.

He needed to talk to his mother. He picked up the phone eagerly now. Two of the phone's three power bars were lit—which really did not tell him much, since the old battery usually gave out after twenty minutes of talking. He accessed the phone's address book by pressing a button. His mother's number was the only one stored on the phone—since he had gone out of his way to save it, and to type in her name and address on the keypad. Once the address book opened, he pressed the button to make the call.

He put the phone to his ear expectantly. His heart was thumping in his chest. He tried to think of what he would say to his mother, but he already felt the tears welling up. When the phone rang once, Shango stood straighter, and willed the tears back down into the depths of himself. When the ringing stopped, and a woman began speaking, Shango opened his mouth to reveal his horrible news. He was so dazed that he did not initially realize he was listening to an automated message. The only thing he heard was "credit expired." The message had to play a second time for him to understand the phone would not be able to make any calls until he bought some more credit. Bewildered, he ended the call by pressing a button on the phone, then he sat down heavily on the bed.

"*Damnit!*" he whispered. As he said it, he looked over at his grandmother's room guiltily—but when he remembered she was dead, he only felt exhausted. He was coming to grips with the fact that he was going to have to walk down to the town in the valley and buy some phone minutes. Unfortunately, since he did not have any money, he would have to get it from his grand-mother's purse. Once again, he looked across the corridor, the same uneasy feeling coming over him. He got off the bed and took a step in that direction, but then he faltered. Maybe he should get dressed first? He nodded his head, happy for the reprieve.

He placed the phone on top of the box with the solar charger, then he went to the foot of his bed, where there was a crude trunk that his grandfather had made from scraps of wood *decades* ago. Inside the trunk, his clothes were folded neatly: three pairs of school uniforms, some underwear, socks, and some dress clothes his mother had shipped in a barrel a year ago. There were also the clothes of Christmas past—sets of clothes that she had mailed two and three years ago. Most of the old clothes were either too tight or so worn that they were only fit for wearing around the house.

Shango grabbed one of the newer slacks, then pulled them on, over his shorts. The pants were now slightly too tight for him, but they were presentable enough that he could wear them in public without the usual sense of embarrassment at his poverty. Because of his shame, he had never brought any of his friends home—and he had never visited his friends' homes either, out of fear that they would expect him to reciprocate. In truth, nobody really knew where he lived. The house was not visible from the road, there were no neighbors, and few people were even aware that there was a path from the road, which snaked through the forest and led to the house. Also, since Shango was honest with himself, he knew none of the boys he played football with after school were close enough to him to *warrant* a visit to his home. He had playmates and classmates, but he did not have friends in a true sense. He did not have *confidants*...

He pulled off his dingy shirt before putting on a trendy-looking t-shirt his mother had sent him last year. He was ready to leave. The only thing left to do was get the money from his grandmother's bag. He was about to head to her bedroom when he glanced at the phone and saw it had only one power bar left. Indeed, the bar was flashing. He would have to set up the solar charger and let the phone charge while he was away. He figured it would be ready by the time he returned from buying credit and talking to the police. He nodded his head, pleased with his plan—but that was when he realized he could get the police to call his mother when he went to the station! Yeah, that was so much simpler. ...And he was strangely relieved now—since this meant he would not have to go into his grandmother's room to get the money. He would let the police take care of everything. All at once, he was eager to be a twelve-year-old boy again: he would let the adults take on those burdens, and sort out all the intractable details they claimed they understood.

Acting quickly, he accessed the phone's address book again, while it still had power. Next, he grabbed his school bag from under the bed, tore out a sheet of paper, and wrote down his mother's phone number.

S hango took the solar charger out of the box and stood looking at it. The main part, the photovoltaic panel, was only about the size of his school notebook. There was a bulkier piece that attached to it via a wire (which had two outlets to plug in equipment). His grandmother had left the phone charger plugged into one of the outlets. Shango plugged the charger into the phone, and was about to pick up all the pieces and carry them over to the windowsill, when he saw the glass was still on the floor—in front of the window. He sucked his teeth in annoyance. The blood was still there as well, but he did not feel like cleaning up the mess right now. He put on one of his slippers before he remembered he had thrown the other one through the louvers, and that it was still outside. He sucked his teeth again, but then he remembered his "town shoes"—that is, the pair of canvas sneakers that were presentable enough to wear to school. They were underneath his bed. He retrieved them from under the bed, then put them on. After that, he scooped all the electrical devices into his arms, walked over to the window, and arrayed them on the windowsill. He waited until the phone made the cheerful sound that said it was charging, then he sighed in relief.

His grandmother would definitely not be pleased that he was leaving the glass there, but he told himself it was an emergency. Now that everything was resolved in his mind, he walked back to his bed to get his school bag—since he usually felt naked when he left the house without it. In truth, he had never missed a day of school in his life. He had never been sick enough to stay home; and in a way, the daily forty-five minute walks to and from school had made him stronger. When he played football with the other boys after school, he would run circles around them; his energy would seem boundless, and they would be in awe of him. Also, in a counterintuitive way, his poverty meant that he ate a healthier diet than his classmates and their families. He could not afford the highly processed, sugar-laden imported foods that had become bizarre status symbols on the island. While others grew fat on this diet, Shango only ate the natural, organic foods that grew on his grandmother's land. It would shame him that his lunch pail usually only contained provisions like yams, callaloo, and string beans—and he would sneak away from the others to eat. However, while he had been cowering in shame, his body had been growing strong.

On his way out of his room, he forced himself not to look at his grandmother. However, he moved faster once he was past her room—in case her corpse sprang at him once his back was turned. Soon, he was outside, pulling the kitchen door closed behind him.

Standing there, he noticed, for perhaps the first time, that there was a disconcerting silence about the place. Only two months ago, they had had ten chickens and a dog. The dog would bark all night; the chickens would cluck incessantly—and go into an orgy of crowing about five-thirty in the morning. Unfortunately, the old dog eventually became sick or senile—and began to disappear for days at a time. When Shango's grandmother realized a mongoose, or some other creature, had been eating the chickens during the dog's absence, only about four of the ten chickens were left. The next day, Shango discovered the dog's decaying corpse while he was walking down the path to school. He noticed the stench of death in the air; and when he went to investigate, he found the corpse lying behind some hibiscus bushes, infested with maggots. There had been nothing to do then, except to let nature run its course. As for the chickens, his grandmother had killed the remaining ones, and salted them for storage—since the mongoose would only return for them later.

The death of all the animals had left an eerie silence about the place. His grandmother had been talking about getting a new dog, some chickens, and maybe even some rabbits, but none of that was going to happen now. Indeed, as Shango walked past the sink, turned the corner of the house, and began walking down the mountain, he returned to the melancholy thought that everything was slowly disappearing from the land. Like the dog, the chickens, and his grandmother, everything was fading back into the nothingness, and soon there would be nothing left...

His grandmother's garden was to his right as he walked. The ditch at the back of the house emptied out into the fields. She had pigeon peas, manioc, sweet potatoes, and plantains—along with beets, cucumbers, pumpkins and tomatoes. On the far edge of her field, there was a breadfruit tree, and coconut trees. A few times a year, she would cut down the coconuts, grate them by hand, and boil them down to make oil. She had peanuts and corn; there were papayas and several other fruits whose formal names he had never bothered to learn. The land was abundant, and a pained expression came to his face when it occurred to him nobody would be here to eat the fruits once his mother took him away to America....

In the center of his grandmother's field there was a huge boulder that had been too big to move. The top was relatively flat, and Shango liked to sit on it and watch the sun setting over the forest. He thought of his grandmother then, because every time his mother and uncle talked to her about coming to America, she would say she was like the boulder—because nothing would move her off the land, and she would be there long after everyone else was gone.

The house rested on four concrete pillars; as the land was steep, the two pillars in front of the house were much longer than the two in back. Underneath the house, in the open space left by the pillars, there were some empty shipping barrels his relatives had sent down in previous years. The chicken coops were still there—but empty now, and creepily quiet. Shango did not like any of it. He moved faster, in order to get away from the place; but as the path was about to enter the forest, he stopped and looked back at the house. The weathered boards needed to be painted—especially at the front of the house. Unfortunately, since the house was on a steep incline, a tall ladder was needed to complete the work. One of his grandmother's old friends had promised to do it, but the vague offer had never resulted in definite actions. Like everything else on the island, the unpainted boards and the promises of his grandmother's friend were all irrelevant now.

As he stood there, he had the vague sense that there was no going back for him now. He would either move forward or he would fade into the nothingness—like everything else his relatives had brought to the mountain. He took a deep breath then, as if cleansing himself of the last remnants of nostalgia. In a matter of days or *hours*, when his mother came to take him away from this place, none of this would have mattered. Reassured by the thought, he moved more quickly.

As for Shango's father, the man was like a myth to him. Somewhere out there, there was probably documentable proof that the man had once existed, but Shango had never seen it. He had never laid eyes on the man. There were no pictures; and since his grandmother had only ever referred to him as "That Man," Shango had never even known his father's name. He did not know if the man was dead or alive—or *where* he had lived—and so, the man remained a myth to him. The few times he had scrounged up the courage to ask his grandmother about his father, she had gone on wild tirades about sin and the weakness of the human soul. More confusingly, the details of the story would always change. Sometimes, his father would be a drug-selling thug; sometimes, from his grandmother's lurid descriptions, his father would seem like a lecherous old man; at other times, the thing in his grandmother's stories would not seem like a man at all—but like one of the restless spirits she said roamed the mountain in search of young, corruptible souls. The only constant in his grandmother's stories was that his mother had been tempted by evil, and that Shango had been the result of their sinful union. With all of that, Shango had grown up fearing the man—the way he feared all the demons in his grandmother's stories.

It was about an eight-minute walk from the house to the road. The path through the forest was getting overgrown, so he found himself pushing vines and low-hanging branches out of the way as he walked. A few times a year—especially during the rainy season—his grandmother would make him go up and down the path with a cutlass, pruning the vines and beating back the unceasing encroachment of nature. Now that his grandmother was gone, the forest path suddenly felt like it was closing in around him. He found himself trotting down the path, beating away vines and bushes as if they were attackers—

Then, at last, Shango swatted aside a final branch, and found himself looking out on the narrow mountain road. The forest path terminated on the inner edge of a long, sweeping curve. To his right, there was a weathered wooden stand that his grandmother used to sell fruits and vegetables to passersby. Across the road, beyond the outer edge, there was a steep drop—a cavernous pit that was at least four hundred meters deep and several kilometers in diameter. The sides were sheer and rocky, but vines and plants clung to them nonetheless. From where he stood, he could see the other side of the pit in the distance. Below, in the depths, there was a thick canopy of trees—and caves that millions of bats would emerge from at night. In his childish imagination, a whole other world existed at the bottom of the pit. Since there was no safe way to reach the bottom—besides repelling, being lowered by a helicopter, or some other extraordinary means that was beyond the vast majority of people on the island—Shango had always suspected a magical world existed in the depths, populated by demons and spirits and all the creatures of his imagination.

When he was ready to step onto the road, he paused and looked both ways for oncoming traffic. He saw nothing—and he did not hear the telltale whine of a speeding car—so he stepped into the road and began to make his way down the mountain. This stage of the mountain road was particularly treacherous, since it was bordered by the pit on the right and the black granite of the mountain on the left. Moreover, there was no guardrail on the side of the road: the gaping maw of the pit merely loomed, ready to devour anything that ventured too close.

The road itself had literally been hewn out of the mountain; and every time Shango reached this section, he would always feel the secret terror that the road would collapse into the pit entirely, taking him with it. Indeed, when he walked this section of the road, he always stayed as far away from the pit as possible, clinging to the mountain-side of the road.

About eight years ago, a devastating hurricane had washed away entire sections of the road; subsequent landslides had rendered it unusable for almost a year. The Chinese had loaned the island one hundred million US dollars to effect repairs, and a Chinese firm had been contracted to do the work. The rumor was that about a third of the money had ended up in secret accounts in the Cayman Islands. Government officials on the island soon started expanding their houses, or building new mansions in secluded enclaves. Exotic cars began appearing on the road; the marina had to be expanded, in order to accommodate the arrival of new yachts. There had been a brief outcry in the beginning—from opposition politicians and journalists, who pointed out that their children, and their children's children, would spend their lives paying for the misbegotten luxuries of their leaders—but since the Chinese firm had done an excellent job on the road, the islanders had gone back to ignoring the obvious corruption in their midst.

Fifteen minutes later, the snaking mountain road finally moved away from the pit. Shango breathed a little easier; but because of the steepness of the mountain, the road essentially became a series of switchbacks. Shango could look through the trees and bushes and see portions of the road below. Sometimes, when the gradient of the mountain was shallow enough, he could bypass the long switchbacks by taking shortcuts through the bushes and trees. However, he usually took the long route, since shortcuts inevitably left him with muddy shoes and soiled clothes.

...His grandmother was really dead. The thought reentered his mind unexpectedly; he faltered, and had to brace himself from the grief. The initial shock was gone: now he was just numb—and exhausted. To keep himself going, he focused on what he had to do: go into town, tell the police what had happened, and let the adult world do the rest.

He was so locked into following his plan that he did not initially hear the car closing in behind him. He heard the tires peal as the vehicle took the corner too quickly; he barely turned his head halfway when he caught a glimpse of the Range Rover's front bumper and grill. Instinct took over, and he jumped to the side of the road. The vehicle zoomed past in a blur, but the gust of wind hit him like a blow. Either that, or the vehicle sideswiped him, because he soon found himself tumbling down the mountain.

He screamed out as he went through a thorny bush; he felt his clothes and limbs being soiled and ripped as he toppled. He tried to stop his descent by putting out his hands, but it was pointless. The wounds on his palm, from when he landed on the glass that morning, were reopening; new wounds—on his arms and legs and back—were added, so that he felt like he was in a blender, being ripped to shreds.

Indeed, his chaotic descent only came to an end when he

collided with a sturdy tree. He hit the trunk with his ribs, and lay dazed and winded for a while, gasping for air and moaning. Maybe another ten seconds passed before he heard the Range Rover's whining engine on the road beneath him. He looked down the mountain, dazed, fighting to focus as the dizziness subsided. The vehicle's tires screeched as it turned the corner of the switchback; and as Shango regained more of his senses, he saw the Range Rover come into view on the road below. The bastards had not even bothered to stop after running him off the road! In fact, Shango heard the vehicle picking up speed now.

All at once, he was overcome with the same rage he had felt at the sight of the blood-filled mosquito. There was a nice rock lying on the ground before him—nice, in the sense that it was the perfect size and weight for throwing. He picked it up as he rose from the ground; then, the moment he was to his feet, he flung it with all his might. He did not really aim in a true sense; and with so many trees between him and the bottom road, hitting the speeding Range Rover was a one in a million shot. Yet, a queasy feeling came over Shango as the rock arched perfectly in the air, gliding between tree trunks and low-hanging branches, as if guided by the hand of God...and then, as the rock smashed into the vehicle's side window, Shango felt as though his heart had stopped and his lungs had shriveled to the size of a pea.

The glass did not shatter entirely, but inside the Range Rover, the sound must have been deafening—since the startled driver quickly lost control. On the narrow road, the vehicle swerved one way, then the other; the driver slammed on the brakes, but that only left the vehicle sliding sideways. Then, Shango was watching in horror as the Range Rover literally flipped over the edge of the road—where there was a deep ravine. For a long while, there was silence, and then he shuddered as he heard the terrible crash. For the second time that morning, Shango fell to his knees.

Yet, after the initial shock, he found himself running down the mountain, toward the road. At last, when he ran across the road and looked down into the ravine, he saw the crumpled wreck was on its back—like a huge, mangled turtle. Its wheels were still spinning eerily; but as the axles were broken, they wobbled as they spun.

From the sight of the vehicle, Shango was sure all the passengers were dead. His first impulse was to run away—to *hide*—but what if they were still alive? He thought about his grandmother again—about her *disappointment*. She was with the angels now—so even if he snuck away and managed to get away with it, his grandmother would know. For a moment, he tried to find a justification for his act: the people in the car had almost run him down; he hadn't meant to do it...but while the excuses were technically true, they could not justify murder. *Murder*...! He felt weak at the word. He was on a whole other level now. This was not something that could be rectified with one of his grandmother's beatings. There was no making this right. Once the authorities found out what he had done, his life would be over. He saw this clearly. There would be no going to America now—no paradise to soothe his pain after a lifetime of hardships and sacrifices. Tears almost flowed at the thought—but there was only one course of action open to him now.

Actually, he was nodding his head absentmindedly when he became aware that sirens were wailing in the air. The sirens were coming from further up the mountain; and from the way they blared, Shango knew multiple vehicles were coming—and that they were coming at breakneck speed.

Two police cars turned the bend in the switchback and came

into view. They had slowed in order to navigate the switchback, but they now began to pick up speed again. After taking a deep breath, Shango stepped into the road to stop them—and to offer himself up to their justice.

The driver of the lead car slammed on the brakes; the second car almost rear-ended it, but swerved to the side at the last moment. Shango stared ahead blankly as both cars came to a screeching halt. An enraged policeman emerged from the lead vehicle, shouting a string of expletives. When Shango only stood there, the man stepped from the car and put his hand on the holster of his gun. He was still yelling—but it was impossible to hear what he was saying with the sirens blaring. The other three policemen had gotten out of their vehicles as well. The men joined in the screaming, and gesticulated threateningly as the first policeman approached Shango—as if instructing their colleague on how to bash in the boy's head.

The approaching policeman's face was hard and set. He looked like he would strangle Shango the moment he was within reach, but when the man was about two steps away, Shango pointed over the edge of the embankment with a trembling finger. Something about Shango's strange mien disarmed the man for a moment, and he stepped closer to the edge to have a look. When he saw the vehicle at the bottom of the ravine, his eyes grew wide, and he began waving wildly for the other officers to come over. Soon, the four men were standing on the edge of the embankment, screaming amongst themselves.

With his duty complete, Shango stepped to the side and waited for the men to decide his fate.

The policemen were all between twenty and thirty years of age, and shared the same tall, powerful frames. Eventually, the one with the highest rank—a sergeant—yelled for one of his subordinates to go turn off the sirens. Next, he told the remaining two to find a way to reach the vehicle. Once all the tasks had been assigned, he returned to his vehicle to report the incident on his cellular phone. Shango looked on in a daze. The sergeant had a gold incisor: Shango watched it in amazement as it sparkled in the morning sun.

The world seemed emptier once the sirens were off. The sergeant was now inside his police cruiser, making an animated report. His subordinate listened from outside the car, with a rapt expression on his face—as if the sergeant were telling the most exciting story he had ever heard. While all this was going on, the two officers the sergeant had sent to the Range Rover had run further down the mountain—about fifty meters past Shango. There, the contour of the mountain allowed them to climb down the embankment without breaking their necks. They were now grabbing tree trunks and large rocks to slow their descent. Shango watched their antics disinterestedly for a few moments—but then he suddenly realized it was odd that they had their guns drawn. Indeed, it was odd that they were ignoring him. Nobody had asked him how he had come to be there, or how the vehicle had capsized. He seemed totally irrelevant to them.

Apparently, the sergeant had instructed the officer waiting outside the car to join his colleagues, because the man ran past Shango now, and headed down the mountain as well. As for the sergeant, he was still talking on the phone, yelling over the static-laced gibberish of whoever was talking on the other end of the line.

Presently, as Shango looked over the edge of the road, he saw the first of the officers was nearing the bottom of the ravine. For some reason, the man was approaching the vehicle tentatively. He gave it wide berth; he pointed his gun as he inspected what was visible of the Range Rover's dark interior. Then, when something caught his attention, he rushed to the back door. It was impossible to open the door—since the frame had been warped by the fall, but the officer kicked in what remained of the glass, then bent down to haul out a body. It was a woman in a nightgown. Her hair was long and bloody. In fact, there was blood everywhere—but Shango was relieved when he saw the woman was moving. Maybe he was not a murderer after all.

In fact, he now found himself thinking that maybe this had been another of God's tests. Maybe God would reward his courage by making America a possibility once more. All at once, everything seemed possible, so he stood straighter and looked out on the world with renewed hope.

The woman the policeman had pulled from the car seemed to be regaining her senses—and moving freely, as though she had sustained no serious injuries. Indeed, the policeman took her in his arms then, and began heading out of the ravine. Shango was almost on the verge of smiling, but that was when he noticed the other two policemen moving to the front of the vehicle with their guns drawn. For some reason, they were now taking aim at whoever was in the driver's seat. And then, inexplicably, they opened fire. Shango found himself thinking that the gunshots sounded nothing like the gunshots in movies. They sounded innocuous, like corn popping. It was all so unreal that he could only stare in disbelief.

Time became warped again, so that entire minutes seemed to pass in a blur. After a while, his mind froze. He saw, but did not see; he was standing there, yet he felt like a leaf blowing in the breeze—

He suddenly became aware the sergeant was standing next to

him. He reflexively stepped back, ready to run for his life—as if the man were a ghost that had appeared out of the nothingness. Yet, compared to him, the sergeant was huge, so Shango again saw there would be no point in trying to run. Besides, it was at that moment that the sergeant put his hand on Shango's left shoulder. The weight was like a load of bricks, and Shango felt like his legs were going to buckle beneath him. When he looked up, there was something like a smile on the sergeant's face—but it was fake, and they both knew it was fake.

"You didn't see nothing here today, you hear?" The fake grin widened after he said it; Shango looked at his gold incisor glistening in the sunlight again, then he nodded his head.

At that, the man's smile became slightly more genuine, but his hand still felt like a load of bricks on Shango's shoulder. Shango's collarbone seemed on the verge of snapping; his shoulder *throbbed*—

"What's your name?" the sergeant asked now.

"Shango, sir," he replied reflexively, the way his grandmother had trained him.

"What's your *surname*?" the sergeant asked pointedly.

"Cartwright, sir."

"Good," the man said, sizing him up. "You seem like a fine young man, Shango Cartwright." He grinned again, and Shango realized the man had said his name deliberately, to show him he remembered it, and that he would put that knowledge to use if he ever had a reason to. From the expression in the sergeant's eyes, Shango knew the man would feel no remorse if that day ever came. The police were like wild dogs on the island—or so his grandmother would tell him whenever she heard of a police shooting in the news. The worse crime got, the more the police and their supporters believed the police had to be worse than the criminals. There was a logical fallacy somewhere, but the sergeant's threat was so clear and nonchalant that Shango accepted it the way he would accept a statement that the sky was blue. If he told anyone what had happened here, the sergeant and his men would gun him down just as ruthlessly as they had gunned down the person driving the Range Rover. Shango saw all this in an instant, and nodded his head to make this fact clear to the sergeant.

By now, the officer with the woman was nearing the top—while the other two were still in the ravine, searching the vehicle, covering their tracks or whatever policemen did when they gunned down people on the island.

The officer with the woman was panting and wheezing now. Since the sergeant saw his business with Shango was done, he removed his hand from the boy's shoulder and went to help his subordinate. The pain in Shango's shoulder stopped immediately, but it felt numb and stiff now. He flexed his shoulder and neck while the sergeant reached down to help the officer over the edge. Now that the officer and his cargo were close, Shango saw the woman was actually only a girl around his age. She was pretty in that peculiar way that signified wealth and privilege in the Caribbean. Her hair was long; her skin was light—but she was in shock. She stared at Shango, and he stared at her—both of them strangely accepting of the horror they had lived through.

The sergeant asked her if she was okay. She stared at him for a few seconds before nodding her head. At that, the sergeant gestured to the officer, who carried her over to the car. Shango turned to watch as the young officer and the girl went past him; the sergeant stopped at Shango's side and stood watching as well. Once the officer placed the girl in the back of the vehicle, he got behind the steering wheel, executed an expert U-turn on the narrow road, and headed back up the mountain. Shango stared at the retreating car, wondering if it was really over—

"Shango Cartwright," the sergeant began again. Shango looked up to see the man proffering some money. It was a large denomination—a note so large he had never actually seen it before. When Shango put out his hand to take it, the man pulled it back, and pursed his lips thoughtfully. "This may be too much money for a youth man like you," he mused. "This is *big man* money. You *sure* you can handle it?"

Shango did not know what to say, so he nodded his head.

"Excellent," the sergeant said too enthusiastically, grinning again, so that the gold incisor blinded Shango as the sun hit it. Shango squinted, then instinctively nodded again as the sergeant went on, "I have a *real* good feeling about you, Shango Cartwright."

For some bizarre reason, Shango felt compelled to say, "Thank you, sir." He found himself thinking that his grandmother would be pleased—but he had the strange sense that none of this could possibly be happening. ...Everyone dealt with trauma differently. Shango's way was to seek refuge in a kind of hyper-rationality—especially when out in public. All his life, he had been fighting a kind of guerilla war against the outside world. All his life he had sought to hide the depths of his poverty from a world he feared would ridicule him. Even now, when he had every justification to be screaming hysterically about his grandmother's death, a lifetime's worth of fear and distrust compelled him to hide behind good manners. He was vaguely aware of the internal contradiction—of the disconnect between how he felt inside and how he was acting—but a lifetime's worth of fear was difficult to overcome, even with reason.

...And his fears were about more than what people might discover about his poverty: they extended into a vast metaphysical plane barely accessible by his conscious mind. He could not explain it, but all his life he had been convinced there was something sinister within him. He would feel it stirring at times, trying to coax him into the darkness. It whispered horrible things into his ears; it compelled him to do things like pick up stones and fling them at his enemies. It *seduced* him—not with the promise of pleasure—but with the boundless possibilities of thoughtless rage. Anarchy lurked in the dark place within him, like a bomb that might explode at any moment for any reason. In this sense, he hid behind decorum and punctilio as a way to keep the darkness from spilling out and devastating a world ill prepared to contain it....

The sergeant was frowning now; realizing something, he took a step back to scan Shango's clothes. "What happened to you?"

Shango looked down at himself, seeing all the mud; there were cuts on his arms. "I slipped," he said simply.

The sergeant thought about asking some obvious follow-up questions, but then shrugged his shoulders. As he did, something new occurred to him, and he glanced at his watch. "How come you ain't in school?"

Shango opened his mouth; all at once, he remembered his grandmother's death, and his original purpose for walking into town. However, as he looked into the man's probing eyes, he instinctively knew this was not the kind of policeman who addressed mundane problems like old women dying in their beds, so he closed his mouth and stood staring up at the man.

The sergeant took Shango's reticence for schoolboy guilt, and declared, in a conciliatory (but utterly meaningless) manner, "Youths must go to school." When Shango nodded contritely, the man continued, "Make sure you go to school tomorrow, you hear?"

"Yes, sir," Shango answered him strongly. Something about the boy's tone pleased him, so that he smiled again.

"You're headed into town now?"

"Yes, sir."

"You going to buy something?"

Shango had no money, but the sergeant was so domineering that Shango thought it unwise to correct him—or do anything to prolong the conversation. "Yes, sir," he answered quickly.

"You going to Gupta's shop?"

"Yes, sir."

"Good," he said, proffering the money again. Shango grasped the end of it, but the sergeant did not release it immediately. Instead, he added, "A youth man walking around with big man money will seem strange to people, and we don't want things to seem strange, do we?"

"No, sir," Shango replied, again digesting the threat in the man's words.

"Good, so take this money to Gupta. Take it to him *personally*, and tell him Daddis sent you."

"Daddis," Shango said faintly. The man let go of the bill then, and nodded his head.

Seeing that he had been dismissed, Shango jammed the bill into his front pocket of his pants, and said, "Sir," a final time. He was about to turn and leave when a car suddenly came charging up the mountain. It was a decrepit Volkswagen Beetle from the nineteen seventies, painted a greenish-brown color that reminded Shango of vomit. The car came to a screeching halt a few meters from where Shango and the sergeant were standing, then a slovenly old man in his sixties or seventies jumped out of with his camera in tow. The man's shirt was hanging out of his pants, and was decorated with various stains—from coffee, ink, and whatever he had eaten for breakfast. He had a grizzled beard, and the kind of puffy, red eyes Shango associated with the pathetic old men who sat outside the rum shop all day. The man rushed past Shango and the sergeant, then began taking pictures of the wreck in the ravine. The sergeant sucked his teeth in annoyance—

"Hey, Charlie," the man addressed Daddis in an offhand manner as he took pictures, "what happened here?"

"Isn't it clear?" the sergeant said menacingly. "A car fell in the ravine."

"Any survivors?" the man asked, turning around for the first time.

"The driver was killed on impact," the sergeant said flatly; Shango glanced at his face, then looked away uneasily when he realized the man had lied.

"Only one person in the car?" the man asked; Shango watched the old man's face curiously, wondering what he knew and what he would be able to figure out.

The sergeant sucked his teeth again. "Yes, only one."

Shango looked up at the sergeant objectively, as if trying to grade his ability to lie. The man seemed good enough at it, but his obvious annoyance with the old man meant he would never be a totally convincing liar. Shango looked at the old man's face next, where he saw doubts stirring. The old man stepped closer to the sergeant now:

"Who was he?"

"We haven't determined that yet," the sergeant droned.

"When will you determine it?"

"Once we look up his license plates."

"There weren't any documents in the car?"

"*Look*," the sergeant began, losing patience, "as soon as we know something, we'll let you know."

"No you won't!" the man shot back. "You *never* tell me anything."

"Then why bother asking?" he said with a sardonic laugh. "We both know you'll just make up lies in that shitty newspaper anyway."

At that, the old man chuckled and bowed mockingly, saying, "Well, Charlie, one man's lie is another man's truth."

"Stop calling me Charlie!" the sergeant fired back. "I am Sergeant Henderson to you!"

"There's no need for false formality between us, Charles," the man began in a singsong voice. "What would your mother say if she could see us now?"

At the mention of his mother, the sergeant was trapped between rage and the awareness that the conversation was on the verge of becoming farcical. He sighed. "Look, since you're just going to make up nonsense anyway, why not do it somewhere else, so we can finish our investigation?"

The words were supposed to put an end to the conversation, but the newspaperman launched into a tirade about freedom of the press and police corruption; the sergeant countered that the old man was a waste of space, that his mother must have been sniffing glue when she conceived him, and other choice words that had both men shaking with rage. Shango found it all fascinating, but he also had enough sense to get the hell out of there and leave them to their craziness.

Suddenly wary, he turned and continued down the road, to the town. He did not look back; and once the men and the scene were out of range, the entire incident seemed so unreal that he began to doubt it could have happened. The only evidence was the sergeant's money. He pulled it halfway out of his pocket and looked at it surreptitiously. Even then, none of it seemed possible.

After a few minutes of walking, Shango's pace slowed: he wondered where he was going, and why he was going there. His original plan—to go into the town and inform the police of his grandmother's death—was now buried beneath an avalanche of complications and hidden terrors. Less than an hour ago, he had had faith in the police and the adult world; he had trusted them to contact his mother and take care of his grandmother— but every few steps, he kept having flashbacks of Daddis' glistening incisor; he saw the policemen in the ravine opening fire on the person in the Range Rover. The police were like venomous snakes hiding in the bushes: going to them willingly seemed like madness. He sensed an irrational fear growing within him, and if he didn't stamp it out now, it would incapacitate him forever. Yet, Daddis' glistening incisor was still there....

He stopped abruptly when something occurred to him: he could use the sergeant's money to purchase some phone credit, then he could call his mother. He nodded his head and smiled vapidly at the thought. Besides, only talking to his mother seemed right now. No one on the island could be trusted. They were all snakes hiding in the bush, waiting for him to venture too close and let down his defenses. Instead of trusting them, he would call his mother and tell her what had happened. It was better for her to deal with the police from afar than for Shango to take unnecessary risks with them. Once he called his mother, she would come for him, and he would get the hell off the island.

...Had the police really killed someone in front of him? Even now, the scene had an eerie, dreamlike quality. For a moment, his mind fluttered over the mystery of the Range Rover's driver, and the beautiful girl in the nightgown, but Daddis' grinning face was still there, reminding him to mind his business.

He began walking again, but he felt doomed—as if time were

running out. He had the sense that if he did not leave the island soon, he would be trapped here forever, with the snakes and monsters. He found himself moving faster, suddenly desperate to reach the town and take the only escape hatch he saw out of this place.

Yet, when he turned the next switchback there was an overlook, from which he could see the town and the valley floor. At certain times of the day, the view was spectacular—especially in the afternoon, when the sun lit up the sky in pastel hues. However, the town, itself had always been ugly to him. From this distance, the place seemed like a conglomeration of shacks. Only about two thousand people lived there, but on Saturdays, when people came for the market, there were maybe twice that. He judged the people there by the filth they left behind. In every gutter and alleyway there were discarded plastic bags, bottles and junk food containers. There were street gangs, for want of a better word, who staked out certain alleyways and intersections. However, they were mostly just bored kids with no prospects, led by men whose only prospect was to manipulate bored kids with no prospects.

Beyond the town, there was a highway that led to the capital. From dawn till dusk, the local farmers would set up their stands on the side of the highway and try to sell their produce to all the people bypassing the town. Sometimes whole families would be seen on the side of the highway; the more enterprising of them would send children as young as three to hold out the produce and prey on the guilt of the speeding drivers. From gangs to families, they were all using one another to stay alive. Everything about the place was ugly, and Shango saw it all in his mind's eye as he stood there—

Another flashback of Daddis' incisor made him shudder—and

he saw his grandmother's corpse in the darkened bedroom, staring menacingly into space. He shook his head to drive away the images, then he moved on.

He was now on the foothills of the mountain. There were a few houses here, which belonged to some of the town's richer families. The gates were all tall; the windows were all grated, and the signs outside the front gates all had messages from security companies, warning trespassers of quick and deadly armed responses. Something about this stretch of the road had always unnerved him, so he began moving faster. He clamped the schoolbag at his side, and bowed his head, as if fighting against a stinging wind.

He was in this position when the Volkswagen appeared at his side. When he looked over, the newspaperman from earlier was waving at him. Shango's mind was so dazed that he stared at the man for a few seconds before he recognized him.

"You want a ride?" the man asked.

When Shango stopped, the car stopped. He glanced into the man's car: the passenger seat was between him and the man. There were some old newspapers and discarded food containers on the seat. The car smelled faintly of toe jam and sour oranges. The combination was immediately nauseating, and Shango shook his head.

"Why not?" the man enquired.

Since he was still dazed, Shango thought about it methodically before replying: "...Not supposed to ride with strange people." That was something his grandmother had always told him, and he had a vague sense that she would be pleased. He went to leave, but the newspaperman went on quickly:

"A wise policy, indeed, young man. Your mother taught you well...but there can't really be strangers on an island with only one hundred thousand people, can there? You and I are probably distant cousins—or maybe I went to school with your grandfather. We're all brothers and sisters, one way or another—members of one big family." As the newspaperman babbled on, Shango thought about the policemen gunning down the man in the Range Rover. That hadn't seemed too brotherly. He thought about his own rage when he threw the rock at the Range Rover. The sequence of events made him grimace. When he looked up, the newspaperman was still waxing poetic about their strong national bonds. The more the man talked, the more Shango knew it was all nonsense. In fact, after a while, the newspaperman's crude attempt to bamboozle him seemed insulting, so that the anger rose in him.

"I don't know anything, sir," Shango cut him off. He spoke with the kind of conscious effort that gratified his teachers when he answered questions in class. His grammar was perfect; his diction and enunciation were precise, and the newspaperman immediately stopped his speech and looked at him uncertainly. After a few awkward seconds had passed, with them staring at one another, Shango continued, "You already know most of what I know."

The newspaperman decided to recalibrate his approach. "Did you witness the accident?"

Shango sighed, exhausted. Yet, for some reason, it seemed beneath his dignity to lie to the man, or play any of the foolish games that people played. "I would rather not talk about it, sir," he said in his schoolroom voice.

"Are you afraid—of the police?" the newspaperman asked earnestly. After all, with his mud-stained clothes, Shango seemed like any of the other half-starved children on the island, who were doomed by their families' poverty. At the same time, there was something peculiar about the boy. As the newspaperman watched Shango, he sensed something more fascinating than the story behind the wrecked Range Rover in the ravine. He had asked the boy if he was afraid, but now, as he stared into Shango's eyes, he saw a strange kind of boldness there—*clarity*. It was not that the boy seemed fearless, but as though some inner strength was allowing him to hold all those fears at bay. What's more, the boy's voice was calm and clear; he did not speak like poor, hopeless boys were supposed to speak. If anything, he was too calm and self-aware. The newspaperman suddenly had the suspicion that the boy had stumbled upon something amazing—some mystical secret that had eluded the rest of them. For the man, it was like coming upon a treasure lying on the street: he had a strange impulse to grab the boy and take him away somewhere, to unwrap the secret in private. The idea was creepy, and when he became conscious of it, he pushed it to the side and instinctively put up his hand to assure the boy he meant no harm.

Either way, by now, Shango had shaken his head in response to the man's question about being afraid. He was not sure if that was true or not, but the voice of adulthood told him fear was irrelevant at this point in time: the only thing that mattered was getting off the island.

When Shango turned halfway and prepared to leave, a kind of wild desperation entered the newspaperman's eyes—a kind of *hunger*. Seeing it, Shango shook his head again: "You already know most of what I know," he said once more, "...and the things you *don't* know..." He did not finish the phrase, but the warning was clear.

The strange maturity of the statement again took the newspaperman off guard. He frowned. "How old are you?"

"I'm twelve, sir."

"What's your name?"

"Shango Cartwright, sir," he said flatly.

"My name is Earl Maitland, Shango Cartwright, and I'm in the business of finding out things people don't think I should know."

Something about the statement seemed self-congratulatory and ridiculous—especially considering the state of the man's car. Whatever business Maitland was in, it did not seem to be going well, and Shango unconsciously smiled at the stupidity of it all. He glanced into the back seat then, seeing a pair of soiled trousers and a half-eaten bag of some cheese-flavored junk food with a grinning cartoon character on the bag. He smiled.

"I like you, Shango Cartwright," Maitland was saying now. "I like you and I respect your decision—if you say you don't want to talk about the accident."

"Thank you," Shango said vaguely.

"...Shango: the god of fire, lightning and thunder," Maitland said abruptly, as if just remembering something.

"Pardon?"

"You don't know who you're named after?"

When Shango frowned, the old man continued, "'Shango was a Yoruba god. Enslaved Africans brought the religion to the Caribbean."

"Oh," the boy said at last.

Maitland laughed at his reaction. "So, you mean you've never been to one of those Shango ceremonies in the bush?"

When Shango shook his head, the old man laughed as he remembered something. "Alfred Mendes once wrote a story about that," he began. "Some upper crust colonials drove into the bush to see a Shango ceremony one night; but at the sight of all those cavorting Negroes dancing to their drums and calling upon their god, they fled, terrified." Maitland laughed at the image, but when Shango's frown only deepened, the old man sighed in exasperation. "You don't know who Alfred Mendes is, do you?"

"No, sir," Shango said, genuinely ashamed.

"Then it's good I found you at such an impressionable age, young Shango—so that I can corrupt your mind with knowledge." The statement was meant in jest, but Shango nodded earnestly anyway, his face grave.

Maitland chuckled. "You remind me of myself at your age." Given the state of Maitland's vehicle, Shango did not know if that was supposed to be a compliment or not. Was he going to end up like that in fifty years? Whatever the case, Maitland's eyes widened as a new idea popped into his mind. "How would you like a job—after school?"

"Doing what?" Shango said, genuinely surprised.

"Helping me to find out things other people don't think I should know: writing letters, making phone calls…that kind of thing."

After the initial surprise, Shango shook his head. "My mother'll be coming for me soon—from America—so I won't be here much longer."

"Really? That's a shame then," he said sorrowfully. "If the best and brightest keep leaving, we won't have much of a nation left."

As the man said it, Shango thought about his grandmother's land on the mountain—and about how nature would reclaim it after he was gone. All at once, he found himself thinking that that might be the best thing for the island as well. Whenever he went into town, his soul would always rebel against their filth. He could not help thinking that it might be best if they all left the island, so that nature could finally triumph over their stupidity.

After Maitland's lamentation on the "best people" abandoning the island, there was a moment of thoughtful silence. Yet, it was a comfortable silence; and afterwards, they seemed closer somehow—as if one of the barriers between them had been pushed aside. Maitland sighed, looked up at him earnestly, and began, "Get in and I'll take you where you want to go."

Shango hesitated for a moment, but something about Maitland's matter-of-fact tone disarmed him. He took a step toward the door before he remembered his clothes were soiled from tumbling down the mountain. Looking down at his pants, some of the mud stains were already crusty from the heat. There were scrapes on his arms; and when he looked down at his hands, he saw they were filthy. In fact, the cuts from this morning—from when the glass shards sliced through his palm—were encrusted with muck. There were traces of blood in the muck, meaning that the wounds had reopened—and that the filth was in his blood stream now. Something about that alarmed him, simply because his grandmother would not approve.

Anyway, with all that, he hesitated once more, not wanting to dirty Maitland's car. He made a nominal effort to dust off his clothes, but Maitland only waved his hand for him to come, before pushing the junk on the front seat onto the floor to make space. Indeed, some of the trash in the man's car seemed *years* old. Reassured that he wasn't breaking some kind of etiquette, Shango got in and closed the door behind him. The toe jam and sour oranges scent was more pungent; for the first few seconds, Shango found himself holding his breath—

"I am a slob," Maitland said proudly as he began to drive. "I make no apologies for it. Slobbery is one of the great pleasures of adulthood, young Shango—as you'll discover once you're grown."

"I look forward to it then," Shango said dryly, to which

Maitland laughed too exuberantly. There was definitely something about the kid, and Maitland found his eyes gravitating over to the boy as he drove. Shango felt a little uncomfortable at the stares. To distract himself, he reached down and grabbed one of the newspapers on the ground.

The newspaper was called *The Provocateur*. Shango had never heard of it—nor did he know what the word meant. However, the graphics and quality were horrible. The columns were all out of alignment; glancing at the lead story—"Government for Sale: Bribery in Clear View"—he spotted two obvious spelling mistakes. The punctuation was a nightmare; sentences ran into one another like train wrecks. Shango tried to understand the point of the story, but quickly gave up. When he looked at the author's name, he was shocked to read "Earl Maitland." He looked over at the driver sharply; Maitland nodded proudly when he saw Shango had made the connection. The man's expression was so self-assured that Shango looked down at the paper again, wondering if his original assessment had been wrong. Scanning the paper, he noticed that Maitland's name was on the next article, and then the next. In fact, Maitland's name was on all the articles in the six-page newspaper.

Shango frowned, then looked over at the man in bewilderment: "*You* did this?"

"Yes," Maitland said proudly. "What do you think?"

Shango looked down at it again. He did not know what to say; but like before, he could see no point in lying to the man. "It's like the inside of your car," he said at last, so that Maitland again laughed too exuberantly. Shango looked over at him uncertainly. Then, remembering the man's sparring session with Daddis, an obvious question popped into his mind. "Why do you do this?" he began cautiously.

"You haven't figured it out yet?" he asked, looking over at Shango earnestly. When Shango shook his head, Maitland continued, "I'm a *madman*."

Despite himself, Shango laughed—for the first time that day. He was not sure whether Maitland was an idiot—or a madman for that matter—but at the very least the man was an interesting idiot.

"Insane times call for insane men, my young friend," Maitland continued desultorily.

Shango was about to smile again, but it was then that the car turned a final corner, and entered the town. Even the large homes and buildings seemed like shacks. Everything seemed to be rusting; all the paint was either chipped or faded from the brutal onslaught of the tropical sun. Stray, mangy dogs pawed at the garbage that overflowed from bins; a few naked children pawed at the dirt, as if taking their cue from the dogs. Shango looked away, ashamed.

Since the streets were all so narrow, he always felt something like claustrophobia when he entered the town. Corridors originally designed to hold a horse and buggy were now typically jammed with two lanes of traffic. Once, when a truck stalled near the town center, traffic had to be diverted from the town for three days, while a special crane was procured from the capital. Little things like that always brought the world to a standstill on the island….

"Where do you want me to drop you?" Maitland asked now.

"Gupta's," he said. The newspaperman nodded: everyone knew Gupta's shop. It was the biggest one in the town, and sold everything from chewing gum to curtains. When Shango bought that dodgy remote-controlled car all those Christmases ago, it had been from Gupta's shop. The shop was the island's version of a

shopping mall; Gupta's family—and *all* Indians for that matter—
were looked upon enviously, since they seemed to have an
entrepreneurial gene that was missing from the island's African
descendants.

Indeed, when Gupta's ancestors arrived from India three
generations ago, they had started out with a stand on the side of
the road. Over the years, the shop had grown into a sprawling
behemoth. The store was a kind of Frankenstein monster, made
from the corpses of other businesses. When the electronics,
hardware, and clothing departments were added, the neighboring
buildings' walls were simply knocked down so that they could be
grafted onto the main store. There was a bar, a night club, a
movie theater that Shango visited religiously when new action
and kung fu movies came out, and some kind of family restaurant
that made the waiters wear strange purple and green uniforms.

Gupta's shop was perhaps the only building in the town that
had been painted recently. Yet, the bright yellow hue was so
jarring to the senses that the building seemed like something
from a fairy tale. In Shango's younger days, Gupta's shop had
excited him—but his innocence as a consumer had been lost
when he bought that toy car for Christmas...

Maitland pulled up in front of the store, then turned to look at
Shango. Now that he was there, Shango felt lost again. He
remembered Daddis' warning—that he should go directly to
Gupta—but as he watched the burly guard standing by the front
door, he wondered if they would even let him see the man.

"Why are you here?" Maitland asked, suddenly curious. Besides,
he sensed the boy's unease. Shango was still staring at the guard.
His hands clutched his schoolbag nervously, yet Maitland could
not tell if it was fear or something else. There was some kind of
mystery there. He had no idea what it could be, but he sensed it,

and his instincts as a newspaperman told him not to let the boy out of his sight.

Either way, Maitland's question lingered in the air. Shango stared at the store for a few seconds after the question had been asked; eventually, he turned his head and looked at Maitland absentmindedly, before returning to the store. "I need a phone card," he said distractedly.

"To call your mother...?"

"Yes," he said, beginning to get out of the car.

"It's some kind of emergency?" Maitland pressed him.

Shango hesitated; but as always, he saw no point to lying—or wasting time deflecting the man's question. "Yes," he said, simply.

"You can use my phone if you wish," he said, taking a cellular phone from his pants pocket.

"...But I have to call *America*," Shango said, looking at the phone confusedly.

"It doesn't matter. It'll be my good deed for the day."

Shango looked over at Gupta's shop. The guard in front of the store twirled his truncheon at that moment—one of those skills that one perfected when one was bored at work. In truth, the guards always made him nervous. There were about a dozen of them roaming the store, looking out for shoplifters and idlers. Daddis had told Shango to go to Gupta directly, but he again wondered if that would even be possible. He had seen Gupta's dark-windowed Mercedes-Benz a few times, and seen the man's picture in the newspaper, but he had never actually laid eyes on the man.

As Shango sighed, the guard caught his gaze. The dull expression in the man's eyes turned into something more menacing, and Shango looked away timidly. With all that, he decided to take Maitland up on his offer. After he took the cellular phone, he reached into his bag to get the sheet of paper with his mother's phone number. When he looked up at Maitland one last time— to make sure it was still okay—there was a strange kind of excitement in the man's eyes. Shango realized Maitland was waiting to hear his conversation, so that he could learn about him and his "emergency." He hesitated, but then he figured he would leave the island soon anyway, so it would make no difference. He began dialing the long phone number.

When he was finished, he put the phone to his ear. He braced himself, trying to think of what he would say to his mother. However, the phone did not even ring. There was a loud beeping noise, then the stern woman in the automated message informed him that the number he was trying to reach had been disconnected. Shango took the phone away from his ear and looked at it suspiciously—as though the problem had to be with the phone, itself. When he could see no error, he put the phone back to his ear, and listened to the looping message two more times. A sick feeling filled him then, and he pressed the button to end the call. For a second or two, he just sat there, staring into space. Had he dialed the wrong number? The phone was in his right hand. He looked down at it, then over to the sheet with the phone number— which was in his left hand. After a few moments, he decided to try again. He began dialing once more—this time double-checking each number as he went along. However, once he was finished, the same automated message played in his ear. He pressed the button to end the call, then stared ahead blankly, unable to digest what this could possibly mean.

"Is everything okay?" Maitland asked then. Shango looked over to see the man's concerned expression. Somehow, he had for- gotten the man was sitting next to him. Remembering he was still holding the phone, he handed it over to Maitland.

"Yeah," Shango blurted out then, as the man's question finally registered in his mind. Still, he was dazed and lost—

"Did you reach your mother?"

Shango stared at the man for a few seconds, until his mind digested the question, then he shook his head. "I must have copied down the number wrong." *Yeah*, he thought as he said it: that seemed right. That was the only explanation. He must have written the wrong number. He remembered his haste from earlier, when he was rushing to copy the number before the phone's battery died. He nodded his head again, suddenly relieved.

"Do you need something else?" Maitland asked, genuinely concerned. Shango saw this, and was grateful—but there was something cloying and off-putting about Maitland's concern. Also, Shango felt he needed to get away from everyone until he could figure out what was going on. He was still clinging to the idea that he had made a mistake when he copied his mother's number. The only thing to do now was to get a phone card from Gupta's shop and walk back up the mountain to his grandmother's. Once there, he could make the call directly from her cellular phone, eliminating the possibility of mistakes.

"Thanks, Mr. Maitland," Shango said now. When the man smiled, Shango began getting out of the vehicle. While he was doing that, Maitland reached over to the glove compartment to retrieve something; once Shango closed the door behind him, he noticed Maitland proffering a business card.

"My number's on it," the man said, "...if you want to talk."

Shango stared at the card uncertainly, then he took it, nodded, and began to make his way to the entrance of Gupta's shop. He did not look back.

There were red silk drapes in the windows of Gupta's office. All six of the windows were open; and as the drapes danced in the breeze, and filtered the morning light, the room had a rich, dreamy quality. The floors were the finest mahogany—and polished to the point where they seemed to glow. As for Gupta, he was a short, chubby Indian in his early sixties. He had not aged well, but he was always meticulously groomed—since he had a barber visit his office every morning. His clothes were custom-tailored to his unique physique. His latest fashion fancy was double-breasted woolen suits that were too hot for the tropical climate. By noon, he would usually have to turn on the air conditioner full blast—but he refused to wear something more practical, or even to take off his jacket. To him, the woolen suits were his right, as a millionaire.

In truth, he did not have any reason to be in his office that morning, but he came to work every day for the same reason he had the barber come to his office every day. The world was held together by men of character and diligence. Without appointments to keep and errands to run, a man's life was pointless—and he may as well be a beggar on the street, putting out his hand for spare change. His father had drilled those words into him—just as his father's father had before him.

During the lean years of Gupta's business, he had lived like a rat in a hole; he had gone without so that his family could climb another rung on the social ladder. However, the lean years were far behind him now. Twenty-five years ago, the first thing he had done to celebrate his success was knock down all the walls on the top floor to make his office. He had given himself "room to breathe," because successful men needed to spread their limbs. It now took him nineteen steps to get from one side of his office to the other; anytime he felt anxious, he would walk the length of the room in brisk strides, counting the steps. In fact, he had situated his desk in the dead center of the office, as if desperate to keep away from the walls and anything that might confine him. There were no cabinets in the office; except for two custom-made chairs in front of the desk, there was no other furniture at all. Gupta had instructed the carpenter to make the chairs half the usual height, so that his visitors would always have to look up at him, and crouch uncomfortably on the edge of their seats like morons.

His youngest son now managed the store's day-to-day operations—and was planning the store's expansion to the capital. As such, Gupta could rest assured that his legacy was intact. Indeed, nowadays, he had time to entertain thoughts that in his youth he would have regarded as *idle* thoughts. On his desk, there was a small jade Buddha, a statue of Vishnu, and several other baubles from his travels. Fifteen years ago, at the onset of a midlife crisis, he had gone on a whirlwind tour of India and other Asian countries. However, he had yearned for a kind of brotherhood with the people there that had been impossible. To them, he had merely been a fake Indian—and not even one of those elite Indians from America or England, who were doctors or engineers. Instead, he had been a glorified shopkeeper from a country most of them had never heard of. Being spurned by the people of his ancestral home had only made him hate the island even more. As a wealthy man, he could move to America or England, or wherever he wished, but the people of those places would never look at him the way they looked at him on the island. Here, he was Gupta; there, he was only a short, pudgy man who could afford expensive hotel rooms. He was *trapped* on the island, but trapped by success, and age, and the demands of ego.

As was often the case with unhappy old men, he now thought of himself as a kind of martyr. He would never be anything other than the king of a corrupt backwater town—but his sacrifices would allow his children to succeed where he had failed. He had a son at Oxford, getting his MBA. Another son was studying to be a doctor in America; and when Gupta's youngest son was ready, he would send him abroad as well. Because of Gupta's sacrifices, his sons would be free of this place. Just as his ancestors had borne hardships so that he could climb the social ladder, this was his burden to bear. There was something transcendental about it: before him, all generations of Guptas had had to suffer so that the next generation could rise; now, at last, they would be free of that cycle. Like Buddhists escaping the roulette wheel of reincarnation, Gupta's sons would move onto a higher plane of existence, beyond the petty squabbles of mortal men.

The phone on the desk rang. Gupta looked at it in annoyance. When he picked it up, a guard greeted him in the obsequious way of all his employees. "Yes?" Gupta said impatiently.

"Sir, there's a boy down here to see you."

"What does he want?"

"He say Daddis send him."

Gupta went to ask what Daddis had sent the boy *for*, but thought better of it. Daddis was a fool that he could manipulate—or at least that was what he told himself. Men like Daddis had been necessary for his success. Daddis solved unsavory problems for him—like the maid who said he had fondled her, and that inspector at the Customs office who had expected him to pay full fees. Daddis helped troublemakers to see the error of their ways. At the same time, the man sending a boy to him was odd. It was never good when one's underlings began sending people to you—and demanding your time—as if you worked for *them*.

Gupta was in a sour mood now, but then he began wondering if maybe some emergency had happened. Why else would Daddis send a boy, if not to deliver an emergency message? Gupta sighed, seeing no other option but to find out what was going on. "Okay, bring him up," he grumbled into the phone.

About forty-five seconds later, there was a deferential knock on the door. Gupta bellowed, "Come!" and looked up from the newspaper article he had been skimming. The door opened and the guard stood on the threshold with the boy. Shango's eyes were clear and bright. He saw Gupta and went to walk over, but the guard put his hand on his shoulder to restrain him. He looked back at the guard confusedly, but apparently the etiquette here was that even though Gupta had told them to come in, they still had to wait in the doorway. The guard was looking over at his master with a kind of cowed expression that Shango immediately found shameful in a grown man.

When Shango looked back at Gupta, they stared at one another. He knew, from the way the man looked at him, that he hated the man and that the man hated him. Shango's clothes were soiled from his fall down the mountain; his shoes were cheap and flimsy, and people who dressed like him had no business entering luxurious offices with mahogany floors and billowing silk drapes. He could see it all in Gupta's eyes, but he refused to bow his head or show any of the obeisance that people of high standing demanded from those they thought to be beneath them. Gupta stared at him, and he stared back. There was a strange stalemate there, and it was so unexpected that Gupta frowned. It was only after five or six seconds had passed that Gupta gestured for the guard to let Shango through. Shango began walking toward him with a calm, confident stride. Gupta looked away and pretended to be busy by shuffling some random papers on his desk. His bad mood was worse now, so there was evil in his eyes when Shango eventually stopped in front of his desk.

"Daddis told me to come to you directly, sir," Shango began in his precise classroom voice. "He gave me this money," he said, taking the bill from his pocket.

Gupta looked at the money, then looked back at Shango suspiciously. "Why'd he send you here?"

"He said a youth man will draw too much attention if he walks around with 'big man money.'"

Gupta stared at him for a few seconds. Like Maitland before him, he realized there was something odd about the boy. There was a strange directness about him. Gupta was not used to anyone taking that tone with him, and he did not like it at all. At the same time, he was still curious about *why* Daddis had sent the boy here. He decided to recalibrate his approach: "Why do you have big man money?"

"He gave it to me."

"Why?"

"Probably to keep me from talking, sir," Shango said curtly. There was an impatient expression in the boy's eyes now. It was the same expression Gupta gave to people he thought were fools, and Gupta sat up sharply when he realized it. He had a sudden desire to crush the boy's spirit: to put him back in his place.

"Let me see that money," he said now, putting out his pudgy hand. Shango stepped closer to the desk and handed over the bill. Gupta took it and twirled it before him, as if looking for a picture of Mickey Mouse, or the fatal flaw that would reveal it to be counterfeit. "This money," he began dramatically, still twirling the bill slowly with his pudgy fingers, "...you think it will solve your problems, don't you, young man? A poor youth like you has probably never seen money like this before."

Shango glared at him, wondering where this was going. "I just need a phone card, sir," Shango said calmly.

The boy's tone infuriated him, so that Gupta cried out, "That's *all* you need?"

"It's why I came here, sir."

When an idea popped into Gupta's mind, he bounced in his chair excitedly, and a strange grin came over his face as he saw the perfection of it. "So," he began, leaning forward in his chair, "you mean if I gave you a phone card, I can keep the rest of the money?"

Shango stared at him confusedly, then shrugged his shoulders. "If that's what you want, then you can help yourself, sir."

Gupta had hoped to see the boy begin to squirm as he faced the prospect of losing all that money, but Shango's gaze did not waver. Once more, they stared at one another; but as the seconds passed, the boy's calm expression only infuriated him further. In the back of Gupta's mind, the voice of reason told him the scene was descending into a farce, but the rage pushed him over the edge. He grabbed the phone on his desk, then dialed a number by jabbing his index finger at the keys threateningly.

"Bring me some phone credit!" Gupta screamed into the phone as soon as the clerk answered. When asked how much credit he wanted, the old man banged the desk with his fist, screeching, "Just bring the *biggest* one." At that, he slammed down the receiver and sat there huffing and puffing. Something about the man's face reminded Shango of a frog that was about to croak, so that he unconsciously smiled.

"You think this is *funny*, young man!" Gupta screeched again.

Shango thought about it objectively and came to the conclusion that denying his amusement was pointless. "Yes, sir," he said.

"You little bastard, don't you *dare* mock me!"

"I wasn't sir," Shango explained calmly, "I was only smiling."

"You were smiling *mockingly*!"

"Was I, sir?" he asked as if he hadn't considered that possibility.

"Yes, you were, you little shit! ...And now you're *laughing* at me!"

Shango had not realized he was laughing until Gupta pointed it out. "I guess I am," he said as if mystified by his body's reactions that morning. "I apologize, sir," he said, sobering.

However, Shango's calm, precise answers still seemed to be mocking him. The man went to launch into a string of expletives when someone knocked on the door.

"Come!" Gupta raged, banging the desk again. At that, a frail-looking girl about sixteen opened the door and began jogging across the room, clutching a phone card in her hand. When she was about halfway there, Gupta screamed, "Hand it to that little wretch over there!" At that, the girl stopped abruptly, looking like she was about to cry. She looked at Shango as if he had tentacles growing out of his head. "Give it to him!" Gupta yelled as she stood there confusedly—but the more the man yelled, the more her muscles refused to move. Seeing her suffering, Shango walked over to her and took the phone card from her hand. Gupta was about to launch into a loud, vindictive speech, but Shango did not even wait. He was walking toward the door now.

"You won't get the rest of the money!" Gupta said feebly, but Shango did not even look back. He did not even flinch—as if none of it could possibly make a difference.

Like the Range Rover incident, the confrontation with Gupta seemed impossible afterwards. The store passed him in a blur, and then he was outside, on the curb, wondering if any of it could possibly have happened. The phone card was still in his hand. He held it up to look at it, then he opened his bag and placed it between the pages of his notebook. Before he crossed the street, he looked back at the store one last time. A different guard was posted at the door now, but they all had the same brutish expression, so Shango stepped off the curb and began walking back home.

Since it was about ten o'clock now, there was a lull in the town. Rush hour was over; by and large, people had reached their workplaces and school houses. In about two hours, they would emerge again for lunch—but the town was relatively quiet for now, and dreary. Something about it was depressing, and Shango began walking faster—in order to escape.

His route out of town took him past his school. Some old women had staked out their positions by the gates, and had their trays with candy and junk food ready for children and other passersby. Shango always wondered how they made enough money to survive; at the same time, all the junk food containers in the gutters attested to a brisk business.

Beyond the school's tall, iron gate, there was a dusty yard. At this time of morning, the yard was empty. The school, itself, was a two-story cement building. As Shango stood there, he could barely make out a teacher yelling at the top of his voice. He had always loved school—and *excelled* in it—but after the morning he had had, he was suddenly suspicious of anything connected to the adult world. Now, as he listened, he heard an entire class chanting something. In his mind's eye, he could see the bored students repeating whatever the teacher said, without thought or any real comprehension. Yet, for the briefest moment, there was something quaint about the sound. For the briefest moment, he yearned for the naïveté of all those students. Their eyes were still closed; their minds were still clouded by the quaint lies the adults told them. They believed without questioning; their faith was *absolute*—but in return, they seemed protected from the horrors that now plagued Shango's mind. There was some kind of trade-off there; and the more Shango thought about it, the more he wondered if he was also blinded by his faith. After all, maybe his absolute faith—in his mother and America—was just another quaint lie. He felt queasy at the thought. In fact, the possibility was so brutal that he immediately pushed it aside, and *shunned* it, the way religious people shunned evil thoughts.

He moved on, hounded by his burgeoning awareness—and frustrated by the fact that he had not really accomplished anything that morning. His grandmother's corpse was still on the mountain; his mother and the authorities still had no idea what had happened. He groaned, but that was when his hunger ambushed him. With all that had happened that morning, he had yet to eat or drink anything for the day. His pace faltered, and he looked about the dreary town uneasily. It was usually his grandmother who made him breakfast and ensured he got to school on time. She had been the vital cog that made the machinery of his life run. Without her, the machine was grinding to a halt, stranding him in the middle of nowhere. His only hope now was his mother and America. A sick feeling came over him when he remembered the automated message about his mother's phone being disconnected, but he again told himself it had to be a mistake. It *had* to be a mistake. There was no other possibility.

Suddenly distraught, he tried walking fast—so that he would be able to get home quicker, call his mother, and put an end to this strange day—but his hunger made him sluggish. Besides, by now, the midday sun was like a stalker in the heavens, following him everywhere…tormenting him. Beads of perspiration appeared at his temples; his mouth was beginning to get that chalky taste that came from dehydration and exhaustion. In truth, when he left the house that morning, he had assumed the police would drive him back up the mountain. He had expected the police to take his grandmother's corpse away today, so that the house could be cleansed of death and sorrow. Yet, like the long walk up the mountain, the thought of again being alone with his grandmother's corpse drained his strength and will. His shamefully childish fears—about mountain spirits and reanimated corpses—were still there, lurking in the back of his mind. Indeed, his muscles locked up as those fears returned, and he leaned against a telephone pole to support himself.

With all of that, his thoughts returned to his original plan. The police station was only a ten-minute walk away—versus another hour in the hot sun if he walked up the mountain. After his encounter with Daddis, the police still left him uneasy, but he was honest enough with himself to see there was no choice. As he saw it, he would have to go to the police sooner or later. Even if he called his mother and had her call the police from America, nobody knew where he lived. He did not exactly have a street address—so, one way or another, he would have to go to the police and direct them to his grandmother's home. Of all the bad choices before him, going to the police now seemed to be the most straightforward one, so he made a right turn at the next corner and headed toward the police station in the town center.

The town's roads were a chaotic network of arteries that only a madman could navigate. They rarely went in a straight line; sometimes they were wide enough to fit two trucks side-by-side; sometimes they were so narrow that only one car could pass at a time. There were no street signs. Sometimes there was a sidewalk; sometimes there wasn't. Brick buildings stood next to shacks, so that the entire thing seemed like one gigantic slum. As he neared the town center, the sidewalks became packed with hawkers selling everything from bootleg sneakers to used refrigerators. In fact, the *density* of the town had always unnerved him—especially around the town center. The narrow, circuitous streets would seem like a labyrinth; the wretched people he passed would seem like minotaurs and other mythological monsters, so that Shango would be overcome by a strange impulse to run for his life. He had never surrendered to the impulse, but he always sensed it building inside of him, like a kind of madness.

To save himself, he stared straight ahead and allowed the rest of the world to pass him in a blur. He ignored the people and the town's trash-clogged gutters—but as he locked away his senses, he inadvertently stepped into traffic as a truck was approaching. The driver sounded a blaring horn that was so powerful that Shango's teeth seemed to shake; coming to his senses, he jumped back, panting and terrified. At least thirty seconds passed before the adrenaline ebbed from his system and his body stopped shaking. After that, he walked more deliberately, and made sure he looked both ways before crossing the crowded streets.

A t the moment, there was a middle-aged woman walking about ten paces in front of him. There was something prim and proper about her: her blouse was freshly pressed; her long burgundy skirt matched her wide-brimmed hat, and her hair was done in a bun, without a single strand out of place. Her steps were quick and decisive; her posture was straight and refined—

But just as she passed an alleyway, a disheveled man leapt out behind her, screaming, "Bock-bi-cow!"

The prim woman screamed, her hat flying off as she whirled. She was clutching her left tit now as the man—known to everyone in town as Chicken George—flapped his make-believe wings and screamed, "Bock-bi-cow!" again. After that, he darted out into traffic, narrowly avoiding being hit by a truck. Yet, as soon as he made it to the other side of the road, he darted back through traffic once more, as if desperate to tempt fate. Still flapping his wings, he screamed, "Bock-bi-cow!" one last time, before disappearing down another alleyway.

After the initial shock, Shango looked on with a guilty smile, thinking that it was impossible for crazy people to get hit by traffic. It was a *guilty* smile because over all the years he had been seeing the man, he had always instinctively thought of Chicken George as a mark of failure by their society. The common myth was that Chicken George had stolen an obeah woman's chicken as a child, and been cursed. Even though Shango told himself the story was nonsense, he preferred it to the stark reality of mental illness and the island's lack of infrastructure...

By now, the proper woman had retrieved her hat from the pavement and straightened out her skirt. Other pedestrians, who had stopped to gawk at Chicken George's antics, had gone back to their business, so Shango crossed the street and continued on to the police station.

M ost of the buildings in the town center had been erected in the nineteenth century, when the island still had some relevance to its colonizers. The chief architect had used a combination of Victorian and Gothic styles he remembered from his hometown in England; but in general, the town center was a pastiche of something that had only really existed in the mind of a homesick Englishman. Worse, with the passage of time, and inadequate maintenance, the two-story buildings were literally falling apart. The paint was peeling; in some places, the cement walls were becoming so brittle that one could dig holes in them with one's bare hands. Everything was slowly turning to dust, and Shango suddenly found himself thinking that the town would share the same fate as his grandmother's farm. Nature would reclaim the land; their failed attempt at civilization would be swept aside, and the farce would finally come to an end.

The crumbling Victorian/Gothic buildings mostly housed administrative offices. The offices all faced a rectangular park that was perhaps the single ugliest feature of the town. In its heyday, the park had had flowerbeds and meticulously trimmed hedges, but now the space was mostly a refuge for stray dogs and people looking for a convenient place to relieve their bodily functions. Plastic wrappers and used condoms now took the place of flowers. The grass and shrubbery seemed diseased: everything had a grayish hue—either from dust or some kind of fungus. Every few years, the town's authorities would enlist a youth group clean it up and plant new flowers. There would always be much fanfare around the event, with politicians showing up to take pictures with brooms in their hands; but like the stray dogs of the park—which ran away timidly at the commotion—the filth always returned once the people were through with their foolishness.

Presently, the park was on Shango's left as he walked down the sidewalk to the police station. In his mind, he began going over what he would say to the police; but as his eyes roamed the landscape, an image of his grandmother's sightless eyes flashed in his mind, and his pace faltered.

Most of the old buildings had inner courtyards. To reach the courtyards, one had to walk up three steps and pass through an archway. Unfortunately, as Shango neared the police station, he saw the gate in the archway was closed. He walked up to the steps and stood staring at the closed gate. There was an imposing-looking padlock on the gate; and right behind the gate, there was a sign posted on a stand, which read, "On break: Come Back in 15 Minutes." Under that, in smaller letters, the sign read, "In case of emergency call 119."

Shango stood staring at the sign, frowning. How the *hell* could the police station be closed? "On break"? What did that mean? ...And the police had made sure to put their sign *beyond* the gate, as if they feared someone would steal it. Shango sucked his teeth, but then he sighed, seeing he had no choice but to wait. He sat on the top step and looked out on the ugly park. One of the mangy dogs was in heat, and three males were circling it. All the dogs were covered with sores, and the thought of their sex made Shango sick to his stomach, so that he groaned and looked away.

As was so often the case with tired travelers, it was only when he was sitting down that he realized how exhausted he was. His limbs all felt like lead. He leaned forward, rested his elbows on his knees, and bowed his head. He wished he could go back to bed—that all of this were only a dream from which he would soon awake. Any moment now, he imagined he would open his eyes, leap out of bed and go to the kitchen—where his grandmother would be preparing breakfast. The thought of it almost made the tears return, but he shook his head and forced them back into the empty place within him—

There was a policeman standing right in front of him! When he looked up, the man had a severe scowl on his face. He was about fifty, with one of those "stout" bodies that may have been powerful in his youth, but which was now mostly fat. His gut bulged over his belt, and his uniform seemed two or three sizes too small. Indeed, Shango noticed the man was holding a bag of food from a trendy American fast food restaurant. The scent was somehow "heavy"—like a liquid entering his lungs. His mouth salivated; he inadvertently ogled the bag, but that was when the policeman sucked his teeth impatiently.

"Youths don't believe in school no more?" he asked rhetorically. "Why you *wasting* time on the steps!"

Shango opened his mouth feebly; when the man leaned over him threateningly, Shango sprang to his feet and took a precautionary step back. Yet, once Shango was to his feet, the policeman spotted an empty soft drink bottle on the step. The sight of the thing seemed to push the man over the edge, because his eyes bulged and his lips began to twitch. Shango watched him uneasily—

"*You* left that bottle there?" he asked in the same threatening manner. Shango followed the man's accusatory finger; but before he could shake his head, the policeman screamed, "You *dirty* children always leaving mess here!"

Shango was so stunned that he could only stare.

"*Pick it up!*" the man exploded, so that the dogs circling the bitch ducked their tails between their legs and ran for cover. When Shango glanced at the man, huge veins were bulging at the side of his neck. In the man's eyes, there was the promise of brutality; and suddenly fearing for his life, Shango stooped down and grabbed the bottle. Then, without any conscious thought, he darted past the man and found himself running at full speed.

He ran without seeing or thinking. Everything passed him in a blur. After about a minute or two, he was out of breath. Looking around, he saw he was in a particularly depressing part of town, where some of the poorer families had their homes. He stopped there, gasping for air and wondering what the hell had happened. Bewildered, he looked back the way he had come. There was no policeman in sight—and he was a safe enough distance from the town center and the man's brutality—but as he stared in that direction, he was suddenly overcome by the burning sense that he had suffered an injustice. Looking down, he saw he was still holding the empty plastic bottle! At the sight of it, the rage exploded in him again. He went to fling the bottle to the ground, so that it could congregate in the gutter with the rest of the discarded trash. However, just then, an old woman came out of one of the flimsy wooden houses. Her head was tied in a colorful scarf, and she immediately reminded him of his grandmother. The rage died away then, and he stared at the old woman longingly. In the entire country, he had no one. All the adults were fools, and he felt the hot tears welling up in his eyes again. The old woman looked at him quizzically then, but he ducked his head and continued running down the narrow street.

He did not stop until he was out of town. When he looked down again, and realized he was *still* holding the bottle, his first impulse was to fling it into the nearest bush. However, his inner dignity restrained him. ...*No*, he thought to himself: the people in the town—*they* were the filthy ones. When he remembered how the policeman had called him "dirty," the same sense of injustice rose in him again. No, he would never be anything like them; and he swore then, with a strange kind of vindictiveness, that he would never let them take his dignity. His mother and paradise were still in the back of his mind; but until he reached the Promised Land, he would remain strong and hold onto those vital things that made him Shango Cartwright. He put the empty bottle in his bag—until he could find a rubbish bin—then he began to make his way up the mountain.

Soon, the town was behind him, and the only sign of civilization was the freshly laid road the Chinese had built. When he

reached the overlook from earlier that morning—where he had
stopped to look at the town—he turned and stood staring. Somehow, the town seemed even uglier to him now, so he turned away
and continued up the mountain.

As noon approached, and the hot sun shone down on him, his
pace slowed further. He was beginning to get a slight headache
from dehydration. His limbs felt heavy, and he had a strange
urge to lie down in the bush and sleep. Every once in a while, a
vehicle—usually a truck—would come speeding down the
mountain; but for the most part, there was nothing, and Shango
had to make a conscious effort to keep away morbid thoughts
about being alone on the island.

That was when he looked down and realized his right hand was
bleeding again. A few droplets of blood dripped onto his pants;
when he looked at his hand, the various wounds all seemed
enflamed. His hand, itself was swollen; and when he flexed it, it
felt stiff. In fact, a dull pain went up his hand when he moved his
fingers. He stood staring at his hand, alarmed by all these new
developments. The filth from earlier—when he tumbled down
the mountain—must have infected it. He began walking again,
knowing that he quicker he got home, the quicker he could clean
his wounds—but he was feeling lightheaded now, and lethargic.

His mouth was so dry that he felt like there was dust in it. His
shirt was soaked through with sweat, and his headache became
more biting as the minutes passed. Yet, like a marathon runner,
he concentrated on putting one foot in front of another. Every
step he took was a step closer to home, and rest, and his mother.
The mental trick worked for a while, but his concentration and
resolve were continually broken by his aching right hand; panicky
doubts entered his mind...and questions about his mother's
disconnected phone were there as well, draining his strength

further—so that a side of him began to wonder if he would ever reach home at all. Once or twice, he even began thinking that maybe he should just lie down in the shade of a nice bush, like his old dog had, and allow nature to take its course....

Around eleven-forty in the morning, he turned a bend in the road and found himself back at the ravine, looking down at the Range Rover. He was amazed that it was actually there. He had expected it to be gone, like a figment of his imagination. His mind flashed back to images of Daddis' glistening incisor, and the policemen gunning down the person in the driver's seat. ... All that had really happened. He was tempted to go down into the ravine and look at the vehicle. Common sense told him they had taken the victim's corpse away, but he wondered if the blood was still there. A grotesque streak in him was curious to see how well they had covered their tracks...but he was too tired to expend the energy. If he climbed down there he doubted he would have the strength to climb back up, so he put the idea out of his mind.

...He had a sudden recollection of the girl the policemen had taken from the Range Rover. She had been the most unreal thing about the experience. He remembered the quiet horror in her eyes. She had stared at him intently—as if she had seen into the depths of him. Somehow, they had understood one another, and it occurred to him she must have seen the same quiet horror in his eyes as he stared back at her. They had both seen death that day. They had both delved into death's intricacies in a way that perhaps few on the island could understand. Maitland and Daddis had been too jaded to understand; his mother and uncle would only be overcome with grief when they found out his grandmother was dead. However, the beautiful girl's eyes had shone with the same stunned horror Shango felt every time he remembered his grandmother's corpse staring back at him in the darkness. He did not know if that connection made any difference; but for a brief moment, he had the feeling he was not alone.

After a sigh, he continued on his way. Some beads of sweat rolled down his temple and into the corner of his mouth. He sucked at them unconsciously, until the concentrated salt left an unsavory taste in his mouth, turning his stomach. He spit to clear away the taste, but it was pointless.

His right hand now throbbed; he could practically feel it swelling. It felt *heavy* now—and warm—but there was nothing he could do but continue putting one foot in front of the other.

Then, when he was coming upon the pit, something tapped him on the top of his head. By the time he looked up, the rain began to soak him. The fluffy clouds were coming over the mountain now. He stared at them in amazement—and yet the rain was warm and soothing, so he just stood there for a few moments with a simpering smile on his face. When he began walking again, his pace was still slow and methodical. There was no point in running, or trying to hide beneath a tree. He felt, in a way, that the rain was cleansing him. His headache abated as his body cooled. He opened his mouth and allowed the cleansing rain to enter him; and for the first time that day, he felt a vague sense of peace.

Two minutes later, the rain was gone, and the tropical sun resumed its assault. His pace slowed; but ahead, by the side of the road, his grandmother's weathered fruit stand marked the end of his journey. He sighed, relieved that he was home, but the dilapidated structure suddenly made him feel melancholy. Most days, his grandmother would be tending the stand when he returned from school. It would be loaded with fresh fruits and vegetables; she would smile and wave to him, and he would know he was home. ...He would never feel that way again, and he felt suddenly empty inside.

He sighed again, but then grew annoyed with his melancholy thoughts. Besides, in a few minutes, he would call his mother and take the steps necessary to end this nightmare. The authorities would come for his grandmother's corpse, then everything would be right with the world. In his mind, his mother would be back on the island in *hours*. She would rush down to take him away from all this. He was so desperate for it to be true that he felt the tears welling up again.

With his destination in sight, he began moving faster. Once more, he pushed aside branches and vines as he navigated the overgrown forest path. The foliage was still wet; droplets of dew were still on many of the leaves—but when Shango looked down, he saw the ground was bone dry. That was the way of the mountain. No matter how fierce the onslaught of rain, the thirsty earth was always dry within an hour. Even when there were floods and landslides elsewhere on the island, the thirsty earth of the mountain remained firm, as if it had a bottomless reservoir somewhere beneath the surface.

As the forest path came to an end, his grandmother's house appeared before him. He stopped and stared up at it. The weathered boards were still ugly, but at least it was home, and it was clean, and it did not leave him with the overwhelmed, claustrophobic feeling he had had in the town. ...His grandmother's dead body was really in there. The thought made the strange anxieties come rushing back, but he was already making his plans in his head. He would go straight to his room, put credit on the phone, call his mother, and then the rest would take care of itself.

He would not have to go in his grandmother's room once—so the nightmare would soon be over. He nodded his head and continued walking up to the house.

When he reached the freestanding sink behind the house, he turned it on full blast and drank heartily. He washed out his swollen hand next, then his head and arms. He felt refreshed, but his right hand was still stiff and swollen. The wounds were all enflamed, but at least they were clean again—assuming the water was clean. When his uncle visited five years ago, a parasite in the mountain stream had wreaked havoc on his insides, so that he had spent half the trip in the latrine. After that, he had had a friend bring him some bottled water from Gupta's shop, and insisted Shango's grandmother use it to cook all his meals. All those years ago, Shango had been ashamed of his island-hardened belly—since it was too crude to pick up local infections. Somehow his uncle's sickness had been a status symbol—like that fairy tale where the people verified the princess's status by seeing if her sleep would be disturbed by a single pea hidden beneath one hundred mattresses. Only when they saw her tossing and turning in bed did they realize she was a princess—and only after Shango heard his uncle crying out from the outhouse did he know that the man's time in America had left him pure.

Shango stared down at his hand now, wondering, on a half-conscious level, if his infected hand meant that he, too, was becoming pure. In truth, the thought was too stupid to stay in his mind for long. Like many stupid thoughts, it required too much effort to take seriously, so he sighed and began to move to the kitchen door.

Upon entering the house, he left his shoes on the mat. He looked vaguely around the kitchen, wondering what he would eat—but calling his mother took precedence over everything. He moved toward his bedroom now. He was so desperate for all of this to be over that he began to jog—but that was when he looked ahead and saw something that made his guts clench. Somehow, the sheet in his grandmother's doorway was untied! The one in his doorway was still tied, but his grandmother's was hanging loose, dancing eerily on the breeze from the open windows. He stopped in his tracks, his muscles twitching—preparing themselves in case he had to run for his life. He had *tied* that sheet—he was *sure* of it.

He held his breath, listening for the telltale sound of footsteps— or floorboards creaking—or any kind of movement behind the sheet. In his mind, his grandmother—or some demon—was going to emerge from behind the sheet at any moment. He prepared himself to scream; his lips were already trembling…but he didn't hear anything—and nothing sprang from behind the sheet—so the panic began to give way to uncertainty.

In the final analysis, superstitions were just the stupid conclusions people drew from unanswered questions. If he let his mind roam too far, he would plummet over the edge. The voice of adulthood was there again, coaxing him away from the abyss. The sheet must have come undone on its own: it wasn't as though he had tied it *tightly*. …That was the only thing that made sense—even though he could not see *how* the sheet could have come undone. As he stood there pondering that detail, he sensed the fears returning, but the voice of adulthood rose to the surface again, pushing him forward. In an instant, before his conscious mind even had time to react, he grabbed the sheet, pulled it to the side, and stood there peering into the room. His heart was racing again; for those first few moments, he was so blinded by the adrenaline rush that everything was a blur. He was like a skydiver jumping out of a plane for the first time: that initial step was a victory over human fears and limitations—but between that time and the moment the parachute opened safely, his fate was out of his hands.

His grandmother's form was still on the bed, in the position he remembered. He stared at the body for any sign of movement, but there was nothing. He began to breathe again. Then, acting quickly, he twirled the sheet and tied it *tightly*. After that, he retreated from the doorway. Like the first time he had fled the room, he did not dare turn his back on his grandmother's corpse. Yet, even when he was in his own room, he kept looking across the hall every few seconds.

The phone card: he remembered his task and took the card out of his bag. The phone was still on the windowsill, charging. He went to it quickly. The glass from the broken louvers was still there, but the only thing he could think about was calling his mother. He grabbed the phone and began dialing the number on the card, to add the credit. After that, he found his mother's number on the phone and pressed the button to dial it.

His heart began racing again…but he was soon standing there in shock, staring into space as the same automated message told him the number he was trying to reach had been disconnected. What did it mean…? He looked down at the phone suspiciously, but there could be no doubt that he had dialed the correct number this time—since he had stored the number on the phone, himself. Had something happened to his mother? He hadn't talked to her in six months, so anything could have happened during that time. His mind went down that path for a few seconds, but there were too many hidden horrors down that way, so he turned back.

…Why would her phone be disconnected? He sat down on the edge of the bed to think. "Disconnected" sounded permanent and formal. Like "deceased" it seemed like one of those words adults used to put a gloss on a horrible loss. Had something happened to his mother? Was he alone now? His mind circled the thought uneasily, but then he began to breathe again when it occurred to him his uncle would have called if anything happened. He was nodding his head unconsciously now—and then his eyes widened when it occurred to him he could call his uncle now. The man's number should still be in the phone's "received calls" folder.

Suddenly hopeful, he tracked down the number and pressed the button to dial it. When the phone began to ring, he felt a sense of relief. He sat straighter, and prepared the words he would say, but when the phone stopped ringing, a recorded message began. There was some cheerful music, and an equally cheerful woman—whom he assumed to be his uncle's wife—declared, "You have reached the Cartwright family. Please leave a message after the beep."

Shango had listened to the message confusedly; but when the beep sounded, he was suddenly flustered. "This is Shango," he began breathlessly, "—from the island..." He hesitated for a moment, realizing a recorded phone message was probably not the place to tell someone his mother was dead. "... You should call me back," he said at last. "It's an emergency." He could think of nothing else to say, so he pressed the button to end the call, and sat there with a dazed expression on his face. After a while, he lay back on the bed and stared blankly at the ceiling. He had no idea what anything meant anymore; he had no idea what he should be *doing*. His life suddenly seemed without options and possibilities—as if he, too had been "disconnected."

In time, when hunger ambushed him again, he left the room and made his way to the kitchen. He moved like someone who was somnambulating. His gaze was distant. He was acting more on instinct—to satisfy the needs of his body—than with fore-thought. Once he was in the kitchen, he stopped and looked around confusedly—as if he had no idea why he had come there. When his belly growled, he went to the cupboard above the counter. There were some condiments—salt and his grand-mother's homemade pepper sauce, along with sugar and some pungent herbs his grandmother swore could cure cancer and any disease known to man—but there was nothing he could eat. None of the fruits were ripe at the moment. A few of them, like the mangoes, were a week or two away—so, if he wanted any-thing to eat, he would have to go out into his grandmother's fields and dig something up. The prospect drained his strength; and just then, he had a flashback of his phone calls to his mother and uncle. The panic threatened to return, but he reminded himself he had left a message with his uncle—and that it would only be a matter of time before his overseas relatives called him back. In fact, he instinctively cocked his head then, listening for the phone's ring. He had left it on his bed, but it now occurred to him he should carry the phone at all times—since his uncle might call at any moment.

He headed back to his bedroom now—rushing as if the phone might somehow ring and stop before he got there. When he reached the room and saw the phone on the bed, he stared at it hopefully. When it did not ring, he picked it up and looked at it to make sure it was still working. It still had three power bars, so he nodded his head in his usual way and put it in his pants pocket.

As he turned to exit, his eyes reflexively went to his grand-mother's dark form lying on the bed. From where he stood, he could hear the buzz of flies and smell the sickly odor of death. The realization of all that lay ahead was too much to bear at the moment, so he found himself fleeing—back toward the kitchen, and the prospect of food.

He got into his outdoor shoes before heading to his grandmother's fields. The farming tools—some shovels, a fork, a hoe, and other gardening implements—were underneath the house, next to the old shipping barrels his mother and uncle had sent from America. Sometimes, his grandmother used the barrels to store crops—since they were the thick plastic variety. Also under the house, there was a cement counter, on which his grandmother had three coal pots. There was of course no gas in the house; so, a few times a year, his grandmother made coal from some of the forest trees—chopping them, burying them in the ground, and smoking them for days, until they were just right. Shango had always found the alchemy fascinating...

Once he grabbed a shovel (and a basket his grandmother used for harvesting her crops) he headed to the fields. He felt like eating mashed sweet potatoes and yams. His grandmother used to cook it with beans or peas, but the beans would take too long to cook. The yam patch was in front of the huge boulder. He rested his wounded hand on the boulder when he arrived: it had soaked up the sun's heat during the day, and he liked the warm, comforting sensation against his palm.

When he was ready, he pulled out a nice thick yam—just like his grandmother had taught him. It was actually too much for one person to eat, but he figured he could have enough for breakfast, lunch and dinner the next day. When he caught himself making long-term plans, an uneasy feeling came over him.

Indeed, if he still had to provide for himself tomorrow, or the day after that, then it meant his overseas relatives had abandoned him. The thought made the panic return, and he instinctively tapped the cellular phone in his front pocket to make sure it was still there. Somehow, the phone reassured him—like a toddler's favorite toy at bedtime.

He had actually missed a day of school. He felt older now—and perhaps harder inside. Many of his illusions about the adult world had been wiped away, but his mother and uncle were still there—beacons of hope in a world of darkness. He had never really spent much time thinking about his uncle—but now, somehow, the man was his only hope.

Actually, he had only met his uncle once—five years ago, when the man came to bring his mother to America. Shango only remembered vague, off-putting things about the man—like his pendulous gut, and his nervous habit of sucking his lower lip. The man had complained the entire trip—about the mud, and the lung-busting hike up the mountain. However, all of that was forgotten now. Indeed, Shango nodded his head at that moment, assuring himself that his uncle would call him back that evening, after he returned from work. By tomorrow, someone would have come to rescue him from this place, and he would finally be able to breathe again. *Rescue*: the sentiment was new, but that was how he felt now. With each passing hour, he became more convinced that if he did not leave this place soon, he would be trapped here forever, like the huge boulder that no one could move.

After digging up a sweet potato, Shango returned to the house. He left the shovel by the shipping barrels, then he grabbed a tall soup pot that had turned black from the soot of the coals. He placed the yam and sweet potato in the pot, then carried the pot up to the sink. He worked methodically, as if had no energy to spare. The adrenaline rush from the phone calls was wearing off, and the old lethargy was reclaiming him.

Once he had washed the tubers, he left the pot to fill up while he went to the kitchen to retrieve a knife. However, when he returned to the sink with knife in hand, and prepared to cut the yam, a strange pain radiated down his arm. It was like the prickly feeling that people had when they sat or slept in an uncomfortable position and their limbs "fell asleep" from a lack of circulation.

He put down the knife and stared at his palm. He was not entirely sure—since he had just put his hand under the faucet to wash the yams—but the cuts seemed to be oozing. They were all open, and he could see into the red, swollen flesh. In some places, he could actually see the bone and sinew. The sight did not actually sicken him, but he knew something was wrong. His mind went to his grandmother's cure-all overproof rum, but his belly was empty; and just then, the pot began to overflow, so he turned off the tap and began to peel the tubers.

The prickly pain intensified when he picked up the pot by the handles and headed to the makeshift cooking area beneath the house. He blocked it out for now, following the demands of his belly. However, twenty minutes later, when the pot's cover began to tremble from released steam, his hand suddenly felt like it was on fire. When he looked down at it, there was a trickle of bloody pus from the deepest cut. The sight set off obvious alarm bells; and now that the food was cooking, he had no more excuses, so he rushed back to the kitchen.

His grandmother's "medical supplies" were in the cabinet beneath the kitchen counter. Since the house did not have a bathroom, the cabinets held everything from toilet paper to toothpaste. In his haste, he forgot to take off his outdoor shoes. He only realized it after he had taken two steps into the kitchen. Guiltily, he looked back at the dirt tracks on the floor—but his hand was burning.

The cure-all overproof rum was in the back of the cabinet. His grandmother had recycled a bottle from the local brewery, but she had brewed the concoction herself and added special herbs that made his nose hairs stand on end and his eyes water. He grabbed the bottle and brought it outside, so he could pour it onto his hand. The moment the concoction hit his palm, he cried out. The previous burning turned into something exquisitely torturous, which left his teeth chattering and his eyes twitching in their sockets. His legs wobbled; new beads of sweat appeared on his forehead. In fact, it was as if he had poured acid into the wounds—because his flesh and bones felt like they were being worn away. The sensation devoured his strength. He stumbled back to the kitchen, delirious from the pain. In fact, he barely managed to place the bottle on the countertop before he collapsed onto the floor. He lay there like a corpse, staring blankly into space. In reality, he may have blacked out for fifteen or twenty minutes—because, by the time he managed to clamber to his feet and meander back to the cooking area underneath the house, the yams and sweet potatoes were finished cooking. There was no point trying to make sense of it.

He mashed the yams and sweet potatoes with a large wooden mortar and pestle that his mother kept beneath the house. The same prickly pain was there as he used the pestle, but he let his hunger drive him for now. He added some salt and seasonings to the mashed tubers, then he ate straight from the mortar, with his left hand. His grandmother would not approve, but once he started eating, he could not stop. It tasted good, but after the first few minutes, he ate mechanically. His mind kept returning to his uncle and mother. Each time, he would pat the phone with his right hand, to make sure it was still there. A few times, he took it out and stared at it—checking that it was still on—before he went back to eating. In time, the hunger was satisfied, and his belly became distended from his meal, but he kept shoving the food into his mouth, in a futile effort to fill his emptiness. His movements became languid; his body felt heavy and clumsy. Exhausted, he barely managed to place the pot cover over the mortar and stumble over to an old mattress beneath the house that the dog used to use as its bed. Within thirty seconds, he was fast asleep.

Something crawled over his arm—like dozens of centipedes. He could feel their little legs dancing on his palm, and he cried out as he burst upright. When he opened his eyes, it was dark outside. He had forgotten where he was: the shadowy outlines of shipping barrels, chicken coops and farming implements seemed like monsters getting ready to pounce. His right hand was burning again. Dozens of huge flies were feasting on his palm. Their little legs were flitting across his skin; but with his haze—and the darkness—he imagined one huge insect. He cried out then, and shook his hand frantically to be rid of them.

Still panicking, he jumped up from the dog's bed, hitting his head against the bottom of the house. He screamed from the pain—and stumbled a little bit from the blow—but he finally remembered where he was. The whole day flashed in a millisecond, draining more of his strength and composure. Somehow, his grandmother was dead. He remembered Daddis, Maitland, Gupta and the policeman at the station. He remembered calling his mother and uncle; for the hundredth time that day, he tapped the phone in his front pocket. He reflexively wanted to pull it out and check if anyone had called; but just then, some nearby bushes began to rustle. More likely than not, it was the wind; but in his mind, he saw the monsters of his grandmother's stories.

Before he knew it, he was running—fleeing to the safety of the kitchen. He tripped over some of the farming implements; there was a horrible clangor as they fell to the ground—or banged into pots and barrels. The clangor charged him further—as if it were some kind of dinner bell for the monsters. He ran for his life! He stubbed his toes a few times, but he did not stop. In fact, he was so terrified that he dared not scream and alert the monsters of his position.

The house was dark and ominous. By this time of the night, his grandmother would have lit all the lanterns, and made the house seem like a home—but now the building only seemed like an extension of the darkness. He slowed as he neared the kitchen door. It was still open of course, but he had the sudden sense that it was a trap. Maybe the monsters were already inside. He had left the door open, so they could have snuck in like his grandmother warned. The doubts had him standing there indecisively for a few seconds; but when the wind blew again, rustling some nearby bushes, fresh terrors prodded him into action. He sprang through the open door and slammed it behind him. He was in the house, but that only meant the darkness was complete now. Remembering the lanterns on the counter, he stretched out his hands to feel for them in the dark. He grasped them, but then he remembered the matches!

He recalled seeing a box of matches in one of the cabinets

beneath the counter—but he could not remember which one. In fact, as the seconds passed, and his fear of the darkness grew into a kind of madness, it occurred to him he may have imagined the matches. He knew there was a set beneath the house—since he had used them to light the coal pot—but there was no way in hell he was going down there again.

He could smell his grandmother; he shook his head to drive away the thought, then he pulled open the cabinets and began fumbling in the darkness for anything that felt like a box of matches. He was overturning bottles and pushing bags onto the floor. He was making a mess, but the terror was his only guide.

By now, his right hand was burning; his body was coated in a layer of clammy sweat, and his throat felt swollen and dry—but the only thing that mattered was finding the matches.

When his hand finally grasped something that felt like a box of matches, he wrenched out the box, inadvertently sending a condiment bottle careening to the floor. It smashed on the ground deafeningly, adding to Shango's terror. Desperate for light, he pulled open the box of matches—but as the box was upside down, the matchsticks tumbled to the ground. Luckily, Shango managed to grab one before it fell. He struck it against the box frantically; when it did not ignite, he struck it two more times before it occurred to him he was striking the wrong end of the matchstick. He turned it around, struck it against the side of the box, and allowed himself to breathe again when it finally burst into flame.

From the dim illumination, he got a glimpse of the mess he had made, but lighting the lamp was the only thing that mattered now. Holding the matchstick in his right hand, he pulled up the glass flute of the lantern with his left hand. When the wick caught the flame, he was relieved beyond reason; yet, still unsure, he scanned the kitchen frantically—lest any monsters were hiding in the corners. When he saw there was nothing, he stood there panting and regaining some of his composure. His speeding heart began to slow. The mess on the floor—with smashed bottles and burst bags—made a queasy feeling come over him. However, that was when something occurred to him.

What time was it?

Remembering the cellular phone, he pulled it out of his pocket and looked at the screen. It read ten thirty-seven! He stared for about seven seconds, not believing his eyes. More troublingly, nobody had called him while he was sleeping. His uncle must have come home by now. He was tempted to call his mother again—half convinced some cosmic mistake must have happened the last time he called her. Maybe the telephone lines had been switched somehow—or there had been some other colossal mix-up at the phone company. Maybe, by now, the cosmic mistake had been corrected, so that he would finally be able to reach her. He stared at the phone for a few seconds before shaking his head. No: there was still a chance his uncle would call tonight; and since he could not charge the battery until the morning, he had to conserve power.

He was proud of himself for using reason at a time like this, but what if his uncle didn't call tonight, or tomorrow, or the day after that...? A sense of dread surged in him for a moment, before seeping back into the cracks within him.

...Why hadn't his uncle called? The terrible options had him staring into space again, but then he chastised himself for not having faith. Maybe this was just another of God's tests. Maybe there was an even simpler explanation—like his uncle coming home exhausted and going straight to bed. There were other plausible explanations, but he was vaguely aware that he was grasping at hope now. He was holding on for dear life, dangling over a precipice of despair. The only thing he could do was hold on...

As the adrenaline rush passed from his system, his teeth suddenly began to chatter. He was sweating, but he felt *cold*. When he looked at his palm via the flickering wick, his eyes widened. The wounds were all enflamed and puss-laden. When he tried to make a fist, he felt as though his hand would pop somehow: it felt that tight. He squeezed one of the pustules with his left hand, and the fluid squirted from it sickeningly, setting off more alarm bells. His grandmother's cure-all concoction was still on the countertop. He grabbed it, and was about to head outside to pour it on his hand, before he faltered. There was no way he was opening the door again.

Looking at the mess on the floor, he realized it really would make little difference if he spilled some of the concoction on the ground. Acting quickly, he opened the bottle and poured some onto his hand. He braced himself for the stinging pain; but now, somehow, there was barely a tingle. His hand seemed numb—as if it were already dead. Suddenly desperate, he put his head back and took a mouthful of the concoction—just as he had seen his grandmother do a few times. His throat and nasal passages felt like they were on fire! His eyes watered. In fact, he could feel the fire all the way down his esophagus, to his stomach. He grimaced and doubled over; yet, in a bizarre way, the pain felt good—since it confirmed that he was still alive.

The terror came and went, like waves on a beach, ebbing and flowing. His grandmother was really dead—and her corpse was down the corridor. As always, the thought seemed impossible.

He stared down the darkened corridor uncertainly. What should he do now?

...And he again remembered the third room at the end of the corridor: the one in which the demon had attacked him. At the thought, his muscles froze, and he stood there trembling. ...Years ago—shortly after his mother left for America—his grandmother had told him about seeing a mountain demon when she was a girl. The demons came into your room at night, paralyzed you, and drained your soul as you slept. The spell they cast over you usually kept you from waking up; but apparently, when the creature came for his grandmother that night, she had been having her period for the first time. Shielded by the mysterious powers of her first menstrual cycle, she had finally been able to see the creature's lumbering form as it climbed into her window and towered over her bed. Terrified, she had clamped her eyes shut, fearful of what it would do if it knew she was awake. Yet, as the minutes or hours passed, she had stolen glances of it via the moonlight. Its skin had been scaly, like a lizard's. It had had birdlike, misshapen claws; and as it labored to breathe, its stale breath had had a rancid, sickening odor, like rotting garbage. When it touched her, its hands had been calloused; at the same time, its movements had been almost tender. It had made a sound, like purring—which, according to his grandmother, was how it bewitched its victims and trapped them in the dream world, so that it could siphon off their souls....

Shango had listened to her story wide-eyed, trembling as she gave all the lurid details of the mountain demon's strange seduction. She had told him the story during school vacation; a few days later, he had taken an afternoon nap in his mother's old room—since it was cooler in there. Yet, no sooner had he closed his eyes than he felt paralyzed and suffocated. He had struggled to move and breathe—but somehow, his lungs had refused to fill with air. He had had the feeling he was not alone—that something was hovering over him, *draining* him. He had struggled to open his eyes, and to *move*—but then, when he chanted a special verse his grandmother had taught him, he had suddenly found himself free. His eyes had opened; he had scanned the room, seeing nothing— but there had been a vile odor in the air, like rotten garbage.

He had fled from his mother's bedroom then, and joined his grandmother in the cooking area underneath the house—where she had been preparing dinner. She had seen the truth in his eyes, and tapped him on the shoulder, as if to congratulate him for remembering the chant and surviving his first experience with the spirit world. Suddenly excited, she had spent the rest of the evening telling him about the spirits. For instance, whenever you woke unexpectedly from a dream that was too good to be true, it was always the work of demons trying to lull you back to sleep. Thus, in her peculiar way, Shango's grandmother had even been able to make his pleasant dreams terrifying...

Since then, Shango had never slept in that room again; he had only gone into it when his grandmother ordered him to get something from it; and even then, he would rush in, grab whatever his grandmother needed, then flee.

...What was he supposed to do now? He stood there timidly for about thirty seconds, trying to find a way he could make it through the night without venturing down the corridor. For a moment, he thought about balling himself up in the corner of the kitchen and sleeping there, but his teeth were still chattering intermittently. He needed to put on something warm—and to dry off the clammy sweat. When he instinctively touched his arm, his skin felt cold to the touch. For whatever reason, he found himself thinking that that was how his grandmother would feel if he touched her. His flesh felt doughy—as if he could pull it off the bones if he tugged on it too hard.

Alarmed, he brought his grandmother's concoction to his lips again, and took another swig. Like the last time, the burning sensation was good—and he felt a little warmer afterwards. Even though there was obviously alcohol in the concoction, he did not feel drunk. If anything, his senses felt more acute. Staring down the darkened corridor, he felt like he could see deeper into the darkness; as he stood there, he could hear the buzz of flies in his grandmother's room, and smell the stench of her. Yet, as the seconds passed, and the burning sensation dissipated as it reached his stomach, his mind became calm. He saw that the only thing for him to do now was walk down that corridor, get into some warm clothes, and get some sleep. When he felt ready, he took another sip of the concoction, grasped the lantern with his left hand, and began walking down the corridor.

He held the lantern high with his left hand, to cast light as far down the dark corridor as possible. In his right hand, he gripped the neck of the bottle as tightly as he could, given the swelling. When a panicky voice in the back of his mind warned him that a demon might be sneaking up behind him in the darkness, he swung around so abruptly that the bottle almost flew from his hand. He stood there panting, prepared to scream or run, but there was nothing. When he thought he heard something in the direction of his grandmother's room, he swung around again. His harsh, irregular breathing unnerved him further—since it sounded like somebody else's. On top of that, the cold, clammy sweat seemed like a foul residue congealing on his skin.

He was relieved when he saw the sheet in his grandmother's

doorway was still tied, but the one in his mother's old room—the one where the mountain demon had attacked him—was dancing eerily on the breeze. Maybe the demon had snuck into the open door while he was sleeping under the house. Remembering his grandmother admonitions about locking up the house at night, his legs suddenly began to tremble. He still had no idea if the things he had experienced in his mother's old room had been a genuine glimpse into the spirit world—or merely the products of his sleep-addled mind—but tonight he was ready to believe anything. He hesitated for a moment; but knowing he could not just *stand* there, he forced his legs to move.

His nose wrinkled as he neared his grandmother's doorway: it was difficult to believe she could smell that bad after only one day. He was so dazed that he began to wonder if he had actually been asleep for days, instead of hours.

At his grandmother's doorway, he felt his heart rate quickening. He raised the lantern high once more, and peered into her room. He could barely discern her form on the bed, but most of her room was darkness and shadow. The angry buzz of flies seemed almost deafening now. It was so loud that it seemed like something physical—something *tangible*—grinding against his skull. When he began to get lightheaded, he forced himself to move toward his doorway. In truth, he was stumbling around now. His vision was not blurry, but he found himself having to concentrate to see clearly. Was he drunk? Maybe: he could not entirely be sure. He just knew he did not feel right.

After raising the lantern high to survey his bedroom, he entered. The outlines of a new plan were already in his head. He went straight for the trunk at the foot of the bed, but placed the lantern and bottle on the floor, since he needed something warm from the trunk. He was moving quickly now—and as he worked, he made sure to position his body so that he could keep an eye on his grandmother's doorway. He kept looking over there every few seconds; and now that his window no longer had glass louvers in it, he looked over at the gaping hole as well, half-suspecting a demon to spring through it at any moment.

He pulled up the trunk's lid and fetched a sweater his mother had sent him years ago. It was grey, and had "I ♥ NY" printed on the front, in letters that were now faded. He pulled the sweater over his head, then closed the lid. Surveying the room again—and the doorway, and the open window—it occurred to him that if he slept in his regular position he would not be able to see the doorway. Acting quickly, he pushed the trunk toward the wall with the pictures of tourist landmarks, placed the lantern and bottle on it, then he dragged the bed toward the far wall. There, he had a good view of the doorway and the window.

With the sweater, he felt warmer now, but his teeth continued to chatter intermittently. His hand still felt stiff and dead; when he looked at it via the lantern, the pustules still seemed grue-some—but he rushed ahead to distract himself. ...Every few seconds, he glanced over at his grandmother's doorway—and the glass-less window. He retrieved his pillow from what used to be the head of the bed, and repositioned it against the wall. He could hear his heart drumming in his chest—above the crickets, frogs, buzzing flies and the other nocturnal creatures desperate to mate and feed.

He was ready to get in the bed, but that was when a shamefully childish thought popped into his head: *What if there was something underneath the bed*—some childhood monster that would spring at him once he closed his eyes? His heart began racing again. He backed away from the bed then. First, he bent down and looked. He saw nothing, except his balled-up towel; but to be sure, he got on his hands and knees to check. Then, realizing his position on the floor left him vulnerable—and that that would be the perfect time for his grandmother's corpse to come to life and spring from the doorway—he jumped to his feet and stood there panting and wide-eyed.

He did not exactly feel sleepy, but he was exhausted—both physically and mentally. He was about to get in bed when he noticed he was still wearing the outdoor shoes. Shaking his head, he kicked them off, got in bed, and pulled the sheet around him. If his grandmother were still alive, she would thrash him for the shoes and for getting into bed in the same mud-stained pants he had worn in the street, but death changed everything. Death made etiquette irrelevant; and just then, the wafting stench of his grandmother's corpse made his stomach turn, so that he grimaced and held his breath.

Even when he was underneath the cover, his eyes kept darting from the doorway to the window. With all that, he did not feel as though he would sleep. He doubted he had the courage to close his eyes—no matter how heavy they became.

He remembered the cellular phone. He took it out of his pocket and looked at the screen again via the flickering wick. It was ten forty-seven now—and no one had called. The despair threatened to return, but he only sighed and placed the phone on the trunk.

However, after placing the phone, he pulled his hand back anxiously, as if the hidden monster beneath his bed might grab his arm and drag him off to hell....

The dancing wick produced shadows on the wall. Shango stared at them as the minutes passed. In truth, he had never had a lantern in his room before. His grandmother had never trusted him to keep one—since she feared he would burn the house down. Besides, by seven at night, he and his grandmother were usually in bed. His grandmother would get up at five in the morning, to start breakfast and the other household chores. She would rise when the sun rose, then begin preparing for bed as soon as the sun set. There was something natural and balanced about it—but his grandmother had practiced the old ways, and Shango again found himself thinking that once he was in America, all the old ways would be forgotten.

His eyes were beginning to get heavy now—but then he suddenly became aware of a scratching sound. It was coming from the wall by his pillow. He looked back at the wall uneasily, remembering that the mountain demon had attacked him in the room on the other side of it.

The sound was low and intermittent. Sometimes, as many as fifteen minutes would pass before he heard it again; just when he was about to tell himself he had imagined it, he would hear it again—and become convinced the demon's claw was scraping the wall. His heart would race for those few moments, and he would hold his breath, so that he could listen.

The last time he felt fear like this had been about a year ago. He had become engrossed in playing a football match after school. He had scored about six goals that afternoon. Nobody had been able to touch him—even the older kids had been no match for his skills, speed and stamina—

Then, somehow, it had been five-thirty. Suddenly coming to his senses, he had grabbed his books and rushed out of town. Unfortunately, when he reached the foot of the mountain, the godlike stamina had left him. His usually lithe legs had felt heavy and stiff as night fell about him. Since there had been no streetlights on the mountain road, the world had seemed darker and more daunting than it had ever been before. He had literally walked in the middle of the road, wary of something pulling him into the bushes if he strayed too close to the edge. He had kept looking around at every strange noise—and by then, they had all been strange to him. When cars approached, he had been relieved for those few seconds of a light and company. Of course, he had had to dart out of the middle of the road—especially when a car zoomed around a bend unexpectedly. The headlights had blinded him at those moments, but the light—and the momentary camaraderie of other human beings—had enlivened his spirits...until the car was gone, and the darkness entrenched itself once more...

By the time he reached the path through the forest, his legs felt like lead. The dark path suddenly seemed like a passageway into hell. He stopped at the mouth of it, staring into the chaotic tangle of bushes and branches. Ironically, home was only five minutes away—if he ran at full speed. ...Yes, that was the only way. He spent about thirty seconds gathering up his courage, and then he sprang from the road and darted into the darkness. Every leaf and twig that scratched his skin seemed like a demon's finger. It propelled him on faster. He was gasping for air; his legs were on fire—yet he would not stop. When his head collided with a low-hanging branch; the pain made something like stars flash before his eyes; his legs wobbled momentarily—but even then, he continued running, as if the Devil, himself were at his heels—

And then, miraculously, he had been out of the path, running through his grandmother's fields. Inside the kitchen, he had seen the lanterns' familiar glow. Indeed, he had run faster at the sight, like a sinner finding himself within reach of the Pearly Gates. Even when he entered the kitchen and saw his grandmother waiting there with a willowy branch to beat him, he had taken his punishment gladly, relieved to finally be in the light.

That was then; now, as Shango lay on his bed, he knew even

the light was not enough to protect him anymore. Back then, he had had his grandmother's reassuring presence to protect him from the monsters. Now, his grandmother was gone, and the house held only death and shadows.

His tired eyes were still darting from the doorway to the gaping window; his ears were analyzing all the nocturnal sounds—the crickets and birds and God only knew what else—for any signs of danger. He did not hear anything out of the ordinary, but when he was resetting his head on the pillow, a huge, shadowy form darted from the darkness beyond the window and swooped toward him! A muffled cry escaped from his lips; he jumped in the bed, his heart racing—

But then the moth clanged into the lantern and fell unceremoniously to the floor, where it lay twitching. Shango stared down at it, still panting as the terror ebbed from his system. Eventually, he lay down heavily on the bed, exhausted beyond reason. He told himself to relax; however, a few minutes later, something scratched the wall again. It was slow and creepy—as if the demon were taunting him.

That was when the lantern began to flicker. Shango looked over at it with wide, trembling eyes. When he looked closer, he saw the lantern was out of kerosene! With the strange passage of time, he had no idea if he had been lying there for hours or minutes. The lantern had probably been low on kerosene when he lit it in the kitchen; he cursed himself for not checking at the time; but either way, the flame was doing a fitful dance on the wick now. It flickered more dramatically, and then he found himself lying in the darkness.

The nighttime sounds suddenly seemed louder. All the creatures seemed to be crying out at once, as if spreading the word that the light was gone—and that he was now easy prey. Shango pulled the sheet up to his neck, breathing shallowly, as if that would somehow hide his presence from the monsters.

Then, somewhere outside, there was a commotion! Something metal clanged against the ground—or at least, that's how it sounded to him. Whatever it was, it was *close*. He held his breath, listening for the telltale sounds of a demon's footsteps. In his mind, he saw a lumbering beast knocking over everything as it passed. His mind flashed with images of fangs and claws; he expected the creature to leap through the window at any second.

His teeth began to chatter again—despite his relative warmth under the sheet. His wide, trembling eyes scanned the darkness frantically. More minutes or hours passed, and then the scratching on the wall became more insistent, as if the demon were boring its way through the wall. Shango inched his way down the bed, to get his head as far away from the wall as possible. Yet, by then, nowhere was safe: the doorway and window were both open to the darkness. And so, in a sign of defeat and cowardice, Shango pulled the sheet over his head and lay there cowering.

That was when a high-pitched squeal came from outside. He had never heard anything like it before, so he pulled his knees to his chest, and lay there shivering in the fetal position. In his mind, all the monsters and demons were closing in on him now; across the hall, he heard something unsettling, like his grandmother's bed frame creaking!

With his heart thumping in his chest, and his trembling, it was impossible to verify the sound. He prepared himself to scream—and to *die*. Yet, it was at that moment that he remembered a chant his grandmother had taught him once. It was something like *zunga-dunga-tunga*—pure gibberish as far as he could tell. He felt like a fool when he whispered it the first few times, but then he miraculously felt something like calm spreading over him.

The ambient sounds of the night became softer and softer—until, incredibly, there was silence. The silence was perfect—infinite and complete—as if God, Himself had come down from the heavens to protect his soul—

Then, abruptly, the silence was gone—even as the peace remained. When he listened, he realized birds were chirping now—instead of crickets and frogs and the usual nocturnal sounds. When he opened his eyes and pulled the sheet away from his head, he was stunned to see it was the dawn of a new day, and that he had somehow survived the night.

W as this a dream, or was he actually awake? He could not be sure about anything anymore. Yet, the sun was rising on the horizon. He turned to the window now. In fact, he sat up in bed and stared outside. It was no later than five forty-five in the morning. The sky was still a pastel hue—like something in a pleasant dream. Unfortunately, a breeze blew then, and his grandmother's wafting stench brought him back to reality. He looked across the corridor, where he saw her shadowed form lying on the bed. A whole day had officially passed. By now, thousands of flies were buzzing about his grandmother's corpse—or so it seemed to Shango. From where he was lying, he could see the swarm circling her bed. The sound of them filled him with a sense of urgency—an awareness that he was running out of time to give his grandmother a dignified death.

He suddenly remembered his uncle's call. The phone was still on the trunk. He reached over and grabbed it eagerly; he stared at the screen with wide, searching eyes—but there was still nothing: no calls; no messages.... He stared at the blank screen as if it would explain itself and tell him what to do next. Should he call his uncle again? He thought about it before nodding his head: there was no other option now. However, no sooner had he come to the decision than the lone power bar began flashing, alerting him that the phone needed to be charged. He stared at the blinking light so intently that his eyes began to hurt. Eventually, he grimaced and looked away.

He lay back down on the bed and stared blankly at the wall, contemplating his next plan of action. There was only one thing to do now: go to the police. Indeed, there were no other choices. Flies were devouring his grandmother, and he was the only one there to make sure she had a dignified death. The weight of it was awesome. He saw everything that he had to do to make things right; but in the back of his mind, the resentment stirred—of his mother and uncle and the adult world. It was only there for an instant, but he felt a little dead inside once he acknowledged it.

H e got out of bed now. When he grabbed the towel from the floor, he noticed the swelling in his right hand had gone down. Scabs had formed, and the healing process was underway. Relieved, he put on the outdoor shoes and headed for the shower. At his grandmother's doorway, he stopped and stared inside. The swarm of flies was a dark cloud over her corpse. The sight seemed impossible—like a badly animated special effect in a movie. He took a tentative step into the room, thinking he would chase away the flies, but it was pointless—and besides, the stench was worse when he stepped closer. His stomach convulsed; he retreated a step, bringing the towel up to his nose as a precautionary measure. It almost made him want to cry, seeing his grandmother like that. He felt like he had failed her, but he swore then that he would make things right. He would go to the authorities now; they would come for his grandmother, and she would finally have a dignified death. The alternative—her being devoured by maggots, like his old dog—was too horrible. In fact, at the thought, he rushed out of the house to shower and get himself ready.

E ven though the water was cold, it felt good against his skin as he showered. He put it on at full blast and stood there shuddering. Afterwards, he felt more awake somehow. His mind seemed clearer now; even after he turned off the tap, he stood there for a moment, thinking about everything that lay ahead. When he went to the station, the police would call his mother and uncle—just like he had. ...But what would happen if they could not reach his relatives either? Indeed, even if the police managed to reach his relatives by phone, they would still take him into custody until an adult came down to claim him. How long would that take? Hours, days, *weeks*...? Where would he stay during that time? In his puerile mind, he imagined a Victorian era orphanage, like something out of *Oliver Twist*, with starving children in rags. Common sense—or some inner hopefulness—told him it could not possibly be that bad. However, after his night of terror, he felt he had to brace himself for worst-case scenarios. Thus, even though his duty to his grandmother was clear, an anxious feeling came over him when he thought about what the adult world would do to him when it found out he was alone.

To distract himself, he again forced himself to move. Soon, he was rushing back to the house. The towel was tied around his waist, and his dirty clothes were in his arms. At the kitchen, he stopped for a moment, looking at the mess he had made the previous night. However, he reminded himself that time was short. He needed to inform the police as soon as possible—for his grandmother's sake. The urgency fueled his muscles; he began to jog once more—but at his grandmother's doorway, he stopped and stared at the grim scene. The stench seemed worse somehow, so that he raised the dirty clothes to his nose to protect himself. He stared, but after a few moments, he realized he was not afraid of her corpse anymore. The dark terrors from last night were gone: now, he saw only decaying flesh.

Remembering the police, he turned to his room now; but at the doorway, he again stood looking at the mess. Guiltily, he thought about the police coming back to the house and seeing this squalor. What kind of people would they think lived there? His grandmother would be shamed. He thought about fetching the broom and mop and cleaning everything, so that the family honor could be preserved when the authorities came. He hesitated for a moment, thinking it over, but then he shook his head, wary of getting sidetracked again—and being led away from his duty.

He was rushing again. He went to the trunk, placed the lantern and the bottle of his grandmother's concoction on the floor, then he opened the lid. The only clean clothes he had left—the only "presentable" ones—were his school uniforms. He grabbed the one on top and dressed quickly—as if he were late for school.

The cellular phone was still on the bed. When he saw it, an excited feeling came over him. It occurred to him his uncle may have called while he was showering. He snatched up the phone and stood staring at the screen with the same wide eyes—but no one had called. He sighed, annoyed with himself for still having hope. He was about to toss the phone back onto the bed, but then he decided to attach it to the charger—which was still arrayed on the windowsill. The sun was rising, so the phone soon made the cheerful sound that said it was charging. Once that was done, he fetched his schoolbag from the corner of the room—since he always felt naked when he left the house without it—then he headed outside.

After he turned the corner of the house and began walking down the mountain, he remembered the food he had made yesterday. He went to the mortar, thinking that he would eat some of the yams and sweet potatoes before leaving; but as he approached, he saw the lid he had placed on the mortar was lying on the ground. Looking in the mortar, he saw that most of the food was gone. In fact, when he looked closer, he saw about half a dozen rat droppings at the bottom. He sucked his teeth angrily. The rat was the only creature he knew that actually shit in its own food. He sucked his teeth again, but then it suddenly occurred to him the scratching from last night—and the loud commotion under the house—must have been from rats. It all made sense now. Indeed, in the light of day, everything seemed clear, and he smiled a bittersweet smile.

It was surreal to walk down the mountain road again. He kept looking over his shoulder, as if expecting another car to mow him down. Whenever he heard a vehicle approaching, he stopped and stood on the far edge of the road. At the spot from yesterday—where the Range Rover had flipped into the ravine—he was startled to see the vehicle was gone. He peered over the edge of the ravine, looking for any stray piece of metal—or even an oil spill—but it was all gone, as if none of it had happened. Nothing changed that quickly on the island unless someone powerful compelled it to happen. However, as he was about to delve into the mystery, Daddis' glistening incisor flashed in his mind, warning him to mind his business. Having survived the night of terror, mountain demons and supernatural monsters now seemed ridiculous to him, but the empty ravine was proof of the awesome power of brutal men....

He lingered there for a little while, exploring his vague thoughts and fears, but his grandmother was counting on him, so he moved from the ravine and continued on his way. Yesterday, his fears and timidity had sidetracked him; today, he vowed he would tell the authorities what had happened, no matter what.

He reached the ugly town about six-thirty, then headed for the police station in the city center. He felt hungry, but he subjugated everything to his duty to his grandmother. By now, the streets were beginning to fill with people. Children were heading to school; adults were on their way to work—or busy concocting whatever schemes allowed them to survive.

As he neared the city center, he spotted some of his classmates; he ducked behind some parked cars to hide, his heart racing. Afterwards, he asked himself why he had hid and what he was afraid of. He could come up with no answer, so he continued on. Indeed, he walked faster, desperate to reach the station and put everything behind him.

What would he tell the police when he got there? He started compiling his story in his mind. It was a simple enough matter to tell them his grandmother was dead, but how would he explain her two-day-old corpse? He had never thought of that before. He could tell them he had come to the station yesterday, and that the irate officer had chased him away. However, something about that seemed shameful. He grimaced as the various scenarios played in his mind: once they started questioning him, his entire story would seem...*suspicious*. What kind of child spent the night with a corpse in the next room? On top of that, the police would take him back to the house to find it a mess, with bottles thrown to the kitchen floor and broken glass in his room. ...What if they began to suspect him of *killing* her? The thought made him stumble over the uneven pavement; his heart raced for a few seconds as all the permutations went through his mind. In the American movies he saw at the cinema, the coroners always had ways of telling if someone had died of natural causes, but was there such a thing on the island? In his mind, he saw the ease with which the situation could get out of control—with wild accusations and sensationalized newspaper articles...but his duty to his grandmother was clear, so he sighed and told himself he would deal with the consequences when they came—

Damnit, he'd forgotten to bring his uncle's phone number. He was sure the police would want to call it. ...But no bother: the only thing that mattered was alerting them that his grandmother was dead. Besides, they could call the number once he took them back up the mountain.

Shango was practically jogging by the time he reached the station—but when he looked, the gate was locked, and the same sign was there, informing visitors that the officers were off on a break! How the hell could they be closed again? He sucked his teeth, but he had no choice but to wait. He was wary of sitting on the steps again—and having an irate policeman yell at him for idling—but he was tired, and there was no point in standing around when there were perfectly good stairs right there.

He was about to sit down when a passing car came to a screeching halt in front of the building. The driver honked the horn angrily to get Shango's attention; and when he looked, he was startled to see the pretty teacher from school—Miss Craig. At the sight of her, there was an instinctive sense of joy. He had spent many school days staring at her dreamily from his desk in the front row. He would spend the hours making up childish fantasies where he would invariably be sitting on her lap or laying his head on her breasts—images that were more redolent of a boy's yearning for his mother than a man's yearning for a woman. Indeed, looking at her now, he felt suddenly unsettled, as if seeing the foolishness of his dreams for the first time.

"Where were you yesterday!" she yelled from the open car window. She had never used her angry voice with him before, and he felt heartbroken. He stood at attention—as if he were in class, trying to redeem himself with a brilliant answer. He opened his mouth, but nothing came out. It suddenly occurred to him he should tell her about his grandmother. She definitely wouldn't be angry with him anymore if he told her *that*. However, a flashback of the last twenty-four hours left his mind overloaded. He had no idea where to begin. His lower lip began to tremble, so that his teacher looked at him curiously. Her angry expression faded away then. Her face softened, and she was amazingly beautiful again. Yet, just as she was about to say something, a speeding car swung around the corner and almost crashed into her rear bumper. The driver began honking his horn, then poked his head out of the window and began yelling obscenities.

With all that, Miss Craig put the car in gear and prepared to move. However, before she did, she looked over at Shango with a stern expression. "You'd better not be late for school today!" she threatened him. Then, with the driver still honking his horn obnoxiously, she sped off, leaving a cloud of exhaust.

Miss Craig's threat was so unnerving that Shango immediately found himself jogging in the direction of school. However, his pace slowed once her car disappeared down the winding road. Guiltily, he remembered his grandmother. What about his duty to her? He grimaced, looking back in the direction of the police station. He could go back to the step and wait, but there was no telling when the police would show up. On the other hand, he could be at school in ten minutes. Miss Craig would be pleased— or at least appeased. He was about to smile, but then it occurred to him, suddenly and brutally, that he would probably never see Miss Craig again once he went to the authorities. They would take him away, holding him until his mother came to retrieve him. The thought broke his heart a little, so that his body slumped.

All at once, he yearned for the normalcy of his schoolboy existence. After everything that had happened yesterday—and everything that would happen once he went to the authorities— he yearned for the simplicity of it. He knew there was something selfish about the thought. The idea of his grandmother's fly-infested corpse still filled him with urgency—and he told himself he would definitely take care of it today—yet he continued walking toward school, driven by Miss Craig's vague threat and the yearning for a fleeting moment of peace before his life, as he had known it up to now, came to an end.

Besides, school would be over at two that afternoon anyway— and his grandmother was not going anywhere. The thought made him grimace again, and bow his head in shame...and yet he was still walking toward the school. Furthermore, there was no telling when the policemen would return to the station. For all he knew, they would keep him waiting for hours, or show up at two in the afternoon, when school was letting out. He was not sure if those possibilities justified his dereliction of duty or only rationalized it. The only certainty was that once he went to the police, nothing would ever be the same again.

S hango stood across the street from the school, watching his schoolmates entering the old, rusty gate. Some of them were congregating by the old women who sold sugary snacks; others were playing in the dusty yard beyond the gate. They all seemed so carefree that he did not know if he envied them or pitied them.

Like yesterday, they all seemed so "young" to him now—even the ones who were older than him. Some of them came from the harshest slums in town; death was no stranger to them, and yet they almost seemed to believe in the world more than those who came from comfortable, middle-class homes. There was a kind of earnestness to them that he doubted he had anymore. After the last two days, even his hopes and dreams seemed guarded. While he would be relieved if he heard from his mother, dark feelings— like resentment and distrust—were settling in his soul, poisoning him from within. Worse, he felt like he was running out of time— and that if he did not hear from his mother by the end of the day, he would never experience real joy again. In a sense, maybe he was delaying going to the police in an attempt to give his relatives more time to redeem themselves. Maybe his uncle had finally heard his phone message and was making calls now. The thought made him stand straighter and nod his head. Maybe the message would be waiting on the cellular phone when he returned to the mountain with the police—or maybe he would go to the police only to discover his uncle had already called them…or, maybe the police would show up at school after hearing from his uncle, and take him away. The various scenarios played in his mind, and he clung to them tenaciously, desperate for one of them to be true.

S hango went to an all-boys' school. Everyone wore the same khaki pants and white shirts with the school emblem. Since he had inadvertently dressed in his school uniform today, he was beginning to think it was fate that he had come here. The uniform made him feel like he belonged to something. He needed that.

Yet, the brotherly spirit was broken when he spotted a towering youth called Grumbles. The youth's real name was Glanville, but everyone, even the teachers, called him Grumbles because he seemed to whisper everything ominously below his breath. Grumbles was the school bully. He had the gargantuan proportions of a sumo wrestler, and the beginnings of an unkempt beard. There were rumors that he was nineteen or twenty, and had been held back in school since he was too dunce to pass. A few students swore he had fathered several children with grown women in the slums, but Shango found it farfetched.

The youth used to make Shango do his homework for him. Somewhere along the line, an understanding had been communicated between them, whereby Shango would hand over his homework in lieu of getting beaten. However, since the youth was such a dunce, the teachers had quickly caught on. One particularly sadistic teacher had pummeled Grumbles' behind with a cane he had had specially made from the hardest wood he could find. Since then, Grumbles had avoided him—and Shango had avoided him as well, knowing it was only a matter of time before he took out his frustrations.

Grumbles' father was a well-known drug dealer, but not a particularly successful one. To be a successful drug dealer on the island, one had to bribe the right people. That was true everywhere, but since the island was so small, the "right people" were often impatient—since they had their own lifestyles to maintain. The island's right people wanted to live like the right people in America and Columbia. They had unrealistic expectations; and so, when the chosen drug dealer started coming up short on his payments, they often ended up killing their golden goose to recoup their losses. Luckily for them, there was never a shortage of young, ambitious thugs who thought they could outwit the system. Grumbles' father was one of them; and more likely than not, Grumbles would be one of them in due time.

Presently, Grumbles walked over to one of the lines where the boys were buying snacks from one of the old women. Just as a scrawny first-year student was walking away with a box of candy, Grumbles grabbed it and began opening it. The scrawny boy began to cry; the old woman he had bought the candy from jumped to her feet and began pleading with Jesus, Paul, Mary— and every other Saint she could name—to come down from the heavens to carry out their vengeance. While she was repeating her incantation a second time, Grumbles sucked his teeth and started yelling back at her, recounting the intimate details of her vagina's stench. It was a daily occurrence.

The shouting match went on for about forty-five seconds, but when Grumbles grew tired of it, he grabbed his crotch in a gesture of contempt to the old woman, emptied the box of candy into his gaping mouth, then nonchalantly tossed the empty container into the scrawny boy's face. At the sight of the crumpled box lying on the ground, the scrawny boy bawled louder—but Grumbles did not even look back as he waddled through the gate in search of more mischief.

One of the old women tried to placate the scrawny boy by offering him another box of candy, but the morning trauma seemed too much for him—because he continued sniffling even after receiving the new box. It was a pitiful sight, and everyone looked away.

Shango groaned as the scene came to an end, then he began walking across the street. As soon as he stepped onto the curb, the school bell began to ring. The boys milling about outside the gate now began to run toward the school. As Shango joined them, he was strangely reassured by the old routine.

The school principal, Mr. Williams, was a fat man in his sixties whose face had a perpetual scowl on it. He was a deacon in the Church, but there were rumors—probably unfounded—that he preferred the charms of young boys, and that he would take special joy when he made the boys pull down their pants and bend over to receive their canings. He was standing in the yard, ringing the bell and glaring at boys he thought were moving too slowly. As such, all the boys were presently trotting to their classrooms. When Principal Williams caught sight of Shango, his eyes softened, the perpetual scowl faded from his face, and something like a smile appeared there for a moment. The transformation was so creepy that Shango nodded timidly before running past the principal at full speed. Indeed, he ran all the way to his class, and only stopped because there was a bottleneck of students at the entrance to the classroom.

Miss Craig's eyes widened when she saw him. Remembering her thinly veiled threats from earlier, he nodded to her in the same uneasy way he had nodded to the principal. Looking vaguely about the room, at his classmates, and the depressing grey cement walls, he began to feel his first doubts about coming here. He remembered his grandmother's decaying corpse guiltily. Yet, now that he was here, he felt trapped. His pace had slowed while he considered his options, but when one of his classmates inadvertently walked into the back of him, Shango became flustered and rushed to his familiar spot at the front of the class. Miss Craig kept looking over at him; each time she made eye contact with him, he looked away uneasily.

Stranger still, when everyone was seated, Miss Craig did not say her customary, "Good morning, gentlemen." Instead, her voice was ominous as she began, "Shango Cartwright, you were absent from school yesterday. Explain yourself."

Shango clambered to his feet and stood at attention. "I was…" —all at once, he was fumbling for words—"…sick," he said at last. He was initially relieved when the word tumbled from his mouth, but then his stomach seemed to knot itself when he realized he had lied—and that it was only the first of many lies he would have to tell about the events of the last two days. He grimaced slightly—but he began to relax when he saw his teacher's stern expression softening. Whether she was reacting to his lie about being sick, or the flustered expression on his face, there was deep compassion in her eyes. If she was feeling sorry for him now, he imagined how she would feel if he told her about his grandmother. In fact, now that he thought about it, the announcement would throw the entire school into turmoil. Miss Craig would hug him, and maybe cry when he told her the details. The story would spread from class to class; everyone would stare at him or ask him how he was doing; and with all that, the entire machinery of the school would ground to a halt. At the thought of their cloying outpouring of grief and concern, he shuddered.

He did not want anyone—including Miss Craig—to pity him. He did not want any of their tears or whispers. In his mind, they would only find out about his grandmother's death when he was leaving for America. In the fantasy, his mother would come to school with him on that final day, bedecked in the finest raiment America had to offer. All his classmates would be in awe of her— and jealous that he was leaving for America. It was one of those half-formed fantasies that fluttered about in one's mind before disappearing back into the nothingness, and he sighed dreamily—

"Shango Cartwright!" Miss Craig blared, startling him.

"Yes, Miss!" he said, standing at attention again as she glowered at him.

"Come here!" she said, pointing to the spot next to her, as if he were a dog. "Come and address the class!"

"Yes, Miss," he said faintly, feeling the life draining from him. He walked up to her tentatively, then nodded to her uneasily as he turned around and faced the class. All the other boys were staring at him wide-eyed, wondering what horrible punishment was going to befall the great Shango Cartwright. Some of them were smiling, gleeful at the prospect of the teacher's pet finally getting his comeuppance. He felt like he was trapped in a nightmare—as if he would look down to discover he was standing there in nothing but a dingy pair of underwear—

"Shango Cartwright!" Miss Craig screamed yet again.

"Yes, Miss," Shango barely managed to squeak—but now, somehow, there was a smile on her face as she began:

"I'm pleased to inform you that you've been chosen to represent our school in an island-wide competition." After that, she began clapping; and at her prompting, the rest of the stunned class began clapping as well, most of them half-heartedly. Shango stared at her, not quite able to grasp what she was saying—and what it could possibly have to do with him.

Miss Craig hugged him tenderly then. It was all surreal. She smelled good: fresh and clean, like flowers after it rained. He lost himself in the scent, and the tender warmth of her body. It was probably only when she pulled away from him and shook him by the shoulders to celebrate that he began to understand.

She was talking again: "We'll be expecting great things out of you, Shango."

"Yes, Miss," he answered reflexively.

"Each high school on the island will put up its best student—which means you'll be competing against older students—but we have faith in you."

Shango nodded as she smiled. Then, again acting more on instinct than with genuine thought, he said, "I'll do my best."

"The competition is in two weeks!" she said excitedly. "You'll be on TV, Shango—on a *Sunday* afternoon." Then, with a starry look in her eyes, "It's a new initiative by our Prime Minister to invest in our youth and identify the leaders of tomorrow!"

There was something vaguely off-putting and cartoonish about her encomium to the Prime Minister. Shango stared at her intently—as if she were speaking a foreign language and he had to concentrate in order to translate. A side of him still believed all this was a ridiculous dream. Still, her smile was amazing as always. He stared at her white, even teeth, losing himself in the perfection of them.

By now, Miss Craig had begun to clap again, followed dutifully by his classmates. Shango nodded his head shyly at them all—a kind of bow—then he began to walk back to his seat. What did it really mean? …Had Miss Craig really said the competition was going to be two weeks from now? Certainly Shango would be off the island by then. *Certainly.* …Yet, the horrible doubts—the *panic*—lurked within him, just beneath the surface.

After Miss Craig's announcement, the rest of the day passed him in a blur. At his other classes—mathematics and chemistry, then history and literature—it was the same thing, with teachers congratulating him and declaring their high expectations. In truth, very little schoolwork was done that day. Yet, when his mathematics teacher called on him to solve a complicated equation, he found that he somehow had the right answer. He had always been able to glance at mathematical problems and give the correct answer in an instant. Similarly, his memory allowed him to recall poems and the other useless things they made students memorize in the Caribbean. It allowed him to pretend to be paying attention when in reality his mind was in a whole other world.

During his chemistry class, he was looking in his bag for his notebook when he saw he was still carrying the plastic bottle from yesterday. Yesterday's strange defiance was gone—or at least lost in the jumble of today's emotions....

At lunch time, when everyone poured out into the schoolyard to play and/or eat, some of his classmates gathered around to question him. Beyond the throng, he saw other clumps of boys pointing at him and talking amongst themselves. There was a strange awe in their eyes—respect, maybe. Students he had known for years but had never really talked to—namely, the popular ones—came over to him as if they had always been the best of friends. Clark Simpson, whose father owned a supermarket that had somehow managed to fend off Gupta's advances, came over and shared his substantial lunch. By then, Shango was too hungry to decline for the sake of family honor and propriety.

Simpson's usual sycophants came over as well, crowding around him and asking him a million questions about himself, as if he were a tourist from Norway or some other distant land. After three minutes of that, Shango found it all tedious—yet there was no way to escape when the popular kids found you interesting. When he tried to get away from them by saying he had to use the bathroom, the entire throng followed him into the cramped room. Shango practically expected one of them to offer to hold his penis when he stood awkwardly above the trough to urinate. With all that, he was relieved when the bell rang and the break ended.

For the remainder of the day, he was plagued by guilty thoughts about his grandmother. He kept seeing her decaying corpse in his mind. On top of all that, his stomach churned nervously every time he thought about what was going to happen that afternoon, when he finally went to the police. After he told them about his grandmother, everything would be taken out of his hands. ...And what if they couldn't reach his relatives? How long would he be trapped in limbo? Given today's grand announcement about the contest, the entire thing seemed like the irreconcilable part of an otherwise good dream—the wild deviation from reality that alerted the dreamer that he was dreaming.

He yawned then, feeling the effects of his night of terror—or the suffocating midday heat, which always had a soporific effect on the school. Even teachers were known to struggle with staying awake when the midday heat hit.

Then, somehow, the school day was over. After Miss Craig dismissed the literature class, Shango stood up uneasily, but she gestured for him to come to her desk. She smiled as he approached. He nodded shyly, but then noticed there was an envelope in her right hand. She offered it to him as soon as he was within reach; then, when he took it, she began:

"Your grandmother will have to sign this form—for you to be in the competition."

"Oh," Shango said as he opened the flap and looked inside vaguely.

When he looked back at his teacher, she exulted, "She's going to be *so* proud of you!"

At those words, something was triggered in Shango, and he inexplicably felt the tears welling up from the depths of him. He hid it by nodding to his teacher and running out of the room. It was not the most glamorous exit, but he would come undone if he allowed himself to be unguarded around her. His intention was to run as far away from her as possible; his mind was already going to the task of informing the police, but as soon as he exited the class, the popular kids were waiting there for him.

Shango figured they would leave him when he reached the front gate, but they followed him, like stray dogs that thought they had found a new master. There was no way he could take them to the police—since they would only ask him a million more questions— so he headed toward the slums, in the hope that Simpson and some of the richer students would balk and leave him in peace.

Unfortunately, by now, Simpson had found his groove in terms of pointless chatter. "Do you like football?" he began at one point. "Me too!" he said before Shango even thought of answering. "I see you playing all the time after school, but I broke my foot last year, so my father doesn't want me playing any rough sports. Do you like tennis? My mother wants me to play, but I'm not that good…" He went on and on like that, so that after a while, Shango did not even pretend it was a conversation. He did not bother to nod or grunt or show any sign that he was listening when he was prompted by one of Simpson's faux questions. However, his sycophants took turns saying things like "Yeah!" and "Me too!" Their strange enthusiasm was fascinating in a disturbing kind of way. Simpson was like a preacher in the throes of a sermon; his sycophants were like true believers in the pews, screaming "Amen!" and "Hallelujah!" Shango wished the boy would shut the hell up and leave, but from the gleam in his eyes, Shango knew he was only getting started.

When the trek through the slums did not dissuade Simpson and his flock from following him, Shango picked up his pace and headed out of town. Indeed, he became encouraged when Simpson finally showed signs of suffering. The boy became winded from Shango's pace; his pointless chatter became interspersed with gasps and groans. Seeing his chance, Shango walked even faster, so that he was practically jogging now. When one of the syco- phants protested, Shango said he had to rush home for an errand. When Simpson asked him where he lived, Shango pointed an ominous finger to the top of the mountain. At that, Simpson and his flock seemed to lose faith, because they reflexively slowed. Seeing his chance, Shango waved generally and sprinted away from them. After about ten steps, he glanced back. They were standing there in a confused clump—with the followers looking to Simpson for guidance. Not wanting to risk getting caught up in their nonsense again, Shango turned and ran on at full speed.

He stopped about a minute later, when he was on the outskirts of town. He had never come this far down this road before, so he only had a vague sense of where it led. Yet, the foothills of the mountain were ahead, so he used them to get his bearings. He turned a bend in the road and came upon a sprawling slaughter house. The odor of death was so thick that he felt like he could practically chew it. It burned the back of his throat and turned his stomach, so that he held his breath and began running again.

By the time the air seemed breathable once more, he looked ahead and saw the road came to a tee. To the right, the road headed up the mountain; to the left, it doubled back to the town. He stopped and looked back the way he had come—first, to instinctively make sure the popular kids weren't still chasing him, and then to calculate the shortest route back to the police station. As best as he could figure, the shortest route was to continue to the end of this road, then make a left turn to double back to the town. It was a twenty-minute walk, and he sighed, but there was no choice.

When he reached the tee, he glanced to the right and saw a police car parked off the road, in a nook they supposedly used to catch speeding drivers—but which they only really used for sleep. Shango's spirits brightened: he could tell the officer in the car about his grandmother, sparing himself the walk back to town. He was practically running to the car now. All he could think about was bringing this to an end, so his grandmother could rest in peace. Through his own bungling and timidity, he had kept his grandmother's corpse waiting for two days. Because of him, she had been denied a dignified death, so he ran with the hope of redeeming himself.

Yet, when he reached the police car, he saw it was empty. The windows were open, and the keys were in the ignition, so he concluded the policeman had to be nearby. Maybe the man was relieving himself in the bushes or something. Just as Shango began to look for a likely spot, he heard something like a scream. He turned in that direction—but stood there uncertainly. Had he really heard something? He instinctively held his breath, to listen carefully, then his eyes widened as he heard the scream again. He found himself creeping in that direction. As he neared the bushes, the screams became more rhythmic. It was a woman screaming! In his mind, someone was killing her—*butchering* her like one of those maniacs in movies. He instinctively found himself moving faster, but when he looked behind the bushes, he saw a scene that did not make sense at first. A man—*the missing policeman!*—had a woman pinned against a tree trunk. The man was holding up both of her legs as he thrusted wildly. His pants were at his ankles, but his shirt hung over his buttock, blocking

Shango's view. The woman was facing Shango. Her eyes were closed and her face was contorted as the policeman continued his thrusts.

When Shango looked closely, he realized the "woman" could not be older than fifteen. Yet, from the man's stubby, cellulite-ridden thighs, Shango could tell he was middle-aged at least.

Shango stood frozen, mesmerized by the raw brutality of their sex. About a year ago, his grandmother had taken him to the country to visit one of her friends. They had sent Shango down to the river to swim while they talked; and there, Shango had encountered a girl his age who was swimming in nothing but her panty. Her little breasts had been budding and Shango had watched them, mesmerized. They had gotten to talking and playing, and then the girl had let him touch her. It had all been like a dream—but at the end of the day, Shango and his grand-mother had headed back to the mountain, and Shango had never seen the girl again.

Presently, as he watched the policeman thrusting into the girl, he wondered if this was how sex was supposed to be. Is that what he was supposed to have done to his playmate in the country? He did not see how it could be enjoyable—and just then, the girl pinned against the tree cried out particularly loud, complaining, "My back getting *scratch* up!"

"I'm almost done!" the policeman said gruffly.

That seemed to placate the girl for a little while, but ten seconds later, she cried out again, and tried futilely to make him let her down. Indeed, the more she protested, the more he quickened the rhythm of his thrusts. The entire thing seemed horrible, and Shango winced, as if it were *his* back getting scratched against the tree trunk.

It was then that the girl spotted Shango and let out a bloodcurdling scream. It took the policeman off guard, so that he stumbled backwards, into a rock. The policeman looked back and saw Shango standing there frozen. Yet, seeing her chance, the girl slipped out of the policeman's grasp and smoothed out her miniskirt. Her skirt was one of those spandex ones, which the policeman had merely pulled up to her waist during sex. When she went to walk past the policeman, he came to his senses and grabbed her arm.

"Where the hell *you* going?" he said, annoyed. His pants were still around his ankles, and his erection was barely visible over his beer gut.

She said something to the effect that she had fulfilled her side of the bargain (Shango could not hear clearly). She was trying to push the policeman off, and he was trying to grab her hands. Now he was arguing with her, saying their deal was not complete since he had yet to have an orgasm. For whatever reason, Shango laughed out; and at the sound, the policeman turned to him, outraged that he was still there.

"Youth, what you doing in *grown man* business!"

At the man's outburst, Shango suddenly remembered why he had come there; and not wanting to get sidetracked again, he blurted out, "My grandmother's dead!"

The policeman sucked his teeth: "Old people dead all the time!" When Shango stood there confusedly, the policeman made a crude gesture with his hand so Shango would get lost. However, while the policeman was distracted, the girl bolted, and ran further into the bushes. The policeman swore when he saw her fleeing; he went to run after her, but his pants were still around his ankles, so he tripped and fell into a thorny bush. At the sight— and the sound of the man's screams of agony—Shango couldn't help but burst out laughing. Unfortunately, his laughter threw the man into a rage; and when Shango looked, he saw the police-man reaching for his gun! Shango turned and sprinted for the road.

He ran for his life, terrified, unable to think. When he reached the road, he instinctively ran up the mountain—back toward his home. After about two hundred meters, he was exhausted—but since he feared the policeman would come charging up the road in his car, he jumped off the road and ducked behind some bushes. There, he crumpled to the ground, and lay panting for about a minute. What had just happened? The entire scene—with the policeman and the girl—seemed impossible. ...*Old people dead all the time*? Was that really what the policeman had said when Shango told him about his grandmother? As he replayed that part of the scene over in his head, a cold, resentful feeling came over him. Every time he tried to talk to adults, they refused to listen. These were the so-called "authorities?"

Bewildered, he sat up and looked about vaguely. A bird in a nearby tree was looking at him curiously—turning its head to look at him with one eye, before turning its head the other way and looking at him with the other eye. Shango and the bird stared at one another; then, when the bird seemed to get bored, it flew away.

Shango groaned and rose to his feet. Before emerging from behind the bush, he listened for the sound of the charging police car. There was nothing; and now that he thought about it, if the policeman was going to hunt anything down, it was probably that girl. The danger seemed to have passed for the moment, but Shango felt lost—and empty inside. He remembered the pledge he had made that morning—that he would tell the authorities about his grandmother, no matter what. However, when he stepped onto the road again, he found himself walking back up the mountain, to his home.

He had laughed at the policeman's antics while they were happening; he had told himself he would go to the police and have them take away his grandmother, but now he did not want any of their filthy hands touching her. They would only befoul her, and dishonor her further…but what was he supposed to do now? When his uncle popped into his mind, he nodded his head too eagerly. Certainly his uncle had heard the message by now, and called Shango back. None of the fools on the island would listen to Shango—since he was just a boy to them—but they would listen to his uncle's well-cultivated American accent. He saw that now. He was a boy, and they were too preoccupied with their adult perversions to pay any attention to what he was saying. The best thing would be for his uncle to take care of everything.

Shango nodded his head, but he still felt hollowed out inside. Indeed, even as he made his decision, he saw there were no certainties anywhere. What if he walked up the mountain only to discover that nobody had called? What would he do then? There was no way he could leave his grandmother to rot for another day. At the thought, he stopped, turned his head and looked down the road, to the town. Prudence told him to go to police head-quarters again—since, presumably, the officers there wouldn't be screwing young girls—but he shook his head after a few seconds.

In a strange way, he felt he had to give his relatives one last chance to prove they had not abandoned him. The cellular phone charging on his windowsill at home was suddenly everything to him. Now that he had caught his breath, he began jogging up the mountain again. In order to keep himself going, he *willed* himself to be hopeful. All at once, he was *certain* his uncle had called. For all he knew, the man had sent the authorities to the house when no one answered the phone. Maybe the authorities would be waiting at the house when he got there. Maybe they had already taken away his grandmother's body. Maybe his grandmother's dignity had already been restored through his uncle's actions. For once, anything seemed possible, so the hopefulness surged in him, like a drug flowing through his veins.

As he climbed the mountain, he began thinking he should have told Miss Craig about his grandmother when he had the chance. He had tried being dignified about all this: maybe he should have gone in screaming and crying, like a child was supposed to. Maybe that would have reassured the adults and prompted them to help him. The thought left something like bitterness in his soul, and he did not like it. There was anger in him now. He began moving faster, as if fueled by that anger— but he felt it poisoning his soul and leaving him open to dark thoughts. The only thing that calmed him and gave him hope was the possibility that his uncle's call would be waiting when he got home. As his desperation grew, the man suddenly rose up as a kind of demigod in his imagination. Everything that mystified and frustrated Shango would be child's play to someone with his uncle's abilities. Once his uncle took care of everything, this nightmare would be over; and like a Biblical character who had suffered in silence and shown himself to be worthy of God's blessings, Shango would soon find himself in paradise. Maybe his mother's call would be waiting on the phone as well. Certainly his uncle had alerted her after getting the message. Yes, everything would be rectified once he got home. All other thoughts were too horrible.

He was panting and drenched in sweat by the time he reached the forest path to his home. When the path ended, he stood staring at the house and the garden. As his eyes went to the huge boulder, he thought about his grandmother's statement—about never leaving the mountain. The recollection left him melancholy—so that he jogged across the field and up to the house.

In the kitchen, the mess was still on the floor. Ants were devouring something from one of the cracked bottles. A long trail of them snaked out of a gap in the floor boards. His grandmother would definitely not be pleased. He had a guilty impulse to grab a broom and clean the house—in order to restore his grandmother's honor—but the phone charging on the windowsill was still everything to him. He took about three steps toward his bedroom before his grandmother's stench stopped him in his tracks. It was as though he had hit a wall, because he stumbled back after the collision. He was coughing now; he held his breath, and covered his nose with the bottom of his shirt, in a futile effort to keep out the stench.

When he looked, he was relieved beyond reason that the sheet in his grandmother's doorway was still tied. Glancing inside, it seemed like there were *millions* of flies buzzing about her corpse. He shook his head, forcing himself to look away. ...The *phone!* Remembering his task, he rushed into his room. He was in such a rush that he walked across his bed in his shoes. Once the phone was within reach, he grabbed it from the windowsill. He was panting as he looked at it; his heart raced, and his searching eyes scanned every millimeter of the phone's display for the thing that would make all this right. ...Maybe ten seconds passed before he allowed himself to acknowledge the fact that no one had called. How was it possible? He kept staring at the display, as if the icon for messages would suddenly appear if he stared long enough. The blank screen mesmerized him—then there was panic in those first few moments after he allowed himself to accept the truth.

Luckily, the panic was quickly followed by the realization that there was only one thing to do now. Indeed, he nodded his head thoughtfully when he saw it. After a few clicks on the phone, he was again calling his uncle's number; the phone was ringing. When a woman answered the phone, Shango could not quite believe he had reached an actual person. It was the same voice from the recorded message—his uncle's wife.

"Hello," Shango blurted out breathlessly. "It's Shango—from the island. ...I called yesterday."

There was a long pause. "What do you want?"

Shango paused as well, taken aback by the abrupt question. "...It's an emergency—like I said in the message—"

But his uncle's wife groaned in exasperation. "You *island* people always calling for something," she said at last. "You don't think other people have problems too?"

When Shango said nothing, her voice became shrill: "*Eh?* You don't think people in America have bills too? *Well?*" she demanded.

Shango had been staring blankly into space, stunned; but at her prompting, he reminded himself not to get sidetracked by another adult who refused to listen. "My grandmother—*your husband's mother*—is *dead!*"

He was expecting stunned silence from his uncle's wife, or at least a softening of her tone, but instead, she screeched "*Good!*" And then, as Shango stood there incredulously, "I *hated* that old bitch!" At that, she slammed down the phone, so that Shango stood there listening to the dial tone. He stared at the phone again—as if expecting to see some cosmic flaw in its design. When he saw nothing, he stared out of the window for a few seconds, his mind moving like sludge. Eventually, a new feeling rose in him, and he shuddered. For the slightest instant, he hated America and everyone in it.

Shango collapsed onto the bed, still in shock. The hollowed out feeling from earlier retrenched itself. He lay there staring at the ceiling; images from the last two days flashed in his mind, so that he grimaced. He rose from the bed then, as if the images were attacking him. Even though he was still exhausted, he felt restless now. There was something he should be doing, but he had no idea what it was. Frustrated, he lay back down on the bed again, his brow furrowing. Looking down, he saw he still had on his outdoor shoes. If his grandmother were alive, she would kill him for having his shoes on in the bed. The thought intensified the panic still further, so that he leapt out of bed once more.

Unfortunately, he still had no idea what he should *do*. He looked about the room absentmindedly. He looked at the glass on the floor, the dried blood, the ramshackle bed he had pushed into the corner of the room during last night's terror. When his eyes came to the open doorway—and the dark form of his grandmother's corpse—the panic reached a new threshold. Somehow, he found he could not breathe. His throat seemed blocked; his mind again began to flash with chaotic images. Terrified, he found himself fleeing the house, as if last night's monsters had returned to devour him. Since he could not breathe, he was soon dizzy. He barely managed to hurdle the ditch outside the house as he fled; then, as everything began getting dark, he stumbled over to the sink and clung onto it to remain standing.

He had a sudden fear that if he lost consciousness now, the demons of last night would drag away his soul. Desperate to remain conscious, he turned the tap all the way—so that the water gushed out—then he put his head under it. When he sensed the darkness retreating, he cupped his hand and gulped the cool water. His shirt and pants were getting soaked by now. He felt water flowing down his back—but he realized he could breathe again. He pulled his head away and took some deep breaths to calm himself and clear his blurry vision. After that, he again cupped his hand and gulped down the water as if he had been dying of thirst. He felt marginally better—and the worst of the panic seemed to be gone—but he still had no idea what he should *do*.

Again restless, he closed the tap and moved away from the house with the feeble gait of an old man. In his grandmother's fields, he inadvertently trampled her beets and carrots. Where was he going? What was he supposed to *do*!

He saw the huge boulder ahead, and wandered over to it in the uncertain way of someone who feared his legs would give way at any moment. When he reached the boulder, he pulled himself up to the flat top, and lay on his back, staring up at the sky. A fragrant breeze came from up the mountain at that moment, and he breathed deeply. Perhaps a full minute passed this way.

He sat up eventually, and turned to face the forest, so that his legs dangled over the edge of the boulder. He always felt calm when he sat up here. Looking about, he suddenly felt this was the most beautiful place on earth. It was peaceful, and that was all he wanted now. When the fragrant breeze blew again, he closed his eyes and breathed deeply. By the time he opened his eyes again, he was startled to find a plan had somehow formed in his mind.

…What if he buried his grandmother here, at the base of this boulder? She had always said she would stay on the land, like the boulder. There had always been a peaceful smile on her face when she said those words, but he was acutely aware that the thought was *insane*. If anyone ever found out what he had done, the adult world would *end* him. Instead of merely punishing him for his crime, they would obliterate him and carry out that peculiar kind of vengeance that people in power saved for those who had willfully circumvented their authority. He would be damning himself if he took this step, and yet he only felt a burning sense of resentment when he thought about the adult world and its rules. They had all abandoned him, condemning him to the horrors of these past two days. Indeed, as his mind replayed the things his uncle's wife had said, he knew there was no point relying on any of those fools. They were morons and perverts, and he could no longer bring himself to defer to them.

The only thing that mattered now was what his grandmother would want. In his mind's eye, he kept seeing the beatific smile she always had when she mentioned remaining on the mountain. Now that he thought about it, this was the first time in two days he had been able to think of his grandmother without conjuring nightmare images of death and decay. She would be at peace here: he knew it in his bones; and as the thought passed through his mind, another fragrant breeze blew from up the mountain— stronger than before, so that the boughs of trees danced in the wind. The breeze comforted him—as if his grandmother, herself had placed her hand on his shoulder. He nodded his head at that moment, surrendering himself to the plan; and once the details were clear in his mind, he jumped down from the boulder and headed to the house to begin his work.

S hango felt a kind of anxious excitement now. For the first time in two days, he was no longer waiting for someone else's approval. He felt freer now. For the first time in days, he was doing something that seemed *right*—but what was equally clear to him was that sooner or later, someone would find out what he had done. When that day came, there would be a terrible price to pay—but given everything that had happened over these last two days, he felt it was a price he was willing to pay. In the end, he was tired, and this was the only thing he saw that could bring the nightmare to an end—at least in the short term. In the long term, there were more horrors; but just as a tired man could only think of sleep, Shango's exhausted mind could only concentrate on those things that would allow him to sleep soundly tonight.

H is plan was simple: wrap his grandmother's corpse in her bedding, carry her over to the boulder, then dig the grave. As he entered the kitchen, he looked at each component as a separate task. If he was going to do this, he had to do it quickly—while he had the courage or madness—or whatever was driving him.

The first thing he did was go to his room and change into some of his expendable clothes—since the work ahead was going to be *dirty* work. He chose some stained clothes he was ready to throw out, then he rushed into his grandmother's room, swatting at the cloud of flies to clear a path to her bed. The flies engulfed him; several flew up his nostrils, forcing him to exhale forcefully to expel them. *Dozens* of others were buzzing against his lips and *face*. They danced on his ears, so that he shuddered and clawed at his earlobes to drive them away. Yet, he felt that if he allowed himself to waver now he would never be able to do this thing. His grandmother had tucked the sheet underneath the mattress; gnashing his teeth, Shango began pulling it out. In fact, he was rushing now—*ripping* out the sheet, then running to the other side of the bed to repeat the task.

When he tried to inhale, the stench almost made him retch. It *burned* his nasal cavity, like poison gas. Unprepared for the full onslaught, he coughed. He tried to hold his breath again, but it was pointless, so he ran out of the room to get a fresh breath. He darted across the hall, to his room. Yet, the air in his room did not seem breathable either. The stench was everywhere, clawing at him like something with form and substance. Seeing the open window, he jumped on the bed again, but since the glass was still on the floor, he actually jumped from the bed to the windowsill. In his haste to get a breath of fresh air, he almost catapulted himself out of the window. In midair, he remembered the battery charger was still on the windowsill. He tried to avoid it as he landed, but it went flying nonetheless. He looked down in quiet horror as the photovoltaic panel smashed against the ground. He stared down at the wrecked panel for a few seconds, as he stood there clutching the wall and gasping for air. However, eventually, he shook his head to remind himself it did not matter anymore. He was not expecting any calls, so he had no further use for the phone. As simply as that, he had turned his back on the outside world.

Once he had taken his fill of fresh air, he jumped back onto the bed, walked across it, then returned to the floor. He felt himself wavering as he stared across the corridor, at his grandmother's corpse. If he was going to do this, he would have to be in his grandmother's presence for minutes at a time. Holding his breath was out of the question. His towel was still on his bed. He grabbed it, figuring he could make a mask. First, he folded it length-wise, wrapped it around his head, then secured the end by tucking it by his ear. He stepped into the corridor then, but even with his makeshift mask, the stench was still too strong. Glancing back into his room, he noticed the bottle with his grandmother's cure-all concoction was still on the floor. He went over to it, cupped his left hand, poured some into his palm, then dabbed it against the part of the towel that covered his nose. The vapors made his eyes water, but the spicy alcohol odor overpowered the stench. To test it out, he returned to the corridor and breathed deeply. That was better. However, since nothing could really mask the stench of decay for long, he rushed into his grandmother's room again. Like the last time, he swatted away the flies. He had to squint as they flew into his eyes. A few of them crawled up the back of his neck, and it took all his will not to run out of the room.

With the heat, and the passage of two days, his grandmother's rigor mortis had eased for the most part. As soon as he was finished pulling out her tucked-in sheets, he began straightening her cold, clammy limbs, so that he could wrap her corpse. Her left arm was stiffer than her right, and he had to struggle with it to lower it to her side. Her eyes were still staring into space. He tried not looking her in the face, but he noticed her eyes were clouded over like fish eyes. When he began pulling the sheet over her body, the first thing he covered was her face.

The mask was beginning to lose its effectiveness. Plus, it slipped a little, and a few flies went underneath—as if searching for a cavity to enter. He had the same urge to rush out of the room, but grunted to drive away the thought. There was no going back now—no retreat from this thing he had started.

The flies seemed to be buzzing angrily now, as if upset with him for taking away their meal. The towel came loose and tumbled to the floor; as the flies attacked his mouth and nostrils, he began swatting again; he held his breath—then tried breathing shallowly—but he refused to run out of the room again.

It occurred to him his grandmother's sheet was not wide enough.

Rather, he saw it would not stay wrapped around her body when he tried to pick her up. Rope: he needed rope. There was some twine somewhere, but he did not want to get sidetracked by looking for it. He suddenly remembered his grandmother had some belts in one of her bureau drawers. He ran over there and began pulling out drawers. He found them in a bottom drawer. She had coiled them neatly. He grabbed four and returned to the bed.

Either he was getting used to the stench or the combination of adrenaline and desperation was allowing him to block it all out. He again started with her head, putting one of the belts around her neck like a noose. As always, he moved quickly to keep himself from thinking about what he was doing. To get the belt around her torso, he had to shove his hand under the corpse. With the heat, the body had become bloated. Beneath her, it was warm and damp—since her bowels had long released. Shango grimaced at the realization, but it only spurred him to move quicker. He notched the belt around her torso, then put another one around her waist. The last one went around her ankles. He was still trying to hold his breath between gasps of air; he was getting dizzy; but instead of retreating, he plunged in. He grabbed the corpse's legs, then pulled and turned the body at the same time, so that the feet fell heavily to the floor. The torso was too heavy for him to lift. He began to panic as he fumbled to get a grip. At last, he jumped on the bed and hauled up the torso using the belts to get a grip. He pulled, and the corpse lurched into an upright position. Using his momentum, he leapt off the bed, pulling the corpse with him. For a second, it seemed to stand on its own. As it began to fall, Shango bent his knees, braced himself, grabbed it by the waist, then began pulling.

Don't think! he chastised himself. Now was not the time for thought. He was dragging the corpse through the doorway now.

His breathing was harsh and animalistic. The stench was beyond comprehension, yet he had to breathe. It was like the corpse was some mummified dance partner. The corpse was taller than he was, and heavier, but luckily his grandmother had a lean, spindly body.

He was in the kitchen already. How was he going to get over the ditch? Acting quickly, he bent lower, so the corpse flopped over his shoulder, then he grabbed the back of its legs and lifted it off the ground. His legs almost buckled, but the adrenaline spurred him on again. He screamed out, like a weightlifter drawing on inner strength. His left leg almost missed the plank over the ditch. He almost went careening over the edge, but somehow managed to propel himself to the other side of the ditch. Unfortunately, with the heavy load, he was unbalanced, so he stumbled into the structure. Acting quickly, he pushed his grandmother's torso onto the sink. The body bent at the waist; there was a clanging noise as the head hit the metal; but by then, Shango's strength gave out. He found himself on the ground, panting and trembling from the effort.

Even then, he did not allow himself to rest too long—or to *think*. As soon as he was able, he rose to his feet. He tried lifting the corpse onto his shoulder again, but his strength was gone. The adrenaline rush had faded away; his legs and hands seemed numb and drained from the initial effort, so he would have to *will* himself to drag the corpse the rest of the way. It took him about a minute to figure out how to resume carrying the corpse. He tried pulling it up from the back, but he did not have the strength. Eventually, he had to insert his own torso between the sink and the corpse; then, grabbing the corpse by the torso, he dragged it along the ground. Once again, he used the belts to get a grip. He was aware that carrying his grandmother this way was undignified;

the belt around her neck was almost sacrilegious; but toward the end, when his legs and lungs burned from the effort, it occurred to him there could be no dignity in death after all. There was no dignity in death, just as there was no dignity in life....

He did not so much reach the boulder as he tripped and stumbled up to it. The corpse landed on top of him, and he lay there panting. After he caught his breath, he pushed the corpse off his body. He stood up slowly, on wobbly, drained legs, then stared down at the swaddled corpse. It was about four o'clock now: there were two hours of daylight left, so he had that long to dig the grave.

The shovel was beneath the house, along with the other farming implements. Shango retrieved it and returned to the boulder. He began digging beneath the boulder. Since the soil was regularly tilled for planting, the ground was relatively soft. First, he dug the outline of the grave, making sure it was long enough for the corpse. When he thought the proportions were right, be began to dig furiously. When exhaustion began to set in, he reminded himself to pace out his effort.

The minutes passed. He lost himself in the act. His arms burned; his hands became so numb that he began to fear the spade would fly from his hands. Yet, the approach of night terrified him, and filled him with strength long after his muscles had reached the point of exhaustion. About an hour had passed by the time the grave was deeper than he was tall. He had always heard graves were supposed to be "six feet deep" but he did not like the feeling of being underground, unable to see what was going on above him. Also, it was exhausting to try to heave the dirt out of the grave. Toward the end, his strength was so feeble that the heaved dirt did not make it out of the hole. He spent minutes heaving the same dirt against the side of the grave. Then, around five-thirty, when long shadows began to fall around him, and everything in the grave became cast in darkness, a sudden surge of panic made him clamber over the sides of the grave, onto the surface. By then, he could not have cared less how deep they said graves were supposed to be.

He looked at his grandmother's corpse grimly. This was it: the last step in his insane plan. Yet, it was too late now for doubts, so he grabbed the corpse and pulled it toward the hole. There was no way to lower the body into the grave softly. He had meant to brace its descent, but gravity took over, wrenching the sheet from his hand. The corpse landed like a sack of bricks in the darkness. Since it did not land flat, Shango had to jump in the hole to straighten it out. Being down there with the swaddled corpse was creepy. His heart began to race; in the hole, his breathing sounded harsh and alien—like a monster's.

As soon as the corpse was suitably arrayed, he clambered over the edge, took a precursory glance around the landscape—to check for the approach of any mountain demons—then got to his feet and stood there panting as he peered down into the hole.

He realized this was the true moment of no return. There was still time to seek out the authorities and submit to their will, but there was a sense of peace in him as he grabbed the shovel and began to fill the grave. Within five minutes, the grave was filled. He was amazed that it was over. He stared down at the mound of dirt, reminding himself that his grandmother was really down there. That was when his mind flashed with something he had seen in a movie once: A hand emerging from the freshly dug earth of a grave, grabbing the victim's ankle and dragging him into the depths. The image made him shudder—so that he retreated from the grave.

When he felt he was a safe enough distance away, he stood there staring again. His grandmother was really gone. All at once, he felt the hot tears rising up in him. Soon, he was bawling, surrendering himself to the grief.

Yet, seeing that night was approaching, he dried his tears and he headed toward the house. He began to strip as he walked, suddenly desperate to be clean. By the time he rounded the house, he had kicked off the ragged pants. Now nude, he went straight for the shower, where he turned on the water full blast. At least ten minutes passed with him just standing under the cascade. The water felt good; and by the time he meandered back to the house to dress and prepare his evening meal, he felt something like peace in his soul. This is how Shango Cartwright began his life of independence.

BOOK TWO
INDEPENDENT

Suddenly, he was awake. He opened his eyes and saw it was morning. He turned his head and looked out of the window: by the hue and luminosity of the morning sky, he could tell it was around five-thirty. He stared at some soft clouds in the distance, but then he sat up abruptly when he remembered burying his grandmother. He instinctively held up his hands, staring at the blisters that had formed from gripping the shovel. The entire thing seemed so implausible that a sudden restless feeling made him leap out of bed. He took two steps toward the doorway, but he could already see his grandmother's bed was empty. The sheets were gone, and there was still a dark stain on the mattress, where her fluids had released. As he stood there, he saw nightmare images of himself dragging her corpse out to the field. He saw himself digging the grave and dropping the swaddled corpse into the darkness. *He had really done it!*

Bewildered, he retreated to the bed and lay down heavily. The entire thing seemed *insane*; but just as the doubts were about to overwhelm him, he remembered his uncle's wife, and his "disconnected" mother, and the idiots in the police department. Indeed, the more he thought about it, the more he came to the conclusion he had had no choice. There would be hardships ahead—when the adult world eventually figured out what he had done. Yet, like yesterday, he knew it was a price he was prepared to pay. His grandmother was resting now—and at peace—he was *sure* of it. The stench of death was beginning to fade from the house; the flies were gone—as were all his irrational terrors from the previous days. Today was a new day, full of new possibilities. That was all that mattered now.

At the same time, he felt something like loneliness when he looked across the corridor once more, to his grandmother's empty bed. From this day on, he would have to provide for himself, and do the things that his grandmother used to do for him. He would have to find money to buy clothes and household items; he would have to pay school fees. More importantly, in order to preserve his freedom and keep the world from suspecting his grandmother was dead, he would have to keep her life going as well. He would have to go check the post office for letters—in the unlikely event that someone actually wrote her. He grimaced when he remembered the vegetable stand and his grandmother's regular customers. He would have to keep the stand going—at least on the weekends. As for his grandmother's friends, they were mostly other old people living similarly isolated lives, so there would be few visitors and few questions. Similarly, now that the cellular phone could no longer be charged, there would be no calls. There was so much to be done—so many variables to account for; so many adults to outwit…yet, in a strange way, the challenge excited him as he rose from the bed and started getting ready for school.

Half an hour later, he pulled the kitchen door closed behind him, and began walking down the mountain. He was wearing his last clean school uniform; the house behind him was still a mess—with glass and burst containers on the floor—but today was

Friday, so he figured he would have the entire weekend to get things right. Once he got back from school, he would sit down and plan how he was going to survive; but for now, all he had to do was make it through the day without drawing undue attention to himself.

He looked over at the boulder as he walked past the house. His grandmother's corpse was really underneath that mound of disturbed earth. He had an impulse to walk over there and investigate, but he was wary of getting sidetracked. Besides, the morning was sunny and warm; the air was fragrant and fresh, and he had the sense that this was a new beginning—both for himself and his grandmother. Death was behind him; life was ahead of him, with all its wondrous possibilities.

The forest path seemed even more overgrown than yesterday. Strangely enough, he felt his heart racing; for some reason, he began to run down the path, pushing aside vines and branches. It was as if the path were a portal to the world of men, which was slowly closing in around him. He had a sudden fear that he would be trapped in there forever if he did not break free. When he finally jumped off the mountain path, onto the road, he stood there gasping for air. He looked back the way he had come—into the tangle of leaves and vines—contemplating his strange journey between worlds. However, when two *huge* military transport vehicles turned the bend and came rumbling down the road, he froze.

The vehicles had open tops. Dozens of soldiers sat grimly in the rear compartments, facing one another. The soldiers' metal helmets looked hot and heavy, and sweat already poured down many of their faces. One of the soldiers caught sight of Shango as he stood frozen on the side of the road. As the vehicle passed, the soldier turned in his seat to watch the boy—as if he feared Shango would pull out a gun and riddle them all with bullets. The man's face wore an odd expression of malice, so that Shango instinctively retreated a step and looked away timidly. The soldier's odd expression—and the presence of so many battle-ready men— left an unsettled feeling in the pit of Shango's stomach. Even after the trucks had disappeared down the mountain, he stood there uneasily, wondering what it could mean.

After standing there for about twenty seconds, he sighed and continued walking. The uneasy feeling was still with him, but as he breathed the fresh mountain air, strange thoughts about adults and soldiers began to fade away. Soon, he was navigating his way down the switchbacks and darting out of the way to avoid speeding cars. Every time he heard a speeding vehicle coming down the mountain, he instinctively stopped and positioned himself on the far edge of the road, where he figured the driver would see him. After a while, it became instinctual for him. So, about fifteen minutes into his journey, when he heard a car coming down the mountain, he positioned himself in a likely position on the far edge of the road. He stopped and looked back, but the car zoomed around the corner at such a wide, reckless angle that Shango was trapped between the car and the steep, rocky cliff. He stood there trembling as the driver slammed on the brakes. The car's tires pealed; cornered, Shango clamped his eyes shut and waited for his fate. For three or four seconds he stood there waiting for the collision. When it did not come, he opened his eyes and saw the car had stopped. Looking up, he realized the driver was gesturing for him to come around to the side of the car.

Dazed, Shango walked over to the passenger window and looked in. He stared at the driver's face for about five seconds before he realized it was Maitland. The inside of the vehicle was still slovenly; it still had that unsavory odor that made Shango think of sour oranges and toe jam. Maitland had been talking excitely on his cellular phone during all this. When Shango made eye contact with him, he gestured for the boy to get in the vehicle. Shango hesitated, but Maitland pulled the phone away from his ear and said, "I'll give you a ride into town." Shango was still reluctant, but when the man on the other end of Maitland's call began talking loudly and excitedly—and Maitland's eyes grew wide and anxious— Shango got into the car, since he did not want to delay the man any further.

The moment Shango slammed the door behind him, Maitland zoomed off at the same breakneck speed. Shango became aware he was sitting on something sharp; adjusting his position on the seat, he retrieved a pen. Maitland was still holding the phone to his ear as he drove erratically. Shango went to fasten his seat belt, but saw there was no fastener. The end of the strap was shredded, as if a wild animal had gnawed it off.

The disembodied voice on the other end of the line was still talking excitedly. With each new revelation, Maitland seemed to press the accelerator harder. Every few seconds, he blurted out things like, "...Really? ...Okay ...That's what I heard! ...Okay... Yes—"

A huge truck turned the corner ahead; Maitland slammed on the brakes, but the car was going too fast to stop in time—and, in that strange, confrontational way of Caribbean drivers, the truck was not stopping either. The driver blared the horn and barreled toward them; desperate, Maitland steered the vehicle into the ditch at the side of the road, so that the car scraped against bushes and vines. A few leaves became dislodged, and flew into the window. Shango braced himself for a loud crash—but the truck thundered past them in a blur, before disappearing around another corner. Shango stared ahead in a daze.

The near death experience also seemed to affect Maitland, because he brought the cellular phone back to his ear and whispered, "I'll call you back." At that, he shoved the phone into his shirt pocket. Now, he put both hands on the steering wheel, but still drove at the same breakneck speed. When Shango looked, there were beads of sweat on the man's brow. Maitland was nibbling his lower lip nervously, and there was a distant, pained expression on his face, as if he were haunted by the horrors beyond the windscreen. When the man grimaced, Shango tentatively ventured, "Are you okay?"

Maitland looked over at him as if he had forgotten he was there. He stared at Shango for two full seconds—then he looked back at the road abruptly, turning the steering wheel frantically to avoid flying off the mountain.

"Sorry," the man apologized once he had regained control of the vehicle.

"No problem," Shango said numbly, as though none of this could really be happening.

Finally regaining his senses, Maitland looked over at Shango critically. "You haven't heard, have you?"

"Heard what, sir?"

"…About Matthew Cuthbert."

"Who?"

Maitland looked over at him, aghast. "You've never heard of Matthew Cuthbert?"

"No, sir."

"You've *never* heard of Matthew Cuthbert?" he repeated, as if he could not believe what he was hearing.

"No, sir," Shango said, wondering what Maitland was getting so worked up about.

"Matthew Cuthbert was the *last* chance the island had to become a progressive democracy—instead of some third world farce!"

"...Oh," Shango said politely.

Shango was about to go back to staring out of the window when Maitland continued, "How can you *not* know who Matthew Cuthbert is?"

"I've just never heard of him," Shango said, growing annoyed with the conversation.

"Well, he was *murdered* last night—*killed* in the prime of his life."

"Oh," Shango said again, but genuinely curious now.

"They stabbed him in his *bed*. First, they poisoned his guard dogs...disconnected his alarm, then snuck in and killed him in his sleep, like *cowards*."

"*Who* did?"

"The *government!*" he said, gesticulating wildly, so that he momentarily let go of the steering wheel entirely.

Shango looked down at the steering wheel uneasily, then back at Maitland's wild, suggestive eyes. Like the last time, Shango wondered if the man was actually saying something or if he was just spouting gibberish. There was something about Maitland— his sloppiness, perhaps—that kept Shango from taking him seriously. At the same time, Maitland spoke so authoritatively about everything that Shango could not help but be cowed. It was like the old men who congregated outside rum shops and yelled loudly about everything from football scores to their sexual prowess. Most of it was obviously drunken babble, but they spoke so definitely that it was difficult to dismiss them entirely. Indeed, as Maitland's outburst about the government lingered in the air, Shango ventured, "*Why'd* they do it?"

"That's what cowards do to protect themselves!" the man raged. "But we won't let them get away with it! We're going to march through the town now. We're going to *mobilize* against this *fascist government!*"

"Oh," Shango said again as Maitland sat there panting.

"...Cuthbert was the best of us, young Shango," Maitland continued in a softer tone. "He excelled in everything—was a *prodigy*. He was a *Rhodes Scholar*—went to *Oxford*, in *England*. He reached those heights, but decided to come back to his country. Instead of cashing in and starting a comfortable life in England or America, he decided to come back to his people, and invest his time and talents *here*."

There was a pained expression on Maitland's face now, so that even Shango began to wonder if the island really had suffered a devastating loss. However, in the end, all he could think was that Cuthbert would still be alive if he had stayed abroad after his studies. Maybe that was the true lesson of the story. Maybe there was no point in trying to build anything here if those in power were just going to tear it down when they pleased....

There was silence for a while. Looking out of the window, Shango realized they were passing the spot where the Range Rover had crashed into the ravine. An image of the pretty girl flashed in his mind; but as always, Daddis' glistening incisor was there to tell him to mind his business. Now that America was no longer an escape hatch for him, he was suddenly wary of the invisible power structure that ran things on the island. All at once, he saw Cuthbert's story in this light—as a warning to let secrets lie hidden.

When they reached the town, it was clear something out of the ordinary was happening. About five soldiers were posted on the main road. Their fingers all hovered ominously over the triggers of their guns; their faces were all hard and grim as they stopped traffic. There was not a physical checkpoint, but the soldiers were going to each car and looking into the windows. Drivers with darkened windows were asked to roll them down. A few were ordered to open their trunks; and of course, all of that caused traffic to back up.

By now, Maitland was leaning forward in his seat excitedly. "Look at how they operate, young Shango," he began. "First they kill, then they make a show of force to scare you into submission."

Shango grunted noncommittally, but he found his heart racing as the car ahead of them was waved through and the lead soldier gestured for Maitland to stop in front of him. Maitland chuckled mordantly before complying.

"How may I help you, corporal," he said in a singsong voice as he stopped next to the soldier.

"Where you going?" the man demanded.

"At the moment, I want to go down this road," Maitland dead-panned.

"What's your business down there?" he said, too dense to catch Maitland's sarcasm.

"I operate a newspaper," Maitland replied, "so my business is finding out why our brave soldiers are stopping traffic in town today."

"Don't worry yourself with all that," he said gruffly.

"Is the Army doing this island-wide?" Maitland asked quickly.

"*I'm* the one asking the questions here!" the corporal growled, losing patience. To show his intent, he raised the muzzle of the gun slightly, but Maitland only chuckled. In the meanwhile, another soldier had come around to Shango's window. The man was wearing shades, and Shango had a strange thought that if the soldier were to pull away the shades, his eyes would be some ungodly yellowish color—like a demon in a horror movie. He looked away uneasily—

"Do you even know why you're here today," Maitland asked the corporal now, "—or did your commander merely tell you to stop every car in town?" The corporal opened his mouth, but then realized he could not answer the question. "...Just as I thought," Maitland said almost sorrowfully. There was a strange moment of silence, where Maitland and the corporal stared at one another; but after a few seconds, the soldier grew frustrated with the entire thing, and gestured for Maitland to drive on.

"Have a good day," the newspaperman said as he drove off, beaming at his pointless triumph.

Shango eyed him curiously, wondering if he was brave or just an idiot. Maitland seemed like one of those lion tamers who grew overconfident and eventually got mauled by the creatures he had supposedly tamed. Sooner or later, an animal's true nature was going to come out. No matter how many stupid tricks you trained it to perform, nature was always going to come out in the end.

M aitland's phone rang a few moments later, and he launched into another animated conversation about the significance of Cuthbert's death. Shango tried following the conversation, but he quickly came to the conclusion it was pointless. Besides, within two minutes, they were at the town center. Maitland parked on a side street; when Shango looked at him confusedly, he gestured with his head for Shango to follow him out.

As they stepped out of the car, he saw there was more activity in the ugly park than usual. Soldiers and policemen lined the perimeter—*dozens* of them. The armed men made Shango uneasy, but Maitland tapped him on the shoulder to encourage him to walk faster. Craning his neck, Shango looked through the phalanx of policemen and noticed some old men holding signs. Maitland was still talking on his phone, telling the person on the other end of the call that he was there. He sounded so excited that Shango looked at the gathering again, wondering if his assessment was wrong.

At most, there were twenty protesters there—if that was even the right word for them. It seemed like some kind of grey beard convention. Several of the old men had canes; at least one of them had those walkers that old women used after they broke their hips. Shango tried to read one of the hand-written signs, but whoever made it had horrible penmanship. He could only make out the word "Justice" and something that looked like "Power." The wretched gathering made Shango's expression sour. Besides, he suddenly remembered he had school.

The road surrounding the park was cordoned off to traffic, so there were people milling about on it. When the boy stopped, Maitland looked back at him. Shango gestured to his school bag; Maitland stopped as well, telling the person on the other end of the call to hold on.

"You're not coming?"

"I have school."

"You're going to miss history being made," Maitland said with a strange, enthusiastic smile. Shango could not tell if he was being sarcastic or if he really believed what he was saying.

Shango looked over at the men in the grey beard convention again, dubious; then, turning back to Maitland: "I'll read the high-lights in your newspaper."

Maitland laughed too loudly at Shango's witticism, as though newly impressed by the boy's mind. In fact, he laughed so loudly that several of the policemen turned around and glared at them. Shango was looking at some of the officers' faces uneasily when one face in particular made his heart skip a beat. It was Daddis! The man was staring at them so intently that Shango could practically feel the weight of his gaze.

Maitland was still laughing. Shango looked up at the man anxiously, but the newspaperman did not seem to notice his discomfort—or Daddis' presence.

"I'll catch you later," Shango blurted out. He was so eager to leave that he did not wait for a response. He merely fled. When he was leaving, he instinctively glanced in Daddis' direction again. The man's eyes bore into his, shining with cold malice. Shango felt suddenly sick to his stomach. He looked down at the ground timidly, picking up his pace. However, after he took three steps, Maitland called to him.

When Shango stopped and turned, the newspaperman began, "Young Shango, don't be afraid to be who you are." When Shango frowned, the man clarified, "Don't let anyone tell you who you should be—not even me. *Trust* yourself." Shango stared at him, thinking about it, then he nodded his head, turned, and continued walking. He forced himself not to look in Daddis' direction again, but he still felt the heavy weight of the man's gaze on his shoulders.

He breathed a little easier once he was away from the town center, but he still felt dazed. There were more policemen walking the streets than he had ever seen. There was a silent tension about the town that he had never felt before. When he had a flashback of Daddis' hard eyes, he found his pace quickening. Half a minute later, he caught himself jogging; he slowed, grimacing.

As he neared school, he ensconced himself behind a group of upperclassmen. They were talking loudly and crudely: boasting about their ability to seduce girls. They were of course talking nonsense—and they all seemed to know it was nonsense, because they laughed uproariously at one another's stories. Something about it was reassuring, and Shango instinctively joined their laughter. When one of the boys looked back and noticed him walking behind them, Shango nodded his head—either as a greeting or an apology for disrupting their nonsense. He walked past them quickly; but when he was moving away, he heard one of them whisper to the others that Shango was "that smart boy."

He had always worn that phrase as a badge of honor, but all at once it made him feel lonely. He had always been Shango the smart boy or Shango the good athlete. He had always had to prove himself in order for people to acknowledge him. For once, he wanted to belong without having to beat out the competition. The boys who gravitated toward him only seemed to do so because they wanted him on their team or because they wanted to copy his homework. For a moment, the realization left him melancholy, but then he remembered Maitland—and the words the man had said about being himself. He was not quite sure he understood what the man had meant, but the words stayed with him and fortified him as he joined the throng of boys entering the school gate.

He felt the new tension as he walked through the schoolyard. One of the boys claimed to have been there when soldiers killed a man who refused to stop at a roadblock. They had found some automatic rifles in his trunk, and there was talk of some kind of revolution or coup taking place. To Shango, such stories seemed too unreal to be believed. They seemed like unrealistic plot twists in a movie. As he listened to the stories, he had the same annoyed feeling he had when he felt a movie was insulting his intelligence—but at that moment, in the distance, there was something that sounded like machine guns firing. There was a hush in the schoolyard then, and they all became true believers.

Indeed, the threat of violence began to excite all their imaginations. Some of the younger boys started playing a soldier game that involved throwing rocks and chasing one another with sticks. In only a short while, the game grew so unruly that Principal Williams, himself had to intervene to stop it. By then, Shango stood by the staircase, watching it all, marveling at how quickly they degenerated into animals...

When the school bell rang, he walked to his home room class languidly. Miss Craig was still beautiful; initially, all his melancholy thoughts left him as he took his seat in front of the class and looked up at her dreamily. Unfortunately, not even Miss Craig was immune to the day's violence. Her usual self-possession and confidence were gone. She seemed more flustered than she had been before. Indeed, during the lunch break, Shango overheard her talking with another teacher when he was heading back from the bathroom. For whatever reason, he lingered outside the door, listening as she declared Cuthbert's death a setup by the opposition party. According to her, his supporters knew his chances of becoming prime minister were slim, so they had killed him to get the sympathy vote and turn the country against the ruling party. As Shango listened, the plot grew so convoluted that it was the first time he had ever found himself wondering if Miss Craig was an idiot. Yet, the thought passed so quickly that he was barely conscious of it. It registered only as a moment of discomfort, soon forgotten in the face of all the troubling things happening around him.

The rest of the day was filled with similar incidents. Between classes, he heard more whispers about soldiers killing people and weapons being found—and Cuthbert's death being the start of something dire on the island. It was the first time Shango had ever thought of politics as something that mattered. Before, it had merely been like the weather—something that everyone complained about but which no one actually had the power to change. There was probably some validity to his original assessment, but when an unexpected storm wreaked havoc on your world, you learned it was time to start paying attention to the weather report.

Then, somehow, he was in his last class of the day—Miss Craig's literature class. It was disconcerting to watch her floundering about, looking for the security and certainty she used to have. Instead of the intricacies of *Wide Sargasso Sea*, she launched into a vague speech about hope for the future. It was only when she brought up Shango's entry in the competition that her eyes seemed to get that old fire. She smiled at him then; he nodded his head shyly and smiled back, thinking that everything was right with the world when Miss Craig smiled.

Yet, she kept going on and on about the contest; and the more she talked, the more something restless stirred in him. It was only after about two minutes of this that his mind stumbled upon a truth that had somehow eluded him: If he competed in an island-wide competition, then certainly they would expect his grandmother, or some other relative, to show up to cheer him on! Why hadn't he seen that before? Moreover, what if he actually *won* the competition? His guts seemed to knot themselves when he realized it. What was he supposed to do now? There was no way he could pull out of the competition—since that would only raise more questions. Besides, Miss Craig would be disappointed, and his boyish sense of valor rebelled at the thought of her beautiful smile fading away. He was *trapped*. He looked so distraught that Miss Craig asked him if he was okay. He smiled meekly to reassure her, but he felt *sick*.

...And then, the school day was over. Shango stood up feebly as the other boys began to file out of the class. Miss Craig called to him as he was about to join the stream of boys. When he turned back to her, she said, "Did you remember the permission form?" He stared at her blankly, so that she added, "—the one your grandmother was supposed to sign."

"Oh," he said. Thoughts of his grandmother set off alarm bells in his mind. He forced himself to remain calm and keep his voice steady when he replied, "Sorry, Miss—I forgot."

"You can bring it Monday," she said, smiling to reassure him it was okay.

"Thanks, Miss," he said, genuinely grateful, but the alarm bells were still jangling in his mind.

When he exited the class, he had a sudden fear that the popular kids would ambush him again, but they were either bored with him or preoccupied with the threat of violence in the air. Either way, his usual Friday afternoon joy was gone. The weekend did not excite him. Instead of rest and fun, he saw only the hard work it would take to keep his lie going. He would have to get the vegetables ready for his grandmother's roadside stand; he would have to clean the house and wash his clothes, and plan the minute details of how he would survive. More troublingly, even though the house on the mountain was still his home, he suspected he would go mad if he spent too much time there by himself. There was something childish and pathetic about the thought, but he had to be honest with himself.

The school cleared out quickly, since all the teachers and students seemed eager to rush to the safety of their homes. More parents than usual were outside the gate, corralling their children to make sure they did not dawdle on the streets. Shango felt the envy and resentment rising in him then—envy of his classmates with caring parents, and resentment of his own family. Yet, knowing neither emotion was going to fill the empty place within him, he bowed his head and moved on.

There were still policemen and soldiers at key intersections. Like this morning, their faces seemed grim, but there was a kind of normalcy to their presence now. The sight of dozens of armed men was no longer jarring to his senses—and so, as quickly as that, a new benchmark had been established on the island.

Shango walked faster, suddenly wary of the town and its people—but the empty house on the mountain was not exactly calling to him either. He felt restless and lost. Remembering Miss Craig, his mind went to the letter his grandmother was supposed to sign. He stopped by a telephone pole, to retrieve his notebook, and noticed the plastic bottle from yesterday was still there. He sighed; but looking around, he did not see any garbage bins. He sighed again, and pulled out his notebook. While he was shuffling through the pages to find the letter, Maitland's business card fell out. He stared down at it, startled, as if it were some kind of omen. That was when a plan began to form in his mind. When he picked up the card and looked at the address, he saw it was only a fifteen-minute walk away. Actively seeking out Maitland seemed like a new threshold in bad ideas. His mind conjured Daddis' glaring eyes to remind him to keep his distance; but as the minutes passed, he found himself walking toward the address on the card.

M aitland's office was on the second floor of a two-story building. Like many of the old buildings in town, it seemed to be crumbling. On the ground floor, there was a dusty antiques store—or, less euphemistically, a junk shop. Some rusty-looking appliances—irons and a stove—were in the display window, but the place was so dark and gloomy that Shango could not tell if it was open or not. Worse, the building was crammed between the mortician's sprawling funeral home complex and another dreary shop that sold those gaudy hats and outfits that old women wore to church.

Across the street, there was some kind of grease-infused business that may have been a garage or a junkyard. Beyond the towering chain-linked fence there were some rusting car frames propped up on cinderblocks—but he also saw some rusting refrigerators as well, and a cast iron bathtub, so he really had no idea what the place was. As he looked, he saw a shack that was either someone's home or the office. An old man was sitting on a can by the door, scratching a stick in the dirt while a mangy dog stared down at the stick as if mesmerized. The entire street had a kind of depressing energy, and Shango's expression soured.

In fact, he was just about to leave when a figure sprang from the bushes behind the shack—

"Bock-bi-cow!" Chicken George screamed, sending the startled old man toppling from the can. Shango was expecting the dog to start barking—and to chase the man off their property—but it tucked its tail between its legs and fled out of the gate, to safety.

That seemed to infuriate the old man more than Chicken George's presence, because he began waving his hand threateningly and telling the dog not to come back. By now, Chicken George was flapping his wings again as he darted out of the gate and sent the poor dog running farther down the street. Once the man was past the fence, he followed the terrified dog for a few steps, before turning to the right and disappearing behind some more bushes.

Shango did not laugh this time—guiltily or otherwise. He had merely witnessed another bizarre scene in a day of bizarre scenes. He sighed. With Chicken George gone, the dog tried re-entering the gate, but the old man threw a stone at it, and called out fresh curses. Somehow, Shango felt sorry for the dog: how could the old man expect the dog to have courage when even he had been terrified when Chicken George first charged from the bushes?

Either way, Shango was about to walk past Maitland's office when he noticed two officers in a car farther down the street. The car was unmarked, but the officers were in uniform—and staring at Maitland's office. Indeed, one had a pair of binoculars. As Shango noticed them, his pace instinctively slowed, but when one of the officers looked at him quizzically, he forced himself to continue walking. He told himself to walk straight past the building without even looking in—but when he was about two steps from the entrance, the front door opened. When he looked up, Maitland shuffled out, carrying a stack of newspapers in his hands. The man's car was parked on the curb, and he walked straight for it. Shango stopped so that the man could pass; and as he did so, Maitland looked down and noticed him.

"Hey!" he said, grinning.

Shango stood there awkwardly for a moment—but seeing the tall stack of papers in Maitland's arms, he asked, "You need help?"

"Yeah, you can open the door for me."

"Sure," Shango said, happy to have something to do.

He lingered for a moment, expecting Maitland to give him the keys, but the man only laughed and said, "The door's open."

"Oh," Shango said. He rushed over to the car then, and opened the door so Maitland could put the stack on the passenger seat. The old man groaned as he bent down to place the papers, then groaned again as he straightened his back. The papers were bundled together with twine, but just from glancing at the front page, Shango saw three obvious grammatical errors. On top of that, the layout of the paper was a train wreck, with misaligned columns and pixilated pictures that made Shango's eyes hurt. When he looked up at Maitland, the man was still smiling at him.

"You came to see me," Maitland said.

Shango nodded his head shyly. "I was just passing through."

"Then I appreciate you passing, young Shango."

Shango nodded shyly again. When he moment lingered awkwardly, he blurted out, "Well, I see you're leaving, so—"

"Nonsense," Maitland protested. Then, tapping Shango on the shoulder, "At least let me give you a ride out of town."

Shango shook his head, but Maitland was not even looking at him anymore. Instead, he picked up the papers in the passenger seat, pushed the seat forward with his knee (so that he could access the back seat) then he tossed the papers back there, as if they were trash. After pulling the seat back in place, he gestured for Shango to sit. Shango hesitated for a moment, but he had the suspicion Maitland was only going to talk him into it anyway, so he shrugged his shoulders and took his seat.

"How did your school day go?" Maitland asked as soon as he got in the car.

"...Strange," Shango answered as the man started up the car. At the same time, he was relieved—excited that he actually had someone to talk to.

"How so?" Maitland enquired.

"All those soldiers on the road, for one thing," he began. As he said it, he glanced back and noticed the car with the policemen was tailing them. Maitland noticed his uneasy expression, checked the rearview mirror, then laughed triumphantly.

Shango looked at him in the usual dubious way, wondering if he was a madman or brave. "...You're not..."—he searched for the right word—"*worried?*"

Maitland only laughed at the question. "If your enemies put so much effort into tracking your movements, then you know you're on the right track."

"I guess," Shango said when he could think of nothing else to say. There was the same uneasy silence for a moment; eventually, Shango ventured, "Your protest went well?"

"We spoke and they heard us," Maitland declared in his usual grandiose way. Then, gesturing behind him, "The car following us is proof that they heard."

Shango still felt he was missing something. "What are you hoping to accomplish?" he said so bluntly that it seemed rude. Maitland again laughed at the question; after a few seconds, he smiled coyly as something occurred to him.

"Let me tell you a story, young Shango. ...Imagine yourself at the beginning of time. The stars and galaxies are expanding into the vastness of space; everywhere you look, electrons are combining into new elements—or being broken down again into their constituent parts. Everything is chaos. However, with the passage of time, you begin to see that there's order behind the chaos. Despite all the complexity, you begin to realize everything is bound by the laws of mathematics and physics. Soon, it becomes child's play to reduce all the complexity to simple equations. You see chemical reactions where before you had merely seen flashes of light. However, just when you begin to think you understand everything, something odd happens. In the blink of an eye, physics, chemistry and mathematics give way to biology, and life comes into the universe.

"Indeed, as you look on in awe, two entities emerge from the universe. One declares himself the champion of chaos, while the other professes to be the embodiment of order. Like the planets, stars and galaxies congealing in the young universe, the entities attract and repel one another. The servant of order calls Himself God, while the servant of chaos calls himself the Devil. They fight one another fiercely; but like all the other matter in the universe, neither of them can be destroyed—only converted into something new. As the battle wages, the stars, themselves become weapons. The entities fling solar systems at one another as if they're children's playthings; galaxies disappear in a flash—but as the two adversaries are evenly matched, the battles are never decisive.

"That's when God makes His greatest creation. He can't destroy the Devil, but he realizes he can change the Devil into something else. Thus, in a master stroke, God takes the Devil and makes him forget who he is. He puts the Devil on the Earth, and makes him think he's an ordinary man; He gives the Devil a wife and family to occupy his time; He populates the Earth with men and women of all varieties, then fashions infinite variations of plants and animals to give the Devil something to hunt and eat. Lastly, as His crowning achievement, God creates joy and pain and contradictions, and sets them loose on the fledgling human race—all in an effort to keep the Devil preoccupied, so that he won't remember who he is."

Here, at last, Maitland paused and looked over at Shango. "That's where I think we are as a race, my young friend. We're background actors in a cosmic play—distractions for the Devil. But when the Devil remembers who he is, there'll be no more need for this farce. When the Devil remembers who he is, and we no longer serve a purpose in God's plan of deception, we'll finally be able to find our own purpose in the universe. ...And so, that's what I'm trying to accomplish, young Shango. I'm trying to awaken the Devil, so that we can finally be free of that original lie."

Shango was frowning, not sure if the story was meant as an allegory or a literal statement of Maitland's beliefs. "You really *believe* all that?" he said at last.

The old man smiled coyly again. "I believe in anything that helps me to think." Then, addressing the doubt in Shango's eyes, "Something doesn't have to be true to serve a purpose, young Shango. Why do you think politicians lie so much?" he added with a laugh. Still smiling, he continued, "Much of the world is composed of well-constructed lies, young Shango, which only serve the purposes of those with the power to lie."

"So," Shango said with a smile, "you want to become a liar, too?"

"Exactly so, young sir!" Maitland exulted, as if again impressed by Shango's mind. "I no longer suffer from the delusion that there are truths out there. If everything God created on Earth was a lie, it's not the truth that will save us. Rather, we need a lie powerful enough to wake the Devil."

The conversation verged on blasphemy; to distract himself, Shango laughed uneasily and ventured, "Maybe you're the Devil and you don't know it."

Maitland looked over at him oddly. He stared for a second, his face blank, before looking back at the road. "Maybe I am," he said at last, "...or maybe it's *you*."

Shango instinctively wanted to snicker, but he did not. Maitland did not smile either—or look away from the road—so the statement hung unsettlingly in the silence.

Maitland dropped him by the roundabout at the foot of the mountain. Shango thanked him for the lift before getting out of the vehicle. When he glanced down the road, he noticed the car with the two policemen had stopped about five car lengths behind them. Shango had forgotten about them during the conversation, but the same anxious feeling came over him when he realized they were still there. What did it all mean? The men were not subtle: they were not *trying* to hide. If anything, they wanted everyone to know they were following Maitland. Shango looked back at the newspaperman uneasily, but there was a smile on his face now. When they made eye contact, Maitland put up his hand to tell Shango to wait, then he reached into the back of the vehicle, pulled one of the newspapers from the stack, and handed it over to the boy through the open window.

"…You said you were going to learn about the protest from my article, remember?" he said, smiling again.

"Oh," Shango said.

When Shango took the paper, Maitland ventured, "If you wish, you can come and see me again, and talk about things—the next time you feel like passing through."

Shango nodded his head, genuinely grateful for the conversation—and the prospect of having someone to talk to in the future. Now, somehow, the loneliness did not seem as overwhelming as before. He stood by the side of the road as the car headed down the highway that led to the capital. The car with the policemen followed—at a slow, ominous pace—like a predator that knew its prey had no way of escaping. As the car passed, the policeman in the passenger seat glared at Shango with dead, malicious eyes. Shango instinctively found his gaze dropping in a show of obeisance; his heart raced, and his body shook from the terrible weight of the man's gaze.

He watched the two cars until they both disappeared around a bend in the road. Something was going to happen—he *knew* it—and yet Maitland had worn a carefree smile. What did it all mean? Was the man brave or just stupid? As always, Shango was unable to come to a suitable conclusion.

Either way, as the seconds passed, he found himself thinking that if the police were to kill Maitland now, there would be nobody with whom he could have interesting conversations. Somehow, he thought of the newspaperman as a friend now— perhaps as his *only* friend. He was trying to come to terms with what that meant, when he looked up and noticed there were four soldiers on the other side of the roundabout, glaring at him in the usual menacing way. After jamming the newspaper into his bag, he headed up the road that led to the mountain.

In his mind, he kept seeing the policemen's car stalking Maitland's. The image made him uneasy, so that his pace was slow as he began the long walk up the mountain. At the same time, he was thankful that he had actually made it through the day without revealing his secret. There were going to be challenges ahead, but today was Friday, and he had survived for three days on his own. He told himself things would get easier once he had time to sit down and think and *breathe* without panic and fear getting in the way of his thoughts. In the months and years ahead, he would have to be strong, and trust himself—not to always make the right decisions, but to find solutions once he inevitably veered off course. The fear of failure would always be in the back of his mind, given all that was at stake if anyone ever discovered his secret, but he had to stride boldly into the unknown if he was ever going to survive. He thought about Maitland then, wondering if that same mindset was why the man was still able to smile.

Unfortunately, when the town was behind him, and he was alone on the mountain road, some of the dark thoughts began to return—not about his ability to survive, but about what survival on the island would strip from his soul. Even though his grandmother had been dead for three days now, this would be the first time he would be returning to an empty house. That was how he thought about the place on the mountain: as an empty house, not as a home. A home, he understood at least subconsciously, was the place one went to replenish one's soul—not merely the place where one kept one's stuff and slept and performed the mechanical tasks of survival. Now that his grandmother was gone, the house would always be missing that special component that transformed wood and nails and concrete into a home. If he was going to survive on the island, he would either have to find a new home or chase death and misery away from the house on the mountain.

He was about halfway up the mountain, lost in his thoughts, when a car came speeding up the road. He was on a relatively straight stretch of the road, so there was none of the panic that usually came when a car zoomed around the corner unexpectedly. Nevertheless, he stopped by the side of the road and turned to watch the car, as had become his custom. It was a BMW sedan with tinted windows and fancy rims. A dancehall song was blasting on the sound system, so that he could hear the car's frame vibrating. He took another precautionary step back as the car closed in on him, but the vehicle blasted by so quickly that the resulting gust of wind almost blew him off the mountain.

The reflexive rage surged in him once more; he raised his clenched fist angrily; he opened his mouth to curse and spew— but just then, as the vehicle was about to disappear around the bend, one of the tinted windows was lowered just far enough for someone to fling out an empty soft drink bottle. The plastic bottle bounced two or three times, then began rolling down the road, toward him. Its meandering journey left him mesmerized for a moment, but when it was about to pass him, he stepped into the road and grabbed it.

Those filthy scum! he thought as he stood there staring down at the thing in his hand. He looked up the road accusingly, but the car was long gone. It was bad enough that they littered the town with their trash, but now they were leaving their trash on his mountain too? *His* mountain: that was the first time he had ever thought of it that way. Yes, there was something solemn and melancholy about the lonely road, but it suddenly occurred to him there was something vital here as well, which nourished him and made the tensions of the day ebb away. He was alone, and yet the air was fresh and fragrant; the trees were lush, and the birds singing in them were melodious. ...No, maybe he was not alone after all. There were living things all around him, living the way they were supposed to live. All the creatures around him now were free of the entanglements and contradictions that seemed to be strangling the townspeople. Thus, on a semi-conscious level, he found himself thinking that maybe the task ahead of him was learning how to embrace the freedom of the mountain, instead of fearing it. Instead of thinking of all that could go wrong, maybe he needed to open his eyes to everything that was right about this place. He stood there thinking about it—or at least letting his mind wander as it pleased—then he sighed, put the bottle in his bag (next to the one from yesterday) and continued up the mountain, to his home.

When he reached the forest path, he again made a mental note that he had to clear away the branches and vines before the path disappeared entirely. The same claustrophobic feeling came over him as he walked through it. Despite conscious effort, he found himself moving more quickly. The vines and creeping plants seemed like snakes about to spring at him. In fact, with each passing second, new irrational thoughts popped into in his mind, so that he was panting and wild-eyed when he pushed aside the final branch and exited the path.

The little house was still ugly and in need of a coat of paint, but at least he was off the path. He looked back the way he had come—into the dark tangle of branches and vines—but then shook his head and looked away uneasily. His eyes gravitated back to the boulder, and the disturbed earth beneath it. His grandmother was really underneath all that. He stared for about thirty seconds, but the thought still seemed unreal; the images that popped into his mind—of himself dragging the swaddled corpse across the field—still seemed impossible. He shook his head to drive away the images, then he continued up to the house.

His pace was slow now—lethargic—but about halfway to the house, a strange thought popped into his mind: What if his mother was waiting up there for him? What if she had come down to take him back to paradise? He knew it was farfetched, and yet he once again found his pace quickening. By the time he turned the corner of the house, something like an expectant smile was on his face—but the closed kitchen door dashed most of his childish hopes, and the remainder were squashed when he opened the door and saw that the mess was still on the floor. He stood in the doorway for a few seconds, listening to the deep silence of the place, and coming to grips with the fact that he was alone.

In time he grew annoyed with himself for having had hopes at all. To survive, he would have to have hope in something, but baseless hopes would only waste his energy and poison his soul with resentments. Sighing once more, he pulled off his shoes, left them on the mat, and stepped inside.

There was a broom in the corner of the kitchen. Once he placed his bag on the kitchen counter, he picked up the broom and began cleaning. It felt good to have something to do. Within ten minutes, the kitchen was tidy again. He took the broom and garbage pail to his room, and continued his work. When he passed his grandmother's room, his gaze lingered on the dark stain on the empty mattress, but he forced himself to look away, telling himself to concentrate on one thing at a time.

The glass from the broken louvers was quickly swept up; the bed was pushed back in place, so that the little room seemed clean again. He felt satisfied as he looked at his handiwork—because somehow, the orderly room was proof that he would survive and make it on his own. ...Yet one thing was still not right: He frowned as looked down at the floor, to where he had organized his shoes. There was only one slipper there—since he had never retrieved the other one when he threw it through the window. Somehow, the solitary slipper threatened the order of the house.

Strangely anxious, he moved from the room now, practically jogging as he exited the house and went in search of the slipper.

When he finally rounded the corner of the house and came to the front, there was some broken glass beneath his bedroom window—and the shattered remains of the battery charger—but the slipper was nowhere in sight. For some strange reason, he found his heart racing, as if the slipper were everything to him. He expanded his search, moving away from the area beneath the window. His eyes were scanning the tall grass now, looking for any sign of the blue slipper—

And then his eyes grew wide when he spotted it on the edge of the forest. He was rushing now—as if retrieving the slipper would make his soul complete again. Indeed, when he finally held it in his hands, a simpering grin came to his face. He knew his reaction was bizarre, yet he was chuckling now—both at his strange reaction and because he was relieved. He was standing there smiling when his eyes came to rest on the most beautiful flower he had ever seen. It was about five meters away, deeper into the forest, beneath the shade of the canopy. It was an orchid of some kind: the luscious petals were orange and yellow—but the colors, themselves, were so vivid that they seemed impossible. He meandered over to it as if hypnotized; when he reached it, he stretched out his hand to caress it—but then retracted his fingers at the last moment, as if catching himself in the act of sinning. He had the strange idea that God had momentarily blessed his eyes with the power to see true beauty—and that he would break the spell if he tried to touch the plant. Looking down, he saw the thirsty earth was dry—almost cracked—yet the orchid was full of life—*vivacious*. None of it seemed possible, so he crouched there for minutes on end, staring at it in disbelief.

He had to force himself to move away from the orchid. Yet, even then, he kept looking back, fearful that it would disappear when he turned his back. The thought was strange, even for him, and he shook his head to be free of it. Yet, even when he was standing in the kitchen again, his thoughts were of the orchid. He returned to his bedroom window and stared down, hoping to catch a glimpse of it, but it was pointless.

Bewildered, he forced himself away from the window and looked for something productive to do. When he spotted the garbage pail and broom, he picked them up and headed back to the kitchen. He left the broom standing against the kitchen wall before heading outside the with garbage pail. Further up the mountain, behind some bushes, his grandmother had a dump. On his way out of the kitchen, he saw his school bag on the counter, and remembered the two plastic bottles, but he recalled his grandmother had a prohibition against burying plastic on her property. The few times he had brought home one of those plastic bottles, she had gone on long tirades about how they gave you cancer and made men's balls shrivel. She had always demanded that he take the bottles back to town to throw away—as if they would somehow infect the land with their disease. According to her, God had fashioned human beings' bodies and souls out of the earth, itself. Thus, when people died, they returned to the earth, so that the cycle of life could complete itself. Indeed, the dead returned their nutrients to the earth, and that rich soil could then be used to create more bodies and souls. However, when one buried plastic and other unnatural products in the earth, the cycle of life was broken; the new people produced from the polluted earth were born with corrupted souls. Like plastic, they could never really return to the earth; and with each new generation, they became more and more alienated from mother earth—the source of all life.

Shango did not know how much of that she believed and how much was merely allegory, but as Maitland had said, he saw the usefulness of believing it and respecting his grandmother's wishes. In fact, for the rest of the afternoon, his grandmother's sayings replayed themselves in his mind. He picked some peas to cook with his yams, but while he was shelling the peas to put in the pot, he thought about his grandmother's explanation of why human beings had two eyes, ears, kidneys, lungs, but only one stomach. According to her, when God created the human race they had two sets of everything; but over time, God saw how greedy they were, so He took away one of their stomachs; he saw how evil their thoughts were, and how much they schemed against one another, so He took away one of their brains; He saw how lustful they were, so He took away one set of their genitalia; He saw how much they lied, so He took away one of their mouths. God did leave them with two sets of eyes and ears, so that they could see and hear; but knowing He had created a monstrosity, He stripped away their other senses until that time in the distant future, when they would finally be able to grasp the beauty and splendor of the world around them.

While the food was cooking, he went into the garden to pick the crops he would sell in the morning. He picked carrots and beets and cucumbers and yams, and put them in a canvas bag. When he was carrying them over to the freestanding sink to wash, he looked up and noticed some of the mangoes were ripe. Spotting a huge one on a lower branch, he leapt onto the trunk and began climbing the tree. For whatever reason, he was smiling now as he pulled himself up the tree.

As soon as he plucked the mango, he sunk his teeth into it and pulled away the skin. The succulent juice dribbled down his chin and arm, but he moaned as he devoured the flesh of the fruit. He had never tasted anything so amazing! In fact, as soon as he was finished with the mango, he grabbed another and began to gorge himself. When he was on his third mango, he remembered another one of his grandmother's stories—about why human beings did not have tails anymore. According to her, Man was a jealous, scheming creature, who was never satisfied with what he had. So, seeing how Monkey used his prehensile tail to reach the highest branches and get the fattest fruit, Man formulated a plan to steal Monkey's tail. Monkey, for his part, was well aware Man was a fool. He would watch Man toiling out in the fields, burning up in the hot sun. To Monkey, Man was the stupidest creature God had ever created, because he had to wear clothes and build a house to live, whereas every other creature could go around naked and sleep under the stars. Everything Man did ultimately only ended up in convoluted failure, which Monkey and his friends would laugh at from the trees. So, when Man told Monkey he'd give him some crops in exchange for his tail, Monkey only smiled to himself, knowing it was only a matter of time before Man's antics treated him to a good laugh. As soon as Monkey handed over his tail, Man attached it and jumped into the tree.

Now Man could reach the highest branches, and gorge himself on all the food that only Monkey and Bird could reach. In fact, Man was so pleased with himself that he teased Monkey for making such a foolish bargain. Even then, Monkey only smiled to himself and waited on the ground—in the shade of the tree.

Man could not believe how much food there was up there on the highest branches! There were fruits and nuts he had never even seen before. He kept eating and eating; his belly grew fatter and fatter, but every time he thought he was full, he would see a luscious meal hanging from a higher branch. By now, Man's belly was sticking out like a pregnant woman's. He should have climbed down to relax in the shade of the tree, like Monkey, but that's when he saw the juiciest fruit he had ever laid his eyes on. It was dangling out on a limb, like a temptress, and Man found his mouth watering at the sight of it. Since it was on the end of the limb, Man had to dangle from his tail to reach it. ...Now, keep in mind Man was already five times the size of Monkey before he started eating all that food. By now, he was about ten times the size—and still trying to support all that weight on Monkey's thin tail. His eyes grew wide as he stretched out his hand to grab the fruit; Monkey's poor tail was straining by then, and just as Man was about to grab the fruit, the tail was yanked off—like a loose thread on an old shirt. Man crashed to the ground so thunderously that Monkey originally thought it was an earthquake. He sprang up from the ground, getting ready to shriek, but when he saw a tail-less Man lying there in a daze, he grabbed his belly and began to laugh. Having seen Man's antics themselves, Bird and Rat and all the other creatures began to laugh as well. Indeed, whenever you heard creatures squealing late in the night, they were probably retelling the joke of how Man lost his tail....

Shango was still smiling. From his high perch, he could see the top of the roof. There were dozens—perhaps *hundreds*—of dents in it from where mangoes had hit it. The further they got into mango season, the more the ripe mangoes would begin to fall. He doubted the roof would last another two years. It already leaked when there were heavy rains; and looking down, he could see patches of rust. If he was going to live on his own, and provide for himself, he would have to find a way to pay for new sheets of galvanized steel. The thought made him grimace; but then, looking up at some huge, succulent mangoes, it occurred to him he could sell them at the stand in the morning. Suddenly hopeful, he climbed down the tree with the same carefree agility, returned to the kitchen, emptied out his school bag, then returned to the tree to pick mangoes. He made four trips up the tree to pick the fruit, then filled a canvas bag with his crop. He felt free and confident now, as if the ripe mangoes were further proof that he would make it. In fact, as he remembered his grandmother's revelation—that the mango tree represented their family's covenant with God—he suddenly saw the ripe mangoes as Divine Intervention. He smiled.

He spent the next few hours cooking and cleaning and performing other random tasks that preoccupied his time and allowed him to believe he was accomplishing something. In general, he was in good spirits, but as daylight began to give way to darkness, he felt a malaise creeping over him again. With nothing to do and no one to talk to, he was in bed by six-thirty. Thoughts of mountain demons were gone for the most part, but in those quiet moments, before he fell asleep, the anxieties were there; his resentment—toward his mother and the other fools of the adult world—was there as well, poisoning his soul. Luckily for him, sleep soon came to whisk him away into the nothingness.

The first thing in the morning, he put his clothes to soak, then he got out the cutlass, sharpened it, and went at the forest path with a kind of savage fury. It only took about thirty minutes to hack away at the most troublesome spots. When he was at the end of the path, looking at the road and the vegetable stand, he stopped to rest and daydream. Only two years ago, he had seen manning the stand by himself as a rite of passage. He had been proud when his grandmother handed over her gnarled change purse and left him to fend for himself. He could still remember his first customer: a smiling old woman driving a quaint English car. She had found it "cute" that he was tending the stand by himself, and had praised him for his ability to tally the bill in his head and give her the correct change. Two years later, the thrill was gone, but there was a new sense of urgency in him now. Starting today, manning the stand would not merely be a chore: it would be his means of survival.

It was about seven in the morning when he finally finished washing his clothes and hanging them up on the clothes line, above his grandmother's fields. With that task complete, he began taking the produce down to the stand. He had to make two trips. He left the first canvas bag by the mouth of the path, then went back for the second one. As he was about to leave with the second bag, he remembered he would need change. His grandmother had a careworn purse that she usually kept in her handbag. He instinctively hesitated before heading to her room— since he did not like its emptiness. He stood in the doorway uneasily, staring at the stain on the mattress; but when he inevitably grew annoyed with himself, he stepped in defiantly. The purse was not on top of the dresser, as it usually was. Some of the drawers were still open from when he had searched for something to bind his grandmother's limbs. The recollection made him anxious, so that he again rushed ahead to distract himself. He opened some more drawers—drawers with neatly folded clothes and underwear and spools of thread and letters bundled together with twine...but her handbag was not in any of them.

He stood up in frustration, scanning the room for a likely location. When he spotted the bag at the foot of the bed, in the shadows, he walked over, grabbed it and fled the room. Why was he fleeing? Why was his heart racing? There was no logical explanation: he just knew he was relieved when he was free of the place.

In the kitchen, he grabbed his schoolbag, which had the about a dozen mangoes. Spotting Maitland's newspaper on the counter, he jammed it—and his school notebook—into the bag as well, figuring he could use them to pass the time. At last, he picked up the second canvas bag, which was also filled with mangoes. The second trip down to the stand was more tiring, since he was loaded with more weight, but it felt good to have something to do—and to be out of the house, away from his grandmother's room.

After setting up the stand, and arraying the mangoes in a way he hoped would be alluring to passing drivers, he sat on a rock by the mouth of the path to read and do some homework. He tried reading Maitland's newspaper, but between the run-on sentences, misspelled words and hyperbole, he lost patience. How was it that Maitland could speak so eloquently yet he wrote like a high school dropout? It was either some kind of willful sloppiness or some neurological disorder—like dyslexia—that scrambled his thoughts. Shango frowned, thinking about it; but unable to reach a suitable conclusion, he sighed, refolded the newspaper, and jammed it back in his school bag.

During the weekend, the mountain road was always dead at that time of morning. When he heard the first few cars approaching, he stood up expectantly and stood by the stand. He stared at the drivers intently, instinctively putting on his most pathetic face, in the hope that they would at least slow down out of guilt. Unfortunately, the cars only zoomed past.

Forty minutes passed before he made his first sale. It was a bookish-looking, middle-aged woman who scrutinized one of the larger cucumbers, caressing it with an awed expression on her face—as if she were contemplating her lover's penis. Shango found the entire scene unsettling, and looked away uneasily to give her some privacy. After she had purchased the cucumber, Shango tried to direct her attention to the mangoes, but she walked away wordlessly, still caressing the cucumber.

Miss Craig had given him a list of words to study for the competition. After memorizing them, he did some mathematics problems that turned out to be so easy that he was finished with everything in ten minutes. He sighed, bored. That was when a minibus turned the bend and began lumbering up the mountain. Shango reflexively stood up and took a step into the road, so that the driver would at least acknowledge him by turning to avoid hitting him. As the bus approached, Shango realized it was full of tourists—or, at least, white people. Some shameful island instinct was instantly triggered in him, so that he smiled and waved. That must have been some kind of international signal for "Buy my stuff!" because the minibus began pulling over. Shango gestured to the neat stack of mangoes, like a magician who had just made an object appear out of thin air. When he heard one of the tourists exclaim at the size of them, Shango pressed home his point by retrieving a particularly large one and holding it up for the tourists to see. As they talked among themselves, he realized they were American. Many of them were looking out of the window now, curious. Even the driver, an islander, had never seen mangoes that size before. When someone asked the price,

Shango gave a slightly inflated figure, but a figure that was no doubt cheaper than anything the tourists would find in their supermarkets at home. That was when a grizzled old man with a bald, sunburned head, demanded to know if the mangoes were sweet. At that, Shango promptly handed the mango over to the man to sample. The man hesitated for a moment, but he sunk his dentures into it when Shango nodded his head approvingly.

When the succulent juice began dribbling down the man's chin, Shango knew he was hooked; and as soon as the others heard the man's moans of delight, Shango found himself running from window to window, accepting money and distributing his product. The original grizzled man bought three more; and by the time the minibus drove off, there were seventeen fewer mangoes. Shango waved at the retreating bus, grinning at his good fortune.

After his first major sale, his salesmanship improved appreciably. He now sprang into action as soon as he heard cars approaching. He found that holding a mango in each hand and waving them slowly was the winning formula. The waving mesmerized most drivers, so that instinct compelled them to slow down and investigate. Getting people to stop was always the key to making a sale—since once people had stopped, they felt obligated to justify their stopping. For many, buying large, succulent mangoes was usually a good justification.

By noon, somehow, he was down to two mangoes. Laden with his grandmother's stuffed purse, he grabbed one of the canvas bags and headed up the path to replenish his stocks. In fifteen minutes, he had picked another thirty mangoes. He had to climb higher into the tree to grab the ripe ones on the outer edge. Once, when he was venturing out onto a limb, his foot slipped on bird droppings or some other slimy substance; and with the mango-filled bag making his movements clumsy, he almost toppled to his death...and he would have died if there had not been another branch there for him to grab. Afterwards, he stood there panting and trembling, then he climbed down slowly and headed back to the stand. Yet, for minutes after the incident, he found himself thinking that if he had died, it might have been weeks or months before someone—like Miss Craig, perhaps—climbed up the mountain and discovered his corpse.

Luckily, selling the mangoes soon distracted him from thoughts of death. One or two of his grandmother's longstanding customers stopped by and commented that they remembered the mangoes from previous years. When the first one asked him where his grandmother was, he panicked, unprepared for such an obvious question. Yet, the woman was smiling, and Shango forced himself to smile as well as he said his grandmother had gone to town. By the time the next customer asked about his grandmother, the lie flowed flawlessly, without any hesitation or thought. He tried not to think about what this new skill meant.

Twelve more mangoes were gone by one in the afternoon. Shango's spirits were high again. Indeed, the fruit put everyone in a good mood: their faces beamed at the sight of them; dour old men found themselves giggling and making small talk. More than once, Shango had had to cut off talkative customers when a new car began approaching. A few times, several cars were parked there, with customers gorging themselves on the mangoes. People departed the stand with smiles—and faces covered with mango juice.

Thus, when a smiling man in a bright orange car pulled over,

Shango prepared himself for yet another sale. The man was perhaps in his late thirties, and had a completely shaven head that glistened in the afternoon sun. He was in a T-shirt, but wore dress slacks and hard-soled shoes. He did not say a word after getting out of the car—something that Shango only remembered in retrospect. Yet, his smile was still wide as he looked over at Shango. It was Shango who directed him toward the mangoes. The man seemed genuinely amazed at the sight of them—as if he had not noticed them before. That, too, Shango would note after the event had passed…

The man picked up one of the mangoes and felt the heft of it: "Wow!" he said; Shango smiled and nodded his head approvingly. In fact, in his mind, he was already wondering how many the man was going to buy. "You picked these?" the man asked.

"Yes, sir."

"Here on the mountain?"

"Yes," Shango said, gesturing vaguely toward the forest path.

The man's eyes went to the path, and hung there. "Oh," he said at last. Then, after some reflection, "I have a store—I could *sell* the mangoes. Do you have many left?"

"Yes, sir," Shango said enthusiastically. "They're just getting ripe now. There are *hundreds* in the tree."

"Wow!" he said again, but in a way that Shango instinctively found odd—too enthusiastic, perhaps. On top of all that, there was something unsavory about the man's smile. Shango's mind was about to go to it when the man pulled out his wallet and retrieved a wad of bills. "You could make some *big* money," he said at last.

Something about the phrase reminded him of Daddis, so that he immediately became wary. He looked at the wad, then back at the man's wide, unsavory smile. Indeed, it was a grin by now. "Okay," Shango said, confused by his uneasiness.

"Can I see the tree?"

Shango hesitated a moment. "Okay." However, when the boy only stood there, the man laughed out loud.

"I meant can I see it *now*? It's not far, right?"

Shango looked in the direction of the path: "No, I guess it's not." He began walking, and the man followed him, still grinning. Shango felt numb—as if this were all a dream. The man followed two paces behind him. After about ten steps down the forest path, Shango looked back at the man: he was still grinning. Shango nodded uneasily and turned back around. However, as soon as he did, he was shoved to the grown. He lay in the dirt, dazed.

When he looked up, he man towered over him, still grinning. Now, for some reason, the man was undoing his belt. Shango lay frozen on the ground, still not quite able to grasp what was going on. However, at the sight of the man's plaid boxer shorts, Shango reflexively began to crawl backwards, like a crab—until he was blocked off by a thorny bush. Something about the sight seemed to please the man, because he laughed out again. When he reached into his shorts and began stroking his hardening penis, Shango began to panic. He tried backing away again—forgetting about the bush—but then yowled as the thorns jabbed him in the back. Through all this, the man only stood there confidently, grinning at Shango's antics.

That was when Shango felt a rock beneath his hand. It was lying right there, as if God had placed it there for his use. He grabbed it without looking, then flung it at the man's grinning face. Somehow, the rock landed right between the man's eyes; he stumbled back confusedly, as if he had no idea what had happened. Wasting no time, Shango scrambled to his feet, his eyes scanning the forest floor for a likely weapon. There was a weathered stick between him and the man. The man was still fumbling around;

blood was flowing from his forehead as he struggled to regain his equilibrium—

Shango grabbed the stick and *swung* it. The man instinctively tried to duck, but in his dazed state, he was too slow. The stick hit him in the head with a loud *crack*. Yet, the blow seemed to return him to his senses, because he began moving faster. He turned on his heels and began stumbling away. Shango had a sudden fear that the man would regain his faculties and overpower him. Desperate, he hit the man in the back of the head so forcefully that the stick snapped in two. The man grunted and stumbled forward, but he managed to stay on his feet—as if the Devil, himself were giving him strength.

Shango began panicking again. He grabbed another rock from the ground, and aimed for the man's head, but he missed. He grabbed another, flinging it wildly. This one connected, but it only hit the man in the back.

By now, the man was nearing the end of the path. Shango grew terrified that he would retrieve a weapon from the car and *kill* him. Looking about frantically, he spotted a stick on the ground— indeed, a *club*, still green from when he had cleared the forest path that morning. He grabbed it, yanked off the few twigs that covered it, and charged the man while he was fumbling with the door handle. Shango rose the club high in the air, then brought it down with a loud thud on the man's already bleeding head. The man grunted again—and groaned—but he still would not go down! In fact, like before, the new blow seemed to jumpstart the man's addled senses, so that he finally opened the door and entered the vehicle. Growing frantic, Shango swung wildly at the man's head through the open window, but only ended up hitting the top of the vehicle. He was preparing to unleash another blow when the man started up the car and shot down the mountain road. Yelling out in frustration, Shango threw the club—but of course, it only fell to the road and rolled over the side of the pit.

Bewildered, he stood there panting. Even after the orange car disappeared around the bend, Shango still stood there trembling and wondering what the hell had just happened. Once the initial terror faded, his body began to shake. ...And what if the man returned later—or *tonight*, when Shango was sleeping? He felt queasy at the thought, so he retreated to the mouth of the path and sat down heavily.

Understandably, he was not himself for the rest of the afternoon. When cars stopped to admire the mangoes, he looked at the passengers anxiously—as if they would attack him too. Luckily for him, the mangoes sold themselves, because his mind was a million miles away. Somehow, by three in the afternoon, all the vegetables were gone. He only realized it after the fact—when one of his grandmother's longtime customers bought the remainder, along with five mangoes. He vaguely remembered the woman's exclamations about how tasty the mangoes were last year, but none of the details—or even the woman's face—stayed with him. Looking at the stand, he saw there were only three mangoes left. How many had he sold that day? He figured it had to be close to a hundred. How much money had he made? The purse in his pocket was fat and heavy. He tapped it, amazed. Nothing that had happened that day seemed possible. He kept seeing the grinning man's confident face—and his engorged penis. *What if he came back...!* Shango felt faint and nauseous every time he thought about it. For once, he wished there were an adult he could go to for protection and comfort. He considered the police, but then reflexively shook his head as his mind conjured an image of the policeman screwing the girl.

In any event, there was something dark and unrelenting stirring in him now, telling him that if he had only managed to *kill* the grinning man he would not be in this position. For a moment, he cursed his weakness—his inability to crack the man's skull open with his blows. If only he had been stronger, his rage would have been able to obliterate the man from existence; if he had been stronger, no one would have seen him as prey to be cornered in the first place. As he stood there, and the darkness consumed him, he wished he could kill them all—all those fools out there—and let his rage purify the island. His jaw was set now; his hands were clenched into fists, but when he brought his hands up to look at them, they were small. His arms were bony, and his prepubescent body mocked all his grandiose ambitions, so he sighed and bowed his head.

Besides, the rage could not be sustained for long. Like a fire ravaging a house, it eventually burned itself out. He felt emptier inside now—and numb—and *lost*. About two minutes passed with him just standing there looking around vaguely, trying to make sense of things that refused to make sense. The adult world did not only annoy him now: it *terrified* him. Yet, his dark, vengeful thoughts instinctively troubled him as well. He feared that if he embraced them, and traveled too far down this path, he would find himself going to extremes. Either he would withdraw from society as some kind of hermit or become a monster. He did not want to define himself by his victimization or his fear or his *hate*. He wanted his relationship to the world shaped by *his* choices and *his* will—not other people's perversions. Yet, he could see no way to defend himself. His arms were still bony; and in the end, he was still only a boy trying to find his way in a world shaped by the brutality of men.

Exhausted, he picked up the remaining mangoes, placed them in his school bag—along with the canvas bags he had used to carry down the produce—then he continued on to the house. Yet, even then, he kept looking back every few seconds, checking to make sure nobody was following him.

W hen he reached the house, the first thing he did was retrieve the cutlass from beneath the house. The hard steel made him feel marginally better. He swung it in the air a few times, reassuring himself that he would definitely be able to crack the grinning man's skull open *now*. Yet, the thoughts were horrible, and he felt even emptier inside as he walked up to the kitchen door and entered the house.

He went to his room, where he stood looking out his window. He found his eyes returning to the path every few seconds, checking for any sign of the grinning man. He grew annoyed with himself, but the solemnity of the mountain—the silence of this place, and his *isolation*—made him tremble inside. *What if the man returned…!* He tried shaking his head to drive away the thought; but by then, the only thing that reassured him was the fact that the cutlass was lying within arm's reach, on his bed.

He began eating the remaining mangoes. There were yams to be cooked, and some beans were soaking, but he did not really have the energy. He ate the mangoes languidly, standing at his window and throwing the skins and seeds into the bushes below.

When the mangoes were gone, he still felt hungry—or, at least, *restless*. He picked up the cutlass and went to cook some real food. He picked some callaloo—since he had a sudden thought of his grandmother yelling at him for eating nothing but mangoes—and cooked it along with the yams and beans. Yet, even when he was under the house, preparing his meal, he sat so that he could keep an eye on the forest path. Even when he was chewing the food mechanically, his eyes rarely strayed far from the path...

After storing the leftovers in the kitchen, he returned to his room and spent the remainder of the afternoon preparing himself mentally for the night. Every few moments, he kept checking to make sure the cutlass was still where he had left it on the bed; he kept looking out of the window, down to the path.... *How had it come to this*? He considered getting out of the house—and going to a place where there were other people. Maybe he could see a movie in town—but then he would have to walk back up the mountain in the dark. He shook his head.

In fact, as night approached, his sense of panic grew. Worried about the grinning man sneaking in during the night, Shango gerrymandered an alarm system for the kitchen door. There was of course no lock, so he tied some empty paint cans to the door knob, so that anyone opening the door would cause the stack of cans to topple. He tested it when he was done, and was satisfied at the clangor—but he would not sleep well that night.

By six-thirty, he was underneath the covers, grasping the cutlass, just in case. He strained his ears for any telltale sound. He jumped up when a nighttime bird cried out in the darkness. The usual nocturnal sounds—of crickets, frogs and all the other forest creatures—now sent his heart racing. By then, the only thing that soothed him was the cutlass. Every few moments, he kept squeezing its handle—just to make sure it was still there. His hand began to ache; and as the hours passed, elaborate scenarios played in his mind—of what he would do if he heard the paint cans topple during the night. He told himself he would hide by the doorway, in the darkness, and wait for the grinning man to come to him. Then, as soon as the man poked his head in the doorway, Shango would swing the cutlass—and keep swinging until the man stopped moving.

He kept telling himself he could not allow himself to hesitate. In fact, as the elaborate scenarios played out in his mind, he even planned what he would do with the dead body. In his younger days, he used to be terrified of falling into the latrine—since he had always thought of the latrine as a bottomless pit, from which nothing ever returned. He would hack up the grinning man's body and dump the parts in there. The images were horrible— and yet, in his terrified state, he had to prepare himself for all contingencies, and give free rein to any demons that might help him survive.

Then, it was morning again. As the early birds sang in the trees, Shango jumped up from the bed, still clutching the cutlass. He threw off the sheet, and held the cutlass as if preparing to strike a blow. He stood there panting for about five seconds, as he searched the room for any sign of the grinning man—as if the man might be hiding in a crevice in the corner. There was of course nothing, so he stood there in bewilderment, trying to figure out how he had reached this place.

Eventually, his eyes went across the hall—to his grandmother's empty bed. As always, her death seemed too unreal—and yet, the incident with the grinning man did not seem real either. He could not vouch for any of it.

As the original panic faded away, he sighed; looking longingly across the hall, it occurred to him some childish fear had kept him from cleaning his grandmother's room. The dark stain on the mattress seemed like a mark of shame, so that he immediately marched across the corridor to begin dragging the mattress outside. He looped the cutlass through one of his belt buckles— since there was no way he would allow himself to be without a weapon while he was alone—then he hauled the mattress off the frame.

Up close, the mattress still reeked of death. Luckily, it was not particularly heavy. There were no actual springs in it: it was essentially just a big sponge covered with a few layers of cloth. He dragged it out of the doorway, and toward the kitchen. However, he had to stop when he reached the kitchen door, because his extemporized alarm system—that is, the stack of empty paint cans—was still tied to the door knob. He rested the mattress against the counter, untying the cans and putting them in the corner, behind the door. When he finally got the mattress through the kitchen door, he propped it up against the freestanding sink. Next, he returned to the kitchen to the get the bar of soap from one of the cabinets. From under the house, he retrieved a bucket and his grandmother's scrub brush, then he went to work. He put the soap in the bucket, filled it at the sink, doused the mattress with the sudsy water, then began scrubbing. It felt good to clean—or at least, it felt good to do something that kept him from obsessing about the grinning man's return.

He scrubbed the mattress with all his strength, grunting from the effort; but after so many days, the stain seemed impossible to remove. The mark faded but did not disappear. Eventually, when he was panting for his efforts, and soaked with the soapy water, he sighed, realizing he had made as much progress as he was going to make.

The mattress needed sun to dry. After he caught his breath, he carried it up to the top of his grandmother's field, where the sloping earth was rocky. There, he left it to dry.

What was there to do now? His clothes were still wet, so he went up to the shower, stripped, and washed himself. The water felt good. After the shower, he walked back to the house, totally nude, carrying his clothes in one hand and the cutlass in the other. It was strange being able to wander the house naked. It was proof that it was all his now—and that he could make his own rules. Yet, no sooner had the thought crossed his mind than he had an image of his grandmother looking down disapprovingly at him from her perch in heaven. Suddenly guilty, he rushed to his room and put on some shorts.

The clothes he had washed the day before were on top of the trunk. He folded the uniforms in the meticulous way his grandmother demanded, then he laid them neatly in the trunk.

It was about seven in the morning now. He thought about trying to sell some more mangoes, but a flashback of the grinning man made him shudder. At the same time, he found himself thinking that he might be safer at the stand than in the house by himself. At the stand, there was at least the possibility of another car passing by if the grinning man returned; in the house, he was alone.

…How much money had he made yesterday? Frowning, he realized he had not counted his earnings. He scanned the room, trying to remember where he had left the purse. Not seeing it in a likely location, he returned to the kitchen. It was not there either. Just as panic was about to set in, he returned to his room and found it under his bed—as was usually the case with things he lost.

After emptying the contents of the purse onto the bed, he began to count. Altogether, he had the equivalent of about one hundred US dollars—about twice what Daddis had given him. He smiled, seeing the fruits of his labor—but he felt a sense of urgency as well, since he had to make as much money as he could while he could. The mangoes were not going to last forever—and none of the other fruits and vegetables could be sold in sufficient quantities to be *lucrative*. Nodding his head, he decided to try to sell some more mangoes.

When he was leaving the room, he glanced into his grand-mother's room—at the empty bed frame. He was glad he had finally washed the mattress, but the room seemed even emptier now. He poked his head in and stood there scanning it somberly. That was when his eyes came to rest on the dresser. Many of the drawers were still pulled out haphazardly from his search for something to bind his grandmother's limbs. Various items of clothing were hanging out of the drawers. Sighing, he stepped in to straighten things out.

He was refolding some blouses in a lower drawer when he noticed a stack of about twenty letters. He had noticed them during the original search, but had been too preoccupied to care. He pulled them out now, and stood up straight to peruse them. Some gnarled twine bound the stack. The first letter had a stamp from America, but when he saw his uncle's name in the return address, the old resentments began to stir.

Curious to see who else had written his grandmother, he untied the twine and began shuffling through the stack. The first ten or so letters were from his uncle. He was about to lose interest when the next letter piqued his curiosity. The penmanship was elegant, with elaborate curlicues—as if rendered by a professional calligrapher. The name on the return address was Nigel Douglass— a good English-sounding name. The return address was in Fern Grove—an exclusive community that was somewhere further up the mountain. Shango had heard about it, but had never had a reason to visit it.

After pulling open the envelope, he hesitated for a moment, wondering about the propriety of opening his grandmother's letter. However, when curiosity got the better of him, he pulled open the flap, retrieved the fine stationery, and unfolded the two pages. The same elegant handwriting filled the pages. The date on the letter was from two years ago. Shango began reading:

I'm writing this letter to show you I'm not afraid. I'm not hiding. I know when you get spiteful enough, you'll drag this letter out in public for everyone to see; you'll show it to my wife; you'll go to the press and use it to say I wronged your daughter. I'm not afraid. I am a man: I lived up to my responsibilities and have nothing to be ashamed of. Yes, I used your daughter for sex; but she saw the usefulness of being used—and of having my baby—and of blackmailing me. Yes, that's what I call it. She got $30,000 out of me and ran off right away to America. You don't think I have friends in New York, who tell me how she's spending the money? Every time you guys demanded money, you always said it was for my son—

Shango stopped reading, his heart racing. He looked at the name on the envelope again: Nigel Douglass. That was his *father?* Bewildered, he tossed the remaining letters back into the drawer, then wandered back to his room, where he sat down on his bed, dazed. He began reading the letter from the beginning, staring with wide, disbelieving eyes.

...Every time you guys demanded money, you always said it was for my son, yet he's still living in that shack on the mountain while your daughter's off in America with the money. In fact, the money's all gone. She just called me asking—no, demanding more. I know you'll go to the public—and my wife—crying about how I took advantage of an "impressionable" young girl; you'll paint me as some kind of monster who never cared for or acknowledged his son, but you're all horrible people. Yes, I'm an adulterer, but scheming people like you are the first to start bawling about your Christian values. You're the worst kind of hypocrites! Like I said, I have friends and family in New York: they tell me what your daughter is doing there. Christian values, indeed! Do what you want. I'm not giving you people one more cent!

When Shango was finished reading, he again stared at the name on the envelope. "Nigel Douglass," sounded sophisticated and dignified—just like the penmanship. His mind lurched off wildly, constructing an image of his father. He went to lie down flat on the bed, but grimaced as the cutlass he had looped through his belt strap cut through the strap and almost sliced through his leg. He stood up and took out the cutlass, then lay down, wondering about the letter.

Blackmail? Remembering the word, he went back to the letter and reread that passage. All at once, he felt like a character in a children's book, discovering he was secretly a prince who had been hidden among the paupers. The prospect excited him— especially now that his resentment of his family was complete. The only thing that made him uncomfortable was his grand-mother's involvement. It all left him conflicted—and curious. His grandmother was not there to answer his questions; his mother was missing, and his uncle's family wanted nothing to do with him. That left only one person: the man in the letter—*his father.*

The revelations of the letter filled him with a kind of dizzy excitement. He walked from one side of his room to the other, suddenly restless. When it occurred to him his father may have written other letters, he returned to his grandmother's room, but the remaining letters were either from his uncle or unknown people who had written his grandmother decades ago. Frustrated, he returned to his room and re-read his father's letter once more. All his life, he had wondered about his father. Now, at last, he had some potential answers. They were only *potential* answers because the man was no more real to him now than he had been a day ago. The only tangible connection he had to the man was this letter.

His father had touched the pages he was now holding. Unconsciously, Shango caressed the page, then winced when he caught himself. What did it all mean? How should he be reacting? Was this strange joy warranted? An avalanche of questions flooded his mind, but the dizzy excitement only seemed to grow and grow.

Since becoming aware his overseas relatives had abandoned him, he had been more guarded about his hopes and dreams—yet, only a fool rejected joy when it presented itself. Despite himself, he smiled, and reread the letter two or three more times, as if new words would magically appear.

Eventually, when the joy became too great for his inner restraint, he sprang up from the bed. It occurred to him he was hungry. He felt like eating fried yam, with onions and the leftover beans from yesterday. The yam was already cooked: he just added the onions and spices. In twenty minutes, he was eating heartily, amazed by how good the food tasted, now that he had joy.

A heavy meal usually made him sleepy, but the restless joy would not leave him. Elaborate fantasies—about his future life in his father's kingdom—were now irrepressible. They threatened his connection to reality, yet he was tired of reality by then. He was tired of loneliness and fear—and soldiers wandering the streets.

To burn off some of his energy, he began pacing the house. When he reached the kitchen door, he looked up and noticed there were more ripe mangoes—*dozens* more. Happy for the distraction, he went to fetch the bags he had used to harvest yesterday's crop. With the joy rising in him, even the grinning man was forgotten for the moment. Soon, he was scampering through the branches. Indeed, today, he felt like he could *fly*.

He made four trips into the tree, and picked at least sixty mangoes. Even when he was walking down to the stand, straining with the weight of the bag, his body felt light and carefree. He again had to make two trips to carry down the mangoes. However, after depositing the first load of mangoes at the stand, he stopped by the boulder to watch the patch of disturbed earth. As always, he marvelled at the fact that his grandmother was actually underneath the mound. He had buried her with his own hands. Bewildered, he reflexively brought his hands up to eye level, to look at them. The hand he had sliced open the first day was almost healed—an implausible recovery he attributed entirely to his grandmother's cure-all concoction. None of it seemed possible. Even his father's letter seemed impossible, so he rushed up to the house to read it once more.

When he finally returned to the stand, he stacked the mangoes in an attractive pattern. However, it was Sunday morning, and there was no traffic. He sat there for about an hour, drifting in and out of his elaborate fantasies, before he heard the first car coming down the mountain. In fact, from the rumbling, he realized it was a truck.

He stood up as it approached, but when the military transport turned the bend, he instinctively retreated a step. Some shameful impulse made him lower his eyes—like a dog showing subservience to its master. In fact, when the transport came to a screeching, jarring halt in front of the stand, Shango looked up wide-eyed and terrified. The brakes seemed to cry out in agony as the massive vehicle strained against gravity and inertia. Shango took another tentative step back, as if the vehicle might somehow explode.

Two dozen grim-faced men were now glaring at him. They, too, seemed unreal—like caricatures of men. Looking at them, Shango suddenly found himself wondering how they were with their wives, girlfriends and children—but then he remembered the policeman screwing the girl.

The man in the passenger seat—a lieutenant—suddenly bellowed, "Them mangoes looking *real* big."

Shango looked back at the stand, as if he had forgotten about his wares. When he looked back, the lieutenant was getting out of the vehicle. Everything about him exuded privilege and brutality. From Shango's past experiences, men like the lieutenant did not merely take what they wanted: they acted as though you were obligated to give it to them. Grumbles, the bully from school, would probably end up being a military commander someday if his life as a drug dealer did not pan out. Shango saw it all in a flash, and retreated another step, to give the lieutenant room.

As soon as the man reached the stand, he grabbed a mango and bit into it. His face beamed as the succulent juice dribbled down his chin. Chewing sloppily, he looked over his shoulder and gestured for his men to come. In ten seconds, dozens of them were before the stand. They stuffed their pockets and filled their bellies. Shango merely stood by the side, watching the scene gloomily. They showed no intentions of paying, and they did not. In fact, after the lieutenant bit into that first mango, they did not even acknowledge Shango at all. Even after they all filed into the vehicle once more, and continued down the mountain, they did not say a word to him or bother looking in his direction. Shango looked back at the stand then, seeing that it was bare. At first, he only stared, not believing what he was seeing; but then, the raw hatred stirred in him again.

If he had been bigger and stronger they would *never* have treated him this way! He was sure of it. He needed to be big and strong too. Even then, his dark fantasies began to churn. In his mind's eye, he saw them all butchered and bloody—and suffering the terrible consequences of his wrath. His eyes bore into the retreating vehicle as if willing it to burst into flames—

But that was when it occurred to him the truck was going too fast to make the bend. Instead of slowing down, it was speeding up as gravity pulled it toward the cliff. Indeed, as he stood there, he heard some of the soldiers screaming. Somehow, all his dark fantasies disappeared in that moment, because he found himself willing the driver to slam on the brakes. The driver tried to swerve at the last moment, but it was all pointless by then—given the speed at which they were going. The next thing Shango knew, the truck was gliding gracefully through the air; for two or three seconds, it was flying over the pit. There would have been something majestic about it—except for the sound of all those hardened soldiers crying out like beasts being slaughtered.

Either way, the illusion of flight was short-lived. In the blink of an eye, the truck nosedived into the pit; the soldiers' screams were sucked into the nothingness, as if God, Himself had silenced them. After that, Shango waited—one second, two seconds— until he heard the terrible sound of all that metal crashing into the ground far below. They were all dead. There was no doubt about it; and even as he stood there in shock, Shango knew nothing could be done for them.

At least ten seconds passed before Shango could move. Like his body, his mind was frozen. More troublingly, when it began to work, it searched for options that did not exist. Even- tually, somehow, he managed to take a tentative step forward, then another and another. With each step, his pace became quicker—more urgent—until he was running down the mountain. However, as he was nearing the cliff, he asked himself why he was running—and what he was hoping to accomplish. The soldiers were surely dead. It was at least a four-hundred-meter plunge to the bottom. The pit was so deep that the bottom was often enshrouded in fog; and even when there was no fog, tall, ancient trees occluded the bottom. As far as he knew, there was no safe way to reach the bottom: the pit's walls were mostly sheer rock face—which was often wet and slippery and treacherous. So, nothing could be done for the men, but he was still curious to see the scene. That was probably what drove him now: morbid curiosity—and the usual eagerness to verify something that seemed impossible.

He slowed as he reached the spot where the winding road transitioned into the cliff. Since the cliff protruded over the pit, he already knew he would not be able to see the bottom of the pit from that position—unless he crawled out onto the edge... which he was definitely not going to do, since he had always been terrified it would collapse, like those cliffs in Road Runner cartoons.

That was when it occurred to him he would be able to see under the cliff if he walked farther down the mountain—where the road was practically perpendicular to the cliff. He began running down the road again, but about halfway to his destination, he became aware something was odd about this section of the road. He instinctively slowed, but he was so focused on getting a glimpse of the truck that the realization registered only as a moment of confusion. Soon, he was running again, driven by morbid curiosity and the need to verify impossible things.

At last, when he reached the next bend in the road, he scanned the patch of forest beneath the cliff. Unfortunately, at that distance—and with the thick tree cover within the pit—there was nothing to see. His only clue was an empty patch in the canopy, where he guessed the truck had knocked down the trees.

What was he supposed to do now? As far as he could tell, there were two options. The first was to go to the police. It was the logical—and *moral*—choice, but he pursed his lips, thinking about the consequences. In practical terms, his going to the police now would only open him up to unwanted scrutiny. If he went to them, they would demand to talk to his parents—and ask questions better left unanswered.

At the same time, human decency called on him to do *something*. It might be days or weeks or *months* before the truck was discovered. The soldiers' loved-ones would certainly be worried during this time. More crucially, despite his relative naiveté, even Shango knew dozens of soldiers disappearing would have profound consequences for the island, given the already tense environment. When they did not show up, the government would assume they had been attacked or kidnapped—or *murdered*. The clampdowns that had started since Cuthbert's death would be expanded; more people would die needlessly. ...No: he shook his head, feeling the cruel weight of responsibility. He could not let any of that happen.

Also, even though there was no tangible reason for him to feel *guilty* about the soldiers' deaths, he remembered the dark fantasies—the *raw malice*—he had felt for them before they careened over the edge. Hadn't he wished for this? Hadn't he just been begging the universe to take revenge on them? He winced.

He was just about to head back to the house—to get ready to go into town and inform the police—when the sun's rays reflected off something in the pit. When Shango concentrated on that spot of the forest canopy, he saw there was something orange and metallic down there. He stood squinting at the spot until a brutal realization made him stagger back. The orange thing in the pit was the grinning man's car...!

His stomach convulsed, so that his heavy breakfast made it halfway up his esophagus before retreating. The sensation was disgusting, and he groaned again. He remembered hitting the grinning man in the head all those times. The man must have lost consciousness after turning the bend. ...Shango had *killed* a man. There was a small boulder by the side of the road. Shango staggered over to it and sat down heavily. Yet, after about five seconds of staring blankly at a shrub across the road, he stood up again, and shuffled over to the previous spot, to peer into the pit once more.

A disturbing thought popped into his mind then: He had either caused—or been at the scene of—three horrific accidents on the mountain. Three times, he had called upon vengeance and darkness, and three times people had died. Reason told him it was just coincidence; but deep down, he considered the possibility that he was a conduit of whatever malevolent forces existed on the mountain. Maybe there was some dark spirit protecting him; maybe his grandmother's soul...but no: he instinctively shook his head, wary of where his thoughts were taking him.

Exhausted, he shuffled back to the boulder to sit down; but after ten seconds, he stood up again, and began walking up the mountain. His pace was slow—lethargic, as if the life had been drained out of him. What was he supposed to do now?

When he passed the spot from earlier, where he had sensed something was different about the road, he stopped again. There were some shrubs missing: the grinning man's car must have knocked them over when he drove into the pit. There were no

skid marks, so Shango figured the man must have been un-
conscious by then. ...At least he had died without knowing the
horror the soldiers had felt when they plummeted to their deaths.
He was not sure it made a difference, but at least it was something.

While he was standing there, he found himself wondering if
anyone else would notice the shrubs were missing. When he
realized he was trying to cover his tracks, his cowardice made
him feel a little sick inside. Yet, remembering the terrors of last
night—when he slept with the cutlass (just in case the man
returned)—he knew he would be a hypocrite if he pretended he
was sorry the man was dead. Indeed, as he stood there staring
into the pit, it occurred to him he was relieved. Maybe the
universe had merely finished off what he had started. Maybe, he
thought at last, *justice* had been done.

The situation was slightly different with the soldiers—since
they had not exactly *attacked* him. Yet, they had not been innocent
either. They, too had wronged him—probably not enough to
warrant death, but who knew what other transgressions they had
committed against the universe.

Indeed, the initial sense of panic began to subside now, and he
looked at everything pragmatically. Before, he had felt he *had* to
go to the police—out of a sense of responsibility for what the
soldiers' disappearance might mean for the island. However, now,
he began to think that maybe the coming chaos was inevitable.
Just as the universe had purged the island of the grinning man,
maybe there were more fools out there who needed to be
cleansed. The idea, he realized almost instantly, was horrible. He
shuddered, as if shaking it free from his soul; yet, as he continued
walking up the mountain, the darkness was there, whispering
horrible things into his ear.

When he reached the stand, it was probably about eight in the morning. All at once, it occurred to him no cars had passed since he set up the stand. What was he supposed to do now? Should he go to the police or do nothing? In fact, he had been asking himself that question for minutes now. There seemed to be too many variables for him to reach a firm conclusion. As soon as he told himself the prudent thing to do was pretend nothing had happened, his conscience erupted with recriminations; as soon as he convinced himself to have courage and go to the police, common sense told him he was a fool. He kept going in circles like that. Frustrated, he began pacing the road, in front of the empty stand.

There was, however, one thing that seemed certain: if he did nothing now, it was unlikely he would ever get caught. Even when the authorities found the corpses of all those men in the pit, nobody would have any reason to suspect him. Yet, as he had feared since he buried his grandmother, the danger of his "getting away with it" was that he was poisoning his soul. Even now, he felt emptier inside—and lonely from the terrible weight of his burden.

That was when a new idea popped into his mind: What if he reported the accidents *anonymously?* He stopped in his tracks abruptly, staring ahead thoughtfully as his mind went through the permutations. He probably could not call the police—even from a payphone—since the authorities would know to be on the look-out for a boy. However, what if he sent them a letter? He could draw them a map to the pit. Indeed, since the mountain road was so circuitous, it might take them weeks to find the men if he merely gave them directions over the phone. He nodded his head as the idea began to take form and substance in his mind. He remembered something: When his uncle visited all those years ago, the man had bought a map of the island as a memento. When his uncle forgot to take it back to America, Shango had claimed it as his own, hiding it at the bottom of his trunk. He realized now that he could trace the relevant sections of the map and include them in the letter. He could mail it tomorrow, when he went to school. It all seemed so perfect that he smiled excitedly. However, as he took a step toward the path, his eyes again came to rest on the empty stand. Somehow, the same rage surged to the surface as he thought about the men taking his mangoes. ...No, he felt no guilt after all, but he would inform the authorities nonetheless, for the sake of his own honor. Nodding his head, he picked up his school bag and headed up the mountain path, to his home.

Like everything that had happened since his grandmother died, what had happened at the pit seemed impossible. When he was standing in the kitchen, he had to fight off the compulsion to walk back down the mountain, to the pit, and make sure he had actually seen what he thought he had seen. Had he really witnessed the truck plummeting over the cliff? In retrospect, everything always seemed unlikely.

Suddenly hungry again—or at least, restless—he ate the remainder of his leftovers. After that, he went to his bedroom to write. He sat on his bed, with his back against the wall and his school notebook in his lap. He sat there for about five minutes, trying to think of an opening line. He could not say anything that might give the authorities some clue of his identity. Yet, the meticulous student in him felt obligated to explain how he knew the things he knew. Stating where the soldiers were would only beg the obvious question of *how* he knew. He did not want to leave any unanswered questions—lest they motivated the authorities to probe further. At the same time, whatever he wrote would have to seem plausible enough that they would not just consider the letter a hoax.

Frustrated, he stood up and went to the window, staring vaguely at the mountains in the distance. Eventually, he sighed once more; then, remembering the map, he went to the trunk. After retrieving it, he unfolded it on his bed and stood staring at it. The map was faded with age and dog-eared. Looking at it now, he wondered why he had even bothered keeping it (given his disdain for the island). He was staring down at the map when it occurred to him he probably did not need a letter at all: he could just write something provocative on the map, like, "The missing soldiers are here!" with an arrow to the pit. His eyes grew wide at the realization.

Acting quickly, he retrieved a black marker from his school bag, then wrote the message directly onto the map, in huge block letters. After that, in a moment of whimsy, he signed it, "Your Enemy." As soon as he lifted the marker off the map, he frowned, wondering what had possessed him. Nevertheless, the more he stared down at the message, the more it seemed right—as if God, Himself, *or the Devil*, had whispered the words into his ear.

After writing the incendiary note, the restlessness returned. He went to the kitchen and shelled the remainder of the peas. When that was finished, he went and looked through all of his grandmothers drawers, in case there were any more secrets. He found his birth certificate in the back of a bottom drawer, meticulously wrapped in cellophane. Somehow, his father's name was on it again. He stood staring at it, amazed.

Still restless, he searched his grandmother's room some more, but when he found nothing else, he reread his father's letter two more times before his boundless energy compelled him to leave the room. In the doorway, he stopped uncertainly, trying to think of something else to do. The sheet in the doorway of his mother's old room was dancing on the breeze. In the back of his mind, the old terrors were still there—but he suddenly saw this as an opportunity to put childish things behind him.

Standing straighter, he walked over to the doorway boldly, then tied the sheet as he had tied his grandmother's. As always, light and openness seemed to chase away all the foolishness. Soon, he was searching through his mother's boxes. Most of them, unfortunately, were just full of clothes. In fact, the only provocative thing he found was a box of condoms that had expired ten years ago. Unsatisfied, he left the room and walked through the house three more times, looking for something to *do*. There was of course nothing interesting enough—nothing that would hold his attention and keep his mind from his father's letter—so the restlessness expanded like a kind of madness within him.

It was perhaps about eleven o'clock now, but time had passed so haphazardly that the incident with the soldiers seemed like something that had happened *months* ago. He again had to resist the impulse to walk down the mountain and verify the implausible images playing in his head. To distract himself, he started searching the house again, but quickly came to the conclusion he would only drive himself insane if he roamed the house much longer. He had to go out. It was as simple as that. In his mind, there was only one destination that could satisfy all the impulses flowing through him: Fern Grove. Yet, he was coy with himself as he headed to the trunk to pick out some presentable clothes. He was coy with himself as he showered, and dressed, and headed out.

One the way down to the road, he noticed his grandmother's mattress drying on the rocks. When he went over to check on it, it was still a little damp, but he did not want to risk it getting soaked if a storm came while he was away. When he lifted it up and began lugging it back inside, the scent of death was only faint. The thought made him feel melancholy—as if his grandmother, like the scent, would soon be gone forever, leaving only vague memories. As usual, his melancholia annoyed him; so, soon as he placed the mattress back on his grandmother's bed, he jogged out of the house. At the kitchen door, he realized he had again worn his outdoor shoes into the house—and that he was slowly drifting away from all his grandmother's traditions. He saw then that there was something sad and lonely about freedom, because even though he could do anything now, all his joyful memories were locked away in those bygone days, when he had been forced to live under his grandmother's rules. To distract himself from the realization, he ran all the way down the forest path—to the road.

It felt good to be free of the house—and to get away from the walls he had begun to feel closing in on him. When he headed up the mountain, toward Fern Grove, he told himself he was only taking a walk. However, he could barely contain his excitement as he began his new adventure. Soon, his mind became overrun with fantasies—about his father loving him and rescuing him from everything that had happened since his grandmother died. Deep within, he knew the various scenarios were unlikely, and he was annoyed with his weakness—since he succumbed to them so easily—but what child did not fantasize about being rescued from unhappiness and hardship? He was a fairytale prince now, returning to the castle after enduring the privations of the outside world. Soon, he would be living happily ever after, just like—

He turned the bend in the road and stopped dead in his tracks. Another military transport was rumbling down the mountain. The grim-faced soldiers riding in the back immediately reminded him of the dead men at the bottom of the pit. The truck blew past him in a gust of foul exhaust, so that he had to brace himself to keep from flying into the ditch.

When he was again standing there by himself, his mind returned to the dead soldiers in the pit. He was just about to reassure himself that none of it could ever be traced back to him when something new and horrible occurred to him. When the authorities finally found the dead soldiers, they would find all the mangoes the men had taken from him! The mangoes were *unique* to the island, so it might only be a matter of time before the authorities came to ask him about them. *Why hadn't he seen that before!* A sick feeling came over him now, so that he bent forward and rested his hands on his knees to support his suddenly frail body.

That was when a dark thought entered his mind: In a month or two, the mangoes would have rotted—or maybe, by then, rats, or whatever creatures lived in the pit, would have devoured them. After that time, whatever remained of the mangoes—skins, seeds, etc.—would be indistinguishable from any other mangoes on the island. If he managed to make it to the end of the school year without anyone discovering the corpses, then he would be free. He nodded his head tentatively—but was he cruel enough to let the soldiers' families and friends wait that long? Was he willing to allow the social fabric of the island to unravel for that period of time? The political factions were already at one another's throats: imagine what would happen if their paranoia were allowed to foment for two months.

...And there was another danger. What if the authorities found the men in a day or two, and saw all those mangoes? It would be obvious to them that the soldiers had visited Shango's stand. After that, men like Daddis would come to him, asking why he hadn't reported seeing the soldiers. He grimaced. Yet, with all the military transports that had passed, he could always say he had failed to make the connection with the missing soldiers. It was a plausible explanation, but he was sure they would ask follow-up questions—or ask to speak to his parents. If it ever reached that point, then he was doomed anyway. In fact, if the police ever showed up to interrogate him, one question would lead to another, and that would be the end of him....

He either had to surrender his freedom or he let dead men stay dead for a few more months. It was one or the other. Now that he saw how the mangoes could implicate him, everything was clear in his mind; but as always, he saw that "getting away with it" might mean dooming his soul.

When Shango began to walk again, his pace was slow and mechanical. The restless energy was still within him, but somehow his body felt like it was in shock. He practically had to force it to move. In the beginning, he did not really have a true destination in mind: he merely walked because it was something to do.

About ten minutes into his trek, it began to rain; two or three minutes after that, the rain was gone. Yet, through it all, his pace was unchanged; his blank, distant stare did not waver at all, even at the height of the downpour; and half an hour later, when his clothes were bone dry again, his mind was still a million miles away, searching for solutions where there were only complications.

It was the idea of his father that began to free him from his stupor. The fantasy—of himself as a prince returning home—began to displace the day's problems. Indeed, as the fantasy took root in his soul, he began thinking that maybe his father would solve all those problems for him. Maybe everything would be resolved quickly, just like in a fairy tale.

At any rate, as he began to regain his senses, he looked about confusedly, at the plush forest. He had never come this far up the road before—not on foot anyway—but as far as he could tell, he had passed no residential areas. There had been no houses; besides the military transport, he had seen no other vehicles. Even for a Sunday morning, this was odd. In fact, it was *ominous*—as if something horrible had happened on the island. Without a TV—or even a radio—to keep him abreast of events unfolding around him, he was totally lost. For all his knew…no, he shook his head, wary of allowing his mind to ponder those dark thoughts. He tried returning to his fantasies about his father, but they seemed suddenly stale and stupid. He shook his head again, frustrated. Besides, this was not the time for fantasies. There were practical reasons for his journey. All his life, his father had been a mystery to him. After all these years, he needed to know something concrete about the man. Even if all he could manage was to stare at the man's house from across the street, he needed *something*.

…He tried to gauge how long he had been walking, but it was pointless. At least forty-five minutes had passed since he began walking up the mountain; but for all he knew, it could have been two hours or more. What if he had passed Fern Grove already? Thinking back, he had come upon at least two forks in the road while he was locked away in his stupor. At each fork, he had instinctively followed whichever road seemed like the main one, but what if he had made a wrong turn? There had of course been no signs, and his vague ideas about where Fern Grove was, were unreliable at best.

Just as he was beginning to waver, a large Mercedes Benz glided past him, heading up the mountain. It did not storm past, like vehicles usually did on the mountain: it *glided*. Its engine purred almost soothingly. He stood there, enchanted, watching it as it snaked its way up the road and disappeared behind a tangle of trees. Then, nodding his head, he began walking again, as if he had received a message from God.

A s he neared the very top of the mountain, the view became spectacular. In one spot, Shango could look through the trees and see the ocean in the distance. He stopped and stood staring. It was beautiful; somehow, his soul felt lighter. He breathed the fragrant air deeply into his lungs, then he smiled vapidly, as if high. He chuckled, acutely aware he was acting silly. At the same time, he resisted his usual impulse to analyze. He had spent too much of the last few days obsessing and planning. For once, he just wanted to enjoy the moment and be at peace.

He was in the rain forest up here. Up here, the world seemed larger—*freer*. When he began walking again, his legs felt lighter. However, as he turned the next bend, he saw the road came to an end. Rather, there was a towering wall ahead of him, and the road came to a tee as it followed the wall. The wall, itself, seemed like something from a medieval castle—something that was meant to withstand the attacks of barbarians. He practically expected soldiers with halberds to appear on top of the wall...but there was no one.

When he reached the intersection, he glanced both ways to get his bearings. The wall seemed to go on *forever*. To the left, it went further up the mountain; to the right, it went downhill for about three hundred meters before snaking upwards again—and disappearing around the bend. The light, carefree feeling was gone from him now. Something about the wall was eerie. He felt, somehow, as if it desecrated the mountain. *Was this Fern Grove?* he wondered. His stomach clenched at the thought....

He decided to turn to the left—probably because the distance to the next bend was shorter in that direction. With any luck, the wall would come to an end as soon as he turned the corner. However, minutes later, when he reached the corner, the wall just went on and on, like the Great Wall of China.

There were still no signs of people—and no cars. Like before, he began wondering if something had happened on the island—some state of emergency, perhaps. Even that black Mercedes Benz had seemed like something from a dream. Suddenly anxious, he stopped and looked back the way he had come. The creepy silence of this place made his skin crawl. There were no sounds—not even from birds and insects—as if even they had been purged. Even the wind did not seem to blow here; he looked up at the trees expectantly, but there was nothing.

He was staring at the wall uneasily when he became aware that motorcycle engines were revving behind him. At first, he was relieved to hear something new—but when he turned, he saw two guards with bulletproof vests, military helmets and holstered guns on their hips. They came storming toward him, then cut him off with their motorcycles—as if he had been trying to escape. Shango only stared in his usual way, as if none of this could possibly be happening.

"Why you *sneaking* around here!" the first one demanded. He was a huge man; with all his gear, he looked like a gorilla riding a child's tricycle. There was something ridiculous about it, and

Shango would have smiled if not for the raw malice in the man's voice. After the man made his demand, he leaned the bike on its kickstand and dismounted in one smooth motion that entailed raising his right leg high in the air to clear the bike. Shango instinctively found the maneuver impressive—even as the man towered over him threateningly.

Remembering the man's question, Shango cleared his throat and began, "I wasn't sneaking, sir—just *looking*." After he said it, he was pleased that his voice was calm. Then, considering the man's question again, the flaw in his logic seemed so obvious that he blurted out, "You didn't see me *hiding*, did you? You can't be sneaking when you're out in the open."

His reasoning seemed sound, but his tone was too condescending to go unchallenged. "You're not supposed to be walking around here!" the Gorilla's partner began to reassert their authority. The partner had a wiry frame and an elongated face that reminded him of a goat's. He, too, stepped off his bike and towered over Shango with his hand reflexively resting on his gun.

Their show of bravado was so farcical that Shango instinctively felt sorry for them. Indeed he saw it all in a flash: they were yet more men with guns whose only power came because rich people sent them out into the world to kill and die for them. They were pawns, guarding whatever wealth existed beyond the wall. At the end of the day, they would head back down the mountain, to live with the very people they were paid to keep away from the mountaintop—

"You don't belong here!" the goat-faced guard bleated when Shango only stood there, lost in his vague thoughts.

Despite the man's yelling, Shango only stared at him confusedly. "Why not?" he asked, genuinely curious.

"Where are your parents?" the Gorilla demanded, losing patience.

Then, still trying to assert authority, he repeated, "You're not supposed to be here!" He seemed aware he had not made a cogent argument, so when a new line of attack occurred to him, he added, "You don't *live* around here, do you?"

"No, sir," Shango responded matter-of-factly.

The Gorilla stood straighter at that little victory, and pressed home his advantage: "Then you shouldn't be here."

However, the reasoning still seemed dubious to Shango. "You can only walk where you live now?"

"You little bastard!" the Gorilla began, ready to spring at Shango and wring his scrawny neck. However, his wiry partner was more circumspect—and wary. Despite Shango's clothes, something about his precise English reminded the man of the snotty rich kids who lived beyond the wall.

"Are you visiting someone here?" the Goat began, wanting to cover all contingencies before he unleashed his wrath. For all he knew, Shango could be some minister's son, visiting his cousin for the day.

Shango thought about it—

"What's in your bag?" the Gorilla demanded, pulling the strap from Shango's shoulder. His partner was still wary, but since the Gorilla was already holding the boy's bag in his hand, there was no turning back now. Soon, the men were searching the bag. For whatever reason, Shango chuckled. There was nothing in there but school books. The men seemed disappointed...and Shango's strange laugh unnerved them as well. By now the guards had lost their momentum, and seemed hopelessly stuck in a rut. The moment might have dragged on indefinitely if a youth had not come up the mountain on his bicycle. Shango and the guards turned to watch him. Stranger still, as the youth drew close, he smiled in recognition and yelled, "Hey, Shango!"

Shango had to stare at him for a few seconds before he realized they went to the same school. The boy was one of the popular kids: one of Clark's sycophants. Shango frowned, trying to remember his name—

"Hi…*Thomas*." To his relief, the name suddenly popped into his head; he was grateful when the youth smiled.

Thomas stopped the bicycle in front of them. It was a flashy BMX bike. On top of that, the youth was wearing something Shango had never seen before: a bicycle helmet. He had on a brand new football kit, replete with a pair of sneakers Shango knew he had no way of affording. When he caught himself eyeing the guy's gear enviously, he looked away uneasily.

The guards had been looking on confusedly. The Goat spoke up at last, addressing Thomas: "You know him?" he said, gesturing at Shango.

"We go to the same school. …Is there a problem?" There was a new confidence in Thomas' voice—something Shango had never noticed in him when he was with the other popular kids.

"No, sir," the Gorilla answered subserviently. In fact, within ten seconds, the guards were on their bikes, disappearing down the road. Shango watched the retreating men in amazement; when he looked back at Thomas, he did not know whether to be impressed or wary of his power.

If Shango remembered correctly, Thomas' father was some kind of high official in the government who sent his son to Shango's school because he wanted him to come through the ranks with "the common man." Unfortunately, it pained the father that his son was only eleventh in the class—and did not excel in anything in particular; as such, despite Thomas' outward ease, when Shango looked at him, he had always sensed the inner sadness of someone who knew he was a disappointment.

"Where you headed?" Thomas asked now, smiling again.

Shango had forgotten all about his destination; he sighed and looked around confusedly, as if just waking up from a trance. "Fern Grove," he said at last.

"The entrance is back that way," Thomas said, pointing the way Shango had come.

"Oh," Shango said, wavering. He did not feel like having another confrontation with guards.

"...I can get you in if you wish," Thomas began. "I live there."

"Oh," Shango said again.

"Is it important?"

Shango looked down at his palm shyly, thinking about it. "I guess so," he said at last.

T wenty minutes later, they turned a final bend and the main gate came into view. In truth, it seemed more like some kind of Cold War border crossing than a mere gate. There were guards in the same bulletproof vests and military helmets as before; there was a steel barricade that kept cars from storming through; and as Shango looked on, he had the vague sense that a new world beckoned on the other side of the border, driven by its own ideology and economic philosophy.

Thomas was walking by Shango's side now, pushing the bike. They had talked, but they had talked about nothing in particular. At any rate, they had not talked about the one thing that begged to be asked—namely, why Shango had come to Fern Grove. There had been no natural way for Shango to broach his secret. Indeed, it still seemed unbelievable to him—like much of what had happened lately. As for Thomas, pride or good breeding had restrained him from asking the question directly; so, for twenty minutes, they had talked about school and their favorite teachers and other polite topics that neither of them had really cared about.

Thomas told him the police had mistakenly gunned down a preacher on his way to church that morning. Supposedly, the man had driven through a barricade without stopping, but Shango suspected that was the excuse they used whenever they shot someone nowadays. Either way, the preacher was dead, and tensions were high...

When they reached the front gate, the guards there treated Thomas with the same strange obeisance as the Gorilla and his partner. Shango found something about it shameful, and he looked away as if to spare the guards the cruelty of his gaze. Now that he thought about it, Thomas was the true prince of this place. Or, maybe all the people beyond the walls were royalty, and the people they hired to maintain their kingdom—their nannies and guards and maids—all knew their place.

Since Shango was with Thomas, nobody said a word to him. Within seconds, they were beyond the gate, in that other world. Shango stopped to take it in, unable to really believe his eyes. Before him, there was the biggest lawn he had ever seen. It seemed to stretch for *kilometers*. It was as if he had stepped into a new dimension: the sun seemed brighter; colors seemed more vivid; and of course, he had never seen houses like the sprawling monstrosities in this place. There were two of them about one hundred meters away—on the other edge of the great lawn. To call them mansions was an understatement. They were bigger than his school—and his school had five hundred students!

"That's a big lawn," Shango mumbled.

Thomas followed Shango's eyes confusedly, then laughed. "That's a golf course," he said.

"What's golf?" Shango asked, frowning.

"It's a game old men and white people play."

Shango looked over at the course again, but saw no one. "How do they play it?"

"They hit a ball with clubs," Thomas explained.

However, the description made it seem barbaric. In Shango's mind, he saw enraged old men attacking a defenseless ball with a club, like some kind of geriatric Neanderthals. There were obvious follow-up questions, but he decided to leave well enough alone.

"How many people live here?" Shango asked at last.

"In Fern Grove?" he asked. When Shango nodded, Thomas shrugged: "There are about thirty houses in here…so, maybe one hundred people."

"Oh," Shango said. Then, shyly, "Do you know where Nigel Douglass lives?"

"Mr. Douglass? Of course. His daughter is *hot!*" He laughed as he said it; Shango instinctively laughed along as well, to show good manners to his host, but it had never occurred to him his father would have other children.

Cautiously, Shango ventured, "How many children does he have?"

"Douglass?"—Shango nodded when Thomas looked over— "…I think Wanda has a little brother."

"Wanda's the girl?" he asked, trying to keep up.

"Yeah."

"How old is she?"

"About fifteen or sixteen." Then, eyeing him mischievously, "You want your shot at her too, huh?"

Shango laughed, but then felt a little uneasy when he realized they were joking about his sister. He sobered so quickly that Thomas momentarily frowned. "…So," Shango began to change the subject, "where does he live?"

Thomas watched him intently. Shango could tell he wanted to ask about everything, but the youth had the patience of a prince. After all, this kingdom was his, so all knowledge—all *secrets*—would eventually be revealed to him eventually. "Do you want me to take you there?" he asked at last.

"Is it far?"

"Not far. I have to go that way anyway."

"Okay, thanks," Shango said, motioning for Thomas to lead the way.

They made more small talk during the ten-minute walk, but it was again circumscribed by the elephant in the room: Shango's secret. The longer they talked, the more stilted the conversation became. Shango would say something inane like, "That's a nice house," and Thomas would tell him what government minister or famous person lived there, and if he/she had a hot daughter. Shango looked around as they walked, still feeling like he had slipped into another dimension. The lawns here seemed impossibly green and uniform—as if an army of gardeners had trimmed each blade of grass separately, with tiny pairs of scissors. Shango felt increasingly ill-at-ease here. Fern Grove was like an expensive china shop: everything around him seemed outwardly beautiful and exquisite, but he was in mortal terror that he would inadvertently break something and be forced to spend the rest of his life paying for it.

There were no fences in Fern Grove—nor were there gates and other property barriers. Indeed, many of the luxury cars parked in the driveways had their windows rolled down. Shango had a strange fear that something would go missing and that they would blame him for its disappearance. In his mind's eye, he saw them sending their armed guards to corner and *brutalize* him.

Thomas, on the other hand, had the carefree mien of someone who had never had a genuine worry all his life. Shango wanted to resent him, but doing so would only be proof of his own jealously and pettiness. In truth, if he could have Thomas' life and still be himself, he would do so, but he suspected he would lose more than he gained if he lived in this place. The people here were probably all happier than he could ever hope to be, but he sensed some Faustian bargain had been struck somewhere. Remembering the medieval outer wall that surrounded them, Fern Grove suddenly seemed like a gilded prison. If one's happiness had to be walled off and gated, then it was a kind of living death—like those comatose people who spent decades hooked up to machines that breathed for them and performed all their bodily functions when in reality they had long ceased to be alive. That was the reality of Fern Grove; and even while Shango was rightly in awe of the machinery that kept the corpse breathing, his soul instinctively rebelled against it.

Douglass' house was modest in relation to some of the others they had passed. It was a two-story modern house, done with glass and steel instead of brick. There were no columns, porticos or any of the other bizarre architectural affectations he had seen on his walk over here.

Yet, now that Shango was here, he felt lost. His father actually lived in that building! The reality of it made him feel like he was being hollowed out. Even though he had come so far, he had no definite ideas about what he should be doing now. The only thing he knew for sure was that he had to get rid of Thomas. There was no tactful way to do it, so there was a final awkward moment between the two boys, as they stood around like two people after a bad first date.

"I guess I'll see you in school tomorrow," Shango said so abruptly that he may as well have said, "Go away!"

Luckily, Thomas' princely patience was still in effect as he smiled graciously and nodded his head. They shook hands, then Thomas got on his bike and zoomed off. Shango watched his retreating form until he made a wide, reckless turn onto the next cross street. It was only then that Shango looked back at the house.

This was the moment of truth, but new anxieties seized him as he considered his alternatives. He had come all the way here, but going to the front door and knocking on it seemed out of the question. He wondered if there was any etiquette for bastard sons introducing themselves to their fathers. He stood there thinking about it, then groaned when he realized he was thinking foolishness.

Dozens of voices suddenly pierced the eerie silence of the neighborhood. Shango took a precautionary step back before it occurred to him the voices were singing "Happy Birthday." More importantly, the singing seemed to be coming from Douglass' back yard. If Shango had not been in a daze, he would have noticed all the cars parked in the driveway—and on the curb.

Someone was having a birthday party back there; and as the song rose in the air, Shango found himself walking across the lush lawn, toward the back yard. When he turned the corner of the house, he saw the yard was *spacious.* Indeed, it seemed more like a park than a yard. There was an in-ground pool, a gazebo and a deck. The fifty or so partygoers were now singing the final stanza. Most of them had congregated around the deck—where there was a table with a *humongous* cake. Shango looked at the scene from behind a pine tree. When the song ended, the people began clapping and cheering—and the cheers became even more raucous when the birthday boy blew out all the candles on the sprawling cake.

Drawn by the scene, Shango moved from behind the tree and blended into the crowd. In a few seconds, he was in the midst of them. He began clapping too—just to blend in with the others. The scent of food filled his nostrils. A short distance from the deck, there was another long table, filled with snacks and punch bowls and pastries. Shango looked at it, mesmerized.

However, it was then that the birthday boy turned around. When Shango looked closely, he was startled to see the resemblance. His stomach muscles clenched; but as always, none of this seemed possible. The birthday boy—his *brother!*—was probably about seven or eight. A woman, whom Shango assumed to be the boy's mother, came over, bent down and hugged him tenderly. The boy endured her affections for a few seconds—but then pushed her off when she lingered too long. Soon, he was running after some of his playmates, who began squealing at the prospect of a chase. The mother yelled for them to slow down, but they were soon out of earshot. The woman lingered there for a while, looking on with a bittersweet expression on her face, as if reminiscing about when he was a sweet baby, snuggling in her arms.

Shango felt like he was invading her privacy, so he looked away. There were some coconut tarts on the table before him. He looked around guiltily, then grabbed one and bit into it. It was heavenly, and his eyes instinctively closed as a kind of orgasmic aura spread over his body. *This is how the gods eat!* he thought to himself. Yet, like a dog that had stolen a chicken leg from the dinner table, he felt compelled to run off to enjoy his meal.

There was a tree by the corner of the house. He retreated to it, hid behind the trunk, and devoured the rest of the tart. It felt good in his stomach, but when he was finished, he felt ill-at-ease once more. There was nobody in his age group at the party— since most of the guests seemed to be the birthday boy's classmates. Also, even though Shango's clothes were clean, they seemed shabby in comparison to everyone else's. Suddenly paranoid, he felt the people at the party would instantly know he did not belong if they looked at him too closely. Instinct told him to hide, but if anyone saw him skulking around the house, he would really be in trouble...

His eyes kept gravitating back to the birthday boy. Presently, the boy and his playmates were running across in the lush lawn, hitting one another with elongated balloons and squealing with delight. Even Shango chuckled at the sight, but then sighed, again feeling like he was invading their space. Besides, there was something too unreal about all this. In the outside world, there were soldiers at checkpoints; people were being *killed*...and then there were the dead soldiers at the bottom of the pit; he remembered the grinning man attacking him yesterday—and the fact that the man was at the bottom of the pit as well. None of those things seemed compatible with the world of Fern Grove. There was something *unnatural* here. Fern Grove, it suddenly occurred to him, was like the mountain demon's spell, lulling him to sleep, filling his dreams with pleasant fantasies, while his soul was being syphoned away.

In truth, the only thing keeping him here was his curiosity about his father; and at the thought, he began looking around again. There were some men in the gazebo, drinking rum and laughing among themselves. Shango stared in that direction, but it was too far away for him to see any of the men's faces—

One of the younger children slipped while trying to dive into the pool, and did an ungainly flop onto his back. At the sight, the other kids started laughing. Then, as the dazed child treaded water, alarmed parents screamed at the children in the pool, threatening them with bodily harm if they jumped in the pool and hurt themselves. There was a contradiction in there some-where, but the children in the pool moped in silence for half a minute or so—until their parents again became engrossed in their conversations. At that point, the children became raucous again. Even the dazed child was soon getting ready for another ill-advised dive.

Shango moved past the long table, and the deck. The gazebo was an island onto itself in the middle of the vast yard—so it was not as though he could walk straight for it. Instead, he walked around the deck, skirting the house. He concentrated on walking at a normal pace—not too fast, lest he drew attention to himself, and not so slow that he would seem like he was sneaking. Throughout it all, he kept his eyes trained on the gazebo, looking for a man with features like his own. In fact, he was staring at the gazebo so intently that he did not notice a man step out from a side door. In truth, the man rushed out, clutching a bottle of rum. Shango bumped into him—

"Sorry, sir!" Shango apologized; panicking, he was going to apologize again, but the moment he looked up at the man's face, the words got stuck in his throat.

The man was going to assure him there was no problem, but when he looked down at Shango, his calm, cheerful expression faded away almost instantly. There was something familiar about Shango's face—something that triggered a recollection of how he had looked as a boy. "...Whose child are you?" the man said at last, his voice hushed.

Shango opened his mouth awkwardly, but then closed it abruptly when the words refused to come.

"...I see," Douglass said after a long pause. He took a cursory glance around, to see who was around them, then he continued, "Come this way." The man headed back through the side door.

Within seconds, Shango was inside the house, following his father through the spacious, brightly lit rooms. He was so dazed that he saw little of it. His mind was sputtering along; his legs hardly seemed to touch the ground, as if he were drifting further away, into yet another alternate reality.

His father took him to his den. He held the door open for Shango, then closed it after him. Shango walked into the room timidly. There were hundreds—if not thousands—of books on the shelves. Moreover, the bookcases were so high that there were ornate wooden ladders to reach the upper shelves. Shango looked up at them, amazed. He had never seen so many books before. Even the so-called public library in town was a farce compared to this. Shango looked at some of the titles, seeing books on everything from economics to philosophy.

While he was engrossed in the books, his father had walked to the far corner of the room, where some plush leather chairs were situated on an oriental rug. As the man stood waiting, the boy stared at him for a few seconds, then he began walking across the spacious room, toward him. His father was a tall man in his forties or fifties. He seemed relatively fit, but his body had the softness of someone who spent all his time behind a desk. He was well groomed (Shango did not know how else to describe it). The man had on a white shirt and dress slacks. He was clean-shaven; his salt-and-pepper hair was freshly trimmed. Indeed, everything about him and his den was meticulous—and fitted the image Shango had gotten from the elegant penmanship in the letter. Yet, like the rest of Fern Grove, Shango was worried he would inadvertently break something in this place—and disturb the meticulous, God-like order.

His father was looking back at him with the same grave expression. "Please sit," the man said, gesturing to one of the chairs. The chairs were at right angles to one another. As Shango neared his father, he could look out of the window and see children playing in the pool. The scene seemed surreal. His heart was racing now. He looked up at the man—at *his father*. When the man nodded his head and gestured to the chair, Shango sat down gingerly; but since he was still overcome by the strange fear that he would somehow break something, he sat on the edge of the seat.

Once Shango was seated, the man took his seat as well. Shango glanced at him: the man looked as if the life had been drained out of him. Shango looked away uneasily—they both did, actually—and sat there in silence for about five seconds.

Eventually, his father took a deep breath; Shango looked over at him expectantly as he said, "Have you eaten?"

"Yes, sir," Shango responded in his classroom voice. Then, not wanting to seem too curt, he hastily added, "There was food outside."

His father nodded, then there was more silence. They listened to some children in the yard squealing with delight.

"...Shango Cartwright," the man began absentmindedly, as if he had been trying to remember Shango's name all that time. "Your mother named you that...just to spite me."

"Oh," Shango said reflexively to fill the silence.

"Those Shango people, with their strange religion...out dancing and beating those drums in the bush in the middle of the night. Your mother would tease me—say I was too stiff...that I should surrender myself like those Shango dancers in the bush...let myself go wild; let the spirits take me, instead of being a slave to things written in books," he said, gesturing vaguely about the room. "...That's what she used to say," he continued; then, looking over at Shango steadily, "Given my position, I couldn't give you my name. I had a wife and child...and your mother knew all this. It wasn't as though I *lied* to her or anything—"

Shango shook his head and put up his hand, as if to say none of that mattered. His father nodded as well, as if grateful. There was more awkward silence, with both of them staring off to the side to avoid eye contact.

At last, when the silence threatened to undo them both, his father began, "I figured I'd hear from you eventually, but I thought you'd be older." He had meant it as a joke, and a strained smile was on his lips for a brief moment, but when something new occurred to him, he sat up straighter and frowned. All at once, his eyes bore into Shango; his voice was harder as he demanded, "Did your people send you here—to get more *money*?"

Shango stared at him confusedly; but then, after a few seconds, a burning sense of shame—and then anger—left him with a peculiar feeling, as if his skin were ablaze. He rose from the chair and found himself moving toward the door. Halfway across the room, a resurgence of the rage compelled him to turn and look back at his father. The man was staring back at him with a frown, still sitting in his chair. From some strange place within him, Shango said, "I didn't come for your money." His voice was calm and steady, and he was relieved. "I never even saw any of it," he continued. "In fact, I'm *never* going to ask you for anything. I'm never going to beg *any* of you. ...I came because I was curious, that's all." He stood there thinking about it, as if pondering his weakness. Then: "The only thing I want now is for you to know my name—so that when I make it, you'll know it had nothing to do with you." At that, he continued walking out of the room.

He saw little of the house as he walked through it; the gated community passed him in a blur on his way out; but during the long walk down the mountain, he realized the stunned, ashen expression on his father's face had pleased him. More than that, he realized he was at peace. He was free now. Once and for all, he had exorcised himself of all his delusions about his family.

BOOK THREE
TRANSCENDENT

E ven when Shango was walking back home from Fern Grove, there were not that many cars on the road. Outside the protective walls of Fern Grove—back in the real world—the people were terrified. There had been reports of armed men attacking soldiers—which joined previous reports of soldiers shooting unarmed motorists and bystanders. The island seemed to be creeping toward chaos; but in truth, Shango's mind had been so thoroughly obliterated by the events of Fern Grove that he hardly noticed the roads were empty. He walked without really seeing. He only came out of his trance when he was approaching the vegetable stand. When he reached it, he stopped and stared at it absentmindedly—as if he had no idea how he had gotten there. After staring at the stand for a few seconds, he remembered all the soldiers stealing his mangoes. The rage was still within him, ready to surge to the surface; but when he recalled all the men were dead now, he turned and stared down the road—to where they had disappeared into the pit.

As always, the scenes flickering in his mind seemed so implausible that he instinctively shook his head. In fact, in time, he found himself walking further down the mountain, to check. When he passed the section of the road where the bushes were missing, he grimaced, but did not stop. Yet, as he turned the bend in the road, and was finally able to see the section of the pit beneath the overhang, the old queasy feeling came over him again.

Since the afternoon sun cast longer shadows over the pit, the orange of the grinning man's car was barely noticeable now. It was only because Shango knew where to look that he spotted it; and objectively speaking, it was unlikely anyone else would notice the orange patch. However, all his old fears were coming back again. If anything, those old fears were stronger now, bolstered by the fact that he no longer clung to the fantasy of his father's "royal" protection. Whatever happened in the coming days and months and years, he would have to bear the consequences on his own.

As for the soldiers' truck, the only sign that it was in the pit was again the open space in the forest canopy. Like the grinning man's car, it was only because Shango knew where to look that he noticed—but an open space in the canopy was never going to mean anything to anyone else. With the passage of time, new boughs and vines would grow—even around the grinning man's car. In a few weeks, there would probably be no sign of any of it; but as always, the relevant question was not if he could get away with it or not. The relevant question was, was he willing to allow the soldiers' families and loved ones to suffer indefinitely? Was he willing to let the social fabric unravel as the various political factions sparred over the soldiers' disappearance? In his heart, he knew his personal sense of honor—his *conscience*—would never allow him to do *nothing*, but he also knew he had yet to formulate a plan that seemed right. In truth, he was stalling—waiting to see how things unfolded before he did anything. There was something cowardly about this position, but taking it allowed him to defer his responsibilities for at least one more day.

Restlessness possessed him. It felt like something tangible, glomming onto his body. He had to keep moving lest it congealed around him and suffocated him. When he returned to the house, he tried to do some reading, but it was impossible to concentrate. He roamed the house aimlessly, looking for something to do—or some heretofore unexplored crevice that might entertain him for a few minutes. There was nothing.

Eventually, he went out into the fields and dug up some yams to eat. Thinking ahead, he planted some peas and squash...but it was still only four in the afternoon when he was finished.

He put the yams on to cook; then, to burn off some more of the restless energy, he grabbed his school bag and climbed into the mango tree once more. He climbed into the farthest reaches of the tree to retrieve the most succulent fruit. He felt like a god up there, above it all. ...But half an hour later, he was back on the ground with dozens of mangoes in the canvas bags but nothing left to do.

After he ate, he lay down in bed, staring at the far wall and listening to the deep silence of the mountain. With nothing to distract his mind, the surreal events of the day replayed themselves in his head. He struggled against his dark thoughts with all his will; his mind sought out all the reasons he should have hope. However, he could not overcome a vague feeling of dread—a strange fear that the empty roads he had seen that day were a sign that he had been abandoned on the island, and that everyone else had been whisked away to paradise.

That was when he remembered the orchid—the beautiful flower he had seen when he was searching for his slipper. He suddenly needed to see it again. ...What if it was gone now? What if it had never actually existed at all—but had instead only been a figment of his imagination? Somehow, he felt as though all his hopes and dreams would be squashed if the flower was gone. He was running now, desperate and frantic...but the orchid was still there, and it was just as beautiful as before. If anything, it was even more beautiful. He smiled, finally allowing himself to breathe. Once again, he crouched down to view it—but this time, merely looking was not enough for him. He stretched out his hand and caressed the petals gently. Next, for some reason, he grasped the thirsty earth, literally raking his fingers through it, so that his nails became caked with dirt. Yet, his smile widened at the strange realization that it was all real, and that he was alive and free.

When the night finally descended on the mountain, he forced himself away from the orchid and returned to the house. Even though the anxieties of daily life were there in those quiet moments—when he was lying in bed, waiting for sleep to take him—he felt stronger, as if his soul had somehow grown over the course of the weekend.

Then, it was Monday morning. He opened his eyes and the dim glimmer of dawn was outside his bedroom window. He sat up in bed drowsily and stared out of the window for a few seconds—at the pastel hues in the sky. He did not feel as though he had actually slept. More likely than not, he had merely been tossing and turning all night. At least two mangoes had banged into the roof during the night, disrupting his sleep. Either he had dreamt strange dreams, or his sleep-deprived mind had wandered off into the abyss. He tried to recall some of the dreams, but it was useless.

Presently, as he yawned and scratched the nape of his neck, the recollections of days past flashed in his mind. His grandmother was really dead—and he had *buried* her out in the fields; his mother had abandoned him; his father was a fool living like a god on top of the mountain…and dozens of soldiers—and the man who had attacked him—were now decomposing at the bottom of the pit.

As those realities reclaimed their place at the center of his consciousness—and the same restless feeling from yesterday overtook him—he felt like a tortured man returning to the torture chamber. He groaned, thinking of all he would have to endure and *do*. Then, as the restlessness reached a new threshold, he sighed and got out of bed.

He had about two and a half hours until it was time for school. Yet, he was so anxious for something to do—something to distract his mind—that he began rushing, as if he were hopelessly late. He grabbed his towel and headed for the shower. In the doorway, he glanced into his grandmother's room and was relieved to find he no longer felt the usual sense of dread. It was perhaps the first time his grandmother's death had not filled him with a sense of panic. He accepted it, as he might accept something that had happened years ago. After all these days—and everything he had endured—his grandmother's room was merely another empty room in a house full of empty rooms. The sight saddened him, and reminded him of his loss, but it no longer terrified him. That, at least, was a sign of progress.

At the entrance to the kitchen, his pace slowed. The canvas bags with all the mangoes were still there. With school, he would not be able to sell mangoes at the stand until the weekend—but all the fruit would spoil if too much time passed. He stopped in the semi-darkness of the closed kitchen, deep in thought. What if he just left them out on the stand for people to take? He could leave a can for people to leave money. He pursed his lips as he thought about it. There was the chance—indeed, the likelihood—that someone would steal the money and just take the mangoes; but by now, Shango did not really feel as though he had anything to lose. The world had already taken more than he could spare.

Acting almost on impulse, he opened the kitchen door before he picked up the first bag of mangoes. It was heavy, and he grunted as he lifted it. At the same time, it felt good to have something to do. Soon, he was heading down the forest path, to the stand. When he reached the road, he was relieved to see two cars zoom down the mountain in quick procession: there really were other people on the island after all; despite all the craziness of the weekend, the world had not stopped spinning....

He left the first bag of mangoes in front of the stand, then returned to the house for the second. The second bag felt lighter somehow—or maybe now that he had managed to stifle some of his more implausible fears, he finally felt like he was awake and *living*. He took one step toward the kitchen door when he remembered the can for the money. The paint cans from his gerrymandered alarm system were still in the corner, behind the door.

Leaving a can for people to leave money still seemed insane, but it was his only choice at the moment. He picked up one of the cans from the floor, placed it on the countertop, retrieved a heavy knife from the cabinet, then jabbed the lid with the knife, so that it made a slot for people to stick their money. He remembered his grandmother had a tube of glue in one of the cabinets. He retrieved it, tore out a sheet of paper from his notebook; then in another capricious moment, wrote, "Leave what you think is fair," on the paper. After that, he applied glue to the back of the paper and stuck it to the front of the can. With his work complete, he picked up the can and looked at it with a whimsical smile. He was still certain someone would steal it, but he was curious about what would happen. In any event, he still felt there was nothing to lose—since the mangoes would only rot anyway.

Shrugging his shoulders, he placed the can in the bag with the mangoes, then he carried the bag down to the stand. Once he was finally there, he took the mangoes out of the bags and arrayed them on the stand. At last, he placed the can in front of the mangoes. Looking at his handiwork, he found himself chuckling.

He was sweating by the time he returned to the house, so he picked up his towel (from where he had left it on the kitchen counter) and went to shower. The cold water again enlivened his senses and made him feel real. In the kitchen, he ate some left-overs from yesterday as his breakfast. The remainder, he put in his lunch pail for later. After that, he returned to his bedroom. Within five minutes, he was dressed and ready to go. He looked around his bedroom absentmindedly, wondering if he had forgotten anything. The map with the provocative message about the soldiers was lying on the trunk. He picked it up, opened it, and looked at it uneasily. He had a sudden thought that if he carried it out of the house, soldiers might stop him at a check-point, search him, then gun him down when they found it. He thought about it for a moment before shaking his head: No, it was a stupid thought. Certainly the soldiers were not that paranoid yet. ...*Certainly*. When he realized he was trying to convince himself, he groaned and left the bedroom—but the map was still in his hand; and when he reached the kitchen, he merely placed it in his bag, along with his school books, his lunch pail, and the two plastic bottles from last week.

He was ready to leave. He looked about the kitchen absent-mindedly once more; when he realized he was dawdling, he left abruptly, shutting the door behind him angrily.

On his way down the mountain, he stopped at the notorious spot from yesterday, where he had seen the orange of the grinning man's car. The car was of course still there; the empty space in the canopy—where the soldiers' truck had fallen—was there as well. He still felt the weight of responsibility—to at least let the men's relatives know they were dead; but as he searched his soul, he again realized he felt no guilt whatsoever. There was no sorrow—even about the soldiers. He stood there thinking about it, wondering if that made him a horrible human being. As always, he was wary of his independence leaving him hard inside; he did not want to tumble over the edge of the abyss, and become a monster. However, in the case of the grinning man, there was nothing he would have done differently. Men who preyed on the weak tended to be repeat offenders; and in the end, whether the grinning man's death was justice or the basest form of revenge, Shango was happy for it—and he would be the worst kind of hypocrite if he pretended otherwise.

He continued walking down the mountain. He was again happy to see there were cars on the road—and that people were still going about their lives. All at once, his father's letter popped into his mind. He remembered what the letter had said about his mother running out of money. Her running out of money probably explained why she had not visited in years. Maybe she had been forced to move from the spacious high-rise apartment she mentioned the last time she visited. What if she was homeless now—living on the street with no way of contacting him? Dozens of melodramatic scenarios played in his mind, but then it occurred to him he was only looking for excuses to explain her abandonment.

At the infamous ravine—where the Range Rover had crashed—he stopped to look at the empty spot where the crumpled vehicle had lain. Images of the beautiful girl flashed in his mind, but just as Daddis' glistening incisor was about to appear, a car turned the bend and zoomed down the mountain. Startled from his reverie, he moved on....

When he reached the town, he sensed a strange new tension in the people. They avoided eye contact; they walked hunched over, with brisk, anxious gaits—as if fleeing from a stalker who might attack them at anytime from anywhere. Shango found himself moving more quickly as well, as if he had caught their disease. His heart raced; his eyes darted about the town, as if on the look-out for threats.

Soldiers and policemen were still at the major intersections, their faces forever grim, their guns ever at the ready. When Shango had a flashback of the military transport nose-diving into the pit, he grimaced. Despite his intention to rush to school and be free of these streets, he felt he was being worn down by this place—as if he were caught in one of those nightmares where the faster he tried to move the slower the world advanced around him.

Also, after seeing Fern Grove with his own eyes, there was something surreal about the shacks and crumbling structures of the town. The garbage in the gutters somehow seemed even dirtier today—as if reality, itself, had been transformed while he was away. He still did not begrudge the people of Fern Grove their happiness. The paradise they had forged for themselves on the mountaintop was still deserving of awe and appreciation, but the stark contrast between the two communities seemed like evidence of a fatal flaw in their society. It was not that one community seemed real and the other was fake; rather, he saw them both as contrasting lies—or as evidence of a vast lie, which was systematically destroying them all.

At the upcoming intersection, some soldiers had cornered someone. As Shango drew close, he realized it was the girl the policeman had been screwing in the bush. Indeed, she seemed to be in the same clothes from that day—the same skimpy, form-hugging miniskirt that the policeman had pulled up to her waist.

The soldiers were trying to "chat her up" as they said in the local idiom. Shango analyzed the expression on her face as she looked up at the men. There was some underlying terror there; but he could tell her natural instinct in everything was to try to flirt her way out of danger. She was telling them no, but she was being worn down—just as the policeman in the bush had probably worn her down. As Shango approached, she looked in his direction. At first, she frowned, trying to remember where she had seen his face before; but then, as she remembered, she cringed and looked away, ashamed. Shango looked away as well, to spare her the weight of his gaze.

While he was walking away from the girl and the soldiers, some of his grandmother's precautionary tales/allegories popped into his mind. They all followed a common theme, with some scheming woman trying to lure a man into a mysterious danger. Whether it was a whore in the bushes or a disguised demon tempting a hapless fool into sin, it was all essentially the same story. Like most of his grandmother's stories, they instinctively terrified him—but for once he sensed something pathological about the way she always linked sex and danger. All at once, he remembered something he had not thought about in *years*: the innocent experiments of his primary school days. He remembered kissing the little girls and lifting up their skirts to inspect their strangely alluring parts.

One girl in particular, Kebrina Bailey, had bewitched him. Something in her eyes—some spark of life—had intrigued him. They would run off into the bushes together to compare body parts, and she would grasp his penis in her little hands, and stare down at it, mesmerized. ...But she had told one of her girlfriends, who had told their teacher—a behemoth of a woman, who scolded Kebrina before the class and went on a long tirade about girls keeping their "treasure" safe from the ravages of boys. The next time he saw her, the spark had been gone from her eyes. In fact, suffering under the cruel weight of adult guilt, she had practically run from him every time she saw him. He had felt a little heart-broken at first; but after a while, he had only felt sorry for her.

When Kebrina left for America a month or two later, Shango had been strangely relieved. She had no longer been there to remind him of the horrible things adults did in the guise of keeping children safe. Yet, he needed to remember now. He needed to be free of all their arbitrary, spark-stealing limitations....

At the front gate of the school, there was a throng of boys. Usually, they were boisterous and animated, but there was something somber about their gathering today. As Shango approached, he noticed they were listening to one of the old ladies who sold candy. The woman's face was bruised and swollen— and wet with tears—as she recounted how some soldiers had brutalized her. Most of the story was in fact gibberish, interspersed with her usual entreaties to Jesus, Paul, Mary and the other Saints, but the boys felt the words in their souls; and by the end, even Shango felt his hatred of the soldiers gestating, poisoning him.

Bewildered, he left the throng and entered the gate, to get away from the strange new religion the old woman was spreading. Yet, beyond the gate, the same tension was in the air. Within the schoolyard, there were clumps of boys standing about, talking in the same somber way. Ahead, he saw some of the popular kids. Spotting Thomas, he waved; Thomas nodded his head in greeting, but the joy and ease of yesterday were gone from him, and he soon turned back to his group. Upon closer inspection, Shango realized Thomas was not in Clark's group today. Somehow, a great schism had formed amongst the popular kids—because Clark was on the other side of the schoolyard, along with others who were supporting the opposition party. As the scion of a prominent member of the ruling party, Thomas had become the leader of the emergent group. Clark's former sycophants were now Thomas' sycophants; and reeling from the great schism, Clark licked his wounds with his depleted troops, and looked over at the new faction gloomily.

Elsewhere in the schoolyard, similar splits had taken place. Former friends now avoided eye contact or viewed one another with suspicion. Shango walked through the schoolyard slowly, looking from one group to another to see how drastically things had changed. Yet, there was an element of farce about these new developments; and after a while, Shango found himself pitying them for their inability to avoid becoming entangled in such foolishness.

Indeed, in practical terms, there were no concrete distinctions between the political parties on the island. There was no ideological daylight between them; they both had the same policies and promised the same things. If there was any meaningful distinction between the parties it was reflected in which communities could expect patronage when the party they supported came into power. Those realities were very real; but, to Shango, the solution was not the rabid tribalism he sensed rising around him. On the contrary, the solution seemed to be a thorough re-evaluation of their political system. In many ways, it was like two "races" (who were otherwise indistinguishable from one another) warring against one another because of their supposed differences. While those embroiled in the struggle could give impassioned, logical-sounding reasons for their racism, those viewing the war from the outside rightly saw it all as irrational and self-defeating. In this sense, Shango felt sorry for them—and was wary as well, since there was no telling when one of their battles might surge over the borders of reason and common sense, and sweep him into their foolishness.

Mentally exhausted, he slunk off to a corner of the schoolyard, beneath the stairs, to be by himself. He felt lonely. He did not have a watch, but he guessed there were about thirty minutes left until the school day began. He was staring ahead gloomily when he suddenly remembered the permission letter his grandmother was supposed to sign. He grimaced. It was still in his notebook. He took the notebook out of his bag, retrieved the letter, and looked at it. There was only one thing to be done, so, after looking about uneasily to make sure nobody was looking, he rested the letter on his notebook, got out his pen, and signed the letter in the angular, barely legible way he remembered his grandmother signing her name. As simply as that, he had committed his first felony.

He had pitied his classmates for their inability to free themselves of lies, yet his entire life was a lie. Everything about him seemed dishonest, and the realization left him with an anxious feeling in the pit of his stomach. He needed to *move*—and burn away some of the restless energy. He was closing his bag when he looked down and noticed the two plastic bottles. There was a garbage bin right by the staircase; as he tossed in the two bottles, he was relieved to be free of them—but there were too many other burdens on his shoulders for the sense of relief to endure.

The restlessness would not leave him; he looked around vaguely—for some new form of relief—but the schoolyard no longer had anything for him. Bewildered, he began walking up the stairs. The door to Miss Craig's classroom was open; and at the thought of her, a faint smile graced his lips for a moment. All at once, he found himself rushing, drawn by the fantasy of her.

Miss Craig was in the classroom by herself, marking papers at her desk. Her face brightened when she saw him. He stepped in eagerly, relieved that there was still beauty in the world.

"Good morning, Miss," he said in his usual shy way.

When she returned the greeting, he felt his stomach tremble slightly as she said his name. The permission slip was still in his hand. He walked over to her desk and handed it to her. She took it, perused it—to make sure everything was in order—then she smiled again. Shango had held his breath as she scrutinized the signature, but he breathed again as she opened the top drawer of her desk and inserted the letter. He had actually gotten away with it! Despite himself, there was a grin on his face now. When she looked up at him quizzically, he looked away awkwardly.

There was a copy of the island's main newspaper—*The Inquisitor*—on Miss Craig's desk. Remembering the soldiers in the pit, Shango started scanning the first page—

"You can borrow it if you like," Miss Craig said when she saw him looking at the newspaper. She was smiling in her usual encouraging way, and Shango nodded shyly as he grabbed the paper and headed to his desk.

However, halfway to his desk, his pace slowed when he finished scanning the front page. He was expecting the soldiers' disappearance to be front-page news, but there was nothing there. He scanned the next page, and then the next, searching for anything mentioning the soldiers—or even the grinning man—but there was nothing. He frowned. By then, he was standing in front of his desk, staring into space. Was it really possible for so many men to go missing on such a small island without anyone noticing...?

"Is everything all right?" Miss Craig asked from the front of the class.

"Yes, Miss," he said reflexively, coming to his senses. He sat down quickly, and smiled half-heartedly, trying to reassure her. However, when he looked down at the newspaper again, his frown returned. He had expected the newspaper to be filled with exposés on all the pointless deaths—and the government's rationale for them—but when he began reading the lead article, he realized it was written in such a way as to imply the opposition party was somehow responsible. It was the first time it had ever occurred to him news could be dishonest.

Indeed, once Shango began to look at the world with opened eyes, many of the things happening on the island began to make sense. Throughout the school day, every time he walked between classes, or went into the schoolyard for a break, he heard his classmates whispering about people being gunned down and weapons caches being found. Most of it sounded like paranoid nonsense, but his schoolmates believed it, and they acted on those beliefs. Predictably, a few fights broke out—between boys from different factions—but through it all, Shango could not escape the sense that they were all pawns: that the true story was all beyond their comprehension, and that reality bore no relation to the neatly packaged thing they were told to believe.

Sometimes people were blind because they were born with an inability to see; sometimes those in power kept the people below them from seeing the inconvenient truths of their society; but more often than not, the people of a society had to be trained to *not* see—and they had to *accept* that training into their souls.

After school, Miss Craig gave him special tutoring for the contest. She made him memorize the exploits of national and regional leaders; she waxed poetic about the accomplishments of the leaders of yesteryear; but when he asked her a few pointed questions about their policies, he could not escape the feeling that the men had all been self-serving fools. In this way, he began to wonder if even her lessons had been part of the vast lie as well.

M iss Craig tutored him until about five in the afternoon. By the time he walked through the school gate, the town was deserted and depressing. The people from that morning—who had rushed to their workplaces and schools to avoid lingering on the streets—had long returned home. Businesses that were normally open another hour or two had already been shuttered. Street vendors were nowhere in sight. Shango walked the streets uneasily. His surroundings seemed vaguely familiar, but it was as if he had taken a wrong turn somewhere and ended up a million miles away from where he was supposed to be. The only thing that had not changed was Chicken George. When Shango was walking the dreary streets by himself, the man sprang from an alleyway and began darting from one side of the empty street to the other, as if dodging imaginary traffic. Shango stopped to watch the man—until he again disappeared down a dark alleyway— then the boy went about his business.

There were still soldiers at major intersections. Bathed in the rays of the late afternoon sun, the grim-faced men seemed even more menacing. Since there was practically no traffic whatsoever, the soldiers gave Shango extra scrutiny. Suddenly remembering he was carrying the map with the incendiary message, he felt his heart racing. If they stopped him now and searched him it might all be over. Terrified, he bowed his head and trotted through the intersection, ready to run for his life if it came to that....

In fact, he ran all the way out of town; and when the ugly shacks were finally behind him, he stopped and looked back the way he had come. He felt like he had just escaped from prison—or as if he had been a miner, stuck down in the depths of the earth all day, breathing noxious gas. He breathed deeply now—as if finally ridding himself of the poison. For the first time since that morning, he felt real again. However, the day was late, and the darkening mountain road loomed before him, so he began jogging again, desperate to make it home before nightfall.

The lack of traffic was creepy. He almost longed for a car to come charging around the bend, but there was nothing. He felt lonely—isolated and stranded in this place. All at once, he wondered if it going to be like this forever. Was he always going to be running and hiding and lying? He saw no end in sight: no peace on the horizon...nothing to give his life hope and meaning.

That was when the contest popped into his mind. He thought about his father watching it on television—and the man's shame at knowing Shango had reached those heights without any of his help...but if all he had to look forward to was revenge and darkness then he knew, instinctively, that he was damned. Besides, the contest was still too hypothetical to seem real. It was only six days away; he had just spent the last two hours learning the obscure facts that would supposedly ensure his victory, and yet none of it seemed real.

When he turned that final bend and headed for the darkening forest path, his legs felt heavy; his clothes were soaked with sweat. He was about to step past the vegetable stand when he suddenly recalled all the mangoes he had put out that morning. The mangoes were gone, but the can was still there. He stopped, staring at the can uneasily. After a few seconds, he walked over to it, telling himself it would most likely be empty. *At least they hadn't stolen the can as well*, he thought with a faint smile. Yet, when he picked up the can, it was heavier than he remembered. He shook it, hearing the shuffle of coins and paper inside. Excited, he pried open the lid with his fingernails, and stood staring in disbelief: there had to be at least the equivalent of eighty US dollars inside! He reached into the can and touched the money—as if fearful it was an illusion. After that first tentative touch, his fingers ruffled through the bills; but, after a few seconds, he inexplicably felt tears welling up in his eyes. All day, he had been fighting the darkness. All day, he had been battling the impulse to view everyone on the island as a monster in the making, and yet this small gesture had somehow restored his soul. To be honest, it would not have made a difference if there had only been a dollar and ten cents inside. The money in the can was proof that there were still pockets of decency left on the island. Somehow, in the midst of so much chaos and dishonesty, there were still honest people out there. The strange tears of joy rolled down his cheeks now, and he let them roll as he smiled and headed up the path, to his home.

As the days passed, he got into a routine. He got up at the crack of dawn, picked mangoes and left them at the stand. After that, he cooked and did any household chores before heading to school. Every time he walked into town, there would be some new horror—some new story about people dying and unrest escalating. In the mornings and afternoons, when he walked by the spot on the road where he could see beneath the overhang, he would stop and stare, reminding himself that dozens of rotting corpses were really down there.

Every morning, when he got to school, he would look at Miss Craig's newspaper with a sense of dread, expecting the soldiers' deaths to be the lead story; but by Wednesday, there was still nothing, and even he began to doubt the images in his mind. Indeed, a strange idea began gestating within him: What if the pit erased you from human existence? What if everything that fell in there was somehow forgotten by everyone else? He began to wonder if the soldiers' relatives even remembered them anymore. If he went to those relatives now, and mentioned the men, he wondered if they would even know what he was talking about. He wondered if pictures of the men, and all other tangible evidence of their existence, had vanished as well. What if the entire universe had rewritten itself, so that the wives of the men now believed they had never been married? What if the children they had borne together had now been erased from existence as well...?

But then Shango shook his head, reminding himself that the universe did not rewrite itself. There had to be a more mundane—but probably no less disturbing—reason why the men's deaths had gone unreported.

He thought about his mother less and less now; and when he did, it was never with his previous sense of yearning. In fact, he did not even resent her anymore—or his uncle for that matter. Neither of them seemed real to him anymore—so being angry with them would be like being angry with a character in a television show. Soon, he felt he would be struggling to remember them, the way he struggled to remember the plots of unremarkable shows. In time, their faces would blend into the vast sea of faces he had seen over his lifetime, and be forgotten forever.

Besides Miss Craig's afterschool tutoring sessions, the only time he felt connected to the world—or, at least optimistic about it—was when he returned home and found the can of money. There were no more tears of joy, but that little reminder of human decency was everything to him now. In truth, he was either shutting down emotionally or attaining a new level of self-awareness. He was either becoming a monster or achieving a kind of God-like clarity about the world around him and what he needed to do in order to survive in it.

Yet, when he looked at Miss Craig's newspaper on Thursday morning—and saw there was still no mention of the missing soldiers—he really began to doubt his sanity. What if he had only imagined seeing the truck plummeting into the pit? Maybe the orange of grinning man's car had only been a delusion as well. If he had imagined the soldiers' deaths, then maybe the Range Rover from the ravine—and Maitland, and Daddis—had all been hallucinations as well.

Whatever the case, he seemed to sleepwalk through the day—and Miss Craig's tutoring session. As always, he could give correct answers when prompted by a teacher, but his mind was a million miles away.

When he was leaving for the day, Miss Craig called him back and handed him an envelope with four tickets for the contest. She praised him for all his hard work, and spoke excitedly of his future success; but again, Shango's mind was a million miles away...

Once he was outside, he wandered the streets languidly, as if blown aimlessly by the breeze. When he emerged from his day-dreams and found himself standing in front of Maitland's door, he looked around confusedly. The street was empty—like the rest of the town. There did not seem to be undercover policemen parked in front of the building anymore, but Maitland's dirty Volkswagen was parked on the curb, so Shango guessed the man was inside.

When Shango looked at the door, he saw it was ajar. Beyond the door, there was a dusty staircase, which led to the second level. The paint on the walls was peeling. Some of the paint chips had congregated in the dust piles in the corners. Shango paused for a moment, wondering if he should go up the stairs. Yet, now that he thought about it, Maitland was the only person on the island he considered even a *potential* friend. He was not sure when it had happened, but he trusted the man. Maitland was a kind of benchmark for him. If Maitland was real, then maybe the other things—the soldiers in the pit and the grinning man—were real as well. Somehow, he had come here in order to re-embed himself in reality. This was clear to him now.

He began walking up the stairs. They creaked eerily beneath him; and in time, he found himself tiptoeing up the stairs, just to avoid the noise. The place smelled like machine oil and some-thing dank and unsavory. His face soured; and at the top of the staircase, he stopped uncertainly. The second floor was actually a huge loft. Looking up, the roof was held in place by an intricate system of wooden rafters. Immediately in front of him, there was a hulking machine, which Shango guessed was a printing press.

At first, he looked at it uneasily, as if it might come to life and charge at him. The thought was bizarre, even for him, and he shook his head to be free of it.

Initially, everything was so still that Shango did not notice the people. However, on the other side of the loft—about twenty meters away from where Shango was standing—someone finally moved, inadvertently scraping his chair against the wooden floor. It was only then that Shango noticed there were about a dozen people standing about or sitting anxiously in the shadows. Maitland was sitting at a desk over there, facing the people. With the shadows, Shango could not see their faces distinctly, but there was something grim about the scene. One of the seated men was talking to Maitland; but from where Shango was standing, he only heard tense whispers.

He hesitated once more, feeling like he had intruded. Yet, as the seconds passed, his eyes roamed the rest of the loft. After a moment of confusion, it occurred to him Maitland probably lived here as well. There was a kitchen next to the hulking printing press; through one door, there was a bathroom; through another, Shango could just make out the outlines of an unmade bed. Of course, there was dust everywhere; crumpled papers were on the floor, along with candy wrappers; and in the kitchen, dishes were piled high in the sink. There were also several bookcases throughout the loft, stacked with hundreds of yellowing, dusty books.

When Shango inadvertently shifted his weight, the floor board creaked again. Everyone in the room seemed to jump at the noise; they turned to look at him, some of them looking as if they were ready to scream. Shango froze, now convinced he had intruded, but when Maitland smiled invitingly and waved—and the others saw the man knew the boy—everyone seemed to relax.

Maitland put up his hand to tell Shango to wait; as Shango nodded and stepped further into the room, the newspaperman went back to his interview.

Ahead, there were several stacks of newspapers on top of a long table. Shango walked to the table instinctively, as if drawn; but when he read the headline story, his jaw dropped. It read, "Dozens of Soldiers Missing Since Sunday." For ten or so seconds, all Shango could do was stare. The story, itself, was written in Maitland's usual disjointed manner, and Shango quickly gave up trying to read it. There was a picture of some of the missing soldiers' family members holding up images of the missing men. Indeed, now, as some of Maitland's interview filtered across the room, Shango realized the people in the room were some of those relatives.

At the moment, a woman—one of the soldiers' wives, apparently—was asking Maitland why the authorities would be lying to them. "What could've happened to them?" she asked, her voice breaking.

All at once, Shango felt lightheaded and dizzy. He leaned against the table to keep from falling. ...Why was Maitland the only one covering the story? He looked back at the stack of newspapers: If only Maitland was reporting the real world, then Shango suddenly wondered what other truths might be hiding in the old man's paper. He started leafing through some of the pages; but in truth, his mind was too dazed to digest much of what he saw. Eventually, he closed the paper and sat on top of the table—since he needed to sit....

A minute or two later, Maitland's interview seemed to end. The people who had been sitting were now rising from their seats. They were thanking Maitland now—for his courage and diligence. Shango listened without digesting what he heard. Soon, the people were walking past him. Maitland walked them to the top of the staircase, promising that he would keep digging until he found the missing soldiers. Shango could only stare.

When the people were gone, Maitland turned back to him and smiled. "Young Shango!" he said with a laugh. "How are you, my friend?" There was genuine warmth in the old man's eyes, and Shango almost felt himself tearing up at the realization.

"I'm okay," he managed to say.

"Have you eaten? You want something to drink?" he said, walking past Shango and heading to the kitchen.

Shango shook his head. "I'm okay," he said again. Then, realizing he was sitting on the man's table, he jumped down anxiously—as if his grandmother would spring from the shadows and box his ears.

By now, Maitland had retrieved a beer from the refrigerator. Once the cap was open, he guzzled it on one go, tilting his head back and then releasing a loud, satisfied, "Ahh!" once the bottle was empty. Shango looked on awkwardly. When Maitland looked over at him again, his face beamed, as if he had just remembered something.

"I didn't know I was dealing with a *celebrity*," he joked as he began walking over to his desk.

"Huh?" Shango said as he followed the man over to what seemed to be his living room. There was a couch there, and a television—in addition to the chairs in front of the man's desk.

"I saw a story about you on the news last night," he revealed, looking back at Shango mischievously.

Shango froze, instinctively alarmed. "*Me?*" he peeped. In his mind, he wondered if they had found out about his grandmother—if they were now tracking him down as a kind of fugitive—

Maitland laughed at his expression. "Yes, *you*—and the other students in the contest."

"Oh," he said, relaxing a bit.

Maitland wore a bemused expression as he contemplated Shango's reaction. "You're not looking forward to it?" he ventured.

"Yeah, I guess. ...I've been studying for it all week. I just came from school," he continued, but there was no excitement at all in his voice.

The mischievous expression returned to Maitland's face: "You weren't going to invite me?"

"To the contest?" he asked confusedly. When Maitland nodded, Shango said, "You wanted to go?"

"Of course," the old man said as he sat down heavily at his desk, sighing loudly again. "We're friends, aren't we? Friends support one another."

Shango smiled shyly. Then, remembering the tickets Miss Craig had given him, he reached into his bag. "I have tickets—if you want to go."

"Of course!" Maitland said enthusiastically.

Shango was looking through his bag eagerly when he came upon the map with the incendiary note. He had forgotten he was carrying it; he paused uneasily as he remembered all those terrible images from the weekend. However, Maitland was still looking at him expectantly, so he continued searching until he found Miss Craig's envelope. When he did, he removed the tickets and stretched his arm over the desk to hand them to Maitland.

Maitland took the four tickets with a smile, but then frowned. "All these for me?"

Shango looked down at the tickets. "Yeah, if you want them."

"You didn't want to take your relatives or something?"

Shango paused, trying to think of a likely response, but the only thing he could think to say was, "Nobody could make it."

Maitland frowned. "You're saying *nobody* in your family can go?"

Shango's stomach clenched when he saw he had bungled himself into danger. "...Yes," he said at last, avoiding eye contact and trying to act nonchalant by putting the envelope back in his bag. When he glanced up, Maitland's frown had deepened. It took all of Shango's willpower to maintain eye contact—since he could see all the questions stirring in the newspaperman's eyes.

Maitland shifted his weight on the chair and looked at him askance. "If none of your relatives are going, then how are you getting to the contest? It's in the capital, isn't it?"

Shango's eyes grew wide at the realization. In all this time, that had never occurred to him. How he could have been that stupid. Yet, he eventually only shrugged his shoulders, seeing he could take one of the minibuses to the capital—

"I can take you if you want," Maitland proposed.

"You?" Shango said, one eyebrow arching.

"Of course. Since you've been so kind to give me tickets, I may as well give you a lift."

"It's really okay?" Shango said cautiously.

At the words, the old man looked at him with an exasperated smirk that made Shango smile. When he nodded his head and put up his hand to show the man he had relented, they both laughed. It was the carefree laughter of friends....

As the laughter was fading away, Shango glanced down at Maitland's desk and noticed the notes from the interview. He sobered, instinctively lowering his voice as he began, "The people who were just here..."

"The soldiers' families ...?"

Shango nodded. "How come you're the only one ...?"

Maitland chuckled. "The people in power own all the newspapers and radio stations—and of course, the government owns the TV station."

Shango had been standing in front of the desk, but now that the heavy topic was in the air, he retreated a few steps and sat down heavily on one of the chairs. "...But why would they *hide* it?" he said at last, frowning.

"Pride, fear...the usual reasons. They can't admit there are forces on the island strong enough to make a truck of their soldiers disappear."

"Forces?" he ventured uneasily.

"Revolutionaries, young Shango."

"*Revolutionaries?*" Shango said breathlessly, alarmed.

"Of course. As I see it, there are two possibilities: either the government did something to them or someone else did."

Shango explored Maitland's logic in his mind. There were of course other possibilities, but there was no way to broach them without revealing too much. He sighed. When he looked up, Maitland was looking over at him with the same excited expression he usually had when discussing politics.

"...So, how long have you known about the soldiers?" Shango asked now.

"Since Monday. I have a friend over at the barracks," he began.

"More spies?" Shango teased him.

As usual, the old man laughed too enthusiastically, but then he pursed his lips as he remembered his conversation with his friend. "...He said one of their trucks hadn't come back, and that they couldn't reach it on the radio. He said none of the officers wanted to talk about it."

"Do other people know? ...Other *newspapers?*"

"Of course they know."

Shango still could not understand it. "But why *hide* it?"

"That's the nature of cowards, young Shango. If they admit they're not one hundred percent in control—that they don't know everything—they fear the people will begin to question them. On the surface, it seems like such a trivial thing. However, when people hold onto power by relying on myths, they can't allow any information that might make people question those myths."

There was thoughtful silence for a few moments. A question had been at the back of Shango's mind since he met Maitland, but he did not know how to broach the topic. "...What happened to you?" he asked at last. When the old man laughed at his blunt phrasing, he went on, "...I mean, how'd you start out?"

"I was a young, idealistic fool, and now I'm an old, idealistic fool," he joked, laughing in his usual demonstrative way.

Shango smiled politely, but he was still curious—or at least hungry for a meaningful conversation with another human being. "...Did you ever marry?" he asked when the old man's laughter died down.

"No," he said with a pensive expression on his face, "I missed my window of opportunity."

"Your *what*?" Shango asked, frowning.

"My window of opportunity: that brief period of time when you're susceptible to love—*and* there're women stupid enough to marry you." Here, he laughed once more, before sobering with a melancholy sigh. "...Thirty, forty years ago, we told ourselves we were revolutionaries—that we were too evolved for bourgeois things like marriage. We convinced ourselves we were changing the world, bringing a new economic order, breaking the shackles of the past...But here we are, all these years later, revolutionaries without a revolution: old fools trying to exist without bitterness, because the world refused to live up to our ideals." He laughed sardonically then, and looked over at Shango: "Whenever you see bitter old men, nine times out of ten, they were idealists when they were young. ...Told themselves they would tear down the old order and erect some new sparkling paradise in its place. …But those kinds of revolutions always fail. Young people tell themselves that problems exist because old people refuse to change—so when they get power, the first thing they do is destroy all the things the old people refused the change.

"However, the true revolution is not in changing the things out there, but in changing the things in here," he said, tapping his temple with his index finger. "Revolution is an *existential* problem, young Shango. *That's* the trick. Exist, and be conscious of your existence, and you've performed a revolutionary act."

Once again, there was silence after the statement. Neither of them moved; they sat looking off into the distance, contemplating the words. Eventually, Shango sighed, exhausted; then, looking up at the window, and realizing it would be dark soon, he got up to leave. "Thanks, Mr. Maitland."

The old man nodded and smiled. "What time will we meet on Sunday?"

"Oh," Shango said, remembering the contest. "I can come here around noon, if that's okay."

"I'll be ready at noon then," he said, smiling again.

Shango nodded shyly and began walking to the exit, his mind still dazed. At the staircase, he stopped, turned to look back at the man, then he nodded and left. When he was on the streets again, his steps faltered. The darkening, deserted town—and the long walk up the mountain—seemed suddenly daunting. He groaned. Yet, the things Maitland had said were still percolating in his mind. A flashback of the distraught family members in the newspaperman's loft made him groan again. The old feelings of guilt returned for a moment, but then a new thought entered his mind. Remembering the map, he retrieved it from his bag and opened it up to look at it. He read the incendiary note once more, frowning at the signature at the end: "Your Enemy." Acting quickly, he fished his marker out of his bag and scratched out the signature. Instead, he wrote, "They're at the bottom of the pit. Please help their families."

Once that was done, he refolded the map and scanned the street again to make sure he was alone. After that, he took a deep breath, walked over to Maitland's car, pulled up one of the windshield wipers, and placed the map beneath it. With his task complete, he walked away quickly, reassured by a vague sense that he had done the right thing. However, as the minutes passed, an uneasy sensation settled in the pit of his stomach, warning him that no good would come of this.

When he opened his eyes on Friday morning, there was a cold, gray mist outside his window. Since the louvers were gone, the rain had wet the floor during the night. In fact, the side of Shango's bed was damp. He sat up on his elbows drowsily before yawning. He felt like going back to sleep, but the usual litany of images made him groan and sit up straighter. He remembered going to see Maitland. However, looking out of the window again, it occurred to him the map he had left on the man's car was probably waterlogged and illegible by now. He sucked his teeth, annoyed with himself. At the same time, he wondered if it might not be for the best. As he had thought yesterday, no good would have come from Maitland finding the soldiers. True, the soldiers' family members would have been able to find closure, but maybe it was better to let secrets lie hidden—at least until the island's turmoil had cooled.

Either way, he felt it was out of his hands now. The men had already been missing for five days without anything catastrophic happening. Maybe the catastrophe would only come if their rotting corpses were found. Maybe those corpses would be the thing that lit the fuse and destroyed what remained of their society.

Eventually, he sighed, turning from the window and his morbid thoughts. Pulling the sheets away from his body, he rose from the bed, yawning and stretching again. Remembering his morning routine, it occurred to him it was time to pick mangoes for the stand. He left the room and headed toward the kitchen. He stepped into the outside shoes on the mat, grabbed the canvas bags, then went outside, into the cold mist. He shuddered as he stepped into it, but pushed himself forward, instinctively yearning for the freedom of climbing. Unfortunately, the mist had left the mango tree so slippery that self-preservation forced him to climb down after thirty seconds.

Deflated, he began to walk to the shower; but after a few steps, he realized the day was too cold and dreary for him to get naked and stand under the chilly water from the mountain stream. Instead, he went to the freestanding sink, where he washed his face and armpits. A downpour started while he was standing there—one of those brutal tropical storms that descended on the earth like something biblical. The wind blew, shaking the trees and sending half a dozen mangoes raining down on the roof like bombs. Shango ducked inside the kitchen door, slamming it behind him to keep out the sheets of rain.

He felt like staying home today. He needed a break—from the ugly town and the wretched politics of the islanders. Yet, fifteen seconds after the downpour had started, it ended abruptly—as if God, Himself, had turned a faucet and shut off the heavens. The sudden silence was creepy; standing there, in the semi-darkness of the closed kitchen, Shango had a desperate yearning for light and open space. He found himself moving toward his room, as if chased by something dark and menacing. When he reached his room, he jumped onto his bed to get to the window, then he stood there panting, as if he had been suffocating. His face soured as he stared out at the gray swirl of clouds and fog. Today was the perfect day to spend in bed, snuggled up underneath the covers... but he shook his head eventually, knowing he would only attract attention to himself if he was absent for the second time in two weeks (after never having missed a day of school in his life). Nodding his head gravely, he went to get dressed.

It was still drizzling when Shango stepped off the mountain path, onto the road. Today, fog obscured the entire pit—and much of the road. All it would take was a slight miscalculation for Shango—or some careless driver—to go plummeting into the pit. Shango hesitated for a moment, still susceptible to thoughts of his warm bed, then he continued down the road. Like before, he could not help thinking that everything was out of his hands, and that the only thing to do was follow fate wherever it chose to lead him. He walked as far away from the pit as possible, hugging the hewn granite of the mountainside. Yet, even then, he was like someone sleepwalking through life. His face wore a blank, inscrutable expression. He had neither a raincoat nor an umbrella, but as the drizzle soaked him, he walked on un-flinchingly, as if tempting fate to whisk him into oblivion.

When he finally reached the town, everyone seemed exhausted as well, as if the rain were draining their strength. Even soldiers stood about lethargically, huddling beneath awnings. Today, they were too preoccupied with keeping warm and dry to bother with the townspeople. The scant traffic moved at a pedestrian pace; actual pedestrians walked listlessly, as if heading to their beds.

Even the old candy vendors in front of the school had stayed home today. The schoolyard was deserted as well, since clumps of boys were taking shelter beneath staircases and awnings. Shango walked straight for Miss Craig's class, still with a dazed expression on his face. As soon as she saw him, she exclaimed and dragged him to the teacher's bathroom, where there were towels. She stripped off his shirt and attacked him with a towel. Shango stared ahead blankly as she berated him about catching pneumonia and being unable to compete in the competition. It was the first time he had ever found her annoying. Even as she rubbed his legs with the towel, and her hand strayed enticingly close to his crotch, his only real desire was for her to leave him alone.

The next eight hours passed in a similar manner. He probably did not say one hundred words the entire day. He somnambulated through most of it; he sat in his classes daydreaming and staring blankly as his teachers prattled on. Today, all his teachers ended their lessons with words of encouragement for him; they made Shango's classmates clap for him; he got a few standing ovations—but all of it only left him feeling more isolated and *unreal*. He grew alarmed when he felt his pointless rage rising, and yet he felt trapped and frustrated by something unnamable.

In the afterschool tutoring session, Miss Craig yelled rapid-fire questions at him, trying to emulate contest conditions. Shango answered her mechanically—but somehow, he got all her questions right. He looked over at her grinning face confusedly. Even when it was over, and she was hugging him and showering him with effusive praise, he was numb inside. Even when he was walking through the school gate, onto the darkening, deserted streets, he felt nothing at all. There was still a light mist in the air. He was vaguely aware that it was settling on his clothes and face; but even then, he walked on disinterestedly, as if none of it could possibly make a difference....

He had made it through another week without revealing his secret or making any catastrophic mistakes. For that, he was thankful. At the same time, he felt as though a hundred years had passed since his grandmother died. He felt *old* now, as if his youth and joyful hopes were in the distant past....

Whether consciously or not, he found himself walking to Maitland's loft; but when he got there, the door was locked and the old Volkswagen was nowhere in sight. He groaned and moved on. When lightning and thunder resounded in the heavens, he found himself jogging down the deserted streets—

But about two minutes later, when he was about fifty meters from an intersection, two soldiers stepped from a side street and began walking before him. As they appeared, Shango's pace instinctively slowed—so that he would not overtake them. In true military fashion, the men walked with their fingers hovering over the triggers of their assault rifles. Shango followed them glumly, already thinking about making a right turn at the next intersection and finding another way out of town. However, that was when a dark figure sprang from an alleyway, startling the soldiers—

"Bock-bi-cow!" Chicken George screamed, raising his imaginary wings in the air like a rooster defending its territory. The soldiers jumped back; but almost instantaneously, they pulled back on the triggers of their guns. Soon, Chicken George was doing a strange, frenetic dance as they riddled him with bullets. It was only when he fell face first onto the pavement that they stopped firing. He was dead. His body did not move at all. The soldiers had shot him at least twenty-five times between them. Shango froze, his heart beating savagely in his chest.

In his mind, if he moved, they would gun him down as well— so he stood there like a statue, his arms extended in an unnatural pose, his face twitching with horror. Indeed, the slightest movement or sound might give him away, so he begged his racing heart to stop its reckless thumping.

By now, the soldiers were searching Chicken George's corpse— perhaps looking for something that would justify their act. However, by their demeanor, Shango could tell they were not concerned either way. When one of them kicked the corpse, the other laughed and did a pantomime of Chicken George spreading his wings.

Was it funny? Shango asked himself, honestly wondering if his horrified reaction might not be the insane one. He waited there, still frozen, until one of the soldiers turned and saw him. As the man's smile died away, Shango's stomach felt like someone had just split him open with an axe. He staggered, but otherwise could not move. Within seconds, the soldiers were towering over him. They said something, but Shango's mind refused to translate the sounds into meaningful sentences. All he could manage was to stare up at them; they repeated their questions, their voices louder, their faces harder and more barbaric. Shango found his lower lip trembling; one of the men grabbed his shoulder, shaking him like a rag doll. Shango clamped his eyes shut; then, despite himself, he began to bawl like a baby. Was this really how he was going to die? He was ashamed of his cowardice and weakness in this moment of truth—

But when he opened his eyes, the soldiers were looking down at him in disgust—as if they too were ashamed of him. While Shango stood there blubbering, the men looked over at one another uncertainly. Then, inexplicably, they began to laugh. In fact, Shango must have been the greatest joke ever told, because the soldiers practically doubled over now as they looked down at the boy's tear-soaked face....

Somehow, Shango had been dismissed. Seeing he was no threat to them, the soldiers moved to the side, still snickering. Shango began to walk—but his stiff, halting gait was so unnatural that the men began to laugh again. Shango willed himself to keep moving—and to move faster. Chicken George's bloody corpse was on the ground before him. The man's blood was flowing into the gutters now. Shango almost threw up at the sight and smell— but he feared he would lose his momentum and freeze up again if he went around the man; as such, he merely stepped over the corpse as he fled.

By now, his face wore a haunted, distant expression. In truth, he was not seeing much of the outside world anymore—and all he could really hear was the soldiers' mocking laughter. Even when the soldiers were far behind him, the laughter was there; even when he was out of the town, walking up the mountain, the laughter was there, in the back of his mind like an invitation to madness.

It began to rain again. After a minute, his clothes were completely soaked. His teeth began to chatter—but even then, the soldiers' laughter was there. He grasped his skull, trying to will the laughter to stop, but it only grew louder. Gnashing his teeth, he dug his fingers into his scalp, as if he could somehow claw the laughter out of his head—

"Stop it!" he screamed at the top of his lungs, so that the words resounded through the forest. In his mind's eye, he could see the soldiers' laughing faces clearly. ...How he yearned to turn their laughter into cries. Five days ago, when he first spotted the grinning man's wreck in the pit, his soul had quaked. Three times, he had called upon vengeance and darkness, and three times people had died on the mountain. The realization had horrified him at the time—but he called upon that darkness now. Indeed, he beseeched all the demonic forces of the mountain to strike out against his enemies and *decimate* them. He wanted their grinning faces *disfigured*; he yearned to hear their screams—

But he began to cry again, instinctively bewildered by his thoughts. Yes, he hated the soldiers and the people they represented. They had stripped him of his dignity and pride. They had *belittled* him, merely because they were stronger than him. He would take revenge, but he would do it like a man of reason. He would rise above them all, and excel on his own merits—just as he had told his father.

Actually, as the defiant thoughts filled and rejuvenated his soul, his tears stopped flowing. He stood straighter. He took some deep breaths, cleansing himself, before he continued walking up the mountain.

His limbs seemed freer now. His mind seemed clearer. ...He was really going to be in an island-wide competition in two days. The thought still seemed surreal; but for once, the prospect excited him. It was time for him to begin to rise in this society— and to prove his worth—so the only option was for him to win the competition. Here, there were no demons to call on—and no gods to pray to. He merely had to apply his will and determination. It was still drizzling and cold, but his teeth had stopped chattering, and his stride had become strong and purposeful.

F or the most part, the strange new defiance guided his thoughts as he marched up the mountain. Yet, when he reached the notorious bend in the road—where he could look into the pit and see the grinning man's car—he stopped uneasily. He stared for a few seconds; but with the mist and the darkness, there was nothing to see. He was about to move on when he looked up and noticed some emergency lights flashing near the overhang— where the cliff protruded over the pit. He stared at the lights, suddenly numb; then, looking at the area of the pit beneath the overhang, he noticed there were some lights down there as well. The lights were in the section of the pit where the truck had left a gap in the canopy. Realizing Maitland must have found the map after all, Shango hesitated for a moment—but the only thing to do now was move forward.

Five minutes later, he was in the midst of them. Over two dozen vehicles were parked on the side of the road—cars and trucks and vans, most of which either bore the insignias of government ministries or media outlets. Shango estimated there had to be at least sixty people milling about. There were soldiers patrolling the scene; reporters and cameramen had amassed by the overhang. When Shango looked through the throng, he saw Maitland standing before them. The man's face gleamed eerily from the flood of camera lights and flashbulbs, and Shango shuddered instinctively—

"How come you're the only one that was contacted about this?" a reporter demanded. "Do you know who did this?"

"I told you already that they left an *anonymous* note," Maitland said in an exasperated tone—

"But how would anyone know the bodies were here," a woman asked, "—unless they played some part in the murders?"

Murders? At the word, Shango felt dizzy and sick. Maybe he had done more harm than good after all, but Maitland shook his head. "Why assume these men were *murdered*?"

"For one thing," yelled another reporter, "you were the one who was contacted: a *known* radical—"

Maitland laughed contentedly, as if the man had paid him a compliment.

"We all know your history," the same reporter continued. "We all know *of* your paper," he began sarcastically, "even though none of us knows anyone who actually *reads* it."

Here, there was laughter from the crowd. Shango looked over at Maitland anxiously, sorry he had entangled the man in all this. However, when he looked, Maitland was joining in the laughter, practically drowning out the others as he bellowed in his usual over-enthusiastic way.

"Well stated, Mr. Purcell," Maitland shot back. "I would expect nothing less from a government mouthpiece." When Purcell scowled and jutted out his chin threateningly, Maitland only laughed louder, holding his belly like a jolly Santa. Then, as a new joke occurred to him, he stopped laughing just long enough to quip, "You people have your heads so far up the government's ass your breath smells like *shit*!" At that, he threw his head back and laughed heartily, while the press corps glared at him and sucked their teeth. By then, he was the only one laughing. His laughter pierced the air like machinegun fire, slaughtering them. In the cruel aftermath, they all seemed like the walking dead, and Maitland looked at them in the same exasperated away.

"You all knew the soldiers were missing for *days*," he continued, "yet refused to report the story. If anyone here is morally suspect, it's you people and your various puppet masters."

Shango looked over his shoulder anxiously. Everyone's face seemed to wear a scowl now. The soldiers clutched their guns threateningly, but Maitland's mocking chuckles filled the void created by the tense silence. When Shango nervously shifted his weight from one leg to the other, the newspaperman finally noticed him in the crowd. The old man nodded imperceptibly then, smiling; Shango went to nod back, but in the man's eyes there was an almost casual declaration that he knew Shango had left the map. Shango stared at him uneasily, as if terrified the man would reveal his secret right there.

However, that was when another reporter yelled, "Stop playing your games, Maitland! Tell us who committed these murders. Was it your *friends*?" Within seconds, Maitland and the reporters were screaming recriminations and counterclaims at one another, waving their arms threateningly in the air. As the reporter behind Shango sprayed spittle on the back of his neck, Shango stepped aside and began extricating himself from the crowd. With all the chaos, nobody noticed him disappearing down the darkening forest path.

On Friday night, horrible dreams plagued him. In the morning, he was jolted from sleep by images of Chicken George's body being riddled with bullets. In the air, he swore he could still hear the soldiers' laughter. ...Outside the window, the sky was cloudless and bright, but Shango felt sick inside. He turned from the window gloomily, resting his head heavily on the pillow. After that, he stared up at the ceiling for about a minute or two. Somehow, he had come to some kind of decision during the night, and he frowned at the realization.

Since his grandmother's death, only Maitland had kept him from total despair. Only Maitland had treated him with any kind of respect—and *listened* to him. He still felt a kind of childish thrill at the thought of Miss Craig's beauty, but even she was not to be trusted anymore. He realized it suddenly: he felt *sorry* for her—since she had given up her soul to a government and a society that was systematically destroying them all. Like the rest of them, she was a blind follower of the thing Shango had come to regard as his enemy. That enemy did not yet have a definite form or face in his mind, but he hated it completely, with all his will. In fact, as he lay there, surrendering himself to the darkness, the only thought that soothed his soul was that one day—sooner or later—he would be strong enough to eradicate that faceless enemy, once and for all.

He groaned. His thoughts were horrible, and that was never a good way to begin the day. He looked toward the window again. The sky was still clear and bright, and he could tell it was going to be a beautiful day. In fact, he lay there dreamily for at least a minute, letting the beauty revive his soul and chase away some of the darkness.

By the time he finally rose from the bed, there was something like a smile on his face. It occurred to him he could sell at least one hundred mangoes today. ...But then he remembered yesterday's shouting match between Maitland and the reporters. Now that the corpses had been found, the chaos of the last few days would only escalate. On top of that, it again occurred to him the authorities would find his mangoes next to the soldiers' corpses. They would certainly come to question him about it if he manned the vegetable stand today.

Thus, the danger seemed clear. Staying home today was the most logical course of action. ...And yet, there was something perverse in him, coaxing him away from his hiding place. It suddenly occurred to him he had a readymade excuse if any investigators approached him. For almost a week now, he had been putting out the can with the mangoes. If approached, he could always tell the investigators the soldiers must have taken the mangoes while he was away. The authorities might still ask to talk to his grandmother—and he could see the obvious danger of exposure if they *demanded* to see her—but his new darkness whispered horrible things into his ear. All at once, he began to see manning the stand as a challenge: as a way of proving himself by *outwitting* them.

He remembered the bloodthirsty soldiers gunning down Chicken George. The men had almost turned on him too, but he had disarmed them with his tears. People looked at him and saw nothing but a pathetic little boy. If maintaining that image was what it would take to survive in this place, then he would do it—as long as it kept him on the path to destroying his faceless enemy. He sensed his bizarre thoughts were leading him to something horrible, but at least he felt real again. He did not feel like a defenseless child anymore. Instead, he was a soldier in a war, deep behind enemy lines. A soldier had the power to fight and to exact revenge on his enemies. A soldier had the power to exert his will on the world—and to *shape* it—and that was all he wanted now.

Two hours later, after washing his clothes, cleaning the house and tending the garden, he picked mangoes and brought them down to the stand. There were still about five vehicles parked by the pit. One of them was a military transport that looked exactly like the one that had careened into the pit six days ago. A news van from the national TV station was there as well; when Shango looked, he saw a camera man and reporter standing by the pit. He grimaced, thinking about all the wild speculation that must have littered the airwaves over the last twenty-four hours. No doubt charges and counter-charges had been made... and Shango was the only one who knew it had all been an accident. He sighed.

The looming prospect of island-wide chaos made his darkness retreat. He wanted revenge—he wanted to *prove* himself, so they would all know he was not that pathetic little boy—but he did not want *chaos*. Everyone lost when chaos reigned, and the fools who stoked it with calls of anarchy and revolution were often its first victims.

Now that the soldiers had been found, the pit became a magnet—not only for the media but for the general public as well. By nine in the morning, there were at least twenty cars parked by the side of the road. There was no way to retrieve the truck from the pit, so all the investigators had to be lowered into it by a winch on the military transport. Throughout the morning, the people who gathered by the pit—reporters, government officials, curious onlookers, and of course, the military—stopped by Shango's stand. He sold thirty mangoes by ten in the morning. Every time someone approached the stand, he held his breath, thinking the person might be an investigator coming to ask him if he had sold mangoes to the soldiers. However, the conversations never strayed from the latest gossip about who had murdered the men and how they had done it.

Supposedly, the authorities had spent all of yesterday retrieving the corpses from the pit. Funerals were already being planned; autopsies were already being conducted; investigators were already compiling their findings; but at the rate things were going, Shango suspected those findings would come too late to keep them from disaster. He had already overheard some bystanders whispering their conspiracy theories. Words like sabotage and treason were already being bandied about. Even if the government's investigators managed to figure out that the truck's brakes had merely failed, he suspected the islanders had gone too far to accept such a simple fact.

Indeed, with each passing hour, the conspiracy theories grew more convoluted. The crowd grew raucous and testy as the various factions yelled accusations at one another. Shango was sick of it all, and yet it was all good for business. By ten-thirty, he had sold at least fifty mangoes. He returned to the tree to pick some more; and by the time he returned, the crowd had grown so massive that the soldiers had to be used for traffic control. There had to be at least one hundred people milling about now, waiting for the officials to make their pronouncements. By then, when Shango saw the investigators' findings would only add grist to the conspiracy theories, he began to despair for the people of the island.

Some of his grandmother's longstanding customers stopped by as well. After two of them pointedly asked him why they had not seen her around lately, the lies came tumbling from his mouth:

"Oh, you just missed her. ...She does not stay out too long anymore. ...She gets tired quickly nowadays..." He went on and on like that. If they pressed him, he mentioned "some bug" that was going around; and since people of a certain age always seemed to believe there was some killer flu wreaking havoc somewhere, he always got a variant of "I hope she feels better soon," as a response.

However, even though he managed to lie his way out of danger, the need for a long-term solution was so obvious that it all left a queasy feeling in the pit of his stomach....

From the way people were talking, it occurred to Shango nobody had found the grinning man's body yet—or spotted the wreck from the road. As he had suspected, unless one knew where to look (and had a sense of what one was looking for/at) the orange patch of the forest floor was meaningless. Shango was tempted to walk down the road and look for himself, but he thought better of it with all the soldiers and government officials lurking about. Either way, as far as he could tell, nobody had even reported the man missing, so Shango returned to his old idea that the universe had erased the man from existence.

By one in the afternoon, he was down to five mangoes. The crowd had swelled into the hundreds. Everywhere he looked, people were talking excitedly. Apparently, the officials were going to make a definitive statement on the soldiers' deaths soon. Even though the rumor had been circulating for hours now, Shango nonetheless felt himself being swept up in the excitement. The usual nervous energy filled him; realizing he had not eaten lunch, he bit into one of the mangoes. In fact, he was chewing absentmindedly when someone from one of the ministries walked up. It was a gaunt man in his forties, whose thick glasses made his eyes seem like specks. The man stopped at the stand and stood looking at the remaining mangoes. Six seconds passed; the man rubbed his chin, as if trying to come to some sort of decision.

Shango was just about to tell the man his price when he began, "Are you usually out here?"

From his tone, Shango instantly knew the man was not interested in buying mangoes. The boy stood straighter and wiped away the mango juice with his arm, willing himself to be alert. "...Only on weekends," he replied.

"What about last Sunday?" the man asked pointedly.

Shango forced himself to remain calm—to shrug nonchalantly and look the man in the eyes. "No, not on Sundays—but sometimes we leave out the fruit, with a can for people to leave money."

The man frowned at the response, and Shango was annoyed with himself, since it sounded bizarre even to him.

"You just leave out things with nobody watching?" he said, looking at the boy fixedly.

Shango nodded before he responded, still trying to scrounge up his composure. "Most of the customers are people my grandmother's known for years," he replied.

"Where's your grandmother?"

Shango felt his legs get go weak from the weight of the question—but then, somehow, a masterstroke of a lie sprang from his mouth, as if the Devil, himself had whispered the words into his ears—

"She's in town," he began, "buying me some new clothes—since I'm going to be on television tomorrow." After the words left Shango's mouth, he stood there in awe, startled by them. In fact, when the man asked him why he was going to be on television, he unconsciously smiled, realizing he had escaped the danger. "I'm going to be in a government contest," he boasted, "—with the island's best students."

"Oh, I heard about that," the man said, impressed; he smiled faintly. "What's your name?" he asked, but when Shango gave his name, he knew the man was only asking so that he would know for whom to cheer. By the time the man asked how much the mangoes cost, Shango knew it was all over. He laughed and gave his price, but while he was marveling at how easy it had been to outwit the man, his dark thoughts—about the investigator's gullibility—made him feel cold and empty inside. After the man was gone, Shango looked down at the empty stand longingly before he headed up the path. There was still time to pick more mangoes to sell, but he did not want to have to lie to anyone else that day.

At the end of the path, he stood looking up at the ugly house, and then the boulder. The day was still young, and yet he felt a restless feeling coming over him. Bewildered, he wandered over to where he had seen the orchid. Like before, he had a strange, anxious feeling that the plant would be gone when he got there. He began jogging, desperate to see it again—

But like before, when he was standing over it, a beatific smile came to his face. He sat down right there, resting his back against a nearby tree trunk. His thoughts verged on idolatry—yet, he could not deny the sense of peace he felt when he stared at the luscious petals. How many religions had started out like that, with one man's irrational peace spreading to the multitudes…?

On Sunday, he again awoke to images of Chicken George's bloody corpse; the soldiers' phantom laughter was there as well, drilling into his head before retreating back into the nothingness. Whatever he had been dreaming had left him with a deep-seated hatred for everyone and everything around him, and he groaned from the horrible weight of it. Remembering the orchid, his first thought was to rush down to the forest, so that he could stare at the flower and revive his peace. Yesterday, he had sat there for hours, daydreaming about nothing in particular until he drifted off to sleep. When he awoke at dusk, he had felt strangely refreshed. Looking out on the darkening world, he had only smiled faintly as he went to fix his evening meal.

Now, as the dark thoughts infested his mind and stifled his peace, he was about to return to the orchid when he realized today was the day of the contest. He sat up in bed excitedly. In his mind, all his enemies would see him on television today. Logically speaking, it was unlikely the laughing soldiers and all those other fools would ever take the time to watch a high school competition; but in his fantasy, all his enemies would tune in to see his triumph. Somehow, even his mother and uncle would view it from America, and know he had succeeded despite their abandonment. In his fantasy, his enemies would come to him after his ascension, desperate to apologize for their past transgressions. It was ridiculous, but the best fantasies often were....

Eventually, he sighed. The fantasy retreated for a moment, but the pending competition continued to fill him with a sense of anxious anticipation. All at once, he felt he would either win the competition and take his rightful revenge, or make some misstep while on air and ruin his life. Somehow, those seemed like the only two possibilities. Common sense told him the safest thing to do was to lose the competition—to stand on stage mutely and avoid drawing attention to himself—but his soul rebelled against it. Too many people had invested their time and hopes in him. Here, he thought not only about Miss Craig's efforts, but his grandmother's as well. He thought about his schoolmates congratulating him on Friday, and the principal looking at him with pride. In fact, for the first time, he felt nervous—since he would disappoint all those people if he lost. He had never really lost anything meaningful before. Whenever he applied himself, he had always excelled. Yet, there was always a first time for everything; and even though he had faith in himself, the universe was cruel—in that it lulled people into believing they could not lose, so that their fall from grace would be even more devastating when they lost.

There was also another reason why he could not lose on purpose. If life required him to be less than he was, then he was not really alive. Before, he had thought of himself as a guerilla soldier, hiding behind the mask of a pathetic little boy. That mask had allowed him to escape death at the hands of Chicken George's murderers—but today, he did not want to hide behind masks anymore. In fact, if he had to hide his greatness in order to survive, then felt it was time for his strange existence to come to an end.

He felt ravenous that morning, so he picked some plantains and fried them with beans and onions. Afterwards, he went over Miss Craig's notes one last time; but by eight in the morning, he was again wandering the house restlessly.

When he picked more mangoes and took them down to the stand, he stood in the mouth of the path uncertainly. All the people from yesterday were gone, so he guessed the officials had come to some kind of decision. His stomach churned as he thought about the consequences, but when a car drove past, and he saw the little girl in the passenger seat laughing with her mother, he felt relieved. Whatever had happened, the world had not stopped spinning.

He arrayed the mangoes on the stand and left the can in front of the mangoes. After that, he walked back up the path, but the nervous excitement would not leave him. When he reached the end of the path and saw the boulder, he wished his grandmother were still there to see his coming triumph. He longed for the old woman; and drawn by thoughts of her, he walked over to the disturbed patch of earth beneath the boulder. The grave was slowly settling; a few sprouts of grass were already growing. Soon, there would be no evidence at all that anyone had been buried there, and he had a sudden, irrational fear that even he would forget. Somehow, he felt it was his duty to keep her memory alive. He had no idea how he could do that *and* keep his secret, but he felt he would be a failure as a human being if he allowed his grandmother's memory to fade away completely.

His dress clothes did not really fit. The slacks were too short, showing the white tube socks his mother had sent last Christmas. His hard-soled shoes were still in the box. He had to retrieve them from where he had stored them in his mother's old room. He had never had a reason to wear them; and when he tried them on he knew his window of opportunity had passed, since he could not even get his heel into the shoe. The dress shirt his mother had sent was actually too big for him, so when he was standing there in the slacks and shirt, he knew the outfit was too ridiculous to wear on national television.

He stripped them off in frustration, but that left only one option: his school uniform. With all the money he had made that week, he could go into town now and buy some new clothes from Gupta's, but somehow that seemed like a waste.

By nine in the morning, Shango was dressed and ready to go. He had agreed to meet Maitland around noon, but given everything that was happening on the island, there was always the possibility that Maitland had forgotten about the contest. Maybe the man had gone to another part of the island to cover a story—or some other emergency had come up. Thus, Shango decided it was better to leave early, just to make sure. He put some of his mango money into his bag—in case he had to take a minibus into the capital—then left the house.

It was odd being in his school uniform on the weekend. He felt as though time had gone wrong somewhere, and that he had become hopelessly disconnected from the world around him. After exiting the forest path, he stopped to look at the stand. Remembering Maitland, he took three of the mangoes and put them in his bag, figuring he would present them as a gift—or have something to eat if he had to make the long journey to the capital by himself.

As always, he stopped when he reached the bend in the road, and stared down at the grinning man's car. Somehow, none of the investigators and curious onlookers had noticed it, and Shango began to wonder if it was only a figment of his imagination. Maybe the patch of orange was only a manifestation of his madness. He allowed his mind to roam the various possibilities, but then he groaned and moved on when he realized he was thinking nonsense.

Forty minutes later, Shango entered the ugly town. Since it was Sunday, the streets were practically deserted. Yet, even in the residential areas, the townspeople had barricaded themselves within their homes, as if taking shelter from a storm. There was an eerie silence about the place. The stray dogs were cowering in the shadows; even the birds and vermin seemed gone from the town, and Shango found himself moving more quickly.

Chicken George's blood was still on the pavement. Shango stopped to look at it. He wondered where they had taken the man's corpse. They had probably dumped it in an unmarked grave somewhere. Nobody was ever going to complain about the local lunatic going missing. Seeing the injustice, Shango felt the rage growing in him—yet, as always, there was nothing to do but keep moving forward....

He figured he would check to see if Maitland's car was there, then he would wander the town until it was time to go to the capital. Maybe he would go window shopping at Gupta's or buy something to eat, or just sit somewhere and think. Yet, he felt haunted; as he approached each alleyway, he kept expecting Chicken George to spring out to surprise him. The first few times, he paused and looked down the alleyway, bracing himself for Chicken George's "Bock-bi-cow!" but there was never anything but the eerie silence.

When he saw Maitland's old Volkswagen, he was initially relieved, but then his soul rebelled against the prospect of waiting two hours in this horrible place. He was almost tempted to walk back up the mountain, where the air was at least fresh and there were no potential ghosts waiting to spring from alleyways.

Like before, he was about five paces from Maitland's door when it opened unexpectedly. He paused; Maitland stepped out of the door holding a box. It was only when the man spotted him and let out a welcoming, "Hey!" that Shango finished walking toward him. As was usually the case, he felt suddenly shy.

"I was just passing," he began to explain his early arrival, "—I didn't mean to bother you."

"Nonsense," he said with a smile. "You couldn't have come at a better time. I have to run an errand anyway, so it may be easier if you come with me now."

"Okay," Shango said, but he was suddenly relieved to have company again—even if it was only to keep the ghosts at bay.

F ive minutes later, they were driving out of town, down a road Shango had never taken before. It did not matter, as long as the town was behind them. The window was open, and he closed his eyes, letting the wind hit him in the face. The sensation made him smile. Maitland asked him how he felt about the contest. Shango paused to think about it:

"I'm going to win," he said at last.

Maitland laughed. "Overconfident?" he joked.

"I have to win," Shango said simply, staring out of the windscreen.

Maitland instinctively wanted to ask follow-up questions, but something about the resolute expression in Shango's eyes told him there was no point. The boy had said he was going to win, so he was going to win.

There was silence for a while; it was Shango who spoke up first:

"What did the investigators decide—about the soldiers?"

"Oh," Maitland said as if he had forgotten. "They said it was an accident—that the brakes failed."

Shango detected skepticism in the man's voice. "You don't believe them?"

"No," he said simply.

Shango watched him closely. "Why not?" he asked.

"It's too easy."

Despite himself, Shango snickered.

"You disagree?" the man asked.

"Sometimes simple answers are the right ones."

"Not in my experience. Not on *this* island."

Shango looked over at him critically once more, wondering where his logic had gone wrong. In all likelihood, Maitland had spent so much time trying to uncover obscure truths that he had come to distrust obvious facts. Like many conspiracy theorists, the more convoluted an answer became, the more plausible it seemed to him. Shango felt sorry for him; but as always, he realized he could not correct the man without revealing too much. Indeed, he began to wonder if this might be the time to reveal all his secrets to his friend. Suddenly ready to shed the burden from his shoulders, Shango cleared his throat and looked over at the old man.

"...The policeman from that day," he began obliquely. When Maitland looked over at him confusedly, Shango clarified, "The day we met...when the Range Rover crashed."

"Oh," Maitland said, remembering. "You mean *Charles*."

Shango nodded. "You seemed to *know* him."

"Charles was my student."

"*Daddis* was?" Shango said, surprised. Then, "You used to teach?"

"Yeah, *years* ago...Charles was one of my best students—maybe even *the* best." He smiled as he recalled something: "I tried to teach him about the pen being mightier than the sword, and he swore he'd teach me that strength came from fists and guns. I'll never forget what he said: 'The rich man builds walls because he fears the poor, uneducated man. The poor man fears nothing, while the rich man's education only teaches him how to be afraid.' ...Well, we've been struggling ever since, waiting to see which one would win: his brutality or my pen."

"Who's winning?" Shango said with a smile.

Maitland chuckled. "Only time will tell, my young friend."

Shango was just about to reveal the details of the Range Rover incident when Maitland's phone began to ring. At first, Shango waited patiently as the old man answered the phone; but five minutes later, Maitland was still ranting about the evil works of the island's political class. By then, Shango again returned to thinking it was best to let secrets lie hidden. Besides, after a while, he became impressed by the way Maitland was able to talk on the phone, steer the vehicle and work the stick shift at the same time. None of it was safe, but it was one of those awe-inspiring skills people acquired when they set their minds on doing stupid things.

E ven when Maitland was off the phone, he continued to rant— ostensibly to Shango, since there was no one else there—but in truth, he was just venting his rage. Shango tried to follow his argument, but like the unreadable articles in the old man's newspaper, Shango soon came to the conclusion there was no point. When pressed, Shango nodded or grunted; but otherwise, he just stared out of the window, at the scenery.

Objectively speaking, the island was beautiful. They were nearing the coast now, and Shango could see the ocean in the distance. The water was clear and blue—aquamarine—and the sky was vibrant and cloudless. The sea air had a good, clean scent—even though he found himself thinking he preferred the scent of the mountain—

Maitland slammed on the brakes and pulled over quickly. Shango looked over at him anxiously before following his eyes and looking through the windshield. About a hundred meters away, a military transport was parked in front of someone's house. A dozen or more soldiers had amassed by the vehicle, brandishing their weapons; as Shango looked on, two old men were dragged out the front door in handcuffs, their clothes disheveled and their faces bloody. They were screaming something, but it was impossible to make out the words at that distance. Shango looked over at Maitland, as if hoping he would be able to translate, but the old man only stared ahead with a horrified expression on his face. He sat there grasping the steering wheel so tightly that the veins on his neck and arms bulged; his face became flushed...but seeing there was nothing he could do for his comrades, the old man's body slumped, like a balloon that was slowly leaking air.

A minute or two later, the soldiers and their captives had all boarded the transport. Yet, even after the vehicle had disappeared down the road, Maitland sat there staring into the distance with a haunted expression on his face. Maybe another minute passed before he put the car in gear and made a U-turn. At first, he took off recklessly, as if desperate to put distance between himself and the soldiers. However, when something occurred to him, he took out his cellular phone once more.

"They got Harris and Smith," he said when the person on the other end of the call answered. "...Protect yourself," he continued, before shoving the phone back into his pocket.

Initially, Shango said nothing. However, at last, he ventured, "Are you in trouble?"

Maitland only continued to stare ahead. Just as Shango was telling himself the man had not heard him, Maitland sighed and said, "The *nation's* in trouble. We're all just bystanders, swept up in it...."

"Why are they afraid of those old men?" Shango asked eventually; as soon as the words left his mouth, he realized they sounded insulting. He put up his hand to apologize, but Maitland only smiled.

"...They fear us because they used to be us," he began. As he talked, he instinctively eased off the pedal, so that their mad flight became more sedate. "We remind them of who they used to be and what they used to believe," he said, looking off into the distance." ...Thirty, forty years ago we were at the same meetings, talking black liberation from imperialists and declaring war on the pathetic old men we had for leaders. Now, *they* are those pathetic old men. They sold their souls to become rich and powerful, young Shango, and now they seek to destroy us—since we're bitter reminders of everything they lost."

Shango was not sure he understood the man's words, but there was a kind of emotional truth to them, so he nodded his head as he stared out of the window.

They did not talk much during the drive to the capital. They passed through a few checkpoints along the way. At first, Shango held his breath as soldiers stopped them and glared at them; but by the end, he took it all in stride—as if he had somehow become battle-hardened during the ride.

The capital was not exactly beautiful, but the parts of it that catered to tourists had a posh feel. Tourism was the process of selling illusions to foreigners; so, at a few intersections, there were grinning islanders in straw hats holding up trinkets for passing vehicles. Shango recalled himself holding up the mangoes as tour buses passed, and felt suddenly ashamed. Maybe those impulses had been bred into them; maybe those raised with the tourism mentality inevitably came to see foreigners only as potential sources of income, instead of fellow human beings...

The national television studio was headquartered in what passed as the island's industrial park. There were warehouses in the area and a few sweatshops that made clothing and some other unremarkable goods for export. The parking lot was practically full when they got there. Dozens of people were making their way to the entrance, all of them dressed in their "Sunday best." Maybe it was only then that the contest became real to Shango. He sat straighter in the seat.

When Maitland finally found a parking spot, they got out of the vehicle and began walking toward the entrance. Maitland tapped him on the back when he saw how tense he seemed; Shango smiled shyly.

A queue had formed by the entrance. Some guards and police-men were checking people's tickets. Maitland was retrieving his ticket from his shirt pocket when Miss Craig came running toward them. Shango literally jumped back, since she seemed to appear out of nowhere.

"There you are!" she screeched, sweating and wheezing from running. When Shango looked up at her confusedly, she grabbed his arm and said, "Come this way. This line isn't for you. We use the *stage* entrance." Maitland went to follow them, but when she glared at him, he froze. Shango looked back at him apologetically, but Miss Craig was dragging him by the arm now. It was only after they had turned the corner of the building that she stopped and faced him. For some reason, her face was hard and her voice was cold:

"Are you related to that man?" she demanded, frowning and gesturing toward the front of the building.

Shango frowned as well, looking at her confusedly. "...No, he's just a friend."

"You need to choose better friends," she chastised him. Then, "Where's your family? Are they aware you associate with such people?"

He did not like her tone at all; and all at once, her beauty seemed to fade away, leaving only an ugly husk. The only thing Shango could do was stare—

"Anyway," she continued, "let's just get you ready—since you're late." At that, she gripped him by the upper arm and pulled him along; but from that point on, he was through with her.

There were more guards at the stage entrance. However, they all seemed to know Miss Craig, because they made way for her as she approached with Shango. She took him to a backstage area, where some of the other contestants and their families had gathered. Through an open doorway, he could see the studio— or at least the audience as they took their seats. He was looking around vaguely when Miss Craig suddenly exclaimed:

"Why are you in your school uniform?"

He looked up at her, feeling himself on the verge of saying something rude, but then she shrugged.

"I guess it's too late to do anything at this point," she mused. "...Are you nervous?" she asked him now. "Do you need anything? Do you remember our lessons...?" She was panting after her rapid-fire questions. Despite himself, Shango smiled.

"Everything's okay," he began. Then, colder than he had intended: "You can leave me now."

She stared at him uncertainly for a while; but then, exhausted by the day's stress, she nodded and headed toward the studio to find her seat.

The other students all seemed to be at least three years older than Shango. Most—perhaps sixty-five percent—were girls. The boys towered over him, yet he felt the excitement from that morning returning. He was just about to smile when his eyes came to rest on one of the contestants. He stared at her for three or four seconds before he realized where he knew her from. It was the girl from the Range Rover—the beautiful girl. She had actually been staring at him for a while, her expression inscrutable. When she nodded, he followed suit—but her entourage of relatives and friends surrounded her then, blocking her from Shango's view. A woman Shango assumed to be her mother was doting on her, fixing her hair and dress. Others were practically yelling their encouragement to her. Unaccountably, Shango felt the resentment rising in him. For her, and people like her, the invisible machinery of the island would always move heaven and earth. Maybe his thoughts were clouded by his time with Maitland—and the dark events of the past few weeks—but now, instead of seeing a person, he saw only her wealth and privilege. Indeed, now that he looked around, his opponents all seemed to be from well-to-do families. He could tell by their clothes and their entourages. Frowning, he wondered how many government ministers had lobbied to have their children and relatives included in this contest. Instead of merely matching wits against them, Shango somehow saw the competition as a revolutionary act: a chance to obliterate the faceless power structure that ruled the island. His ambitions were grandiose and ridiculous, but a new resolve entered his eyes now.

While the other students and their entourages talked excitedly amongst themselves, Shango stood there silently by himself. It was not that he did not feel he needed anyone—it certainly felt good to know Maitland and Miss Craig would be in the audience, ready to cheer him on—but he was acutely aware he did not *need* their cheers. There was an entire reservoir of strength within him, waiting to be tapped, and he smiled imperceptibly, knowing he was ready.

A few minutes later, a stern-looking woman in her sixties came to tell the entourages to find their seats. Once they were gone, she addressed the contestants, congratulating them and laying out the contest rules before the broadcast started. There were eighteen competitors. They had been randomly assigned to three groups of six. The top two from each group would advance to the final round. Shango listened attentively, but otherwise showed no emotion.

The stern woman's final act was to assign the contestants to their groups. Shango was to be in the first group. He took note that the beautiful girl was in the third—and that her name was Paula Browne—but then he grew annoyed with himself for noticing.

F ifteen minutes later, he was being marched out onto the stage. The announcer was a giggly fat man in his forties who was supposed to be affable. The audience laughed at his jokes, but Shango only found him annoying. The six contestants sat at a long table, while the announcer stood at an oblique angle from them, behind a lectern. The audience, which was composed primarily of the contestants' entourages, seemed tense. Shango saw only a sea of shadowed faces. The announcer made some comments and made a joke that was supposedly funny—since everyone else laughed uproariously—but Shango only sat there stone-faced, preparing himself.

Each station had a buzzer in front of it. The contestants were told to get ready, and then it all began. Shango felt like he was having an out-of-body experience. Obscure information was suddenly on the tip of his tongue: the colors of the rainbow, the countries Columbus had visited on his various voyages. In math and science, no one else even had time to press the buzzer. He reiterated the intricacies of scientific laws like a university professor. When the announcer jokingly asked him if he wanted to give someone else a chance to answer, Shango merely said "No, sir." The announcer laughed uneasily, not sure if Shango was joking. When Shango's expression remained grave, the announcer again laughed uneasily before moving on awkwardly.

The first group was not even close. Shango *obliterated* them. One girl began to cry during a commercial break. Shango was ruthless. The other contestants looked at him with a strange combination of awe and hatred. Shango did not care. If anything, it pleased him. In the aftermath, his vanquished competitors slumped offstage, where they sat in a near catatonic state, asking themselves what had just happened. He felt no sympathy, and he found himself thinking that if he somehow lost, he did not want any sympathy either—no insipid, "You tried your best" comments…

Yet, his competitors' crestfallen expressions began to irk him, so he wandered away by himself. He went to the bathroom and washed his face. When he returned, he noticed the beautiful girl—Paula Browne—was looking at him intently. He ignored her, took a seat in the corner, sat back, and closed his eyes.

The waiting made him restless; it grated against his nerves to listen to the contestants in the second group missing answers that seemed obvious to him. Frustrated, he stood up and walked outside. The guards—and the contest's producers—were reluctant to let him leave the building, but he assured them he would stay within view of the guards…

It felt good to breathe warm, fresh air—instead of the cold, filtered air of the studio. He stood against the building, watching traffic zooming by, birds flying in the sky, and anything else that would pass the time. He breathed deeply.

Half an hour later, he was called into the studio for the final round. Paula was one of the finalists. Despite himself, the reality of her made him lose focus. When he was on stage with her, his mind kept drifting to thoughts of Daddis' glistening incisor. With his distraction, she answered the first two questions. The audience seemed to love her, because their applause was like a roar. She was the embodiment of everything they celebrated, and it was only that realization that brought back his old ruthlessness. A strange madness seized him; he was overcome by the desire to see her crying like his first round opponents. Driven by that madness, he rang the buzzer and practically shouted the correct response to the next question. A minute later, he had already caught up to her score; by the commercial break, he was twenty points ahead. During the break, he forced himself not to look at her—not to think of anything but his brutal will.

Halfway through the next series of questions, Shango was the only one with points. He heard Miss Craig in the audience, cheering raucously when he answered an obscure literature question. However, he made the mistake of looking over at Paula after answering a question on Boyle's Law. There was a bizarre expression on her face—something like joy. He checked the other four competitors' grim faces, then looked back at her. They sat staring at one another—perhaps the way they had stared at one another that first time—realizing they would perhaps always be bound by their shared journey into the darker places of human existence. While they were staring at one another, one of the other competitors had the chance to ring the buzzer. When she gave the wrong answer, Shango buzzed in with the correct one. However, the ruthlessness was gone from him by then. The competition, which he had previously viewed as way of proving his superiority, now just seemed silly. Toward the end, when his lead was insurmountable, he stopped buzzing in—literally giving others a chance as the announcer had joked. He sat there numbly, staring blankly into space. It all seemed so anticlimactic that he did not understand the wild applause and congratulations that came his way when the final round was over.

He was on his feet now, shaking hands with people. Paula patted him on the shoulder, still smiling with an odd gleam in her eyes. Shango merely nodded. ...Somehow, Miss Craig and Principal Williams were on the stage now, congratulating him. A man who was supposedly the Minister of Education was there to shake his hand and to declare that Shango had just won the equivalent of five thousand US dollars. None of it seemed possible. The broadcast ended on that note, with the announcer thanking everyone and congratulating Shango. In all the chaos, Shango kept looking over at Paula, wondering what her strange joy could possibly mean.

With the show over, the audience was getting up to leave. The minister was a chubby man in his late fifties. He was flirting with Miss Craig now; and for some reason, she was giggling at his inane comments. It was only when Shango saw Maitland step onto the stage that he smiled. Soon, they were shaking hands.

However, while Maitland was patting him on the back, Miss Craig suddenly confronted Maitland with, "Why are you even here?"

When Shango looked over at her, there was a scowl on his face; even the minister was glaring at the old man, and Shango felt his skin growing hot. Before he even had time to think, he blurted out, "Mr. Maitland's my friend!" He looked up at the startled old man then, nodding. "He's my *best* friend," he said, trembling at the realization. In fact, he almost felt he would cry, and paused to keep the tears at bay. He lowered his voice and eyes, fighting to maintain his composure now. "That's why he's here," he continued. "He drove me here when there was no one. He's been a *friend* to me—"

"Well, someone else can take you home," Miss Craig interrupted him. "He does not need to be here," she said with a dismissive wave of her hand.

Shango opened his mouth, feeling he could actually curse her; his lips were already trembling; his hands were clenching—

"If it's fine, then I'll leave you, young Shango," Maitland said then.

"But Mr. Maitland…"

"I did have some errands to run," he said somberly, "so if someone else can take you…"

Shango lowered his eyes; Maitland continued:

"I'm so proud of you, young Shango—not just for winning, but for remembering who you are." He nodded again, and smiled. When he held out his hand, Shango grasped it strongly before the old man left him. Shango stared at his retreating form, but the old man did not look back. Afterwards, the place seemed emptier without him; and when Miss Craig tried to say something upbeat to restart the festive mood, Shango heard nothing at all.

Paula and her entourage came over to congratulate Shango. A corpulent older man said he was Paula's father. The man patted Shango on the back and praised him liberally; but in truth, much of it passed Shango in a blur. Apparently, Paula's father and the minister were great friends, because they hugged one another and spoke obliquely about some business at "the club." When the entourage left, Shango was vaguely aware that he was to go out with them to celebrate. By then, he was merely going with the flow. Even though the contest was over, and he had ostensibly achieved his objective, he felt as though none of it had really happened.

Five minutes later, he found himself in the passenger seat of the minister's BMW, looking over at the policeman who was the man's driver. In the back seat, the minister canoodled with Miss Craig while her coquettish giggles echoed unsettling in the closed vehicle and made Shango's skin crawl.

To block it all out, he stared out of the window—at the streets of the capital. They were driving through a posh area now—a tourist haven with trendy shops that offered "duty free" merchandise for tourists. The lagoon was to the left; a cruise ship was anchored in the harbor, like a monstrous beast tied up by its master.

Sulking in his seat, Shango wished he had gone with Maitland—but he realized as well (at least intuitively) that he had done the old man a favor by parting ways. From the scene earlier today—at his comrade's home—Shango guessed Maitland had more than his fair share of problems without the added responsibility of keeping Shango safe. When one was in danger, it was some-times more reassuring to know one's friends were far from that danger. Yet, even though Shango knew there was nothing he could do to help the old man in his coming battles, he felt like a horrible friend for allowing him to fight those battles alone.

By the time they parked in the restaurant's parking lot, Miss Craig was walking hand-in-hand with the minister. Shango did not know if he was jealous or ashamed for her. The minister was probably twice her age. Worse, the man was not exactly handsome either. It had never occurred to him Miss Craig might be the kind of woman who would be attracted to a man merely for his power and prestige, yet he could find nothing else about the man that might appeal to her. At any rate, he was annoyed with himself for thinking these thoughts—and annoyed with her, since her antics forced his mind to dwell on such frivolities.

Shango walked ahead of them as they made their way around the restaurant to get to the front entrance. At the entrance, about two dozen people were talking excitedly; most, if not all of them, had just come from the contest—since Shango recognized some of his competitors. When Shango looked back, he saw the minister clapping another one of his old friends on the back. He groaned and stepped to the side to wait. Unfortunately, Shango was a star now. Someone began snapping his picture; a woman, who said she was a reporter, started asking him inane questions about how he felt and if he was happy. At one point, when her questions began to grate against his nerves, he found himself saying, "I assure you madam, I am happy." The woman laughed at his precise phrasing, perhaps thinking he was trying to be droll; Shango forced himself to try to smile, in order to reassure her and curtail further questions about his happiness.

He nodded his head and tried to move on, but that was when a short, middle aged Indian woman stepped before him, congratulating him profusely. He wanted to be annoyed with her, but something about her sweet, matronly face kept his darker thoughts in check. From her excited chatter, his mind extracted something about running a charity and being proud of him. He thanked her for thanking him and was thinking about how he would get away when she said:

"Oh, where's my husband. I'm sure he'd *love* to meet you." She began looking around frantically, and then waved when she finally spotted her husband standing in a group of old men. It was Gupta. The man looked over glumly when he saw his wife standing there with his old adversary. As his wife pressed him, he extricated himself from the group and came over like a disobedient child called by his mother. Gupta's wife introduced Shango to him; Gupta dutifully shook Shango's hand and nodded his head with a fake smile.

Shango considered the bizarre couple then. She was sweet and gregarious, while he was so obviously a frustrated old bastard. Yet, maybe that contradictory pairing was why they were so successful as a couple. Gupta butchered the meat and she made marvelous meals out of it. He was all blood and guts, and she was delicate seasonings and artistic presentations.

Shortly after that, the minister came over with Miss Craig, saying he was hungry. When they entered the restaurant, Shango saw even more of his vanquished opponents from the contest. They were seated with their families, receiving consolation and praise. The girl he had made cry in the first round seemed to have recovered, because she waved at him. He nodded his head and smiled. Now that the competition was over, his strange ruthlessness seemed totally bizarre and unwarranted. In retrospect, even though he was glad he had won, he felt no real pride. He was aware he had built up the competition to something it could never really be. He had waged war against people who had been no match for him, and so he almost felt like a bully. ...Had he really won the equivalent of five thousand US dollars? He vaguely remembered that announcement at the contest, but now it seemed too farfetched to be believed.

Paula was there, still smiling at him in that peculiar way. The maître d' was a slender, effeminate man with a thin mustache (like some really bad stereotype). He talked excitedly about how he had a "really nice" table set up for the minister—to which the minister grunted his approval, as if to say he deserved nothing less than a really nice table.

The "really nice" table was about two tables away from Paula's. It was right next to the window, which seemed to be its main selling point. Shango sat facing the window, so he could look out on the lagoon and the tourists wandering the streets; Miss Craig and the minister sat with their backs against the scene, perhaps preferring to look around the restaurant and be seen by their friends. At any rate, as the minister whispered something in her ear, and she began to giggle again, Shango was acutely aware he had become the third wheel in their budding romance. He sighed and stared vaguely out of the window. When he glanced to the side, he realized Paula was staring at him intently. He still could not figure out what that look in her eyes *meant*. He wished he could talk to her—away from all these people. Yet, at the same time, he feared being alone with her. He feared the secrets behind her smile—even while his mind was quickly becoming obsessed with them.

The waiter came; the minister ordered lobster for Miss Craig and Shango, then laughed pompously at a joke that Shango did not really catch. Feeling trapped, the boy sighed again. He was just contemplating the long, torturous hours ahead when there was suddenly a commotion at the maître d's stand.

"Ma'am, you can't go in yet!" the effeminate man protested, but the woman stormed in nonetheless. She was heavyset and middle aged—with a florid expression on her face that warned the world she was not going to take any nonsense. When Shango looked, she was marching in his direction. He instinctively recoiled, thinking she had somehow come to bash his brains in, but she went straight for Paula's table instead.

"So, I see you're alive after all!" the woman began sarcastically. Apparently, she was addressing Paula's father, because she glared down at him.

"Mrs. Armstrong," he began formally, not even deigning to look up at her, "now is not the time—"

"Then when *is* the time? *Three* weeks now my husband's missing!" she raged, holding up three pudgy fingers as she slipped into the local patois. "He go to work for you, call me *from* work, yet you don't want to answer simple questions about what happened to him!"

When Paula's father ignored her, the woman's rage exploded!

"Eh, Mr. Big and Powerful, you think you can make this go away? You think you can shut me up and bribe police to look the other way—"

The head waiter came up, whispering for her to calm down, but that only seemed to enrage her further; when the man put his manicured hand on her shoulder, she pushed it away and glared at him so threateningly that he retreated two steps and stood there cowering.

She turned back to the table, a vindictive look entering her eyes. "All you fancy people in your nice clothes…You don't think my husband used to tell me about what was going on in your house? *Eh?*" she demanded when Browne remained mute.

"Madam, this is not the place!" the man bellowed again. Shango watched his face twitching with rage and ineptitude—since he saw there was nothing he could do to stop her—"

"Don't 'madam' me you, old *pervert!* …You're all high and mighty in public, but behind closed doors you're a *demon*, sneaking into your daughter's bedroom at night—"

Several people gasped. Shango probably did not even comprehend what she had said at first. He was merely lost in the spectacle of high class adults shouting at one another like street vendors.

"Lying down with your own *daughter!*" the woman screeched now, pointing an accusatory finger at Paula. Shango followed her hand, still dazed. He blinked several times in quick succession, as if his mind were sputtering, unable to start the process of comprehension and interpretation. When Shango looked around confusedly, everyone seemed to be staring down at his or her table—or off into the distance—as if even then trying to erase the woman's accusations from their minds. Indeed, no one was looking at the woman anymore, as if refusing to see her. Her accusations were merely something to be forgotten now, and ignored in polite society.

When Shango looked back at Paula, he realized she had been staring at him all that time. He stared back at her; and in time, it occurred to him she was looking to see if his view of her had changed—if he saw her as damaged now, or corrupted. In the entire restaurant, they were the only ones looking up. Even Paula's doting mother had a dull expression on her face as she stared down at her plate, pretending not to hear.

Amazingly, the girl smiled then—a beautiful smile in the midst of so many ugly realities. Sometimes beauty was a mask for ugliness; sometimes it was like the sun, shedding light on everything and banishing darkness from the deepest crevice. All at once, Shango realized why she had smiled at the contest. She had seen that Shango was more than what he seemed to be—that he had been more than the poverty his mud-stained clothes had implied; he had not merely been a passive victim of the horrors around him, but had instead *transcended* them. Staring at her now, he saw she had somehow managed to transcend her own horrors—

"Eh!" the woman began again, still glaring down at Paula's father, "You think you can keep secrets on this island? People *told* me the last thing they saw was my husband driving away with your daughter—taking her away to safety because of what he had seen…and you *still* think you can keep secrets?" She sucked her teeth, but the dumb silence of the people in the restaurant only seemed to frustrate her. Maybe it was only then that she saw the true monster was not Paula's father, but the society that knew the truth and did not *shun* that monster.

As the woman stood there deflated, Shango was finally able to digest the whole picture. The person Daddis' men gunned down in the ravine had been the woman's husband. Shango's eyes grew wide as he saw it all. However, by now, the woman had lost most of her fire, seeing the extent to which society protected its monsters. Bewildered, she took a few wobbly steps back, turned, and made her way tentatively out of the restaurant.

As she was doing so, two police cars came to a screeching halt in front of the restaurant. Shango—and everyone else—watched them via the window. In a moment of shock, Shango recognized Daddis and the very same policemen he had seen at the ravine that day. The underlings ran ahead and apprehended the woman as soon as she came out of the door. Daddis stayed behind, the brutality shining from his eyes as he watched the scene. The woman did not fight. The policemen did not even have to handcuff her. They held her by her shoulders and placed her in the back of one of the police cruisers.

Daddis nodded his head when he saw the work had been done. He was about to return to the car when he looked through the restaurant window and met Shango's eyes. When he did, he froze. In his eyes, there was the same malevolent expression from weeks ago, when he saw Shango standing with Maitland in the town.

The man seemed to calculate all his options in an instant; but seeing he could do nothing at the moment, he turned and walked briskly to his car. Within seconds, the police cars disappeared in a cloud of exhaust and burning tire rubber. Shango felt sick inside, knowing no good would come of this.

Ten seconds later, people were already pretending nothing had happened. Polite conversations resumed; some people were already joking that the woman had merely been crazy. Shango had never been as disappointed in the human race as at that moment. The lobster came, but he was in no mood to eat. He kept looking over at Paula. Maybe that was the only thing that gave him hope and kept him from total despair. Somehow, she was managing to survive...but was it enough to merely survive?

"I'm not feeling well," he told the minister and Miss Craig. "Is there any way I could be taken home?"

"I'll call my driver," the minister said, taking out his phone. In truth, the man seemed happy to get rid of the boy; and as the man went back to eyeing Miss Craig suggestively, Shango was happy to be done with them as well.

When the driver was there, Shango simply got up, leaving the happy couple to whatever they were doing. As he turned from the table, he paused for a moment, nodded to Paula—as if to say they would meet again, and that they should both stay strong until then—then he left.

It was night when he reached the town again. Somehow, he felt no need to hide anymore, so he had the driver take him all the way up to the vegetable stand. The mangoes he had put out earlier were gone, so he merely picked up the can and made his way up the dark path, to his home. He realized he felt no terror at all when he was walking through the forest by himself. There was no running, no jumping at unknown noises in the darkness... Now that the island's secrets had been exposed, all those childish fears were behind him.

H e slept soundly and peacefully. In the morning, he opened his eyes and stared out at the cloudless, azure sky. He had gotten used to waking up to terrifying flashbacks of the previous days' horrors, but today he only felt numb. He recalled winning the contest—and the revelations about what had really happened at the ravine...and Paula's smile. The good seemed to cancel out the bad, leaving only the numbness. He had a sudden desire to talk to Maitland; he remembered Daddis' menacing stare, grimacing.

Sighing, he got up and started his day. Forty-five minutes later, he was walking down the mountain. He paused only briefly to look for the grinning man's car. Vines or other plants seemed to have covered it completely, because there was no sign of it today. Shrugging, he moved on.

He did not realize it at first, but the soldiers were gone from the town. He wondered what had happened behind the scenes to change the government's response. Maybe they had captured, killed or otherwise neutralized all the so-called radicals on the island. Maybe, Shango thought strangely, all of it had merely been the product of another powerful man's desire to keep secrets hidden. Whose toes had Cuthbert inadvertently stepped on? All at once, perverted intrigues seemed to lie behind all their daily horrors; yet, like Paula's molestation, Shango suspected the truth was lying out in the open somewhere. Now that his eyes were open, there was no telling what terrible things he might see, so he proceeded cautiously as he waded into the filth.

A s soon as he entered school, the congratulations began. The boys in the schoolyard surrounded him. Even the two factions of popular kids seemed to have reconciled, because there was suddenly a sense of unity and common purpose everywhere. Miss Craig was a little hung over and drowsy, but she praised him so much her voice soon became hoarse. Other teachers led standing ovations for him once he entered their classes. He thanked them, and was gracious, but he still felt numb inside.

In fact, his uneasiness grew as the day progressed. He kept seeing Daddis' malevolent eyes. He cursed himself for not going to Maitland first thing in the morning, to warn him—or to receive his protection, or whatever it was that he wanted from the man. By then, all he could think about was making it to the end of the day, so that he could go to his friend.

However, after school, the popular kids ambushed him again. He tolerated them as best as he could; he walked with them toward the gate, and answered their questions—but he did not allow Clark to bombard him with faux questions anymore. Instead, he answered them methodically, forcing them all to adopt his rhythms. At the front gate, he was about to tell them bluntly that they should part ways for the day, but that was when he looked across the street and saw Daddis sitting in an unmarked car. He swung around immediately, his heart racing—

"I forgot something in class," he lied; then, before the popular kids could ask him any further questions, he ran back the way he had come. ...What was he supposed to do now? The only reason Daddis would be there was to take him away. Shango felt sick; he ran faster, desperate to flee...but was there anywhere he could hide at this point? When he reached the staircase, his steps faltered. There really was no place on the island he could hide from the man—unless he stopped coming to school and stayed holed up on the mountain. He grimaced, nibbling his lower lip nervously.

When he looked back, the popular kids were waiting for him, and looking in his direction. To buy himself some time, he continued walking up the stairs. However, once he reached the second floor, and was out of sight, he ran to the back of the school, where there was another staircase. This one led to a storage room that mostly had junk the school had never gotten around to throwing out: decrepit furniture from the nineteen seventies, cracked blackboards, and the like.

The back staircase overlooked someone's private property. There was a fence there, but some of the boys used the yard as a shortcut. Acting impulsively, Shango jumped down one flight, to the ground, leaped over the fence, then ran across the yard, to where there was another fence. A dog, he realized, was chasing him. Terrified, he vaulted over a tall wall, and then somehow found himself in an alleyway. He only had a vague idea of where he was; but as the dog continued barking, he ran for his life—

Maitland: the man suddenly popped into his mind—as an oasis in a wasteland of nightmares. At the next intersection, Shango stopped to get his bearings; when he figured out the direction of his friend's house, he began sprinting. In ten minutes, he was there. Maitland's car was in front of the building. He paused; but seeing no more policemen in unmarked cars, he entered the building and ran up the stairs.

"Mr. Maitland!" he screamed halfway up the stairs. At the top, he opened his mouth again, scanning the loft, but the familiar stench of death was in the air; and when he turned his head and looked up, he froze. Maitland's corpse was hanging from one of the rafters. There was no doubt that he was dead—and that he had been dead for hours. His tongue was hanging out of his mouth, his eyes bulged from their sockets, and his face, itself was swollen and blacker. The man's pants were soiled, from where his bowels had released. Shango saw but did not see. He had the same disconnected feeling he had had after seeing his grandmother's corpse that first time. There was some adult thing he should be doing, but his mind was unable to tell him what it was.

Presently, as the wind blew through the open window, the corpse turned slowly on its axis; the flies circling it were like rogue satellites hurtling into one another. When planet Maitland made it halfway through its orbit, Shango noticed the man's hands were tied behind his back. For the first time, he noticed the overturned chair on the floor. Either someone had tried to make this seem like a suicide—and had foolishly neglected to untie Maitland's hands—or they really did not care about covering their tracks, and this was merely a warning for others. It was probably only then that Shango saw all the horrible contours; overcome, he sank to his knees and began to sob. He was on all fours now, groveling on the ground as the grief wracked his body. He was in this position when the top step creaked loudly behind him—

Shango swung around, wiping away his tears hastily to restore his blurred vision. However, Daddis was already there, towering over him. Shango saw, right away, that there was no point in running. When Daddis gestured for Shango to rise, the boy complied. His tears had stopped flowing by then, and he saw everything with terrible clarity. It was not that he accepted his fate: fate did not care if you accepted it or not; fate did as it pleased, and all Shango could think was that he would keep his dignity in these final moments, regardless of where fate took him.

Daddis placed his hand on Shango's shoulder—almost tenderly this time. "I left this here for you, youth man," he explained, motioning to Maitland's corpse. "Learn from this, and you'll live a good, long life."

Reflexively, Shango nodded—not in agreement, but because good manners almost demanded that he show the man he understood.

"I'm not going to harm you, youth man," Daddis continued, his voice solemn now. There was something almost professorial about him as he explained, "For you to learn from this, you have to understand why I did it. I didn't kill Maitland out of fear or anger. I killed him to give his life meaning. I did it out of *mercy*— and to save you from following his pointless path.

"You come from country people, right?" he began now.

At his prompting, Shango again nodded reflexively.

"Good, so you know when one animal gets sick, you sometimes have to kill the rest of them to keep the disease from spreading. I don't want to see you catching disease too, Shango Cartwright. I just saved your life and you don't even know it. In ten, twenty years...when you're old enough to see I saved you, you'll *thank* me."

Here, he paused, allowing Shango to digest his words. When he saw the boy understood, he nodded gravely and released Shango's shoulder. "Go home now," Daddis said then. "Go home and live a good life...and *learn* from this."

Somehow, Shango found his legs moving. Soon, he was walking down the stairs; in time, the ugly town was behind him, and he was walking up the mountain road, but he had no real destination in mind. He was like a dead man on his feet. There was nothing left for him now—no hopes, no friends—and yet he was beyond tears and sorrow at this point. He had reached that point of exhaustion when the only respite seemed to be death, itself.

At the end of the forest path, he looked up at his ugly home and felt nothing. Remembering the orchid, he meandered over to the patch in the forest, but his body slumped when he saw the luscious petals had finally begun to wilt. Bewildered, he forced himself away, now desperate for something—*anything*—to give his life some meaning. Spotting the boulder, he stumbled over to his grandmother's grave. Even more grass covered the grave today; and in another week or two, there might be no evidence at all that he had even disturbed the earth. Before, that thought had left him distraught, but he saw again how nature healed itself. When left alone, nature corrected all the violations and desecrations of men; and in that, at least, there was hope. It was not enough to sustain him forever, but it seemed enough to get him through these dark moments...

He was standing there, allowing his mind to drift on these thoughts, when he became aware of voices and footsteps behind him. After he turned, he saw two people—a man and a woman—emerge from the forest path. Both of them were wheezing and flushed, and the woman waved to him excitedly when she spotted him. Shango saw, but did not see. The woman's long, blond hair seemed fantastical against her caramel skin. She had taken off her stiletto heels to walk up the path, and Shango looked down at the neon blue of her toenail polish. The same color was on her fingernails—and it matched her blouse and earrings. The man with her was not an islander—Shango knew this right away. The man was tall and strong, but there was a softness about him: his muscles came from half-hour sessions in an air conditioned gym, instead of actual labor in the real world.

The woman was running up to Shango now. Soon, she was hugging him tightly and calling his name; the man stood by the side, smiling. It was only when the woman pulled away from him and looked him in the face that Shango noticed a vague resemblance to his mother. She was speaking excitedly now:

"I came yesterday, but nobody was home, so Sheldon and I returned to the hotel. You wouldn't *believe* my shock when I turned on the television and saw you in that competition!" Here, she hugged him again, and kissed him on the cheek. Yet, by now, Shango was so dazed and exhausted that he convinced himself he was hallucinating.

The woman was making a conscious effort to speak with an American accent, but since she was not exactly pulling it off, it just sounded stilted and *odd*. With the wind, she kept sweeping her blond hair weave over her shoulder. Shango had a strange impulse to rip it off and stomp on it, as if it were some kind of monstrous parasite, devouring her brains. Her makeup was gaudy as well, following the same neon blue motif. ...No, this could not be his beautiful mother after all. The thing in front of him could only be a warped projection of his depraved mind. Something about that reassured him, so that he sighed and looked off into the distance, hoping his delusion would disappear if he ignored it—

"Sheldon's my new husband," she said now, disengaging from Shango and gesturing to the man standing on the sidelines with his hands in his pockets and sweat streaming down his face. The man nodded and smiled when she looked over at him, but Shango was bored with his hallucinations by now. His mind went to what he was going to eat—

"What happened with the phone?" the woman began now. "I've been calling for a week." When Shango only stared up at her blankly, she quickly continued, "Sheldon left the rental car parked by the path. We have a nice hotel. Sheldon got rooms for all of us. *And*," she said, grasping Shango by the shoulders, "your papers are finished! I'm here to collect you, son. I'm taking you to America! Now, you, me and Sheldon can live like a family. Mummy can come too—I did her papers, even though she always said she wanted to live her last days here." However, she frowned then. "Where's Mummy? ...Why was her bed empty when I looked in her room yesterday?"

Shango only looked on blankly, still convinced the woman was a figment of his imagination. When he looked at her husband, the man seemed bored and aggrieved. He was holding the small of his back now, as if he had strained it on the walk up the mountain path. As Shango caught his eye, he seemed visibly uncomfortable, and blurted out, "What's wrong with your son? He doesn't talk?" Shango only stared at the man, before returning his gaze to his mother.

Outraged, she reared her hand back and slapped him across the face. Shango did not even flinch. In fact, he felt nothing, and only continued to look up at her in the same indifferent way—

"I won't have a son of mine acting like an animal!" she screamed. However, his continued indifference disturbed her, and she unconsciously took a step back. "What's wrong?" she said, her voice timid for once. Looking at her now, he realized, suddenly and completely, that he did not love her anymore. The people he had loved—his grandmother and Maitland—were gone now. His body quaked a little with the fresh grief of Maitland's passing, so that he bowed his head and sighed. By the time he looked back up at his mother, he did not *hate* her; he did not begrudge her for her obvious happiness at finding a "good American man." Yet, he saw, just as clearly, that he hated the child he used to be. That child had been a fool, and he was suddenly determined never to be foolish again.

His mother's lower lip had begun to tremble with the burgeoning awareness that something horrible had happened in her absence. "Where's Mummy?" she asked again.

Shango looked up at her fixedly, then he sighed and straightened himself out, as if he were about to answer a question in class.

"You're standing on her grave," he announced in his precise classroom voice. Then, as his mother stood there in shock, with her eyes bulging and her lips trembling violently, Shango left her and headed to the sink to wash up. Soon, he heard her wailing; her new husband rushed to her side to support her, but Shango did not even look back—since he had no more time for foolish things.

ABOUT THE AUTHOR

David Valentine Bernard is currently in the Caribbean, completing his PhD in the sociology of development. Before starting his studies, he worked as a data manager at a New York City HIV/AIDS program. *The Thirsty Earth* is his sixth novel. Visit the author at www.dvbernard.com.

FOLLOW SHANGO AS HE GROWS INTO HIS DESTINY.
BE SURE TO CHECK OUT

WHEN THE DEVIL REMEMBERS WHO HE IS

BY DAVID VALENTINE BERNARD
COMING SOON FROM STREBOR BOOKS

For security purposes, Shango's department was housed deep within the bowels of the building. All cellular and electronic signals were blocked; according to one technician's boast, a nuclear bomb could go off outside and they would still be able to continue their work uninterrupted…as if even the end of the world was nothing compared to the work that took place within this room….

On Shango's computer screen, there were thousands of lines of programming code. The application had crashed, so he was searching the code for the bug. Unfortunately, after a while, his mind began to wander; his soul began to rebel against the sterile stillness of the office, and his vision became blurry. When the lines of code began bleeding into one another, he clamped his eyes shut, hoping to clear his vision—but his eyes still burned when he opened them.

He felt as though he had been sitting there for days. Outside—beyond the walls of this place—the New York City streets were alive with motion and energy; but inside, the sterile stillness was like a death shroud on his shoulders.

Presently, as one of the overhead fluorescent lights flickered, Shango craned his neck and looked over the top of his cubicle. On the other side, a gaunt Asian with large, lachrymose eyes was staring open-mouthed at his screen. Altogether, there were ten cubicles in the room; when Shango looked, the other programmers were also staring wordlessly at their computer screens, as if mesmerized.

The programmers in the room were the best of the best. They had the brain power to work on the cure for cancer or complete the next great innovation that would revolutionize human existence. Instead, they worked on programs that allowed their financial firm to conduct millions of trades in a minute and make countless billions with other people's money.

At the thought, Shango's gaze instinctively went to the far side of the chamber—where there was a glass partition. Beyond the partition, the supercomputer sat in its own refrigerated room, like a dark monolith. All their so-called wealth was stored on it; all their work and sweat—their hopes and dreams—had been digitized, so that they could be beamed across the world at a moment's notice. The dark monoliths were the pagan gods of their times. Their civilization had created all-knowing, all-seeing beings to shepherd them through their lives, but Shango could not escape the feeling that their souls were being devoured by the things they had foolishly come to worship....

Eventually, when his eyes returned to his screen, he sat straighter and resumed his search for the bug. His eyes still burned; reflexively, he looked down at the time in the lower right-hand corner of his screen. It read 11:36 AM. He stared at it for three or four seconds, amazed that he had only been sitting there for two hours.

...At least it was almost lunchtime. At the realization, his mind went to the beautiful woman he had spotted in the park recently. He smiled unconsciously at the thought of her, but then grew annoyed with himself—both for his stray fantasies and his overall inability to concentrate. All at once, a new sense of defiance began to grow within him. Sitting straighter in his chair, he took a deep breath and leaned in closer to the screen. He frowned, *willing* himself to concentrate. Then, at last, he felt "the old feeling" coming over him. It was as if a spigot of brilliance had been opened in his soul. His nerve endings tingled; he felt like he was outside of his own body, able to go anywhere he pleased—and *do* anything—merely by directing his will.

In an instant, all five thousand lines of the programming code flashed in his mind; all that complexity was broken down and analyzed. The previous burning in his eyes became a warm, comfortable sensation; colors seemed more vivid; all the stray sounds in the air—the buzzing from the overhead fluorescent lights and the intermittent tapping of computer keys—became hushed, and he leaned back in the chair, suddenly aware of everything he had to do to fix the program.

Ten minutes later, he pressed the button to execute the software, then looked on with quiet satisfaction as it ran flawlessly. The old feeling remained with him for a few moments—the sense that everything was within his grasp, and that he could accomplish anything merely by *willing* it. The feeling was both exhilarating and disconcerting—but as he had done over the years, he forced himself not to think about the magic too deeply, lest it wore off.

With his work done, he allowed his mind to turn to thoughts of lunch—and the beautiful woman in the park. He smiled then—and rose from his cubicle—but the other programmers were so engrossed in their work that nobody even noticed him leave.

He walked down a long, empty corridor. The walls were white; the same fluorescent lights buzzed overhead. There were security cameras there as well, and Shango always felt uncomfortable at the thought of some anonymous overlord observing him. At the end of the corridor, there was an elevator. Shango had to press his security card against the console to access it. When the door finally opened, he stepped into the cramped, empty space. There was another security camera in the ceiling; as the elevator doors closed, Shango looked up at the camera uneasily, then he forced himself to stare straight ahead, at the dull metal of the elevator doors.

Strangely enough, even after the elevator began its ascent, he was overcome by the sense—indeed, the *suspicion*—that the thing was actually transporting him deeper into the bowels of the earth. As the seconds passed, the suspicion grew into something more frantic. Shango felt trapped—*doomed*—

And so, as soon as the elevator door opened to the lobby, he sprang out. He breathed deeply, as if he actually had been suffocating. However, the lobby was abuzz with workers going out for lunch, and the sight of all those other people began to stifle the madness. He was not alone after all. He was no longer trapped within the bowels of the earth; his soul was no longer at the mercy of dark monoliths. He sighed.

Beyond the glass enclosure of the lobby, a beautiful summer day beckoned. He nodded unconsciously and joined the stream of workers heading in that direction. The thought of the park was already reviving his soul. He wanted to feel the warm rays of the summer sun on his skin—

But everyone had to go through turnstiles to enter and exit the building; those coming from outside had to stand on line to have their bags x-rayed; and with all that, a bottleneck had formed. Each worker had to press his or her security card against the console for the turnstile to operate; two guards looked on threateningly, ready to pounce at anyone whose ID did not work. Shango allowed his mind to go numb as he waited his turn....

At last, he was beyond the turnstile, moving toward the exit. Unfortunately, he again had to wait at the revolving doors. The frustration was building within him now. He felt like screaming—like going on a mindless rampage against everyone and everything in the building ... but soon, he was outside, breathing the warm summer air. The air was not exactly fresh, but at least it seemed real, so he breathed deeply and again allowed the madness to leave him.

He was so preoccupied that he did not initially notice the man screaming from the sidewalk. It was a gaunt white man in his fifties or sixties with disheveled hair and soiled, rumpled clothes. Three guards stood within a few paces of him, ready to restrain him in case he tried to make a run for the entrance.

"We're all gamblers in a casino economy!" the man raged. "That's what they've made us: gamblers with no other choice but to turn that roulette wheel. But like all casinos, it's not the gambler who makes the money, it's the casino owner: *the casino man*. That roulette wheel isn't a game of chance!" he screeched, pointing an accusatory finger at the building. "We're all going to lose eventually! That's the nature of the game. Yet, most gamblers get so excited when they win ten dollars that they forget they've already spent one hundred trying to win the jackpot! ...Meanwhile, the casino man is laughing all the way to the bank. The casino man *never* loses. He makes up all the rules and runs his scam so well that the penniless gambler will borrow and steal other people's money so he can rush and give it to the casino man!

"Hell, the casino man runs his scam so well that the gambler doesn't even believe he's gambling anymore. Instead, the gambler will say he's *investing*. 'Invest and soon you'll be a casino man, too.' You believe this crap?" he said with a chuckle.

It was only when the man put his head back and began laughing dementedly that Shango shuddered and came to his senses. The man was obviously insane, but there had been poetry in the madness. Shango had lost himself in the cadences and stanzas. More troublingly, while he could rightly say the man's rhetoric was simplistic, he could not say it was *wrong*, and this troubled him. The man began ranting again; but when Shango looked up, he noticed one of the guards looking at him oddly—as if to ask why he was standing there, giving that fool his attention. Shango moved on quickly; but even after he crossed the street and entered the park, he still found himself fighting against the effects of the poetry.

Only when he reached the meadow, and saw the beautiful woman sitting on her usual bench, did he feel his mind relaxing. He took his seat at a bench about thirty meters away from her. As usual, she was dressed in bland office wear, but whatever she wore always had a certain flair, simply because she was wearing it. To Shango, it was like those ridiculously expensive "lingerie" items that women were duped into buying. When a woman was truly sexy, even the droopiest, cheapest grandma drawers became sexy. The woman made the clothes sexy, not the other way around, and Shango smiled unconsciously as he looked across the meadow, at the woman.

She was reading a newspaper. Her long legs were folded elegantly, and her wild tresses of natural hair were dancing in the gentle breeze. His smile widened, but the odd thing was that he had sworn he would never actually approach her. For a week now, he had been watching other men try their luck. Day after day, she slaughtered her suitors with indifference. Their jokes and pick-up lines never drew smiles or even annoyance—only indifference. She stared back at them with her cold beauty until they slunk off. From businessmen in five-thousand-dollar suits to construction workers with bulging biceps...from intense-looking artist types carrying pretentious tomes, to hip-hop gangstas with baggy pants...she was immune to them all. As far as Shango knew, she had yet to even utter a single word to one of them; and when her cold beauty left them devastated, stumbling away on wobbly legs, Shango would always feel a morbid thrill in his soul.

In fact, he suspected her beauty was even more devastating up close— which is why he congratulated himself for staying at a safe distance from her, where he could admire the broad strokes of her beauty without being brutalized by the exquisite details.

When he became conscious of his thoughts, he groaned. He knew everything about his strange voyeurism was shameful. In fact, it was pure idleness, and he bowed his head, deep in thought as he tried to reconcile it all. There was much to consider—not only about the woman, but also about the work he did at the company. ...Minutes passed; he was sitting in the same position on the bench, with his head bowed, when he suddenly became aware someone was standing over him.

When he looked up, he was startled to see the beautiful woman was there. As he had guessed, her beauty seemed almost oppressive up close; he stared at her, willing himself to remain calm—and to resist becoming another one of her victims. When the moment lingered awkwardly, she smiled, so that it took all of Shango's inner strength not to come undone—

"I guess you don't remember me," she mused.

He frowned and sat straighter. "I know you?"

She sat down next to him and turned to face him. Her eyes narrowed: "Don't you?"

She was staring at him expectantly; he tried placing her face, but all he could think was that her beauty was eroding his will—

"Okay then, Shango," she said, getting up.

"Wait, you *really* know me?" he said, amazed.

She looked down at him with an exasperated smile. "Of course." She began walking away.

"Wait," he said, suddenly desperate, "—give me a *hint* or something."

She paused, but shook her head: "From spying on me all week, you know I don't converse with strange men."

"You can't spy in a public place," he said with a smile. "Besides, you're talking to me *now*, aren't you?"

"Of course," she said with a shrug. "I'm *talking* to you. People talk to their dogs all the time—but those aren't conversations, are they? A conversation is a *mutual* exchange—and that can't happen between us until you remember me." She did not smile; it did not seem like she was being coy or hard to get—nor did she seem angry that he could not remember her. Rather, now that she saw he did not know her, she had simply retreated into her cold beauty.

Shango stared at her, bewildered. "...I'm a *dog* now?" he said with a chuckle, trying to joke, but all her smiles seemed gone forever.

"I'll be here tomorrow," she continued. "If you remember me by then, then we'll try again." She prepared to leave—

"Wait," he protested, "by your logic, you'd never talk to anyone new—since you only talk with people who already know you."

She shook her head. "You still don't understand. I talk to new people all the time. However, I save conversations for friends. ...There's nothing as useless as trying to have a conversation with someone with no memory of you—no *emotional connection* to you. You may as well be talking to yourself." At that, she turned and left. He put out his hand plaintively; but from her demeanor—and the startling clarity in her eyes—he knew it was pointless.

A minute or so later, when she disappeared behind some trees, all he could say was, "Damn!" All at once, he realized he was in love with her—and that he had been in love with her since he saw her a week ago. He frowned in her direction, wondering how the hell it had happened and how he could possibly know her. He definitely would have remembered a woman like *her*. He scoured his mind, going back to when he started eighth grade in Brooklyn. With his luck, she had been some anonymous ugly duckling from one of his classes, who had since blossomed into an unrecognizable goddess. Maybe she had been one of his friends' friends, whom he had met once, in passing. Frustrated, he groaned and stood up, knowing his mind would obsess over her for the next twenty-four hours. He was already trying to remember where he had stored his school yearbooks—and anything else that might jog his memory. "...*Damn!*" he whispered again.

While he was standing there, his cellular phone began ringing. Startled, he took it out of his pocket and stared at it. From the phone number, he could tell it was someone from his job. He grimaced. He viewed workplace cellular phones as a new form of slavery. Now, workers were forever bound to their companies: forever within range of insipid emails and unrealistic requests. Once, while he was sitting in the bathroom stall, his boss had called, frantic about the status of a module he was working on. While the man was huffing and puffing on the phone, Shango had almost blurted out, "Can I at least wipe my ass first!" He glared at the phone now, but then sighed and pressed the button to answer it.

An unnaturally chipper woman responded—unnatural in the sense that there was no warmth in her voice. It was a corporate version of a pleasant voice. "Is this Shango Cartwright?" she began.

"Yes, ma'am," he said mechanically.

"I'm calling from Baxter Becker's office. He'd like you to come to a meeting he's having now with the executive team. You're not far from the office, are you? You weren't at your desk."

Shango stared ahead blankly for a second. Baxter Becker was the Chief Executive Officer of the firm. A sick feeling came over Shango for a moment, but he soon regained his composure. "The meeting's *now?*"

"Yes, come up to the penthouse conference room. They're waiting." She put down the phone.

Shango looked down at the phone confusedly. The entire conversation had to replay itself in his mind before he came to his senses and began jogging back to the office.

His mind swirled with images of the beautiful woman and Baxter Becker as he sprinted across the street to avoid a speeding cab. There was a police cruiser in front of the building now. Two officers were trying to talk the disheveled man into the leaving, but when the man began screaming louder—about freedom of speech and corporate greed—they hauled him away for disorderly conduct. By then, all the poetry was gone, and Shango looked away uneasily.

Soon, he was inside the building, beyond the turnstiles; he got on a packed elevator and headed toward the penthouse. His mind still swirled; he felt unfocused. With all his running, he had begun to sweat. He wiped his brow with the back of his hand, then stood there grimly.

The higher the elevator rose, the emptier it became as workers exited onto their floors. For the final leg, Shango was again by himself, staring at the dull metal of the elevator doors. ...Then, he was there. The doors opened and he stepped out, onto the rich mahogany floor. A receptionist was there. Shango stepped up to her desk; as soon as he said his name, she smiled in recognition, said they were waiting for him, and directed him to the double doors to the left of her desk. He straightened his tie as he walked; he wiped off more of the sweat, and willed himself to be calm, but his mind still swirled.

What could the CEO possibly want from him? If they needed some new application designed, they would have gone through Shango's boss. ...But why else would they call him to such a high-level meeting? Logically, he did not think he was being summoned for some kind of reprimand. More likely than not, he would be congratulated for something. One of his programs had probably made them more millions... but all this was definitely *odd*.

When he reached the double doors, he stopped and looked back at the receptionist. As she nodded encouragingly, he took a deep breath and pulled open one of the heavy doors.

The room was cavernous. About twenty people were seated at an oblong table. All conversation ceased when Shango entered. He stopped abruptly, wondering if he should have knocked. However, from the far end of the conference table, Baxter Becker smiled and gestured for him to enter. Becker was a tall, slim man with "salt and pepper" hair that seemed somehow too perfect. The only available seat was at the foot of the table, opposite Becker. They had saved it for him. He did not like the cabalistic smiles on their faces—the knowing glances at one another. *Why the hell was he there...!*

He sat down. The woman to his left smiled at him. When he reflexively nodded back, he noticed the three gigantic plasma screens on the wall. There were charts and figures on them—financial projections that promised even more billions for the company—

"Cartwright," Becker began abruptly, the moment Shango was settled, "—you're originally from the Caribbean, aren't you?"

"Yes, sir," Shango droned.

At Shango's reply, the people in the room looked at one another gleefully; Becker grinned at the Chief Financial Officer, who was in the seat next to him. While Shango was looking around confusedly, Becker ventured:

"Do you mind if I call you Shango?"

"No, sir," he replied, his mind numb.

"We have a *glorious* opportunity for you, Shang," he began excitedly. Apparently, leaving the "o" off Shango's name was hipper—or proof that they were closer now. Shango found it annoying, but he nodded encouragingly, hoping Becker would get to the point.

The man paused dramatically, then leaned forward in his seat. "What I am about to say is sensitive information: *top secret*." He looked at Shango gravely—as did the others at the table.

"I understand, sir," Shango replied.

There was a dossier in front of Becker. He leafed through a few pages, then looked up at Shango again. "Now, Shang," he continued, "the island you are from"—he returned to the dossier, and scanned the pertinent page, putting on his reading glasses to do so—"they've fallen on some pretty tough times." He took off his glasses and looked over at Shango with the same grave expression. "Since gaining independence, the country's lurched from one disastrous government to another; the treasury's *bankrupt*, and they have no way of ever repaying their massive debts."

When the man paused, Shango dutifully said, "That's right, sir." He lowered his eyes, instinctively ashamed of the place he had not seen in thirteen years. He had spent the years trying to exorcise the island from his soul. Being associated with it now—in front of the executive team, no less—made him feel like a child again. The shame *burned* in him; his mind suddenly flashed with a horror image of Maitland's corpse hanging from the rafters, but—

"We're entering a new era of business history," Becker continued joyously. "We're taking entrepreneurialism—indeed, capitalism, itself, to its rightful place: its *logical* conclusion."

Shango stared at him as if he were speaking Klingon or some other contrived language. When he realized the man was waiting for his response, he droned, "I see, sir,"…even though he was totally lost.

"We just finished marathon talks with the leader there. What do you call them again—Prime Directors?"

Shango blinked confusedly: "Prime Ministers, sir."

"That's right!" he said, grinning widely; the other members of the executive team grinned as well. Shango watched them uneasily, since he still had no idea where they could possibly be going with this. "Anyway," Becker resumed, "it's all ours now! We'd like you to be our representative on the ground. This is a *huge* opportunity for you—for *all* of us!"

Shango frowned, totally lost. "*What's* ours, sir?"

"The *island*—we just signed the papers!"

The other people in the room began talking excitedly amongst themselves. Shango felt he could not possibly be understanding them correctly. He shook his head, then sat straighter in the chair, as if trying to wake himself up from a dream. After replaying Becker's last sentence in his mind, he shook his head once more: "…It's still a democracy, sir," he began, quieting the room. "You can't *buy* it."

The Chief Financial Officer, a sallow little man in his sixties with a face like a mole or some other burrowing creature, corrected the flaw in his logic: "We can if they *choose* to be bought." The CEO nodded at his colleague's insight—indeed, the statement was so straightforward that it seemed tautological—but as Becker looked over at Shango's aghast expression, he realized the statement lacked the artfulness necessary to make it *palatable*.

Becker put up his hand now—a gesture meant to placate Shango. "There's going to be a referendum on the island after we make our plans public. That's where you come in."

One of Shango's eyebrows rose as if to say, *"What?"*

The CEO began talking quickly: "As with any transaction, people have to be shown what's in it for them."

When the man paused, Shango nodded tentatively.

"That's why we want you—no, we *need* you—to talk to the people of your country—"

"But I haven't been on the island in *thirteen* years," Shango pleaded.

"That's why you're an asset: you have our expertise—our grand vision and *excellence*—but you understand how they think. You know what they need to hear to make this deal happen."

Despite himself, Shango chuckled.

"This is a great opportunity for you!" the mole-like CFO chastised him, as if Shango's reaction showed ingratitude.

As the entire scenario flashed in Shango's mind again, he shook his head. "I design computer applications that automate our global trades. I have a master's degree in *computer science*. In college, I majored in *mathematics*. I'm not a *politician*—"

"But you're still one of *them*," the CFO growled, his annoyance growing.

Shango laughed now, amazed by how quickly he had gone from "one of us" to "one of them." He looked back over at Becker, since the CEO seemed more reasonable. "Why don't you use someone from marketing—or public relations?"

"We are already using them," Becker began. "However, we need your…insights."

Shango read between the lines: they needed a black face—preferably one with island roots—to sell this to the people down there. If he refused, his career would be over. They would not fire him or anything so obvious, but all his avenues for advancement would be closed. He sighed. "…What exactly are you expecting me to do?" he said, frowning.

"Just be our eyes and ears—and *voice*—on the ground, that's all. Help us show them how much we can help them." Then, as he sensed Shango's resistance, he added, "What the poor countries of the world have lacked is the creative engine that comes with true business acumen. They haven't had the expertise to navigate the global marketplace. For too long now, we've *neglected* them. We've left them to flounder